- 3 ω/σ

ANTHONY ADVERSE

———◆———

VOLUME TWO:
THE OTHER BRONZE BOY

———◆———

ANTHONY ADVERSE

BY HERVEY ALLEN

WITH A NEW

INTRODUCTION BY THE AUTHOR

AND ILLUSTRATIONS BY

EDWARD A. WILSON

MOUNT VERNON · PRINTED FOR

THE MEMBERS OF THE LIMITED EDITIONS CLUB

AT THE WALPOLE PRINTING OFFICE

MCMXXXVII

VOLUME TWO

BOOK FOUR

In Which Several Images
Travel Together

· BOOK FOUR ·

24. THE TABLE OF THE SUN

Tʜᴀᴛ great continental knee that curves southward to thrust the leg of Europe into the boot of Italy also encloses its gulf with a twinkling garter of mountains. These are not always clearly to be seen, but once glimpsed are provocative beyond most vistas, even if the traveller is an experienced one. In winter and other doubtful seasons the gulf hides itself in rain, or mists which sweep down like the swirling skirts of cosmic dancers from the slopes of the Maritime Alps.

But in early summer before a sirocco blows it is quite another thing. Then the sky over the gulf is turquoise, and the Mediterranean Homeric blue. By night the planets appear to lower themselves and burn nearer to the earth, and the stars to march higher as they do in tropic latitudes. Dawn comes from Italy, and if you are so lucky or so wise as to be on deck at that early hour, you need have no fear of an anti-climax in your destination, for before you lies Genoa rising unbelievable, white marble terrace above white marble; red tiles, churches, towers, villas, orchards, and castles ringed in by a noble amphitheatre of hills.

It was thus that Anthony Adverse first beheld it from the deck of the *Wampanoag* one summer morning while the ship's cutwater slipped contentedly through the untroubled seas. Never since his first bright sight of the world from the top of the tree at the convent had he seen anything quite so beautiful. Something of that first, fresh exaltation now returned to him as he leaned over the rail, gazing his eyes full.

They were tacking in slowly against a land breeze, now on a wide reach to port and now close hauled to windward, while the crew slowly took in sail. The sweet, heavy scent of orange groves and the intangible coolness of jasmine and new-mown grass rolled to him across the water. Only now, after nearly an hour of light, the olive orchards were beginning to stand out greyly amid the brighter green of the pink-topped oleanders.

The light widened and the sea grew bluer. Just a few minutes before it had been dark violet. How could he ever sleep; miss a moment of it? Why did men have to die and leave a world like this? Life could not be long enough on a star so beautiful. He wondered if Captain Jorham, who was at the wheel while the steersman helped take in sail, saw or felt anything similar.

Philadelphia called them below to breakfast.

Anthony had slept like a child every night since leaving Livorno. His senses were keen, yet soothed and washed limpid by the clear sea air. There was a tang and a zest about everything—about the movements of his arms, of his hands and fingers. He could feel the most delicate surface texture of things. In the quiet ship he could hear the slightest sound. Captain Jorham looked at him and grinned.

"Feelin' pretty keen, eh? I used ter myself. Glad to get away?"

Anthony had to admit that he was. All the little objects of furniture, houses; people that had annoyed him; the pain of familiarity with a thousand things that he wished instinctively to avoid but that had possessed some irksome claim upon him had vanished. He was no longer accountable to them. He need be sorry for nothing. Just now he was too happy to regret even those he loved—had loved! What a magical thing was this, the mere transporting of the body!

He within, he felt, remained the same. He himself had not moved. It was merely the outside world that had shifted. The encumbrances about him had vanished.

So he sat in the cabin that morning inhaling his coffee slowly, feeling the surprisingly healthy warmth of it, watching the green water slip by outside the porthole and enjoying one of the noblest of illusions immensely. Travel had set him free.

The blocks rattled on the deck as the ship came about again. Mrs. Jorham galvanized by the smell of coffee opened her panel and thrust her head, dressed in brown curl-papers and a night-cap, through the narrow aperture. Captain Jorham, seating himself upon the chest marked "Jane," began to feed his wife biscuits and bacon. From the biscuits from time to time he gallantly knocked out the weevils. It was a sign that he was in the best of good humour.

" 'Strordinary female bird walled in," thought Anthony.

The lips of Mrs. Jorham pointed, came out of the slot, and surreptitiously pecked her husband on his leather cheek. Then she looked at Anthony and rearranged her cap. Properly embarrassed by such intimate domestic details and endearments before a stranger, she smiled, pecked her husband once again, and closed the panel with an overpowering air of virtue and dignity. Throughout the entire meal her manner had been that of a lady-Putnam. That was it. She was not a toucan, she was a Putnam! Anthony saw that even on shipboard, in the intimate presence of strangers and of the ocean itself, Mrs. Jorham contrived to remain elegant and refined. It was a perfection which knocked out the weevils in their own dust. It was "Putnamism." Captain Jorham, who participated in it distantly by marriage, was proud of it, too. He set down the mess-kid in which only the wriggling weevils remained, triumphantly.

After Philadelphia cleared the board the captain took some papers from his desk and spreading them out on the table with a knowing air, dipped his pen, and beckoned to Anthony. As he sat down beside him he noticed that Captain Jorham not only reeked of tobacco but also was redolent of rum.

"Sign here," said the captain, without previous palaver.

Anthony leaned over the paper, which he found to be a roster of the crew. The captain's stubby finger pointed to the vacant line marked *mate*.

"Died o' smallpox at Lisbon," vouchsafed Captain Jorham.

But Anthony still hesitated with McNab's first lesson in mind.

"It's all fair and above board," continued Captain Jorham a little anxiously. "Didn't yer old man tell ye about it before ye left? He and I arranged it all before supper that night. Ye're to be carried as second mate. That'll keep the Frenchies from askin' any questions about ye at Genoway. I'll tell ye how it is. It's mighty ticklish work these days bein' a neutral and tryin' to make ports and pick up cargoes with the French lordin' it on land and the king's navee on the water. It all depends pretty much on what cargo ye carry. But if I can git a nice cargo of fryin' ile over to Havaner it'll sell high. That's what I'm pushin' into Genoway fer. There's a sight of it piled up there now. Cost nothin'! It's worth the chance. It would go plum against the grain to run empty to Havaner. I'm layin' to pick up some fine blocks of marble for ballast, tew. I expect even the British ul have a hard time calalatin' *that* as contraband. And the French'll let us clear all right if we don't have English refugees aboard. Na-ow if ye just sign on as mate, between ye and me sort of *ex-officio*—no wages, of course,—ye can pass tolerable fer Yankee born. Better say Virginny, though. Your talk's a lot more like that. Ye don't use your nose proper to Bosting way. I'll tell ye another thing, tew, if the British board us at sea it may save yer bein' pressed, ye bein' a mate. Look here!"

He pointed out on the rolls the names of six seamen with the notation, "Pressed at Sea off Ushant, February 6, 1796, by H.M.S. Ariadne."

"A fast frigate or she'd never have done it. Most chasers we just sink in the blue, but there's a few on 'em can overhaul us with a followin' wind. That leaves us six hands forward to git home on. Old 'uns all. That English snotty that boarded us did know how to pick his men. Even the babies now have practice in that, dang 'em! Still it ain't such a bad berth bein' a mate on board with a lady in the cabin."

More than convinced by this time Anthony signed. The captain looked pleased and relieved. He opened up "Elisha" and taking out a bottle poured out a double tot.

"Wall, *mister*," he said with a twinkle, "here's luck to ye, and a fast first run."

The panel opened slightly as the lady-Putnam sniffed through the orifice.

Anthony saw trouble come into the woman's eyes. Her mouth trembled a little, but she said nothing. At last with a look of unhappy resignation she closed herself in again.

The captain drew his hand across his mouth and went on deck. As the ship beat in toward the harbour he descended twice again for a spiritual interview with "Elisha." Before they passed the Molo Vecchio he was in a genially prophetic humour and moved with a superbly confident roll. It was in this semi-rapt condition that the skipper felt himself most able to cope with a bargaining world. "Well iled." But the precise amount of lubricant necessary to fill the *Wampanoag* with a profitable cargo was hard to gauge. There was one curious thing about it, however. Liquor had brought the captain luck. A cargo of parrots once proved remunerative beyond all sober expectation. He gave a slight hitch to his trousers.

"Goin' ashore, *mister?*" he asked with a grin. That a young gentleman like Anthony should be his mate tickled him immensely. In his present mood the joke seemed colossal. "Get yer togs on."

Anthony dived into his chest hastily to get his purse and coat. As he opened the chest for the first time since leaving, he found

a letter addressed to him in the engraved strokes of Mr. Bonnyfeather. He opened it very impatiently now and read hastily.
He reproached himself for this, but with the early morning
noises of the new city coming through the port he could not
control his impatience.

It was a prolix letter of instruction how to proceed about the
collection of the debt. Mr. Bonnyfeather had apparently foreseen all possible contingencies. They were under nine heads.
Bother! This could wait till Havana. How coldly it was written. The old man addressed him as if he were nothing but an
agent. There were several enclosures, some drafts on Spanish
bankers, and two other letters.

Il Signore Carlo Cibo, Regla, Habana, Cuba

That could wait, too. How cramped the old man's signature
was getting now. Well, his hand . . . Then his eyes fell on
a postscript.

*P. S. I have not cast this epistle in terms of affection lest I
should have no eyes left to see with as I write it. Wherever you
are when you read this, remember the hand of him who writ it
is (as ever in the past) extended to you in blessing (and even
from the grave). I have put this in your chest myself. Do you
look under your great-coat for further remembrance, my son.
Thine,*   *J. B.*

He sat down on his bunk holding the letter which swam grey
before him. How had it been possible for him to forget all past
benefits in a few hours? He felt he should like to stab himself to
make the hard heart in his breast capable of feeling as it should.

Yet, perhaps gratitude was like sorrow, you could not feel it
all at once or it would overwhelm you. He looked at the open
chest. He could see the madonna wrapped up there in something that made her look like a mummy. Preserved, eh? So the
past was still with him. But he would not disturb her now. And
he would look under the great-coat later on. He could not bear

to receive anything more from that hand "extended even from the . . ." Oh, for just one day without any past behind it and no future before! The old man must still be well in Livorno.

Livorno? Where was that? Was there such a place? It was the noise and smell of Genoa that were coming in through the port.

He roused himself. In order to act it would be necessary to shake off the past, to remember it only in its proper place. Be grateful, yes! But not now, not this morning—in Genoa. He closed the lid of the chest with a bang right on the nose of the madonna and all the rest.

But he had forgotten his purse. He had to open the chest again for *that*. As he put back Mr. Bonnyfeather's letter which he had unconsciously clutched in one hand all the while, the other enclosure fell out before him.

To the Reverend Father Claude Aquaviva Xavier, S.J.
At the Palazzo Brignole, Genoa.
A.A., Deliver this in person. 'Tis the old summer school of the Jesuits in the suburb Albaro. Fail not in this if time permit.

So Father Xavier was in Genoa! Here was the past with a vengeance. How long it had been since he had thought of him! He had sent him his last childish letter to Naples years ago, and he had not answered the last from the priest. Meant to, of course. Naples? These priests of the suppressed Jesuits moved about now from pillar to post. Probably Father Xavier had had no easy time of it. His heart smote him. He might have written him. But it was just after Faith . . . damn it all! How much there was in that chest! Well, he would try to see him. The direction was in Mr. Bonnyfeather's hand, his last request as it were. This time he closed the chest deliberately and locked it, clapped on his hat and went on deck. Captain Jorham eyed him.

"It ain't sea-vility for the mate to keep the captain waitin', mister," he said as they stepped into the boat.

Philadelphia, grinning and sweating, rowed them through the crowded shipping of the old semi-circular harbour. Looking up, Anthony saw the tricolour waving on the massive Fortress of Sperone towering above them on Monte Peraldo. Bugle calls floated down faintly. Here and there along the miles of walls inland the sun glinted on cannon or flashed on bayonets. All the churches were built of black and white marble. There seemed to be any number of their striped façades and towers.

They landed at the Porta Lanterna and it was four mortal hours before the French officers in charge of the port were finished examining papers and quizzing Anthony who had to translate for the captain.

It was not easy to convince the military authorities that a neutral ship was not a legitimate prize of war. They rowed out and made sure she was empty. But they looked disappointed. Captain Jorham had cause to be grateful for his "mate." Finally with his papers reluctantly signed permitting him to purchase "ship's stores, olive-oil, marble, and statuary," he was allowed to go.

"Stat-*uary*," rumbled the captain, "stat*oo*-ary?"

Anthony laughed. The French had been slow to understand about the marble blocks for ballast. Statuary was made out of marble, marble was statuary. Meldrun! let them buy them both, neither was contraband. The captain kept looking at the document.

"By God, mister, I got an idear!" he suddenly roared.

It was some minutes before Anthony's back stopped stinging between the shoulders as they walked along.

Genoa was a welter of small, crooked streets with narrow, high houses, hunchbacked, twisted, and set at all angles. A perpetual dank shadow lived here as if at the bottom of an old well. Even the stones seemed to be rotten. An odour as of old cheese wrapped in a goatskin weighed on the senses.

The streets swarmed with half-naked urchins, women with baskets of fish or equally redolent dirty clothes on their heads. Soldiers slouched by on unmilitary errands, and every fifth or sixth person was a dark, scurvy-looking priest with a sallow, grimy countenance. Here, about the Porto Franco, where their errands lay that morning, Anthony could scarcely believe that he was really within the walls of the noble city set in green hills that he had seen from the ship.

They passed under endless arcades where the plaster walls had turned black with ages of grime. Festering piles of rubbish and garbage, rag piles, and unspeakable refuse piled against the walls. Yet between the outward-facing arches along the curb the merchants of macaroni and polenta kept their stalls, especially where the sword-like streaks of sunlight descended upon their heads.

The quantity of oil which the captain desired seemed unheard of. Even with his new mate to do the talking, the bargaining took them well past noon. The Ligurian dialects were often difficult, and the Genoese laughed at Anthony's Tuscan. When at last all was completed it took another hour or two to assemble carts to haul the jars to the quay. Captain Jorham was too wise to take his eyes off his purchases for a minute, or to pay until the last jar wrapped in straw ropes was safely deposited in the official confines of the Porto Franco. Then he was forced to see that the custom officials there had good cause to remember him.

But even at that the captain could rub his hands with satisfaction. Since the French had come, trade in Genoa was at a standstill. For that reason he was able to purchase supplies and provisions for the voyage at less than cost. His eyes sparkled, and to Anthony's alarm he showed some signs of being about to clap his newly acquired mate on the back for the second time that day.

Under ordinary circumstances Captain Elisha would have now returned to the ship to take his grub and save his pennies, but the liquor he had taken that morning was already dying out in him by noon. And he had secretly embarked on a long sipping wassail which engaged him for about four months every three years, when he began to hear the stealthy approach of certain footsteps overtaking him out of the past. It was his peculiar habit during the approach of the shadow feet, to mix wine with rum and porter into a potion known as "A Dog's Nose" for the reason that there are no whiskers on it and it drips. Rum and porter he had, but little or no wine.

Also he desired to purchase marble for ballast and to sell that usually unprofitable item at Havana for tombstones. It could be replaced there by ordinary stones, said to be abundant in Cuba. As a cautious measure he desired holes to be drilled in those marble blocks to secure them when once aboard. Then he was pleased with his "mate" for slinging the lingo so well. He intended to use such abilities further.

For above all there was the great "idear."

This was nothing less than to take full advantage of the permission to purchase statuary, so accidentally conferred upon him that morning, and to fill the vacant bunks in the fo'c'sle of the *Wampanoag* with "idols," to wit: various examples of life-size ecclesiastical statuary, saints, madonnas, and bambinos manufactured at Genoa in vast quantities cheaply, and hence doubtless salable at substantial profit to the less-artistic faithful in Havana. Indeed, the churches in Cuba, as Captain Elisha assured himself, although his data was based on only a few visits of irreverent curiosity, were lamentably bare of "idols." Some Protestant qualms assailed him, but the idea he felt was truly inspired.

Standing on a sunny corner he mopped his brow with a green duster while all this passed rapidly and somewhat confusedly through his troubled old mind. He was hungry, likewise he was very thirsty. Mrs. Jorham was safely "on board." Well, he would get her a present. He would get himself plenty of wine, see the ta-own and make his macaroni mate do the talking.

"Come on, mister, let's find victuals and drink. Lead the way. Captain's and owner's charges."

Anthony was willing. He had been afraid they would go back to the ship. Now he might be able to get time off to see the town—and Father Xavier.

He hailed a French officer passing across the way, an amiable fellow, who led them gayly along a decent, little side street under wrought-iron balconies into a trellised courtyard covered by one huge vine. A party of French officers sat at a big stone table in the centre, their sabretaches, swords and sashes heaped up like tangled trophies on the stone benches. There was a litter of bottles, half-devoured salads, cheeses, loaves, and the remnant of a fine ham garnished with cloves on the wine-stained table-cloth. Corks popped and flew about with oaths. They raised a shout when their comrade appeared. Captain Elisha's eyes brightened. He sensed distraction.

He and Anthony sat down in a corner. A woman with a red petticoat flapping about her bare calves came and placed a small wooden table before them. On this she set a bowl of grape vinegar, a dish of fresh young garlic, salt and a brown loaf.

"Onions," remarked Captain Jorham, "are a *sovran* remedy for scurvy."

He forthwith fell to and proceeded to eat the entire bowl of garlic, dipping each pearl-like bulb in the vinegar, sprinkling a little salt on it, and then plumping it into his mouth where it disappeared slowly, wagging its green tail nearly to the end. But just before the end, each tail was bitten off at precisely the same distance and spat out upon the floor. After the "onions" he inserted a piece of bran bread off the edge of his knife and rammed it home as if to keep the bullets in place. He looked about him complacently and noted that he was sitting in the centre of a demi-lune of tender garlic tips all pointing outward. He counted them; one to forty-three.

"Scurvy's an awful thing if it gets to you," he said, "makes your fangs loosen." He spat experimentally through his own front teeth again. They were firm. Still he looked a little uneasy about something.

"Liquor, mister," he said, "somethin' hot and stirrin'! I feel them onions prominent in my midst. *Ugh!* that's better!" The captain plugged with his spoon thoughtfully. "I heard of a schooner from Bermudy what started oncet with a cargo of cedar casks and onions for the whalin' grounds off the South-Shetlands. Them onions was sealed in they casks to keep. That was where trouble started. Afore that ship reached Jamaiky the casks swelled up like a cargo o' new-fangled French balloons. Onion gas! The ship went skiddin' along on her side. They couldn't tack her. They had to stave in them casks or they'd a floated clear o' the water and made leeway clear to Afriky. Well, sir, I'm beginnin' to feel like that schooner now. *Whir-oosh!*"

One of the French officers, a man with a long, red beard smeared with salad oil and particles of cheese, looked at him in disgust.

"I'm floatin'," said Captain Elisha, "I'm risin' like bakers' bread. I'm like a bloater when he's tickled, a dead cachalot in the sun. Nothin' but strong cordial will belay it." He reached for the vinegar. Anthony stopped him alarmed. Just then the woman returned with a jug and a large smoking dish. Captain Elisha applied himself to the jug. His throat rippled.

"Coolin'," he said, "but nigh as sour as vinegar." He put it down. Anthony tasted the wine. It was Lachryma Christi. His teeth went on edge. He ordered the sweetest thing available, Mountain-Malaga. The captain gulped a glass of it. He still rumbled but looked more comfortable.

"That's the antidote, mister, now let's sample the grub. I'm blown up fer full capacity."

It was a large basin of rice and boiled chicken. They polished this off between them. It was enough for Anthony. He ordered some muscat of which he was very fond. The captain was captivated with it. After two bottles he looked around on a new world. The "onions" were hopelessly buried.

"Na-ow I allow I'm beginnin' to be hungry." He looked at the empty dish regretfully and at his mate expectantly. Anthony called the woman and ordered further refreshment. Having now some gauge upon the captain's capacity and being enthusiastic with burgundy himself, he commanded a feast.

The captain cut himself a large quid of tobacco, which he stuffed into a round place in his cheek, while he continued to look on approvingly. The woman somewhat awed departed. They heard her giving excited directions in the kitchen. Meanwhile the captain extracted what solace he could from the tobacco, evolving in the process great quantities of saliva. Presently he had attracted the notice of the party of French officers who began to bet on his aim.

At some distance on the pavement before Captain Jorham a small lizard was basking innocently in the sun. The captain's front teeth were bared from time to time and immediately afterward the universe of the lizard dissolved in brown juice. It moved each time like a flash. The eye could not follow it. At a distance of about four feet nearer the wall, and farther away from the captain, another and browner lizard seemed to appear. It was about twenty feet to the wall.

The bets began to become interesting. At each saurian remove the stakes became higher and the odds against the captain rose. But the major with the red beard and salad oil, looking at the mahogany tinge of the captain's teeth, bet a meagre fortune upon him. The major was an artilleryman. Two more shifts of the devastated lizard confirmed the major's faith touchingly. He now staked his watch and placed it on the table. The trajectory he hastily calculated was then about twelve and a half feet, allowing for the curve of the parabola. It was a long chance. But the captain fetched the lizard. The unfortunate, and by now suspicious, animal paused once more, but this time near a hole in the wall. Whatever happened it had only two inches to flinch, and it was now nearly twenty feet away from the captain. The latter ruminated slowly, accumulating ammunition with a lacklustre look. The stakes were by this time reckless even from a military standpoint. Captain Elisha straightened himself, every eye upon him. Suddenly the lizard was washed into its hole. A yellow rainbow had collapsed accurately upon it.

The consequent enthusiasm was loud and prolonged. The major, who had won a month's pay, insisted that the captain should join him and his companions in celebrating so remarkable an event. The artillery, he maintained, had been gloriously upheld. Anthony participated in the reflected glory. The whole party gathered about the big stone table while Anthony translated for the captain the round of congratulatory toasts that followed. Outwardly unperturbed but inwardly ravished, Captain Jorham sat grey and bleak as Plymouth Rock in a gale of laughter. Nevertheless he was adequate to the international occasion.

"Confusion to the British."

The table roared back at him with delight. The major would have embraced him but even Captain Jorham renigged at the salad oil beard. Instantly he was more popular with the others, captains and lieutenants who had only moustaches. In the offing much more food now appeared. The captain resumed his seat and began to feed. Between dishes they plied him with wine. He drank all and everything, setting down his empty glass each time with obvious regret. For the first time in his life, surrounded by enthusiastic friends, he became entirely gay. Into the frozen swamp of his feelings burst a warm April light. He began to croak and to bellow

> *"Yankee skipper comin' down the river*
> *Ho, ho, ho, ho,* HO."

"Incroyable, magnifique! Allons, enfants de la patrie!"

The little courtyard rocked with song. Taking the cue from his mate the captain waved his glass, too. The woman in red petticoats stood by loyally. Shouting something to a mysterious "Batcheetcha" in the kitchen she produced a stage thunder there amid the pans. Things were pounded in a pestle. The two timbres of sizzling denoting roasting and frying arose simultaneously. Chickens died noisily several times. The major was a generous man. Cloths whisked and dishes clicked. Everybody began to eat and drink all over again as if their stomachs had expanded as the generous wine enlarged their souls.

They ate tagliarini, they ate ravioli, they ate cocks' combs and sheep-kidney minced with mutton chops and liver. They imbibed tender pieces of shredded veal fried and heaped upon a vast platter like a miraculous draught of shrimps. They ate chickens and spaghetti and mushrooms and ducks. When all the others were satiated Captain Jorham continued. He polished off a heap of sausages fried with garlic, topped that with a dish of green figs, and washed it all into place like a glacial drift that finds the worst is over and warmer times have come again—with waves of Madeira.

A happy silence compounded of satiety and pure human affability settled down upon the party. They looked at one another with complete approval and admiration. A Gascoigne major whose forefathers had been petty, brawling, and carousing nobles gazed into the eyes of Captain Elisha whose grandfather was an English regicide, and belched little nothings into his ear.

"Surely," thought Anthony, looking at a rat-like quartermaster opposite him, "no more gallant band of heroes has ever assembled to do honours to strong souls from the sea like Captain Jorham and his mate."

It mattered not that nothing which Captain Jorham said could be understood intellectually. What was the intellect? Indeed, where was it? The very sounds the old sailor made were enormously popular. He who had overwhelmed the lizard! Mark you, at six metres! When he told a joke and laughed, the courtyard howled. Two brown, dirty little boys sat in a crook of the great vine looking down from the pergola above. They chattered like little monkeys with their arms about each other watching a feast of lions. Yet even they, Anthony felt, and all the rest he thought felt with him, were part of this pleasant perfect society. To be approved, included, and considered. Yes, everything was perfect. Everybody was delightful. He was. They all were.

He had never drunk quite so much or enjoyed it so greatly before. Wine ran in his blood. He was absolved from all responsibility. The world, though slightly hazy, sparkled like a thicket in the sunshine. The pattern of vine leaves and the shadows on the floor under the trellis were revealed to him as beautiful beyond hope of imitation.

For the first few bottles he had still felt himself as a spectator, at times even a disapproving one. Then, as he had returned again and again to the scarlet glass, he seemed to emerge completely into another atmosphere. Delight, warmth, a delicious lightness and a complete identification with a perfect world ensued. He was convinced that this was the way things really were. A sober vision simply did not reveal them or put one in touch. Everything now became very clear, a little enlarged. The edges of things were framed in amber and the vistas beyond became supernal; bathed in auriferous light. Never had he felt so at home with his fellows as with these men in this courtyard. All of these people, all of them, men that he had never seen before today, were friends. The capacity for trouble had been removed from the universe. He was one in a brotherhood of a paradisiacal company.

Wine, the sun and vines had done this. The sun? He looked up at the sun through the vine leaves. This delicious wash of grape shade and shifting light under the trellis was like being at the bottom of a lake, a lake of air. So he was! He remembered that now. And it was in this kind of light under the plane tree that he had first come to life. No one could remember original darkness. He remembered the full, simple, unquestioning joy of light now. The clear light and the warmth and joy that had become part of him, that was still in him. Nothing could ever destroy that. It was what he was. Like the face in the miniature, that face! He crowed like a child again, moving his hands and feet slowly, feeling them. He thought; he dreamed.

It was the sun that brought all of this food and wine and joy out of the earth. That gave light, that made the eyes live. In that light moved shadows, men and things that ordinarily seemed to be to the light what shadows were, projections of something else. You could never quite understand what was throwing these shadows when you were sober. You forgot the origin of them and so you did not see things, and men themselves. But now, now he felt near to these fellow beings and things at last. He could see them as they actually were. You could draw close and know them. The darkness between them was gone. In the sunlight all were of one substance. All were part of this glory of heat and light beating down into the little courtyard. The very food and wine they had eaten came from it. They ate it and it became part of them. All were of one substance, men and things. All of it came out of the light.

Everybody was always eating and drinking everywhere. He longed to tell them about it but he could not. It was the sun that laid this daily table around which humanity gathered. Or something that made the sun. . . . He rose to his feet overpowered by so sublime a thought, striving for words. Only thick, lowing sounds came from his lips. He could not tell them. They shouted back at him but he did not understand. He felt sad. He wandered off somewhere. The world seemed to open out before him. The light became brighter. It flashed; streamed.

A vast table whose gleaming cloth stretched out like a white road to the horizon lay spread out before him thronged by all the nations of men. He could see them coming and going. Beyond the horizon there was nothing, nothing but clouds rising out of an abyss. He too could draw near to the table and partake with everybody. He dragged his feet a few steps farther and seemed to be standing on the table himself. He sat down on it. The table-cloth shone like the sun on water, dazzled.

He did not want to eat after all. He felt dizzy. He put his hand to his head and leaned against something. An hour passed, another. After a while the horizon cleared enough to see again. The monster table of the sun had vanished. He was sitting on the curb before the door of the restaurant looking up the Strada Balbi, long, white, blinding and silent in the late, hot afternoon.

Oh, yes, he knew now where he was. It was Genoa! He had been thinking about something. About a sacrament? Something like that. An ancient love feast? Oh, well, nonsense! How long had he been sitting here? Where was the captain? They had something to do. What day was it now? But what did he care about time! He turned and walked back into the courtyard steadying himself. He had a great drink of water. It tasted flat. The woman was laughing at him. Everything was clearer now. He must have slept a long time. Only a sense of tremendous well-being and a little irresponsibility remained. After a while the floor grew steady. Bon!

Captain Jorham lay sleeping, leaning back in a chair propped against the wall. A fly was crawling over his bald head slowly.

Those princes, those best of all good fellows, where were they? Vanished. Yet there was something tangible about them. The major had paid the bill. " 'For the honour of the French

Army,' signore, he said," thus the woman pocketing Anthony's coin. He felt relieved. All that for a tip! Now he knew he was sober.

Inside the skull over which the fly was crawling the captain was not really asleep. His brain had merely slipped the cogs of time backward some twenty years and transported him hence. He was sitting on a bench before his door in Scituate, Massachusetts. Just across the bay over there was Abner Lincoln's house and mill by the stream. The mill wheel was turning. The swallows dipped and left rings in the shallows. It was sunset. Overhead Jane was putting their child to bed. He could hear her singing and the feet of the child padding about on the floor. Now his wife was humming and rocking the baby monotonously. A note of foreboding crept into her voice. Suddenly the mill across the stream started to grind. It seemed to be uttering the letter "R" for minutes at a time. It was grinding up something. His child! Run, do something about it! If only he could move his feet. "*Rrrrrrr.*" He reached up and brushed the fly out of his ear.

Better! The mill had stopped. Dreaming? Why wake up? How happy he and Jane had been until . . . let him hear the child's feet again. Dead! Oh, yes, he had forgotten! He was afraid he *might* hear them again, at night. No, no, not dead! Yes, *dead!* Good lord! "Do not cry, Jane. We will go to the cemetery tomorrow." But it is already tomorrow. "Come, you can take your knitting." He started for the cemetery, and woke with his feet slipping. After a few minutes he remembered. The child was dead years ago. Poor little baba! But he must forget that, not hear the feet, on the deck, anywhere. . . . Shove it down, put the lid on it, live only now. "Remember, Elisha, it is pleasant here now, better now, better *now*," insisted one part of him to the other. "You can always take a drink and make it *now*. Take a drink, take a drink!" Captain Jorham arose from his chair roaring for liquor.

"This is the way I put soft shoes on my baby's feet, mister," he said as he downed a glass. "Can't hear 'em then." Anthony was sure the captain was still very drunk. Yet he looked sober.

They stayed the rest of the afternoon at the Café of St. Lawrence the Martyr. They had another little nap while it rained. Felt better, all well. The time seemed to have come to sally forth. The captain, Anthony was relieved to find, was now in a gracious Madeiran mood.

———◆◆———

At six o'clock of a particularly fine June evening the city of Genoa was already beginning to bestir itself smoothly for the moonlight night that was to follow. After the shower it was very clear, cool. Long, deepening shadows lay across the streets. Yet the sky was suffused with the red light of the approaching sunset. The air was blue and sparkling, just exhilarating and soothing enough to be grateful as an aftermath to the wine which still warmed them. Responsibility had nobly died.

Scarcely caring where they were going, they threaded their way through a maze of streets so narrow that no vehicles could pass. It was far too late to think of going after the marble blocks. In the mood in which he found himself Captain Jorham was willing to go anywhere and readily fell in with Anthony's suggestion that they should visit Father Xavier in the suburbs. Afterwards they could have supper, more wine, return late, or make a night of it. Yes, the marble and statuary could go till tomorrow. Everything could wait until tomorrow. Just at present they were like two fish swimming indolently and without particular direction, suspended, and suspiring in a golden, liquid atmosphere.

Bell-jingling strings of mules going home, sedan chairs for hire, painted private chairs for the nobility preceded through the dark tunnels of streets by carriers with linen lanterns on poles, passed and crossed and recrossed one another in all directions as if a festa were going on. Tall, narrow houses frescoed in glowing colours with pictures of saints, gods, and angels rose all about them, flinging their balconies half-way across the street. Beneath streamed a medley of motley costumes whose weird, cloaked fashions and screaming colours blent with the voluble soft voices and grotesque street cries into the total spectacle of the life that thronged and flowed, gathered and dispersed, gestured and hurried onward.

It was with some difficulty that Anthony prevented the captain from climbing into a gorgeous but lousy sedan whose bearers kept turning up at every corner and offering themselves. God knows where they would have got to in that. He linked his arm through the captain's. He occasionally wobbled a little yet. Keeping a sharp eye on their pockets, they passed on. Suddenly they left behind them the zone of premature evening in the narrow streets and emerged by pure chance on the Strada Nuova where day was dying brilliantly.

The endless street stretched on up into the hills above, narrow, clean, lined with rows of marble fronts where a few lights were already beginning to twinkle on the balconies. The long rays of light struck along it like a cañon. Only illustrious people could live on a street like that. Beggars were out of place there even in Genoa.

They shook off a man with sore eyes who had followed them holding his inflamed lids apart. Calling a gay little carriage drawn by two mules with pompons and bells they left the beggar toiling and cursing after. The fat driver on the tasselled box was in no more hurry than his team. They trotted on indolently inland toward Albaro, rising every moment a little higher and gradually leaving the crowded port behind. It was now that to his great joy Anthony rediscovered the noble city which he had seen from the ship like a happy morning dream. All day he had lost it amid the narrow streets of the stinking water front.

Although the approach to the suburb of Albaro itself is through ribbon-like lanes giving entrance to long, silent villas painted with vast frescoes which the sea air has dimmed—subjects holy, profane, and grim—yet there are many spaces where the main road passes in an arc over crests and opens upon sweeping vistas of the heights above and the sea below.

It was a little after sunset when the mules and driver as if by mutual consent came to a halt at one of these spots. The breathing of the animals, gradually becoming more regular after the labour of the ascent, as they slowly and more slowly inhaled the restful quiet of the evening air, finally seemed to die away altogether and to become one with the silence of the evening. All in the carriage were in unconscious sympathy with this relaxing rhythm, and the process continued to penetrate even further into their minds as they looked about them.

Lofty hills with fortresses on their crags from which banners of evening mist were already flowing leapt above them. On the lower slopes white villas smouldered in the sunset, set deeply in an ever darkening green intaglio of gardens and lawns. The twelve miles of the city's defences streamed and tumbled like the wall of China across the heights. In the valleys of the Bsagnio and Polcevera an opalescent fog had already begun to gather. Out of it flowed the dark rivers under their bridges into the still flashing bay.

Genoa, the wide far-flung city, lay there at their feet, encircling the light-twinkling harbour with the beautiful curve of its white arms, gathering the ships to its breast from the ruined Chapel of S. Giovanni Battista on the rocky seashore to the Porta Lanterna. Beyond all this, limitless and smooth with distance, stretched the violet tables of the open sea. Westward it glowed with submarine fires that reflected themselves upon the sky, and as they cooled and went out, blotched the long horizon with glazed patches of floating scarlet veiled by narrow clouds touched by the lingering pencils of the sun. Slowly even these melted, showing stars behind. It seemed now as if everything earthly were dissolving into the sky. It was like the hood over the Virgin's head, thought Anthony. Even the hills slowly expanded and blended into the same engulfing shadow that was swallowing the sea.

At the centre of all this dying world sat Anthony. Only the mules, the dim outline of the driver on the box above, and the captain beside him still remained outside of his mind as another reality. The wheels had for a while been holding him up, he felt, but soon he knew himself just to be floating in the body of the carriage on a sea of twilight. Then no carriage. He and the outside world merged. Or he held it all within him as a slowly darkening image. The place where his eyes ended and the world began had again been swept away. It was a timeless, spaceless levitation . . .

Only a moment ago his being extended thus had felt limitless. Now as darkness grew he was slowly withdrawing himself again into a point bounded by stars as they came out one by one and grew clearer. Soon he would be back within his head again. Something already had begun to remain outside.

The mules stirred. The carriage moved forward a few inches on solid ground. He looked down and saw his own hand on his knee and felt it. He looked around at the face of the captain. He also had lost himself, Anthony could see.

His face had grown wide and peaceful, glimmering. The lines of stress and hard care and sorrow were relaxed on his forehead and cheeks. His lips framed themselves wonderfully about the smile of a younger man. Much had been forgotten and caressed away as though Elisha Jorham had once participated in vivid happiness and the vision remained, one which he only needed to be reminded of to resume.

"This is Elisha himself," thought Anthony. "I hope that he can see me as I am, too." He moved slightly. They looked at each other long and silently in the low twilight. They were both at home with and comforted by the unspoiled glory of the world. That was an important discovery for friendship. Then the captain suddenly resumed the mask which experience had provided him. His face hardened.

"Well," said he, "what little thing happens next, mister? I'm trustin' my events to you now, see?"

"Nothing that matters much, sir, I suppose," replied Anthony shaking the stars out of his head.

"Wall, na-ow ye never can be sartain I calalate. Let's make sail anyway. We've got to be goin' somewhere."

The captain was getting sleepy. He began to nod shortly afterwards. A quarter of a mile farther brought them to the door of a small inn.

"I'll turn in here while you drive on and see yer friend," said Captain Elisha. "It's bed and not victuals I want now. But be sure to call fer me in the mornin' even if you make a night of it.

That's orders, mister. Don't leave me stranded, mate," he added anxiously, "I can't swing the lingo, you know."

Anthony reassured him. He would call him for an early breakfast. "Good! It's marble and statoo-ary tomorrow, and that may take longer than buyin' ile. They're never in any hurry around cemeteries." The captain yawned. "But you can't live that way; do business."

Anthony left him comfortable enough in a bedroom under the eaves where the moonlight was already beginning to filter through the tiles.

"Looks like one of Jane's crazy-quilts," murmured the captain fingering the covers dreamfully. "Say, mister . . ."

But Anthony had already driven on.

25. THE VILLA BRIGNOLE

Half a mile across the valley from the inn Anthony was driving along the endless garden wall of the Palazzo Brignole. It had once been a summer school of the Jesuits but was long since deserted, as most of that suppressed order had fled to Russia or Poland. The hoofs of the mules echoed against the cracked and peeling stucco of the outbuildings in the empty moonlight. The driver turned in reluctantly enough through a rusty iron gate, and unhitching under a shed, began to make himself and his team as comfortable as the fleas would permit. Supper seemed remote. He was heard to wish fervently that il signore would not be long.

"An hour or two at most," replied Anthony, who then began to pick his way gingerly across a weedy terrace, fingering the letter to Father Xavier. The address upon it now seemed improbable, for in the moonlight he stumbled over piles of rubbish and old stable litter while tribes of owl-eyed cats fled wailing before him.

Even in Genoa Father Xavier could scarcely have found another dwelling which expressed so well the departed grandeur and the present desolation of his order. The vast uncompromising façade of the Palazzo Brignole stretched itself before Anthony on the crest of a series of terraces. Its flat face looked blindly at the moon as if it too were oblivious to change. Its lower apertures were stopped with rubbish like gagged mouths. From its upper windows the cracked and wrinkled shutters, like so many grey cataracts over innumerable eyes, told of nothing but seething darkness in the cells behind them. Two ruined arcades, extending from the house at right angles, stumbled with collapsing arches down the giant steps of the terraces and enclosed within their shattered arms the long approach that had once been a landscaped garden but was now a melancholy wilderness.

It seemed to Anthony as he looked up at the great house, from which not a light shone nor a sound emanated, that the garden was rushing down upon him over its arcades in tangled masses of shrubbery and flowing outlines of serpentine vines. It was a river of dark vegetation in sinister spate. What made it worse was that it had once been meant to be as artificial as a canal and neat as a priest with a new tonsure. It was some moments before he could force himself to follow the cats and plunge into its moon-shadowed mazes toward the house itself. At this hour it was a garden fit only for those that could see in the dark.

He tripped over roots that had forced their way through an old pavement cracked in a thousand directions. At other places the walks gave oozily under his feet. Everything was overgrown with weeds, gaunt, or blackly flamboyant. Frogs croaked in the stagnant stone basins, and as he rose turn after turn up the ruined steps, statues with mossy faces started out at him from their vine-tangled niches or lay prone with leprous spots upon them as if dead in the moonlight. Once he thought he saw a lantern gleaming far before him. But it was only a solitary firefly signalling vainly for an answer. The house remained pale and lampless, and grew even huger and more lonely as he approached it.

At last he stood upon the last pleasance, peering in through an open portal whose doors had long lost their hinges and were now leaning drunkenly against the pilasters of the cavern-like vestibule. Into this he did not care to venture. Indeed, he would have ended his mission here had it not been that now for the first time his ears were saluted by a sound other than that made by frogs and crickets.

At first he thought it was water dripping musically into some abandoned well, but as he stood listening intently the ghost of a tune emerged. Someone was negligently touching the strings of a harp. The sound grew louder. It seemed to emanate from the silent, wandering barracks before him. For a while it had come from nowhere, and the effect of the soft music in the moonlight had been so eery as to halt him where he stood. But to the notes of the harp were now added the slightly flat tones of a feminine voice practising the bravura. One, the highest note, was a dismal failure and made him laugh. It was an entirely human anticlimax. He strode through the vestibule eagerly and almost immediately found himself in the inevitable littered courtyard beyond.

From a porter's lodge in one corner of the quadrangle came a few gleams of light and the sound of the harp, although the heavy shutters were closed. There were even heavy bars on the windows. He walked over and knocked at the door but there was no reply. The music had stopped instantly. He heard a few stealthy footfalls behind the shutters and the light went out. At first he was inclined to be angry at this reception, but then he could not help grinning. He knocked again. Silence.

After a long interval a queer voice said softly, "I am not at home. I went away years ago. Let me alone."

"Signora, or ma donna," he said, "I am not a brigand, I do not wish to disturb you. I am looking for a priest, Father Xavier. Do you know him?" He waited anxiously but still there was no reply. Some time passed. Then he knocked again, this time impatiently.

"You must call for him in the court. Call loudly," said the tired voice within. "He is getting a little deaf I think. He no longer cares for my music." That was all. After a while the light reappeared and the harp resumed.

He turned away again. The four walls of the high villa frowned down upon him with tightly-barred windows. The moon looked over one corner of the roof a little tilted. Best do as he had been told!

"Father Xavier, oh, Father Xavier!"

"*Ier, ier, ier,*" mocked the echoes, dying away into a solemn gibberish. The harp dripped and tinkled, and the flat voice in the lodge ran through an eery, windy bar or two again. Somewhere in the shadows a chorus of cats began insultingly. He felt enormously irritated. It was warm and damp here, too. He was sweating. The place was decidedly . . . decidedly so!

"Father Xavier!" he roared again in a sane determined tone.

"What is it, my son?" said a familiar voice so close to his shoulder that he wheeled about, startled in spite of himself.

A few feet away stood a slight, emaciated figure with a black robe fluttering in the night breeze that sighed through the archway. There was a small crucifix hanging from its belt. This, and a shining tonsure of thin, grey locks glinted in the moon. Only the face was the same. At the sight of those familiar features, which standing out above the shadows seemed to be glowing with a quiet light from within, Anthony was transported by the fascination of fond memory into the past. He seemed to be standing again in the court of the Convent of Jesus the Child. Each looked at the other searchingly.

"My father, is it possible you do not know me?" said Anthony.

"Anthony, my son, my son!" cried Father Xavier. "I would rather see you here tonight than an archangel. Where have *you* fallen from?"

35

He came forward and put his hands on Anthony's shoulders and looked up into his face.

"I used to look down at you. You remember?"

Anthony could feel how old his hands were. A feeling of pity swept over him. An irritating cadenza of the woman's voice interrupted them. Suddenly he felt embarrassed.

"I have a letter from Mr. Bonnyfeather for you," he said awkwardly.

Father Xavier laughed. "A formal introduction I trust— 'Anything you may be able to do to further the fortunes of so estimable and prepossessing a young gentleman will be esteemed as a service rendered to your obedient servant'—eh? So, we are on the formal basis of manhood. Come, my son, I shall receive you as I am sure you deserve, letter or no letter."

He laid his hand on Anthony's arm and led him across the court to a little door with a grille in it, a door so narrow as to be successfully concealed behind a large pillar. Taking a candle from the niche where he had left it, Father Xavier extended a shielding hand before the flame and they began to ascend a series of narrow stairs.

The ramifications of the old house were unimaginable. A thousand closed doors loomed mysteriously on a hundred corridors going nowhere. Anthony suddenly felt an overpowering sensation that he had been here before. It seemed improbable that the priest could ever find the way to his own room again. The silence was oppressive, but somehow as they went higher it was not so hostile as it had been on the ground floor. Inside, the house was merely asleep, not dead. People could come back here and be happy again. It was not like the garden. In summer the house was warm and dry, dusty.

They had both unconsciously fallen into their old step as if sauntering again through the corridors of the convent. Father Xavier walked as though he had a child beside him. Anthony's steps became shorter and faster. He did not notice it but the priest did. The light from the candle made the enlarged, blue veins on Father Xavier's hands stand out in knots. A still, porcelain light filtered through his thin, shielding fingers and fell upon his face as if the glow upon it were from within.

As they walked on through endless corridors and up confusing flights of well-like stairs, Father Xavier gave the impression that with all this paraphernalia of the building about him—with the glimpses of frayed frescoes starting up before the candle and dying away into the darkness like the gliding fringes of a delirious dream—the priest had nothing whatever to do. He alone, in all the passing phantasmagoria of vaguely glimpsed scenes of nature and the works of man, held the light which revealed them—and let them go again. Only his face shining as from within remained. Yes, Father Xavier looked that way tonight. Anthony wondered what such impressions might mean.

At last they paused before a door apparently no different from a hundred others they had passed but to which Father Xavier unhesitatingly applied his iron key.

It swung open upon a small apartment under the leads. The moonlight poured in through a dormer window. Beyond was a glimpse of a few pale stars. Even with only one candle and a little moonlight Anthony felt at home in the place immediately. Father Xavier motioned him to a shadowy chair, and when some more candles were lit, he saw it was one of the old, red ones with tassels that had so intrigued him as a child at the convent. Through what vicissitudes had it been since then, he wondered, to come here?

It was marvellous how with the closing of the door the very memory of the labyrinthian chaos of a house that was below and around them had vanished. They might have been in a comfortably furnished, opaque bubble hung somewhere in space, utterly safe from and independent of the outside universe. A few embers from the faggots which had cooked the priest's supper still glowed and made the place, if anything, too warm. Father Xavier threw the window wider and they heard the notes of the harp at a great distance below them.

The priest turned and touched his forehead significantly.

"She is composing an opera which will never be sung," he

said. "An old cousin of the Brignoles who has been permitted to live on here in the lodge these ten years now. It *is* a little weird at times. Let us close it out tonight. What do you say?"

He shut the window again and going over to the fire poured some water on the embers. As the last hissing died away he extended his arms along the mantelpiece, leaning back and looking at Anthony.

"Do you remember my old room in the little house?"

"I now feel as if I had never left it, father."

"Here are some of *your* books, the ones with the pictures in them," said Father Xavier smiling and running his hands affectionately over the backs of the leather bindings, without turning to look at them. "That was where your world began, was it not? Ah, those were good times at the convent after all. Better than we knew. And now, to think of it, we have ten years or more to talk away between us. Why, a lifetime would not be long enough for that! Have you not found it so, Anthony?"

"I remember some days I think it would take ten years to tell about. I do not think I shall live long enough to find out what really happened in some of them, father. And yet looking at you now it all seems as though I had only dreamed them. I could almost imagine that harp down there was our old fountain in the court splashing away under the plane tree. That sound of water comes often at night. I hear it then."

"So, does it go that way with you? Yes, we often return to ourselves at night, to what we were, or are. Tell me all about yourself, my son. It is long since we have had a good talk. Do!"

He took down a long pipe from the mantel. "Do you smoke? No? I do. It is one benign, fleshly indulgence to which I have finally succumbed."—He began to rummage around in various curious receptacles for another pipe, carrying his guest's attention from one thing to another, but giving him no chance to speak.—"You must inure yourself to the weed before its true virtues can be evoked. Try this. Just one or two whiffs at first, if you do not really care for it. Real Virginia, very light and sweet. Old. I keep it in this jar with a little damp sponge." He lifted the pipe rapidly and brought a lighter. The stem was in Anthony's mouth and he was drawing in the sweet smoke almost before he knew it.

"I *am* a little cold after all," said Father Xavier, looking at the fire regretfully. "A second till I change into my wool." His voice now came floating in from his little bedroom just beyond. "I am quite luxurious here you see," he added as he secretly put on a stole under his gown.

Anthony had taken a few whiffs of the pipe. The first few were pleasant but he did not care to go on. He felt himself to be floating just a little free in space, his feet not quite on the floor. It was not dizziness but the beginning of levitation. He was no longer connected with anything in space—with nothing except Father Xavier's voice. That was the only reality—and himself.

"Now tell me about yourself, as you said you would," said Father Xavier, coming back into the room and seating himself opposite with an air of one who has come to listen to a moving story. He wrapped the loose gown a little closer over his chest. "Tell me everything. What *did* happen that day I brought you to the Casa? You had an encounter with a goat, didn't you? I remember something about that."

"Ah yes, the goat!" Anthony began, and without being aware of it launched forth into what gradually and surely grew into the minute autobiography of the years since he had left the convent. If there was anything that he omitted he could not remember it. All the people, the house, the books, the benign and sedate Mr. Bonnyfeather, Toussaint, Faith, and Angela crowded into the little room under the eaves of the Villa Brignole where Father Xavier sat with two fingers across his breast holding his woollen gown. At which two fingers Anthony somehow could not help but look as he went on and on.

At first he was aware only of a certain pleasure in the sheer narrative of his own affairs with so good and trusted a listener. Then a kind of exaltation overtook him on the wings of which his story began to move, but always inward toward the core of his being. He was scarcely conscious of the little exclamations, encouragements, and an occasional query from Father Xavier. Their voices seemed to blend, and it seemed to have been suggested to Anthony that he should ask certain questions of himself rather than that he should answer another person's. He even took a certain vague pleasure in inflicting pain upon himself as he related his struggles and doubts, or discussed the perplexing books on Mr. Bonnyfeather's shelves, the curious philosophy of Toussaint, that day in the room with Arnolfo. Now, strangely enough, he could tell everything, even the burning of that night with Faith. It was a relief. Somehow it did not seem so terrible now that he had told it. Father Xavier said nothing disturbing. So he could tell him of his love for Angela too, and the vision afterward.

As he began to speak of the madonna, *his* madonna, he began to understand that all he said, all his story of the days he had lived and the nights he had dreamed, were bound up and made one intelligible thing to himself by the feeling about a picture of her that he carried within him. It was inexplicable but it was so. She was the one permanent thing he had known. How could words compass it? It was not the little statue. That was only his particular familiar image of her, an inheritance from childhood. Into what had she grown? How could he tell it to Father Xavier?

"You see what she is lives in me, yet that is what I can speak to when I must speak to something beyond me—or be left alone —or die I guess. Shall I say that in her I, and the world, and what she is meet? At her feet! That is not it, but it is how words put it. It seems to me now I came here just to tell you that. I know it now! I came up from the sea, and through that evil, tangled garden with the dead statues, and into the court tonight. And I heard the music of the mad woman, and then I called to you, and you were there. We are not alone in this deserted house, are we? Tell me we two are not alone, my father. There is something beyond us and yet in us and with us. I believe you know. It is not all like walking up through those meaningless corridors tonight, my father. Thou knowest?"

His voice ceased and the candles burned steadily upright.

There was not a sound except the *tick* and *tock* of the pendulum over the mantel.

Then he saw the two fingers on Father Xavier's breast move. His hand was moving in the air and his lips in absolution. His gown fell apart where the fingers had been holding it, revealing the stole. Neither said anything for a while. On both of them had fallen a great peace. It seemed to Anthony that now he was free of the past forever. But the clock went on. It was after midnight. It was the morning of July 14, 1796. The clock and the calendar both said so. But in the souls of the priest and the young man it was no time at all. After a while Father Xavier got up and going over to a cupboard took out some white wine. Anthony now remembered he had had no supper. They both felt stiff. A small blaze in the grate and some wine and bread brought them back to the warm room again and the present.

Father Xavier then made up a pallet in one corner of the chamber and insisted that Anthony should lie down. He pulled up a chair close to the fire, and wrapping his gown about him again, stuck his slippers up before the little blaze. Propped upon one elbow Anthony watched the firelight glancing across the priest's strong but sensitive profile. There was something exquisite and smooth about it, but a strength there that might be stern. His eyes were a little sunken and the grey locks of the tonsure gave him the look of a venerable youth.

"I am sure," said Father Xavier at last, "that we are *not* alone." The clock seemed to interrupt him again.

"You must tell me about yourself, father," said Anthony. "Here I have taken up the whole long evening about my own precious affairs."

The priest smiled a little sadly.

"I have been busy upon the errands of my order. For a while at Naples, then in Sicily. A starving time there. These are very sad days for us. We Jesuits no longer whisper into the ears of kings. It is very difficult to bear the scorn of the world and to reconcile the bull of the Holy Father against us with obedience to the order—and the service of Jesus Christ. It is difficult in practice, that is. I have stayed in Italy, but I have been hunted at times. Indeed, I lately have been very ill, sick in body and mind." He leaned his head on his hand.

"I was educated in this house, before I went to Rome. Did you know that, Anthony? In the old days it was the summer school for the novices. Please God, it may be so again!" He seemed to be seeing things in the coals and went on in a lower tone.

"Many years ago in the days of the Colonnas it was the Villa Brignole. My mother was one of that family. Now that the Jesuits have been driven out it has fallen into their hands again. I have relatives here. They have let me stay on in these rooms quietly until I am stronger and times are better. Since the French have come things are so disturbed I need hide no longer. There is food, an old servant, and my books. I am writing one myself about our holy martyrs for the faith. It has meant more than I can tell you to have you come here tonight. Most of the work of my life seems to have crumbled. But I take courage in you as I see you now."

"Then so do I, father," said Anthony. "You first encouraged me. Indeed, without you . . ." He could not go on.

They were both silent a little again.

"Perhaps, you had better give me the letter from Mr. Bonny-feather now," said Father Xavier smiling.

"I had forgotten all about it! Forgive me. I seem to have been interested only in myself tonight. Believe me, it is not entirely so."

Father Xavier reassured him. "You can in part blame me for that tonight. But give Mr. Bonnyfeather some of the credit for having brought us together again," he added as he broke the seal and began to read.

As he read further his brows wrinkled. It was as he had thought. All had gone well with Anthony in the matters of this world. More than well. But Mr. Bonnyfeather was in doubt as to his ghostly state of mind. "I have not neglected it," wrote the old man, "I have done what I could, but my ignorance is great and in your absence I have, alas, felt myself somewhat helpless. Sir, you will forgive me, but I am old. Some things have fallen through my hands. Perhaps I should blame myself for having turned the boy over to the Frenchman.

"Perhaps? Yet I would have you remember, too, that he was to be prepared for the world and that is not a seminary . . . In the matter of first communion I have been most remiss. He is going on the long journey I mentioned above, so to your care and wisdom I leave the matter. Also in the matter of the will I would have your wisdom exercised as to whether he is to be told now the full extent of his benefits. Do as you think best." So the priest read on for several pages. "And this enclosure to you is only an earnest in advance of that other money matter of which I have spoken." Father Xavier sat pondering for some time.

"Anthony!" said he.

"Yes," replied Anthony sleepily, "sir?"

"Rouse yourself. I have some things I must talk to you about. How long will you be in Genoa?"

"Not over a day or so at most. The ship must sail . . ."

"Yes, I see," said Father Xavier. "Then you must take the sacrament at my hands tomorrow. At least I am still an ordained priest," he added with a proud melancholy half to himself. "I know a chapel where we can go together."

Anthony was sitting up now clasping his knees and thoroughly awake. Somehow he felt a little reluctant. He was not sure. It seemed hurried. He recoiled somewhat.

"I have never taken the wafer, father,—you know?"

The priest nodded and tapped the letter. "So I am told."

"I must pick up the captain too at an inn near here. We have much to do tomorrow—and my confession?"

"It was tonight, have you forgotten already?" Anthony winced. No, he had not forgotten. That was it. Somehow he felt that the confession had been drawn from him. It was unpremeditated—and yet?

"I would not put pressure on you, Anthony—but you are going on a long journey," said Father Xavier looking into the fire. His expression was very sad. He continued after a while. "God knows I would give you more preparation. There are many things I would talk about with you. There is one thing I must say to you tonight lest in my weakness I forget it. There is God and His son as well as the Madonna. No, I would not disturb you in what I may call your faith, in the comfort she has brought you. Continue, but let it lead you on. I would put it this way for your peculiar case. Do you from now on consider that which she holds in her arms." He paused to consider his own phrases. "So Christ came into the world, but so did he not go out of it."

Their concentration on each other was again intense.

"Tomorrow early then," said Anthony after a little, and felt himself relax. He lay back gladly again.

Father Xavier rose. "You have made me very happy," he said. He put a little crucifix on the table and left a candle by it. "There is a piece of worldly news which I was also bidden by Mr. Bonnyfeather to convey to you if I thought it wise to do so." He snuffed the candle carefully. "Well, I *do* think it wise. You are to be his heir." He stayed a minute looking fixedly at Anthony. Then he turned and went into his bedroom. The candle remained burning by the crucifix.

After a while Anthony got up and put it out. He found it impossible to do anything more than say a Pater Noster. He was in a sleepy tumult within. The night had been an exhausting one. He tried to feel grateful in his heart—and went to sleep.

———◆———

They were awakened next morning by the lusty bellowing in the court below of the man who had driven Anthony the night before. He was much worried about the disappearance of his fare. Anthony stuck his head out of the window and a hearty exchange of divergent views as to the advantage of spending a supperless night in an abandoned shed went on.

"But you always sleep in your carriage," remonstrated Anthony; "why should I pay you extra for it?"

"Si, signore, but always under a dry archway and with wine in my own belly, and hay for the mules. Last night there was famine, fleas, and fog. The cushions are soaked with dew and I in agony from rheumatism. I shall catch the miasmic fever, I shall die. My wife and ten children, my aged mother, my two aunts . . ."

Anthony laughed and tossed something down to him. "I hire you for all day, with meals at restaurants, wine included," he said.

The man picked up the coin and kissed his hand toward the window. "Pardon, signore, I did not understand I was retained by a nobleman. I remain then till you appear." He looked ridiculous bowing there in the court so far below. An obsequious mouse, Anthony laughed again.

"Will it all go as easily as that did? The heir is feeling generous this morning, eh!" said Father Xavier from the next room.

"Very," said Anthony, "and awfully hungry."

"I am afraid you have forgotten something, my son," smiled Father Xavier, standing by the door with his hat under his arm. "We could not eat now, you know. There is holy food for us this morning."

An inexplicable reluctance swept over Anthony. His promise!

"I am sorry. In the joy of the bright morning, after last night, after finding you, I felt like a boy again. I had forgotten."

They emerged into the court and took their way rapidly to the garden. Along the lower terraces a few wisps of mist were still smoking. The rest of the place lay flashing with dewy laurel thickets, flower-beds a riot of colour, and living green steeples of cypresses pointing up through the tangled vines. The sunlight glinted from a hundred little ponds and rain-filled basins. Down at the far gate tossed the scarlet pompons on the mules' bridles.

Anthony stopped and took a deep breath of the cool air just beginning to be tinged with the heat of the coming day. It was, he felt, right, and a fortunate thing to be alive this morning; just to be alive. Then he remembered their errand again and looked a little guiltily at Father Xavier.

"Rejoice," said the priest, "it is not sinful to be gay and happy. We are not bound on a sorrowful errand. Do you not suppose that I am happy about it too? Ah, yes! I am afraid from Mr. Bonnyfeather, and from those books of his, you have imbibed a sombre tinge about the matter. The northern races, you know, do not have a talent for religion. It is, after all, an affair of the heart, liable either to sour or to effervesce if it goes too much to the head. It is between the heart and the head that the church mediates. But come! You would not have me making a homily to you here with that shattered Calypso grinning at us from the grass!"

They began to descend the sweeping steps of the approach. Through the gaping gateway behind them came the distant notes of the harp. Father Xavier shook his head. Anthony wondered if she had been playing all night.

"Sometimes for two days and nights at a time, then she sleeps—and so do I," said Father Xavier.

It was a little uncomfortable, thought Anthony, to have his thoughts replied to this way out of the thin air. There was something in the tone of the harp that had reminded him of the garden the night before, damp moon shadows and dripping moss.

"But very beautiful here this morning," continued Father Xavier; "in full day or by the light of memory it can be very lovely even in its ruin. And I remember it when it was kept to the old marchesa's taste. I spent my childhood here and by a curious chance my novitiate, too, after the fathers took it over, years ago. A long time ago now it seems."

They had descended somewhat into the shades of the vegetation and dense paths.

"To that little pool over there I can remember coming with my mother and sailing a toy boat, a divine little *Argo*, I assure you. And it was in this grotto I spent a year alone as a novice. You see, Anthony, this is my—my convent." He lifted a heavy branch and they stepped through into a space of open green with an artificial grotto in the rocks behind it.

Before this cave staggered pitifully enough even though in dull green bronze a large figure of a water carrier. Once from the mouth of his receptacle had gushed a refreshing stream into the basin before him. But that now lay cracked and empty with a few plants struggling in its many fissures, dependent for their sustaining moisture solely upon the accidents of heaven. Already in the growing heat of the morning they were beginning to droop. Yet the eye scarcely noticed their small and ordinary tragedy. It was inevitably fixed by the terrible predicament of the water carrier himself. Above his patient human limbs the empty, lead pipe that had once conducted his secret supply was now uprooted and writhing like a snake determined to trip him.

They stood for a minute looking at this. Father Xavier picked a small flower from the basin and put it in his pocket. His lips moved. Then they went on along the terrace and down a flight, along another terrace and down, and still another— and climbed into the carriage at the gate.

26. THE STREET OF THE IMAGE MAKERS

THE hard road, dustless with the damp of night still on it, and shining before them, clicked cheerfully under the wheels. Under the spell of the exhilarating miracle of motion an enchanted seascape opened itself before them. The Mediterranean sparkling from headland to headland rolled away northward toward France. The still, white town at the foot of the distant hills with the sun upon it might have been an eternal one. For a moment the mood of the day-before possessed Anthony again. He could apprehend the vision of the table. He could not see it any longer, but he felt that he was united again with all men in the bounty of that feast. The feast of the sun and wine! "It was an affair of the heart." The words recurred to him with startling clearness. The head had nothing to do with it. Why meditate?

What was this that Father Xavier was trying to tell him about the holy communion as they drove along over these ineffable hills? What of sorrow and pain and mercy; of the meaning of certain words? It was true that he could not really hear them. Meaning should be attached to words like these. What was it he was about to do? Something for Father Xavier! It would be his pupil who would do it then; who would take the wafer. Not Anthony, not Anthony Adverse. He would not do it. No, that was it, that was it exactly. He, Anthony, would *not* do it. Presently he would have to tell Father Xavier that he would not. That was going to be hard. He sat back for a minute against the seat and felt the grit of the road crunch reassuringly under the wheels. *Clip, clop, clip, clop,* rang the iron shoes on reality.

"Thus the communion of saints . . ." said Father Xavier.

"Father," said Anthony suddenly, interrupting him, "I must talk to you now. I must tell you that I cannot take the wafer this morning. It is impossible. It would not be I. You would merely be giving it to me. Don't you see, it would be neither the head nor the heart? Not now at least." His eyes widened. "Not now . . ."

Father Xavier had gone grey. He looked as if something within him had crumbled. He sat very still.

"In the house," he thought, "in the house, before we left this morning. Now it is too late. I had prayed for this but it is not to be given to me. The work of my own hands . . ."

They were climbing a hill again, with no visible ending. The mules began to walk dragging the weight behind them slowly upward.

"Will it always be like this, I wonder?" thought the priest— and then bit his own tongue.

"Forgive me, forgive me, my father. I am sorry to have given you pain," said Anthony. "I would not be so sudden in telling you but . . ."

"In God's time and not mine," replied the priest. The colour slowly came back to his face. "Let us say no more about it. Now where are you going today? Perhaps I can help you. At least I know something about Genoa." He smiled, still quite pale.

It was not until many years later that Anthony understood that he had been present at a miracle that morning after all—a miracle of self-control.

At the top of the hill he unexpectedly found himself driving past the inn where he had left the captain the night before. A hearty "Avast there, mister," apprised him of the fact and revealed Captain Elisha gesticulating from the door with a napkin, while wiping egg from his moustache.

There was something about his portly figure, poised on its thick legs like a tree that has gripped the rocks and withstood tempests, which caused Father Xavier to appraise the mariner with approval, nor did a slightly puzzled twinkle in the captain's steady blue eyes escape him. He had seen a deeply concealed but unsolved trouble effervesce in humour like that before.

Captain Elisha on his part soon ceased to regard the kindly priest as a "foreigner." Anthony was more relieved than anyone. It had been impossible for him to imagine upon what grounds these two could meet. It was simply to be as man to man over the breakfast table. Their legs were soon under it.

"I swan to Jesus, mister," said Captain Jorham pouring a little coffee into his rum, "ye're the first mate I ever did have servin' under me that spent his shore leave with the clergy. Beggin' yer pardon, father. Not that I have any pec*oo*lar objectshune. There's wus ways of killin' time I heard tell on. Didn't know Mr. Adverse was of the persuasion." He grew more offhand as he felt himself getting into deeper water.

"You see, Mr. Adverse was a pupil of mine a good many years ago," vouchsafed Father Xavier, "I used to teach him geography and Latin."

"Wall now then," said the captain glad of so naturalistic an explanation of his mate's intimacy with the priesthood, "I did hear him tell ye was by way of bein' an old friend. Sort of a reunion then, eh?"

"Exactly," said Father Xavier.

"I met a priest in Canton oncet that had a whole school o' Chinee orphans. He was a good man for all they might say at home. Heard he was murdered afterwards. One of them slow demises they devils goes in for. Begin with yer fingers and toes and work in." He began to cut up a piece of potato graphically. "It's wonderful how little holdin' ground the soul needs. I've seen a Chinee shaped like an egg and his eyes still bright. Fact! . . . Course it's different with children. They just up anchor and goes." He looked troubled.

"What was the priest's name?" asked Father Xavier.

Captain Elisha could not remember but Father Xavier did. It had been one of his own order. "I have his story in my book."

"Wall, I swan—to man!" said the captain. He began to tell them about his voyages to Canton. They all felt at ease with one another. "Seemed like that poor fellow died jes' to make us better acquaint," he averred finally.

"That has been one remote result," said Father Xavier half to himself. "Who knows?"

Anthony observed that the captain was doing well with his "coffee." The mood of the evening before seemed likely to continue. After a while they got up and smoked a pipe outside. Anthony indulged in one, too. He did not care much for it yet. But after the experience of the night before he had made up his mind to go in for tobacco. It might pay to investigate it as well as wine. He felt just a little light in the knees as they climbed into the carriage. The captain had Anthony interpret while he paid his bill.

"And you might ask the woman," he said, "if they have a child in the house."

"Si, signore, just learning to walk. I trust its cries were not disturbing. She is very little yet."

The captain looked relieved. "'Taint the cryin'," he said. His face seemed to forbid curiosity about his inquiry.

Soon they drove on, merrily enough, it seemed to Anthony. He glanced at Father Xavier curiously. All seemed well there, too. But it had been profane food that morning after all.

"Is your hunger fully satisfied, my son?" said Father Xavier quietly in Anthony's ear. His face did not change. Anthony did not answer.

Not one to neglect any aspect of opportunity, Captain Jorham had been quick to see in the accidental presence of the priest that morning an expert aide and adviser in the purchase of church statuary. As they drove down the hills back to Genoa he began without further ado, or any sense of embarrassment, to unfold his scheme for improving the condition of the church in Cuba.

Somewhat to Anthony's surprise Father Xavier consented to serve in an advisory capacity. Indeed, as the priest listened to the captain's rather remarkable plan unfold an amused smile seemed to be hiding itself in the deep shadows under his eyes. But his mouth remained grave.

Yes, he could undoubtedly aid the captain in making the proper purchases. "It is in the Street of the Image Makers that you will find what you are looking for, I think. As to the marble blocks—I do not know whether I can help you, but I suggest that you ask some of the masons and sculptors at the place that I spoke of. Do you want to go there now?"

Captain Jorham assured him that he did. The less delay the better. Father Xavier directed the driver.

Just where the Albaro Road approaches the city gate they passed a small chapel with a fresco upon its outside walls so striking as to cause Captain Jorham to stop and descend to examine it. Outside the door there was a little money box for the benefit of souls in purgatory. Just above it on either side of the grated portal, behind which an altar could be seen, was an enormous picture of souls frying in hell. The sympathy of the artist had evidently been with the devils who were undoubtedly enjoying themselves. A small baby for the extreme trespass of not having been baptized had had both its thumbs cut off and could find nothing but a hot coal to put in its mouth. This seemed to hold the captain, although the main exhibit was an old-man-soul with a grey moustache and carefully parted hair who was being put feet first into a furnace vomiting flames. Various minor activities of a somewhat frank and painful nature were being carried on in the background. These occasionally caused Captain Jorham to "swan to man." He paused for some minutes, thoughtfully.

"I hope, father," said Anthony taking the opportunity while they were left sitting in the carriage, "that you are not shocked at the captain's scheme for taking the saints to Cuba. I am not responsible, you know."

Father Xavier smiled. "Far from it," he rejoined. "I regard Captain Jorham, and men like him, as respectable means to higher ends. Sailors, soldiers, shopkeepers, and the like are usually commendable in themselves. One should consider what is using them and why. In this case I have my own idea that the end may be a worthy one. But let us say no more, he is returning." They heard a small coin fall in the box. The captain climbed in tilting the carriage slightly. For some distance he seemed inclined to get the priest's views on infant baptism. From these he could derive small comfort.

"Er—na-ow that picture," he went on, "is that your idee of the hereafter?"

Father Xavier was non-committal though not reassuring.

"I'll tell ye some o' the parsons on the Cape could get p'inters from it," he resumed. "It would fill a church down Truro way every Sunday. It's not wasted here I guess. Nope! Do you know I calalate we're all like to be surprised by the way etarnity really is. Nearest I ever come to it was oncet off the Andamans when a bolt of fire fell into the sea right plumb off'n the starboard quarter. Left me blind for a week, it did." He paused dreamfully as if remembering something, closing his eyes.

"What did you see on the other side of the lightning, Captain Jorham?" asked Father Xavier very quietly.

The captain opened his eyes and looked at him. "I'm not giving away etarnal information for nothin' ara-ound here," said the captain. The thought of the coin he had dropped in the box for the baby remained with him. With it he had secretly bought a little comfort and was now indignant at himself for having done so.

They were now well within the town again driving through

crowded streets. A seemingly endless number of twists and turns finally landed them in front of an apothecary shop that was built into the side of a hill. They told the driver to wait and entered.

As they did so a number of shabby men who were waiting near the door hurried forward to meet them. "We want medicines only," said Father Xavier. Whereupon these physicians, for such they were, sank back disconsolately into their chairs.

They left the light of the street behind them and continued to walk along a bottle-lined passageway that gradually grew darker.

It was some seconds before Anthony's eyes became used to the deepening shadows or comprehended the meaning of a bright patch of sunlight some distance ahead. The air became dank and cool. They ascended a few rock steps, where some white mushrooms flourished, and then suddenly came out of the long tunnel into a drench of sunshine just beyond.

"This," said Father Xavier, "is the Street of the Image Makers. Without me, my son, I do not think you could have come even so far."

"Swan to man, if we ain't come clean through the hill into a lot of old stone quarries," exclaimed the captain shoving his hat back. "Thar's the sky."

The captain was correct. The Street of the Image Makers descended straight before them into a huge, rocky pocket in the hill which had once been an immense stone quarry. From the surrounding white cliffs tall, forbidding houses turned their bleak backs upon it, and from dizzy ledges goats looked down indulgently upon the place. In fact, the only entrance, that through which they had just come, had been mined in ancient times. Hence, where the tunnel ended the street began. It was merely a gash in the living stone, a gradually widening continuation of the tunnel now open to the sky like the bed of a dry canal.

In the walls of this marble prism shops and dwellings had been hollowed out from time to time, and their fronts carved in the various styles which the caprices of the owners had dictated. Before several doors an arcade rested upon Ionic pillars, one solid piece of stone. Another shop affected a classic façade with a temple-like entablature resembling a rock tomb. Some had severely plain fronts pierced by doors and windows only, but even around these openings skilful chisels had traced wreaths of flowers and vines. Farther on the street widened away and descended into the heart of the abandoned quarry, where at the end of its gleaming vista sparkled a dark blue pond.

Completely removed from the noise and sweaty confusion of the city, the first impression of this little community was that of a sepulchral place set apart from the living interests of mankind. It seemed to brood upon its peculiar affairs exclusively, as if the inner moods of its troglodytical inhabitants were reflected by the single eye of the pool in the marble at the end of their curious avenue.

"This is where most of the holy images, shrines, and ecclesiastical carvings in this part of Italy are made," said Father Xavier. "Look, that is a forge over there." He pointed to a hole in the rock topped by a little chimney pot from which smoke and flames were issuing. "There are also several small potteries scattered about. Sculptors work here in both stone and wood. Those who apply colour are a separate fraternity and live farther down the street. I would not be surprised if the images of the gods had been made here when Genoa was a Roman town. Some of these places, you can see from the weathered carvings, escape the memory of man."

The priest's remarks had by now brought them before the arcaded shops. From these a continuous muffled thudding proceeded. Looking in, they saw a number of workmen with wooden mallets beating upon chamois skins. Stepping to the first window Father Xavier called loudly for "Messer Stefano." An artisan in a leather apron appeared at the door. Tall, thin, and very dark, there was something Egyptian about the man, as he stood peering out into the sunlight with hawk-like eyes, small gold earrings, and a short leather apron.

"Stefano, I have brought you some customers," said Father Xavier. The man hastened to lay aside his tools.

"This is the potentate of the whole street," whispered the priest to Anthony. "A rather remarkable fellow. You will have to do all your bargaining through him. Humour him. He regards himself with some justice as an artist and a philosopher."

The thudding in the shop had ceased. Only from the forge down the street a thin troll-like clinking could still be heard. As Father Xavier explained the nature of their errand to Messer Stefano at some length it seemed as though not only the padrone but the place itself was listening.

"Go on with your work in there," said Stefano after a while. The hammers of the gold beaters resumed.

"Since the captain here speaks nothing but English," concluded Father Xavier, "you will have to conduct your negotiations with Signore Adverso. You will find him not without a natural insight in this affair, a young gentleman of honour and sensibility, a former pupil of mine." The workman bowed slightly.

"And now," said Father Xavier, turning to Anthony unexpectedly and with a smile that was almost tremulous, "you see I have brought you as far as I can. It is time to say good-bye. Let it be here then."

"To see you again, and when, my father?"

Father Xavier wrung Anthony's hands and hurried up the street. At the mouth of the tunnel he turned. Anthony raised his hand in farewell. He saw that the priest was blessing him. Then he disappeared into the shadow of the tunnel behind.

"If the signori care to, I will show them about the street," said the voice of Stefano smooth but not obsequious. He led the way into the shop.

"All the shops here are now under my direction," the man continued a little proudly, "but the gold leaf is my special care. Would you like to see?"

He drew aside a chamois skin revealing the beautiful, yellow metal underneath spreading out from a lump in the middle in one shining sheet. He showed them the process. "Under a skilful hammer, you see, there will be no holes."

The captain was much impressed. "Wall, sir, I used to think

my dad could make gold spread further than any living man. It would have hurt his pride to see this. He was pretty talented though. When I was nine years old he brought me a penny after a successful v'y'ge to Nassau. Sir, I had to show him that coin every Thanksgivin' for ten years. I've kept it so durned long I larned the only Latin off it I ever knowed. '*Expulsis piratus, resti-too-shia commercia.*' Kick out the pirates and reopen the stores," he translated, flushed with his own learning. "And that penny was only copper, and here it is."

Stefano had managed to catch the Latin. "We are not pirates here," he said grievously displeased. Anthony was forced to explain. The man summoned a vague laugh from somewhere and laying down his hammer led them out again.

"You will find each little place given up to its own specialty, signore," he explained. "Trade in images has not been very good for nearly a hundred years. My grandfather remembered a better time. With the makers of holy images it now goes hard. War, it is always war! Few churches or shrines are being built. No one makes vows. It is mostly the women and antiquarians who buy now. I have been forced to control things here in Genoa. I buy up even the old figures and retouch them. Only a few of the most popular blesséd ones still sell. In here we make nothing but bambinos."

He threw open a door for them at the side of the street. Inside a number of boys and girls were preparing plaster and pouring it into moulds. From a drying kiln at one end of the room a girl returned with a tray full of white baby dolls and laid them before an old man who sat with brushes and various paints before him. They watched him a while.

"Do *not* vary the smile, Pietro," said their guide. "How often must I tell you? It is that one beatific expression of Buonarrotti's which I desire you to repeat. What do you know of ecstasy?"

"Si, si, padrone," said the artist deprecatingly as he retouched a few cherubic lips. "But memory plays me tricks with these smiles. I once had children of my own. You should have let me stay moulding resignation into holy hands. I was good at that."

"Not so good as you think," said Stefano as they went out.

"It is very difficult to have to make these artists always do the most perfect thing and keep repeating it," he continued as they went along farther. "So many of them have their own ideas. And that would be well enough, signore, if this street were given over to secular art. But you see, in my case, in what *I* have undertaken to do here, the perfect examples both in life and art have already been given. It is restraint therefore and imitation that are needed . . .

"Si, I have thought much and often as to the effect of these statues upon those who will acquire them. They are to bring to mind the very image of the holy one whose intercession is sought or whose example is to be followed. In that, as in everything, a certain technique is necessary. Have you ever thought of that, signore? Without a technique, a bodily method for faith, morality, religion itself would perish. Without the church as one immortal corporation, without the methodology which it inculcates and even turns into a habit, the memory of divine things would be lost. Or it would be left in the minds of women to be told to babies. It is true most vital things *are* remembered that way from generation to generation. But our religion is not so simple as that. There must ever be images, concrete moulds into which it can be poured." He flung up his hands excitedly. "But, pardon me, I do not wish to bore you. You see this is my life work, my enthusiasm, this small street. It is not altogether that I live by it. I live *in* it." He checked himself somewhat embarrassed.

"Tell me what you think," said Anthony. "It is seldom that people will do so. I have often thought about what you are speaking of. Tell me, you would not have them worship the image itself?"

"I would not stop them," said Stefano. "What can you do with such minds as that but give them something outside themselves to adore? Let them play in their divine doll house. Let them dress their saints and be happy. Those who plague such people with abstract ideas about God are foolish. Is it not better to leave them with an image which may lead to something beyond?

"I am not speaking of philosophers and savants, my friend. They are idolaters of ideas. With them both the image and the technique of the ways of life they would inculcate are always lacking. Hence their dreams must be renewed every generation in adults, by the few who can read and understand. God forgive me, I hope I utter no heresy," he crossed himself, "but I have often thought it is not such a mystery after all that God should have embodied himself in human form. Otherwise he would have remained to us unknown, imageless, a vague voice in the winds, mystery in the landscape, the theory of some teacher, or the beautiful dream of an artist in some idol ugly or beautiful as sin. In Christ he became a body, the way, and the life. I believe; I know that." He wiped his brow with his sleeve.

"What is the man saying?" asked Captain Jorham, a little alarmed at being left out so long.

"He is talking about the image of God," said Anthony with secret enjoyment.

"Holy smoke, *resti-too-shia commercia*, let's be gettin' on!" snapped the captain.

"I see that your friend does not fully understand," said Stefano.

"What I was trying to tell *you*, signore," he hurried on in a lower voice, "is that in all my images here I have, for reasons that you can now surmise, tried to embody nothing but the most perfect attitudes and gestures. I have studied the works of the old artists in the days of great faith, and have chosen for each saint or bambino or madonna, even for Christ himself, those features which have been found to have the most appeal. Each one of these images is a lasting and a silent preacher. Come, let me show you something wonderful now."

He took out the key for the door before which they now stood. "These are too precious to be worked on except under supervision. The model here is of great value. It is part of the French spoil from Milan. Not now, not of this Buonaparte, but of the French kings many generations ago." He threw open the door.

"Only I and my assistant work here," he said. "All of these

models are from my hands. See, here is the original." He pulled a cloth off an almost life-sized figure in the centre of the room where the light fell upon it from the door.

It was a Virgin and Child carved in some soft grained stone. Just the head and bust of a peasant woman wrapped in an ample medieval garment. The stone had been coloured and gilded and a great blue fold of the virgin's cloak swept down over her breast. In the folds of the deep hollow slept the child. It could not be seen from the front. It was completely concealed in the hollow. Only the folds of the cloak and the position of the woman's hands conveyed the fact that something infinitely precious was concealed there.

Stefano pointed to the hands and paid them the compliment of saying nothing at all. Then he turned to the models.

"You see we could not afford to reproduce this in stone," he said. "These are clay replicas. When they are first baked the colour is a little garish but if properly placed in the shadow the effect of the lines and the whole figure is admirable. I think we have caught what those hands are saying . . . and the wonderful sweeping fold!" He ran his hand over the bulge of the blue scarf with satisfaction.

"It is well reproduced, Messer Stefano," said Anthony, "but not so durable as the original I suppose."

"No, signore, but light, even porous, and easy to transport," said Stefano lifting one of the images. "See!"

"The biggest thing we've seen yet," said Captain Jorham. "You might start with one of these, mister." He peered over the edge of the fold. "Just as I thought, she's got a baby, too! The hul thing's complete. Better start in and make your dicker now. This is the kind of thing we want. Nothing small and cheap. How about some o' they life-sized figurines?"

With some censoring of the text Anthony translated.

"If it is large figures," said Stefano, "come this way."

He led them directly across the street and up a few steps into a kind of stone lean-to with its rear wall in the rock itself. Here standing in solemn tiers were twenty or thirty life-sized figures of saints and a large thorn-crowned Christ with the conventional anatomy of the bleeding heart exposed. Its expression of agony was so intense as to make a large St. Lawrence stretched out on his gridiron over terra cotta flames comparatively genial.

"That's the stuff," said Captain Jorham. "Some of them are a little cracked, too. They ought to be knocked down reasonable. Git busy, mister. Why not the hul lot?"

Stefano was surprised at the wholesale gusto of his customer. A little disgusted, too, Anthony could see. For that reason he began by bargaining for one of the fine clay figures of the Virgin they had just seen across the street. The man seemed somewhat mollified by this. After all the young gentleman did understand the pride of an artist.

"As your masterpiece," said Anthony, "we will give you for the model ten crowns less than you ask. And that, as you know, is more than meeting your expectations. For that reason, and because we shall be taking all of this old stock, you must make me, on worn figures at least, a more reasonable rate."

After an hour and a half of chaffering, by which time the captain's hat was shoved clear back on his head and his hands deep in his pockets, an agreement was in sight. Another half hour and it was agreed that Stefano should retouch and repaint where necessary. All of the "old holy ones" were to be made bright and new. It would take two days for the paint and gilding to dry. Anthony would call for them then and take them to the *Wampanoag*. It was also arranged that they should be transported in carriages. "Every respect must be shown them," explained Stefano. The excitement in the streets at so extensive a flitting of saints would undoubtedly be considerable. After some demur Captain Jorham agreed. He had once seen a religious riot at Lisbon.

"Tell him we'll even put 'em to bed when we get 'em aboard," he said. "I mean it. It won't do to have any of these people breakin' loose in the hold. Besides somethin' might shatter 'em if the cargo shifted. Now how about them marble blocks for ballast?"

But this could not be arranged. It would take weeks to drill the holes.

"Never thought of that," said Captain Elisha. "Ask him about some plain marble slabs. I can batten them down I calalate. We want weight, weight! There ain't profit in water ballast. The crew drinks it."

It was possible to arrange for the slabs. Captain Elisha looked much pleased. The total outlay had not been large and he had obtained more statuary than he had thought possible. They adjourned to Stefano's hut and sealed the bargain over a bottle of bad wine. By sunset they were back on board the brig.

"And a couple of days will just give us time to load stores, water the ship, and do a little calkin' along the water line where that Portegee bumboat rammed her," mouthed the captain through a mouthful of Philadelphia's grub, "and lay in a few kegs of wine," he added, looking his wife in the eye. "Say, Jane, don't 'e look solemn about that. Wait till you see who's comin' aboard to keep you company. Taewsday mornin'. Whew!" He paused for a minute with his fork and knife held bolt upright.

"Right on that Putnam sideboard is going to be a heathen idol—with a baby. It's the prize o' the hul lot. It goes to Havaner in the cabin!" He cut a piece of salt pork at one blow. "As for the rest of 'em, there's five empty bunks in the fo'c'sle. I'd like to see the British come aboard now with a press gang. They'd have to prove Jesus Christ was born in Sussex. Still," said he rapping on wood, "some of them post captains could do that all right. It ud take God A'mighty to stop 'em. That it would." He poured some hot water into his rum.

"Mister, you're a macaroni mate and you can't hand, reef, nor steer. But you're goin' to have a hul starboard watch with haloes, and a cargo of tombstones for ballast. There's only one thing I got to say to you as captain of this *holy* ship. I don't want no miracles occurrin' when I'm below. Do you hear? *That goes!*" He left the fork quivering in the table.

"Now you get your charts and we'll lay out the course."

The lines about Captain Jorham's mouth began to be a little more drawn as he imbibed a large pitcher of "dog's nose." He gradually became silent and morose as the evening wore away and his wife knitted and knitted.

"More baby clothes?" said the captain at ten o'clock by the chronometer when they prepared to turn in. She nodded and closed the panel. The captain drew off his heavy boots.

"Mister," said he, "*you'll* do the navigatin'? You kin?" He looked anxious.

Anthony felt sure of it. He took out his new sextant that Mr. Bonnyfeather had given him. The latest London make, he noted. By degrees and by degrees he would soon be slipping over into new latitudes. He went on deck for a while and looked again at the city.

In his room at the Palazzo Brignole, Father Xavier fumbling in his pocket for his pipe found the flower he had picked from the empty basin in the garden that morning. It seemed to him as it lay in his palm that he had also permitted that to wither. His hand shook slightly. But what could one do with wild flowers? Leave them to the winds of God? A sorry argument about predestination failed to comfort his soul. His dreams were sorrowful.

On the *Wampanoag* next morning they began to bend on a suit of new sails.

27. THE PILLARS OF HERCULES

Captain Jorham had miscalculated. Nearly a week passed before the *Wampanoag* could put to sea. Much against his better judgment, because he was so short-handed, he was forced to ship some "Spanish riff-raff" and a few "select" British deserters hanging about the docks at Genoa. The latter, after they sobered up, proved willing hands enough. At least they could be counted on to keep a weather-eye peeled for king's ships. And above all else Captain Elisha was anxious to give British cruisers a wide berth.

At last the brig was watered and her cargo stowed. Five saints were lashed in the fo'c'sle bunks and the grumbling men told to swing hammocks. Late one afternoon they hoisted the anchor merrily enough and a few hours later sunk the peaks which gird in the Gulf of Genoa under the northern horizon.

Under a complete suit of new sails the ship bowled along famously. Philadelphia, happy with an ample supply of olive wood, his favourite fuel, sang at the door of his little galley now surrounded by chicken coops. Forward, two pigs, a milch goat and her kids, and a number of ducks and geese swelled a bucolic chorus that sang of good fare to come.

Captain Jorham had reverted to a kind of man-o'-war discipline for his now motley crew, a discipline with which as an ex-privateersman he was familiar. One Jeb Collins, a middle-aged down-easter with iron-grey hair and a rasping voice, had been appointed "quartermaster" with the authority but not the wages of a second mate. Under the press of sail which the brig was carrying, both of the watches were kept pretty constantly on deck. Captain Jorham had not seen fit to appoint Anthony to either. He took one himself and gave the other to Collins. In the strong and continually freshening breeze pouring out of the east he carried sail till the weather shrouds sang a higher note.

Mrs. Jorham was the only member of the crew who persistently kept below. She sat in her cabin and contemplated with an indignation which only she could control the large terra cotta figure of the Virgin Mary that now occupied the place of her copper coffee urn on the Putnam sideboard. A little less than life-sized, the statue seemed to have thrust aside the urn, which was Mrs. Jorham's chief pride, in wanton intrusion. It occurred to Mrs. Jorham that the Virgin kept wrapping the folds of her ample, blue cloak about her with a calm aloofness that amounted to provocative disdain.

It was only an added exasperation to the captain's wife to find that in the deep fold over the statue's right shoulder a baby lay concealed. Aside from sectarian scruples about "idols," she had also certain personal reasons which made even the statue of a woman with a child in her arms, especially when it was snugly ensconced in her own cabin, peculiarly hard to bear. Besides, as she continued to look at it—and she could scarcely avoid doing so—in the atmosphere of her lonely reveries the thing began to take on the elements of a living personality. She caught herself giving it from time to time a caustic piece of her mind.

That her husband had inflicted this reminder upon her seemed a piece of deliberate cruelty and reproach. Her only consolation was, if he had not been drinking he would not have done so. But in the obstinate state which the captain had now reached, and took care to increase from day to day, remonstrance would be useless. His only reply would be to mix himself another dog's nose. Furthermore, with the primary cause of her husband's drinking Mrs. Jorham was to some extent forced to sympathize. Indeed, she reproached herself in a Biblical manner with having been responsible for it.

Up until now the captain had kept the deck. But the delay at Genoa had advanced his potable calendar considerably, and she foreboded his early and complete retirement to the cabin in no very complacent mood. Meanwhile she sat there reduced to silence, minding her knitting, and brushing away an occasional mist of stinging tears. Under these circumstances she felt it would have been some company and no little protection to have had the new mate keep to the cabin more than he did.

Anthony, however, kept the deck early and late. He was anxious to pick up every item of nautical lore that might come his way, and that in as short a time as possible. His position on the ship was, he realized himself, somewhat ridiculous. To the crew as well as to the captain he was already known as the "macaroni mate." Neither the captain nor the men paid much attention to him at first. He was, as Captain Jorham had said, strictly "*ex-officio*." He had been inclined to accept this position more or less, but during a dog watch at Genoa Collins, the quartermaster, had leaned over the bulwarks with him one evening while they watched the lights of the city coming out one by one, and unburdened his mind.

"Before we git into the trades, Mr. Adverse, you'll find yourself in real charge," said the quartermaster. "I know the skipper, and he ain't d-ue to last tew long as things are going na-ow.

Ye're mate on the roster, and ye'll find that mate ye'll have to be. Na-ow I'll dew all *I* can, but you might keep that in mind. Authority's authority, and ye either are, air ye ain't."

So Anthony kept it in mind. To be lost on the Atlantic with a ship and crew—to be lost there! It haunted his dreams. He could only pray that Captain Jorham would last. But wishes soon became ridiculous. Already it was a miracle how Captain Elisha could keep going as he did.

"He counts on gittin' us through the Straits," said Collins. "And then—"

"Ah, and then!" thought Anthony. He was glad he had spent his life more or less about ships around the docks at Livorno. The nomenclature and the lingo were familiar. He began now to memorize commands. But above all he began to furbish up his navigation. He even wished he had listened to the mad Mr. Williams' theory of lunar longitude. The *Wampanoag's* chronometer was obviously a joke. He made a few friends among the older members of the crew. Once at sea he went up on the yards to shake out or take in sail. Collins at least was for him. That was one comfort. And he had learned the ship from trucks to keelson at Genoa while she was lading. After a week he felt the men respected him even if they laughed. He laughed with them, and kept the deck. The first noon out he brought up his sextant but the captain would have none of it.

"Lay off that mister, till I give the word. I don't need that contraption to tell where we're at na-ow."

"The old man's awful techy about shootin' the sun," whispered Collins. "He'll try to go by dead reckonin' when he kin."

So the new sextant went back to the cabin. But the men had seen it, and some of the old hands who had sailed with Captain Jorham before looked pleased.

The captain's method of navigation, since his faith had been shattered some years before in his pet sextant, was, although he did not condescend to explain it, abundantly plain. In the Mediterranean it consisted in coasting from one well-known landfall to another. In wider, ampler oceans of late years his progress had become truly wonderful. Each voyage had rivalled that of

Columbus in view of the possible mysteries ahead. One grand fact had consoled him. Sailing east from *Amurakee* one was bound to reach *U-rup*. Undoubtedly the converse might also be true. At any rate he was about to put it to a pragmatic test. In the meantime in a comparatively small place like the Mediterranean he felt at home. With two ex-whalers for lookouts he continued to crack on sail unmercifully.

Once the bend in the coast by Genoa was out of sight he took a long southern slant till he raised the peaks of Corsica. A day later the fishing boats making for Ajaccio allowed him to mark himself down as about 42 N. and 8 E. After that it was comparatively easy going for a while. The east wind, which held and continued to freshen a little every day, suited him well. On that tack the *Wampanoag* was at her best. He merely squared away a little to be sure to pass to leeward of Asinara and then ran down the coast of Sardinia as far as S. Pietro.

"Call it thirty-nine North," said Captain Elisha. "Gib is just thirty-six and away, and away west."

But he frowned a little as he looked at the chart. The bulge in the coast of Africa was somewhat confusing. He wanted to give Port Mahon and the Balearics a wide berth on account of British cruisers. To make, as he put it, "a good southing" before he squared away before the wind for the Straits. Part of Africa, however, appeared to be in the way. And Algiers was an unhealthy neighbourhood. Between the horns of this dilemma, Algiers and Minorca, he lingered over the chart for an hour or two. The application of a third dog's nose he was glad to see had straightened out the coast of Africa. "Well, he would hold on south; take a good plenty south." And he did so.

Next day the wind showed every sign of freshening to a blow. With some difficulty Collins got permission to reduce sail and finally to send down the royal and t'gallant masts. Not only the ship but its new mate now rode much easier. Watching the yards roll against the sky while the spars came down had given Anthony his first serious qualms. Nothing, however, could persuade the captain to follow the example of several other ships and head west. Collins was obviously worried at this obstinacy.

"Git a sight today if ye kin, Mr. Adverse," he managed to say while the men were lashing the lower topmasts to the shrouds with extra precautions. "This here weather looks like a little patch o' clear before a big blow. For God's sake take advantage of it. I'll try to keep the skipper below at noon. Seems like I could smell Afriky."

When Anthony came up with his sextant a few hours later both the deck and the horizon were momentarily clear. Taking advantage of a patch of clear sky just at noon, when the scud which had been driving for some hours luckily opened out overhead, he made his first observation at sea.

When he worked out his position he made it to be much farther south than the captain's longest guess would admit. Africa must be not far over the southern horizon. He said so, but somewhat too diffidently.

Ordinarily Captain Elisha would have given heed and taken the credit to himself. Under influences more potent than the calculations of his merely titular mate he now argued and held on. He was convinced at dawn by a frantic voice from the masthead and a not too distant glimpse of a long beach dead ahead where breakers bared their fangs and endless sand dunes smoked in the gale. For a few hours he was somewhat sobered. The ship was instantly put before the wind which swept her westward. The trend of the coast soon caused them to man the port braces and give the brig a safe northern slant. After that they all breathed easier.

"Drunken man's luck it wasn't a lee shore," muttered Collins to Anthony. "We'll git more wind sure before tonight."

The incident proved a fortunate one for Anthony. In the estimation of all hands he advanced considerably. A certain subdued humorous tolerance with which he had so far been treated now gave way to a more serious acceptance and respect. From that time on his appearance on deck with a sextant was hailed by the older members of the crew in particular with a secret sigh of relief. The vagaries of the captain's navigation even when sober were only too well known. It was not long before Anthony discovered the cause.

The captain's sextant, he found after a little checking, had once been repaired and its angle altered. Evidently it had had a fall some time prior to the American Revolution. Consequently the more accurate the observation the more certain the error. It was only a few seconds—but at the end of a voyage! To amuse himself he worked out a table of compensation.

But of all this he determined for the time being to say nothing. In the captain's present mood it would do no good. And knowledge was power. Excellent seaman as Captain Jorham ordinarily was, should the mixing of dogs' noses continue, Anthony was by no means certain how much responsibility might not yet rest on the inexperienced shoulders of his mate. It would be well to keep safe what little claim to authority he had. With this Mrs. Jorham and the now greatly perturbed Collins agreed.

Indeed, from the time of their brief glimpse of Africa dead ahead Anthony worked out the course daily with the aid of the quartermaster. The captain was already moving in spheres without parallels, a diviner ether and an ampler air. The cabin itself had begun to take on a peculiar air of unreality which Anthony could scarcely account for. In this both the captain and his wife seemed to have an equal share. He took the charts out of this realm of speculation into the more sober and ecclesiastical fo'c'sle.

"Necessity makes strange bedfellows, indeed," Anthony thought as he and Jeb Collins fumbled over the charts, laying out the compass bearings for the day while surrounded by several bunks full of Christian martyrs and saints. The whale-oil lamp overhead swung with the motion of the ship causing murky shadows to chase over the face of the map like little clouds over a miniature landscape. The face of St. Lawrence who was lashed on his gridiron to the forward bulkhead grew alternately dark and pale. Beneath him the terra cotta flames continued to flicker. Someone, Anthony noticed, had put a tarpaulin over Christ. St. Catherine's wheel was hung with oil-skins and gear.

"It's a turrible time on this little ship when the skipper begins wallerin' in grog," remarked Collins looking about a little apprehensively. "Luck's usually with him even then, I dew allow, but it don't seem right to tempt it tew far by lashin' all these heathen people in a Christian fo'c'sle. 'Sides, 'tain't shipshape. I kivered that awful bleedin' heart myself. Looked like murder and mutiny on board."

He turned to the chart again with a distinct look of relief.

"Lay it a good deal north of west, Mr. Adverse. Ye'll be wantin' to give them Sallee rovers a wide berth and yet not nose tew near Minorca. Call it nor'west by north, that's about right till tomorrow allowin' fer what you said the variation is. She logs about ten knots in this breeze. Ye can see where that ul git you tomorrow noon. Hope ye can git the sun then. Maybe? But as I've been sayin' all erlong it's comin' on to bla-ow. We're not far enough off the coast yet to suit me."

They went up on deck together. Astern, between the low slate-coloured cloud that covered them like the roof of a cave, and the leaden floor of the sea below, was a long bright streak, green, intensely clear, and apparently gaining on them fast. A flock of gulls streamed past screaming, going downwind. Beyond the clear streak Anthony thought he could see land. A long range of sombre hills wrought with a freedom that only ruthless nature could attain were lifting sullen, tortured peaks above the horizon. Suddenly a hellish glow of sunset flashed redly from peak to peak. As if returning an answer their dark battlements lightened and winked with sheets of internal flame. Their pinnacles started to wither away. From beneath them endless lines of mad cavalry with white tossing manes came galloping down on the ship. The rumble of distant artillery rang around the horizon, a volley of bullet-like hail spattered the sails and deck.

"Land O," roared the lookout.

As if warned by instinct Captain Elisha instantly appeared on the quarter-deck.

"Ready about, take your stations for stays," he roared through his speaking trumpet.

"Stations!" howled Collins. "Git 'em up, Mr. Adverse, don't lose no time. There's no chance to strip her now." His whistle shrilled.

"Put the helm da-own," bellowed the captain.

The *Wampanoag* shot around into the wind her canvas slatting and thundering. Warned by the pother overhead as much as by Collins' now profane encouragements the men were at their stations before the ship teetered into the eye of the wind. As if she had received a sudden blow from a furious fist the *Wampanoag* was taken aback.

"Haul taut! Mainsail haul!" bellowed the enormous trumpet. The aft sails moved around together and filled with a loud report. The yards were braced up. "Let go and haul," commanded the trumpet. Anthony saw the foreyards come round and the canvas bellow out. The jibs were sheeted home. With a great bound under the first full impulse of the gale the brig dashed off on the opposite tack. The men went about coiling up ropes as if nothing had happened.

The cause of all this had been a glimpse of Cape Carthage to leeward. The manoeuvre was repeated again several times that night. The captain remained on deck for hours until he had worked well out to the northward into the open sea.

Under the outward buffeting of the elements and the internal refreshment with which Philadelphia constantly supplied him, the captain seemed that night to surpass the usual limits of human personality. He stood behind the steersman with his legs braced far apart in what appeared to Anthony to be seven league sea boots. The foam and spume streamed off his oilskins that fluttered in occasional wild glimpses of moonlight like infernal rags. As the night wore on his voice took on more and more of a brazen quality. He drove his crew and his ship hour by hour clawing off the coast of Africa, thrashing along now on a short, mad stretch to leeward, and now beating up into the teeth of the wind. The rigging shrieked and the bows of the *Wampanoag* thundered and foamed. In the tireless figure on the quarter-deck at home in the storm, Anthony thought he could glimpse a more colossal emanation of the man who had been at one with the world when he sat in the carriage at Genoa watching the sunset. It was the curious quality of this man that he seemed during the night to grow in stature, to be an antidote for fear. Perhaps it was the immense brazen voice from the trumpet that all obeyed. Perhaps? When the dawn broke Anthony was surprised to see again that Captain Jorham was really not so tall. A rather short figure if you looked closely.

About dawn the brig was put before the wind again. From now on it would be a straight run for the Straits. During the night she had been stripped of canvas and was driving with nothing but a reefed foresail, a spanker, and a jib to keep her from yawing. There were two men at the wheel, for the seas were now coming on so fast from behind as to kick her stern at times almost clear of the water. The drag when she settled back again was terrific. Four arms on the spokes were none too many. They shook out a reef in the foresail but it was not enough— another. She continued to plunge more determinedly.

"It'll never do to broach to na-ow," shouted the captain in Anthony's ear as an unusually large wave rose and combed just aft of the taffrail only to break and go hissing by.

"Na-ow's the time to get a little more drag on her for'd. Do you see, mister?" he roared, pointing to some of the crew busy rigging preventer stays to the foretopmast, "I'm going to give her a double reefed foretops'l."

Presently there was a report as if a small cannon had been fired and streams of ripped canvas whipped about frantically, beating the crew off the yard. Collins drove them back and made them cut it loose. It was snatched to leeward.

"The old sail," said the captain. "Thought we'd try that first. Na-ow watch. Ye might have to do this sometime."

He went forward banging on the scuttle for the other watch who came tumbling up. The new sail was hoisted and bent on slowly with extra lashings. When it opened out they let it blow away clear of the lower yard. For a moment it stood out flat and clear like a horizontal banner streaming forward. At that instant the captain roared and it was sheeted home to the lower yard with an even pull on both tackles.

The brig leaped ahead. The men at the wheel wrestled with the spokes over a brief "S"-shaped course that soon flattened out into a clear wake of bubbles left straight behind. Aft, the waves still rose now as before, followed, but fell astern. Captain Jorham returned to the quarter-deck and spat over the side. He cupped his hands to shout. "Never let 'em slat back on ye. Ye hev to sheet home *jes'* so. If ye let the blocks whip back and tangle, ye're gorn!"

They stood together a while watching the ship tear through the crests and race down into the hollows beyond as if in mad pursuit of some invisible prey. But she rose now and seemed to be lifted ahead, the sails booming as they came up out of the valleys of water into the full force of the wind.

Under the pressure of her increased canvas the *Wampanoag* was whipped forward at startling speed. Anthony could feel transferred to his own body her wild desire to twist and lay-to which the men at the wheel constantly checked. It must be certain, he thought, that something would go. In reality it was only a good hearty gale, but to his inexperience it seemed a hurricane. When the gusts came he waited for an ominous crack overhead, having no adequate idea of the relative strength of yards, cordage, and ship's timbers. So he stood for hours, watching, but nothing happened. The ship had been made for this, he had to admit at last.

The bell was struck with the spray and rain streaming off it. The men at the wheel and the watches were relieved regularly. Old Collins heaved the log. The wind keened through the rigging, and the turmoil of waters raced by. As the sun sank at last in a red mist and the horizon narrowed to the ship's dimensions he began to feel confident again. Soon even the ship disappeared except for a few feet of deck and a dim tracery aloft. He was alone in the universe standing on something. A few feet aft the bearded face of a sailor smoking a pipe seemed to be floating without a body over the feeble glow of the binnacle. Only when the ship rolled could you sense the man's body eclipsing a few misty stars. A faint glimmer from the stern windows followed and followed over the tossing wake. The sound of hissing and foaming was muffled by monotony. An endless, meaningless story told in a mad liquid tongue, it was. Its constant narrative was unimportant, only its cessation or a complete change of tone could be significant. It was the same with the sails. They would go on that way and go on—till the wind changed. He turned and went below.

As he slid the scuttle hood over his head and descended into the cabin the piping of the gale and the song of the rigging was suddenly cut off and made infinitely remote. It was a relief to escape it. Then the curious face at the aft end of the cabin was looking at him. He paused half-way on the ladder listening, missing the noise of wind and water, only to become aware gradually of the internal life of the ship.

It was a kind of suspended motion accompanied by muffled cracklings, strainings and squeaks, groans and the hushed swishing of water under the keel. The floor of the cabin tilted always to another angle, poised, tilted again, slid, and climbed. A long gurgle of bilge water bubbled and stopped like a drowned flute at every subsidence. Clothes suspended from hooks pointed to the middle of the floor only to find the ship's sides nuzzling them. *They* had not moved. And to all of this there was a kind of inexpressible rhythm, a repetition which no one could predict or remember. But it went on.

Yet the main impression of the cabin bathed in its smoky yellow light was that those who sat there were waiting for something inevitable to happen. As Anthony stood on the ladder and looked about him he was instantly aware of it. Yet he could not account for it at all. It was like listening behind a closed door for someone he knew was there but who made no sign. Mrs. Jorham was knitting. She did not even look up. Philadelphia was laying the table, noiselessly. Captain Jorham was nodding with his mouth open. Yet they were waiting—not for him. The shadows slipped slowly from side to side. The lamp hummed as if a moth were in it. The Virgin wrapped her cloak about her and looked in its folds. He came down slowly, peeled off his heavy wet coat and sat in his bunk. The air was not so fresh down here. He was tired and perhaps a little dizzy.

The same impression that he had going to Genoa came over him. He was not moving at all. The sea outside, the shadows, the events in the cabin were all coming out of somewhere and going past him. He, watching this vague panorama, remained still. Yes, the long corridors in Father Xavier's house with all the frescoes in the wall had gone past him. It was all like walking in a treadmill. The convent, the days at the Casa and the streets of Livorno, Faith, Angela, Vincent, Genoa—tonight in the cabin was going by like that. It had all come out of the darkness into the light of his eyes and returned into the darkness again. Dreams of it remained in memory. There was more, more to come. You could not stop it. You walked to the last rung in the treadmill—and then? Travel! He laughed silently as the side of the ship pressed itself against him.

Mrs. Jorham beckoned for him to come and eat but he could not. He felt decidedly dizzy and tired after the long day. He wished the ship would stay still. It kept moving about *him* as the centre of everything, sickeningly. He began to talk to Mrs. Jorham in a low voice through which now and then over his own monotone he could catch the loud ticks of the clumsy chronometer. It sounded like a treadmill. What she replied he could not remember. After a while he went on deck again. In the darkness—he was glad of the darkness—he was very sick.

The fit passed. For a day or two he was dizzy, then very clear again. The motion of the ship no longer troubled him. He was going with it now. He forgot it although the wind had increased if anything. Captain Jorham had added a storm staysail in the teeth of it and the brig rode steadier.

Anthony often wondered what would have happened to them if Captain Jorham had taken to his bunk before they were clear of the Straits. For days now it had not been possible to get a sight of the sun. The ship had been swept steadily westward in a smother of spume half the time with a pall of rolling, dark clouds driving over her and billowing down so low sometimes as to seem about to touch the masts. Through all this pother of the elements Captain Elisha carried his ship by dead reckoning and sea instinct. To him the currents, the tides, the very colour of the water were guides. They scarcely had a glimpse of the stars. At last there were some signs of a break in the gale. The men in the tops watched eagerly for a landfall.

It came suddenly, and unexpectedly to starboard. One day at noon the pall overhead lightened, the sun struggled through. Before them the wind seemed to be tearing the clouds to rags. Without the least warning, as if a curtain had been raised, long lines of snow-capped mountains were seen marching on their right. Sixty miles inland the wild hills of the Sierra Nevadas rose above the brown plains of Granada with continental fragments of dark cloud-bank breaking against them, clouds rolling up in white mist, filing through the passes, and being driven and harried westward along the slopes. An interplay of swiftly moving titanic shadows turned the long coasts of Spain fading away before them to the southeast into a Satanic country lit inland by infernal gleams.

"That's Cape Gata," said Captain Jorham, indicating a point of land with a few white houses and a fierce surf leaping up about a small, stone battery. "And it's darn lucky if there ain't a British frigate anchored under its lee." He gave the *Wampanoag* a sharp sheer to the south. "We're too far north this time. Sartin we *did* miss Algiers all right, by about two hundred miles, and there's a nasty current along here that helps the British right up to Port Mahon. We'll jes' hev to run for it now. Gib is about a day's sail away."

He turned and whistled loudly through his fingers.

"Lord send this wind holds. Mister, do you know what gettin' through the Straits means? Sounds simple na-ow, doesn't it? Wall, sir, in 'ninety-two I was hangin' out at Luff's boarding house at Gib with five other skippers, mostly British, for six 'tarnal weeks while the west wind bla-ew and bla-ew. There's alers a five to six knot current settin' in through the Straits but a long westerly bla-ow makes it worse. There's eddies then that jes' swallers fishers and small craft. Wall, the seventh week I says to myself, ' 'Lisha, you're gittin' barnacles on the sole o' your trousers,' says I. So I ups anchor and in two days I beats out after p'intin' back and forth between Tarifa and Tangier till I thought I'd wear out the gudgeons. Y' see I knowed all o' them five other skippers was up on O'Hara's Folly with glasses lawfin' like loons. Y' see? Na-ow somethin' happened to the current and one arternoon I jes' sailed up to Trafalgar. Nor that ain't all. I got a cargo at Cadiz and took it round to Lisbon. 'N I filled up with wine and shoes there for the garrison and come back on the same wind, and there was all five o' them Britishers still settin' ra-ound the table at Luff's with corns on their tails. '*Officer, give me one penny for de bread, I say, officer, give me one penny for de bread,*' says I, stickin' my knot in over the geraniums. Wall, *sir*, there was enough crockery come through that winder to furnish an admiral's galley. And that's true, and that's the Straits." He whistled again through his fingers shrilly. Collins laughed.

Next morning Calpe and Abyla, the two immortal pillars, rose superbly before them towering above the surrounding mountains. The gale was blowing itself out. But there was a choppy sea tossing in the Straits. They passed a British ship of the line wallowing drunkenly into Gibraltar with her topmasts housed and only her courses set. The great rollers swept her sides, now exposing her gleaming copper and now leaping to her third line of gun ports, smothering her in spray from time to time. The *Wampanoag* fled past her and down the narrow gulf with a line of mountains on either side and the strong wind behind. The topmasts were being sent up again. Before the Rock lay behind them the brig was once more a tall ship.

They burst out into the Atlantic with long curtains of rain overtaking them as the gale finally blew itself out in a succession of dying squalls. A rare display of rainbows grew and withered, arching away into the hills toward Tangier. Land birds came and perched on the masts. Gulls cried peevishly behind till a fierce lanner came and drove them away.

"Golondrina, señor," said a Spanish sailor to Anthony, scooping up a tired bird from the deck and warming him in his hands. "From my country, over there." The man had a young, ardent face and sensitive fingers that trembled over the bird. Anthony felt sorry for him. The sailor stood leaning over the bulwarks gazing at the white villages among the mountains. Suddenly he pointed toward a lighthouse with a small, red-roofed town clustered about it; orange trees, and barren hills behind. He took off his red, tasselled cap and his eyes shone.

"My town," he cried, "Tarifa! Pardon, señor. Ah, the girls of *my* town! They have the true gracia. Have you seen the Andalusian women yet? No! Your eyes have not yet then been completed!" He leaned over the bird in his hand. "See, its head is small but it has true wisdom there, señor. It knows enough to fly home. El saber nunca ocupa lugar. Fly, golondrina, to the little house under the tower," he whispered. Anthony could not hear the rest. The man smiled and cast it into the air. It circled and made off for Spain. "The last point of Europe!" the sailor cried, stretching out his arms, "my town! You return, swallow, and I, I, Juan Garcia, I go to Cuba and there are no graciosas there. Ah, adiós, hermosa, bendita sea la tierra que tu pisas."

"It *is* a beautiful place," said Anthony looking after the departing bird, "Europe, old and noble."

"Sí, sí, señor, sí, sí!" The young sailor's face glowed.

"Pipe down, onion," shouted Collins from the wheel, glaring with his cold blue eyes.

The man's face darkened. He turned with a magnificent gesture to Anthony. "Señor mío, le beso a usted la mano; y sí hay algo en que le puedo servir tien usted—aquí!"

"Belay that," thundered the voice. But the youth stalked forward ignoring the quartermaster.

"Don't let 'em hornswaggle ye, Mr. Adverse," warned Collins. "I'm tellin' ye. A louse like him has enough garlic on his breath to start a kippered herring fer home let alone a bird. For a peso he'd stick a knife in your back."

"It's a beautiful morning, isn't it, Collins?" said Anthony suddenly, and looking him in the eye. "I'm proud to be the first officer of a ship on such a day. Did you ever hear this, Collins?

> 'Loud uttering satire, day and night, on each
> Succeeding race and little pompous work
> Of man.'

That you Collins?"

"Not egg-*zactly*, sir, not day and night, sir. I wouldn't say that." The man shifted his quid. "Sartainly not to the *first* officer on a beautiful mornin'."

He twisted his lock. They looked at each other and laughed.

"All right, then," said Anthony, "all *right!*"—and went below. Collins gave a slight whistle, but not for more wind. They were in the Atlantic now and the only man on board who could use a sextant was to be respected. A little later Captain Jorham came up with his glasses and swept the horizon. His legs were behaving independently and that was a bad sign.

Another bad sign was the topsails of a great English convoy coming down from the direction of Cadiz. Captain Jorham had no desire to bring down some fast sloops of war to investigate his intentions. He soon lost the convoy by cracking on every yard of canvas the *Wampanoag* could carry.

The little brig bloomed out sail after sail till she towered from deck to royalmasts with everything that would draw. The stu'nsail booms were got up and rigged. The jibs were guyed out. Above the royals were skysails. A balloon sail was the skipper's especial pet. It fluttered now and then when she luffed a little. The skipper sat on the bulwarks and kept his eye on it and, "Ease her, ease her," and "now a rap full," he would say to the man at the wheel, "and hold her there."

"Aye, aye," muttered the hand, nervously turning his quid.

"Yankee skipper, comin' down the river," hummed the captain to himself, unconsciously patting the ship's rail.

"Now you're walking out like a flea onto the belly of the world, old gel.

"There's nothin' but blue water between here and Bermudy. Mister, it's clearin' fine," he said, turning suddenly to Anthony. "You can take all the sights you want to na-ow. That there promontory to the south is Cape Spartel, and yonder north over the convoy is Barbate. We're just about the middle o' the entrance to the Straits and that's so nigh exactly thirty-six North and six East that you can mark that off on the chart and take it as your jumpin' off place for the v'y'ge. Na-ow lay a course for jes' west o' the Azores, say, thirty-two—forty. You might sight

Corva. Keep nor'west of it if you do. You'll pick up the North-east Trade thereaba-outs this time of year, and from then on it's plain dumb-fool sailin' to the Indies. You jes' let the wind push you. Run from any sail ye see and don't borrow no trouble. Me—I've got a good deal of trouble on my mind. Na-ow I'm goin' below, and don't you call me unless you're chased or it comes on to bla-ow. Short of suthin', call it nothin', and *leave me with God!*"

He collapsed his telescope with a final snap, and hitching a little sideways scuttled below like a crab.

"Sounds to me like Old Stormalong's resignin'," said Collins as the captain's shoulders disappeared into the cabin followed soon after by Philadelphia with a steaming pot of coffee. "But it'll take more than coffee and a dog's nose to sniff us safe past the Azores unless we want to fetch up on one o' them palmy isles. I remember oncet in the Pacific, when the skipper went off on a long spell like this. We jes' drifted round like the ark for a month, and no doves never came back neither. What do you Noah about that?" chuckled the quartermaster closing one eye solemnly. "Wall, he finally sobered up and brought her round the Horn.

"Mr. Adverse, if I know the signs of the skipper's weather, 'n I ort to, arter sailin' with him since 'eighty-two," continued Collins hemming and hawing a little at having to discuss his captain's vagaries, "it's goin' to be right wet from here to Havaner. And that leaves it pretty well up to you and me." He took a turn or two considering.

"Na-ow," he took another turn and hitched his trousers.

"Na-ow, how would it be if you left the deck to me and I left the navigatin' to you, 'cept fer heavin' the log and markin' up the slate and sich like. I'm askin' you since you're mate now *o*-fficially."

"Is it orders you want?" asked Anthony admiring the wise little bantam of a man with a black silk handkerchief knotted dapperly about his tanned neck and a silver whistle thrust in his pocket.

The quartermaster nodded.

"Very well then, take charge of the deck," said Anthony. "I think I can find out where we are. I have my own sextant, you know."

"That's *one* blessin'," said Collins. He tugged at his forelock. "I'm glad you realize the sitooation, Mr. Adverse. But I wonder if you dew? Let's git rid of ears yonder and I'll partikilarize."

He went to the wheel, and sending the man there forward, began to con the ship himself, running his eyes over the sails constantly and taking advantage of every puff and slant to get the most out of her. Presently he had Anthony in his place, directing him with one hand on the wheel himself.

"Ye have to develop a feel for the thing and that comes slowly. Steady na-ow, bear da-own, sir. Ye keep a kind o' constant balance against the pull. It would never do to be taken aback carryin' everything as we are now. It might yank all the sticks out of her. Ye have to watch like a hawk for squalls, tew. A small cloud on the horizon and white water comin' down fast, that's trouble! I'm going to strip some of the canvas off soon as we're sure the skipper and the Almighty are tetertate like he indicated they would be soon. Less hurry the more speed when ye're short-handed like we are. The old hooker's a fast one though!"

Feeling the ship as it were in his grasp, Anthony stood fascinated but with every sense alive, watching her sway over the long grey seas; hearing the wash and gurgle about the rudder behind. To the quiet voice of Collins which continued in his ears the sea was providing a half-musical accompaniment.

"Na-ow as I was sayin', when I sent the man for'd—every sailor has ears and eyes in the back of his head, ye know—as I was sayin', our sitooation *ain't* comical. It's like this. The skipper's off again. He usually goes on till he has the *squeegees*. That may take two weeks, or yet a month. 'Tain't snakes. It's his dead baby what comes back. He hears her. Na-ow it won't do to let the crew get wind o' that, cause they'd *see* her. Ye see I know. This here is my 'steenth v'y'ge with the cap'n.

"He's a kind o' curious one. There ain't a better skipper afloat. He made a fortune or two on some Canton runs. Then he married him a wife—below now—and built a fa-ine house at Scituate, lookout and all. Meant to settle down. Wall, they lost their only little gal. About three years old, she was. And after that he started to go to pot on land. They dew say his house was baby-haunted. Nobody won't live there since. But I dunno. Anyway him and his wife up and cleared out. He left her to home for one v'y'ge and it was then I heard tell her baby came back. Anyway the Missus wouldn't stay on, and he'd drunk up his money or lost it on some venture or other. The *Wampanoag* is all he's got, for the house can't be sold or rented. There's lots of skippers laughs at him for havin' his Missus aboard, but believe me, he needs her, and I'll say she *dew* look after him wonderful. Besides, she never said it, but I'm sure she's scairt to stay behind.

"Wall, you see how it is. I said fer ye to look after the sun and the charts, but you'll have the cabin on yer hands too, Mr. Adverse. That won't be easy. *Ye got to keep the old man below.* Give him liquor and humour him. Git him over it. If he gits on deck there'll be hell to pay. Wait till he begins to hear that baby walkin'. Paddlin' footsteps on the deck, Mr. Adverse! Mrs. Jorham'll do the rest. She knows how to peter off after the horrors. A little less every day. As fer me na-ow, I'll get the ship to Havaner if ye can give me some notion where we are every day or so. Na-ow then I'll take her over, I expect."

He resumed the wheel and squared his shoulders as if he felt the mantle of authority settling on them.

"Coil that loose end up, you swab," he roared at one of the Britishers who was sitting on a pail near the galley. "And git for'd. Step lively. Ye're dead from yer ankles up and yer feet are asleep. Do you think ye can put yer bum on a bucket and let it *draw* barnacles on this ship? Send that man aft to the wheel again."

The sailor slunk off shuffling his bare feet uncomfortably. Anthony went below. Already the cabin seemed more eery. Now he knew what they were waiting for.

When he came on deck some hours later to take the sun Collins had already reduced sail considerably. The skysail and royals were gone and the balloon sail had vanished. It was a clear day and he managed to get a good sight.

"I forgot to tell ye that the nigger knows about things in the cabin," said Collins looking on over the figures. "He's been with 'em fer ten years. They own him. I don't want yer to mistake me, Mr. Adverse, in sayin' what I did about the skipper. Ye won't, will ye? I'm no sea-lawyer, ye know." The man looked at him with some doubt and anxiety in his honest eyes.

"You can depend on it I understand, Collins," said Anthony.

"Then we'll say no more unless we have tew. Na-ow where do ye make it today?" They fell to over the chart with perfect understanding of each other.

The seriousness and sheer necessity of the work they were doing and the manifest trust and regard of the seasoned old sailor caused Anthony to ponder a little as he went below to check over his figures again and again. This was the first bit of work he had ever done which seemed vitally important, for a moment an end in itself as well as a means. Over that little sheaf of figures he had completely forgotten everything else. There was not anywhere even a little rainbow of play lurking about it. On that basis, then, he and Collins had met. Here was a platform that he could stand on with many an honest man. "With many another honest man," he corrected himself.

He was a man. "By God," he thought, "I've grown up! What a lucky thing Mr. Bonnyfeather put that sextant in the chest. What a gift!" Suddenly he saw that old gentleman from an entirely new angle. He *had* worked. "I am his heir." He made sundry good resolutions. On the chart of the Atlantic Ocean he marked down the exact spot where he had overtaken his majority.

28. THE SEED OF A MIRACLE

T HE passing of time on a long voyage Anthony soon discovered was not announced to the inner-self by bells, chronometers, or even by days and nights. He could apprehend its duration only as a succession of varying moods superinduced by the weather and the latitude. And in these moods, he also noticed, the ship herself, as a positive personality with a certain will of her own, one to be humoured rather than baldly controlled, seemed to participate.

The mood on starting from Genoa, for instance, had been a briskly busy one gradually relaxing into routine and habit until the gale had overtaken them. Then from somewhere off the coast of Tripoli to a spot in the Atlantic southwest of Gibraltar they had been harried by the storm. It was true they had profited in distance by that harrying but the sky had been leaden and down-billowing, the ship had been plunging and wallowing; rain, spray, and green water had delayed them. No one could be comfortable for a moment. A kind of business-like melancholy and glum endurance punctuated by anxiety had gripped all alike.

But as they turned northward for the region of the trades, an entirely new mood held the whole ship. The wind piped only a little, and quite merrily. The brig still swept along but paused now and then to dance a bit and to dash a capful of spray back playfully. The air was cool and the sun was bright. Melancholy had vanished. A certain active ease and happy relief could have been noted in the *Wampanoag's* log. This, as they pressed west, and the air became gradually hotter, lost its mercurial quality and threatened to end in a vague feeling of sloth. The wind faltered. Off the Azores in late July one moved like the ship—reluctantly. As yet they were not in the refreshing track of the trades. A sticky south wind came in puffs over the port bow.

Meanwhile—the time consisted mostly of meanwhiles—with no direct responsibility for the ship, and with the course for the day agreed upon, Anthony found time to ransack his chest from top to bottom and to improvise a splendid, solitary mode of existence which was so pleasing to his natural soul that it eventually caused him alarm. He left the madonna swaddled just as Faith had packed it. Under the great-coat where Mr. Bonnyfeather had asked him to look was a tight canvas roll containing one hundred guineas. There was also a large box of beautiful calfskin quartos which Mr. Bonnyfeather had had newly bound for him. These he proceeded to devour from Addison to Zeno.

Now he was able to read what, when, and as long as he wanted to, and to think things out even if it took half the day. With an almost complete cessation of events, and with no new people to meet and adjust himself to, he had opportunity to think over his whole existence; to arrange and to classify; to trace cause and effect; and to evaluate.

His entire past now lay behind him in a distant perspective out of which he could pick and choose. In it he thought he saw himself as he actually was. Out of it he began to reconstruct himself as he thought he would like to be. Hence resolutions and resolves, heart burnings and yearnings, regrets, hopes, a few tears and not a little laughter as he lay in the shadow of a boat; lulled by the slow motion of the ship, the sound of the wind and water, and the disappearance of time. All the sorrows and delights of comparative solitude had become his.

Of a few things in his own nature he became acutely aware. He no longer merely accepted them as unchangeable. Some things he would change. There was, for instance, his difficulty in seeing clearly the difference between his own visions and the outside world. Was this because his senses laid hold of things so fiercely and yet so delicately that the images of them were burned into and transformed by his own nature into something else? If so, how did that world, that something else always becoming within him, correspond to events without? On what basis of reality could he proceed? Which world should he accept? Was there a working compromise that he could find?

So far there seemed only one place where the two worlds met. It was in that ideal, or state of being, which was represented to him by the madonna. He could see now that it was a personal accident that she, his particular image of her, had become his visualization of the being in which both inner and outer worlds met and by which they were controlled. Something must control both life and reality, he saw, vision and fact, man and nature. To that something he felt akin as if some portion of it were in him. Yet *he* was also in nature; yet the material world lay without! It was not only the motion of the ship which now caused him to reel as he tried to understand all this.

He would not worry himself any more over the fact that his private image of that in which his own nature and the world met was wrapped up in a rag in his chest. That might be absurd, or it might not. It was convenient to have some image of this necessity. He did not have to be literal about it; he could accept it as his habit, as an aid—and, as Father Xavier had suggested, the image might hold in its arms further developments.

It was a very ancient image that men had found pregnant for millenniums. If he tried to make a new one it might become mathematical, he felt, and he feared that. Why? he wondered. Figures represented thoughts only. There was more to life than thought. Feelings! A figure of a figure—zero was that! So a mathematical madonna would be more ridiculous than a clay madonna. He could not apply even a pronoun to a mathematical image. A word?

Could he make it a word? Perhaps *the* Thing *was* a word. "In the Beginning was the Word." Ah, he had almost forgotten that. The Word, eh? But a man had written that? Had God written it? Suppose he had, what would be the difference in understanding it? A man would have to understand it. And a word must stand for something. This word then had no Image. *The* Word had no Image! Why had it been said that way? "In the Beginning was the Word and the word was light." What did, what could light have to do with it? In the shadow of the boat he stood up and prayed to be able to see. He groped, drawn by a great necessity to try to know all things; all things in one.

All things in one! In that idea there was some glimmering of hope, he thought. In his mind he marshalled what he had already thought. He tried to put it together and go on. Suddenly in his intensity of feeling he felt that he had ceased to think by stages, logically, one thing after another. All of this process was collapsing; telescoping as it were into one, a toneless, colourless state of apprehension in which he understood without making sentences for himself why the Word had no image. In it objects and what reflects them meet. "IT IS" is alive, it is "I AM."

An intense feeling of exaltation accompanied the process of this discovery and then a flashing shock. He stood leaning against the boat, tired, with his eyes closed. Dazzling fire images chased themselves over his darkened eyeballs as if he had been looking at the sun. "Some minute copy of this force that resolved both the inner and the outer world into one must be inside myself. Or I am indeed undone," his lips moved. The fire streaks on his retina began to arrange themselves into a pattern like that of the sunburst behind the madonna's head. "That image again, always that!" He opened his eyes and looked at the sea to rest them.

"If the light hurts yer eyes ye ought to wear a sunshade," said Mrs. Jorham, who, he now discovered, was sitting near and watching him. He had been absorbed in himself, he knew, but she must have brought her rocking chair on deck almost noise-lessly. She must have been sitting there a good while. He resented it.

"It's *not* the sun," he said.

"Oh!" She stopped rocking a minute to look at him. "Jes' seein' things, eh? Didn't know ye was troubled that way."

"Well, I am, Mrs. Jorham," he replied a little tartly.

"Um!" she mumbled.

He hated to be questioned this way. "Good Lord!"

"Wait till ye *hear* 'em," she said suddenly, dropping her knitting.

Oh, yes, *she* heard things. The woman had her troubles. He remembered now. She took up her knitting again.

"I find a lot of comfort in this." She held up the big socks with the needles in it. "It's kind o' like makin' the sheep go over the stile, ye know. Ye jes' keep countin'. I'm sorry for ye, Mr. Adverse, 'deed I am."

"Oh, thank you, Mrs. Jorham," said Anthony. But she would not be repulsed.

"Want to come and hold the yarn?" she said. He shook his head.

"It's real bad then? But sakes alive, I know something better than this. Come on down and I'll show ye my sewing."

At first he thought he could not, but she turned and looked at him expectantly. He laughed at himself and went. After all why should he, Anthony Adverse, be so superior? Wasn't it only last night that he had seen himself climbing into a bed with Miss Florence Udney? She had been there perfectly plainly. Florence! He had touched her on the hips. Round and smooth.

89

He could still feel her by him today. Very soft, well— Perhaps he could afford after all to look at Mrs. Jorham's sewing. Anyway she was getting it out of the basket .

"How wonderful women were!" The basket was full of beautiful things: A quilt cover all puzzled together out of little triangles of silk stitched microscopically; baby clothes; a fragment of lace work on pins, showing a spider spinning its web. What a design, very delicate, quite spidery! "Made with rows of single Brussels' stitches," said Mrs. Jorham. More baby clothes, a small cap embroidered with tiny violets; that must be for a doll. You could hardly say. Some babies were very small. Table things worked with blood-red roses and tawny leaves. Doll clothes, undoubtedly doll clothes, hemmed. They must have been hemmed in Lilliput. And Captain Jorham's shirts having buttonholes worked in them and a big "E. J." on the neck.

"Marvellous!" What a good way this was to forget God. "In the beginning was the Word . . ." his mind seemed to echo. Oh, bother! Look at the sewing.

Mrs. Jorham put a worn, silver thimble on her finger and began to select various needles and coloured threads out of her neat little basket where ribbons and the eyes of four pairs of scissors stared at one from the lid. She laid out some square patches and began a sort of monologue to herself about the art of sewing which Anthony was allowed to overhear. A man could be interested in it if he wanted to be. . . .

"And the Word was God." Ah, yes, he had forgotten *that!* "The Word was God." That was where a personality, an image for the Word, came in. It was God said, "Let there be light. And there was light." What did light have to do with it? For goodness' sake, Anthony, can't you listen to the poor woman? She's talking. Listen you . . . you . . .

"Sewin' is kinda like playin' on the harpsichord. Ye got to get yer fingers used to it jes' by plain practice. There's the needle and there's the thread. Some of the stitches ye make look like notes. After a while ye can run 'em together without thinkin' about it, and that's when ye begin to enjoy it. That's when ye begin to play whole tunes. Looks like a melody, doesn't it?" She held up a pillow cover. "Larned that out Canton way. Them butterflies are the same both sides. This here vine's done on linen with flax flourishin' thread. Land, ye'd think that vine was growin' there, wouldn't ye? I used to do samplers, but that's too easy. Straight-stitch embroidery on tammy-cloth's nice. But it's appliqué work I like, flat stitch and outlining with back-stitch. A few corded outlines and fancy stitches, or the ground with back-stitch settin' in. Some uses a goose or a weighted cushion but I jes' hold my hands like this. See!" She made the needle fly and the flower began to grow. . . . .

"But what *did* light have to do with it?" the obstinate voice demanded. "Hell's fire, wait and find out," he answered himself. "Mrs. Jorham is doing the talking."

"Did ye ever think how many kinds of stitches there are? Look here, I'll show ye some on these patches. Here's a plain running-stitch. Everybody tries that, even children. Next is back-stitchin'. You take up six threads, draw it out, then you go three threads back and pull it through six beyond. Real fast! This way!" Her needle seemed to devour the cloth. "Right to left, of course, only crazy people and Chinee go contrary. Then there's hemming. You have to know how to fold the cloth. There's plain hems, and ornamental hems what runs along the edges and in and out zigzagging over the sides, and then stitches with a loop. And you ought to know how to fasten threads off-and-on. That patch is done for. Now give me two more. This is sewing.

"An antique seam, and an open work seam, and you can make an open-hemmed-double-seam. Now let me have a big patch. Gathering is what I like." She wrinkled the cloth and flashed the needle through the little waves on the patch so fast he could see only a darting point of light with the thread following. "Na-ow ye pull it together. Ain't that nice? *Whee!* Now if ye want ye can just pick out yer crinkles into couples or fours and start smockin' 'em. I used to make curtains for doll houses that a way; made some for . . ." She stopped. "Land sakes, I've bruk the needle! Give me another, the big one. I'll show ye how to galloon, but first here's whipping. . . ."

"Whipping?" said the voice of Captain Elisha who raised his head from the table where he had apparently been asleep. "Whipping is what ye ought to have. It's ye that's temptin' her aboard this ship na-ow with all yer makin' of doll clothes. I know! She'd never have followed us if ye hadn't come along. It's her mother she wants. Y're turnin' this cabin into a nursery. Can't fool me. I know y' aren't makin' them baby clothes for Abner's brats. It's for her. Where's that doll?"

He got up and began to hunt around peevishly.

"Elisha, ye go and lay da-own. It's bad enough without havin' ye on my hands, *tew*. Ye know very well ye asked and begged me to come. And I told ye what would happen. I told ye. Didn't I?"

"Yes, woman, I ain't blamin' ye for losin' her. But ye oughtn't to be temptin' her on with that doll. It's waitin' for her to come fer it that does me in. Give me a drink.

"God!" said he freezing to the spot where he stood. "What's that on deck now?"

"Only a rope end, Captain Jorham," said Anthony. There was a stir up above. They heard the sheet and its tackle drag across the stern bar.

"Sounds as if the wind's shiftin'," said Captain Elisha. He started for the door and then shrank back. "*Ye* go up and take charge, mister. Get on with ye. Ye're in the trades now. I got real trouble da-own here." He collapsed into his chair. In a great hurry Mrs. Jorham began to mix him a drink. Anthony left the atmosphere of terror which had momentarily gripped him too and gladly ran on deck. It was true. The ship had already come about and was headed due west with a steady, sweeping breeze behind her. The trade winds at last!

"There's nothing ahead of us now but blue water for days and days," said Collins coming up looking relieved. "We can sort of settle da-own now. It's wonderful how different jes' a few minutes of these breezes makes a man feel! A few minutes ago my shirt was stickin' to my back, now look—" he let it billow out behind as he stood looking astern with satisfaction. "The old slant jes' petered out. I saw the jibs flap, and the next minute she was all a-flutter. Just had enough way on her to pay off. Wall, the skipper was about right. We picked 'em up south a bit o' where he said. I'll lay her dead west till ye get yer sight tomorrow and we can set the new course then. If this wind holds, Mr. Adverse, we won't have to start a rope till we git nigh to Barbados." He lowered his voice. "How's things in the cabin?"

Anthony told him.

" 'Pears to me like it's comin' on sooner than I expected. So she's givin' him liquor, eh! Only does that when he's right nigh the wust. Ye can expect that baby aboard almost any day now I'd say. Don't let it wear ye da-own. Las' time I got so I was listenin' for her myself. Near the Andamans that was. And a crack of lightnin', tew. Oh, the skipper told ye, did he? Wall, ye can stay on deck most of the time and jes' keep an eye down the companion. He's about paralysed na-ow I s'pose. Na-ow I'll go and git all sail set. We can crack it on right."

Under the urge of Collins' voice the *Wampanoag* began to burgeon again with stu'nsails and royals. The jet before the cutwater leaped high and higher as each new sail was flung out. The brig swept forward with a swift even motion. All noises blent to an even monotone. They had entered upon the long, stable mood of the western passage.

◆—◆

Collins had been too sanguine. The captain showed few signs of having reached a crisis. He slept, awoke, grumbled; pretended to turn a few pages of a large Bible laid open before him; drank again, and laid his head on his arms. A low sound like a saw in difficulties drifted up the cabin ladder all day long. Mrs. Jorham knitted her sixth pair of socks and waited with a fixed, blue fear in her eyes. Before the heels of the next pair were woven she expected a visitor. When no one was looking she went to a drawer in the sideboard, unlocked it, and took out a diaphanous doll. On its clothes she had lavished the last scintilla of her skill as a needlewoman. She hid it in her bunk and resumed knitting slowly.

To escape the tenseness of the cabin Anthony now spent most of his time on deck. He had a mattress brought up and slept by the cabin door. A good deal of the time he took the wheel.

It was a joy to con the ship over the smooth tables of sea towards the dark line that receded ever before her. There was scarcely any perceptible motion to the water. He became aware of the movement of the ocean now as a rhythm felt rather than movement seen. The earth itself might have been breathing and the ship rising and falling on her breast. A mile ahead a long field of weed would slowly rise and then sink again. Many minutes later the ship would answer in her turn as the horizon like a vast disk tilted slightly. For days a great, white bird, whose name Anthony did not know, followed them on motionless pinions hour after hour, as if it knew the future and were waiting for something momentous to happen to the ship. One evening with a strange cry it departed swiftly over the edge of the world in answer to a call.

As they drove westward the patches of weed increased. Then there would be great lakes of clear, blue water twinkling with a cobalt light across which the ship seemed to hurry faster. Out of one of these virgin spaces, like motes out of an eye of space, a school of porpoises suddenly rose one morning and began leaping in a succession of infinite arches before the bow. Jolly fellows with mottled bellies, they preceded the vessel like heralds of her happy royal progress across the depths.

When Anthony looked at the weed-patches with the small-glass he saw crabs and strange urchins gesticulating there like fiddlers of the ship's transit through their unknown realms. All seemed calm and happy in these latitudes. A tunny that one of the men gaffed from the chains, as though he had speared the spirit of these seas, died in spasms of rainbow colours as if its fishy ghost could only manifest itself exquisitely even in departure. All day the flying-fish scudded before them. At night he heard them flop in the water or fall with a bony clatter on the deck. When someone with a boathook fished up a branch of tree with nuts on it, it seemed to be the herbage of another planet. So far behind them now, so infinitely remote before them was even the dream of land.

But if the ocean was beautiful beyond Anthony's utmost capacity to feel, it yet furnished only half the mood of that super-equatorial aisle of the earth-star. Above them and above rose and towered the unthinkable limpid and liquid with its lights appointed; glowing; darkening; ever shifting against sameness, the impalpable womb of clouds. Islands of shadow, glittering groves of slanting rain shot with rainbows appeared and vanished; shifted and melted on the level, molten plains around about. Once a waterspout trailed its smoking skirts uncomfortably near, only to go spinning away to leeward like some cosmic dervish weaving its wasp-like waist up into the dark funnel of the pall above it. Then there would be days of intolerable blue with only wisps of cloud at dawn and nothing but the noise of the sails and the whisper of the sea punctuated startlingly by the clang of the ship's bell.

The men sat about the decks picking oakum or spinning rope yarn, washing damp bundles of old clothes and hanging them up to dry, singing now and then brief snatches, and talking in subdued lazy tones. Even Collins could not find enough for them to do. All the old sails were patched. All the boats and bulwarks were painted, the brasses polished, and the anchor chain made rustless. The standing rigging was slushed down. And still they were only a little over half-way across.

A small fiddle was permitted to squall away in the fo'c'sle and even to come on deck. But after a week it gave up. The presence of the vast silence through which the ship was moving made it too absurd to be tolerated. A game of banker began under the lee of the galley and went on. To Anthony at the wheel eddied back now and then a whiff of burning olive wood from the galley fire, bringing mornings in the cart with Angela vividly to mind. Indeed, the plains about Pisa sometimes seemed to mirage themselves before him when the smoke was strong.

Mixed with it were vivid whiffs of tobacco from the sailors' pipes. In that weed he now began to find a solitary solace himself. Tobacco made his body content to be still.

The intolerable vastness of things was now eating itself into his mind. At first it had been oppressive but now he began to feel as if there were a window in the top of his skull that gave on irreducible nothing. A certain element of terror accompanied this. In the vision of the universe which it opened up there was a gaunt possibility of madness, a terror of space, that had drawn a little too near. He could not quite close it off. He had once made the mistake of climbing into the maintop and looking up too long at the stars. Suddenly direction had vanished and he found himself clutching the mast. The circles and circles beyond circles of his geometry had for a while been a comfort. But now he could no longer bound nothing with a compass. Always there was the maw of more and more. No compass opened wide enough.

The constant taking of observations and the necessity to think in terms of arcs and spheres gave him, as he watched the horizon before him, a palpable sense of the huge ball across which the ship was slowly crawling. That was tremendous enough. But to recollect that this frightful sphere was hurtling eastward, and that he was going with it at a speed really beyond thought, made him feel like clinging at times to the wheel, waiting as it were to be thrown off into space like a drop of water from a grindstone. Once under the rising full moon as he looked astern he thought he saw the long, silver streak of water racing; streaming steadily east into the very mouth of the dead planet. Slowly it rose above the line of ocean, serene, but terrible. And then he was being hurled along under it going around again toward the sun.

That night he took a lunar for longitude. Despite all he could do he could not divest himself of a sense of horror as the disk of the moon swept down over the fixed star he had chosen. Through the glass he saw the edge of the moon was sawtoothed. There was something about the motion of all these bodies in the sky, especially at night, that was a little mentally sickening.

Strive as he would he could not divest himself of an emotion about them even when, as he had to assure himself, it was merely mathematics he was practising. Even to take a shy look at the infinite seemed to cut him off from the entire ship's company. To glimpse the mood of it even for a few hours had, he felt, changed him somehow permanently. Something within him that he had not known was imprisoned there had been fed with the raw meat of heaven. It was now aroused and clamouring for more. Along with this went a sudden increase in his apprehension of geometrical problems. Theorems which he had once been forced to prove to himself ponderously now suddenly became axiomatic. He became ambitious as a navigator and determined to check his longitude by an observation of Jupiter's satellites. This was a matter of some little difficulty as it was necessary to rig an improvised tripod for the captain's little telescope and to wait for a perfectly calm night.

Collins accomplished the tripod. But it was harder to persuade the captain to let him have the glass, a good one once taken from a prize. He did so only after considerable cajoling. Captain Jorham had not been sleeping lately. He was now very restless. From time to time that day Anthony had heard him and his wife talking. When he came into the cabin they always stopped. There was an air of great tension about both of them, Anthony noticed. But he was now so engrossed in his own little experiment on deck that he paid no particular attention to it. Matters had gone on so long in the cabin he had come at last to take them for granted. Besides—tonight it was calm! And tonight he was going to observe the immersion of Jupiter's inner satellite. How grand that sounded! As he began to focus the glass the nice intricate reasoning behind the observation and the way to use the tables kept running through his head.

The planet hung like a distant lamp half-way to the zenith. In the glass at first he saw nothing but black, then a few sparks of stars. Now he was on it! It was a great, grey, moon-shaped thing. Out of focus of course! He twisted the eyepiece toward him. Now! There it was, the whole beautiful system! An intensely shining, little disk with three bright sparks arranged in a line to the right. If the ship would only stay perfectly still! That was a little better now, clearer. There was the other spark on the left. Much farther out than he had thought. God! How beautiful they were, silver, but silver that was alive. Calm, orderly, perpetually reordering themselves in repetition endlessly repeated and shining that way forever, glorious, lovely—calm! He could never drink in enough of that light. Let it keep sliding into his eyes and become part of him. This was mental drink.

He let Collins look. "Four of 'em, eh! Four moons! That doesn't seem right, does it?" He went back and unlashed the wheel again.

It would take almost an hour yet before that little moon would touch the planet's disk, if his calculations were anywhere near right. He began to walk up and down the deck stopping once in a while to refocus. "Why not hurry it up and be done with it?" something prompted him. "You fool," someone else replied. He laughed. Yet his little moon evidently was moving. And the sea was very, very calm. Almost no wind tonight. The sails flapped. She was just keeping way on her. That was lucky. They had had only a few really calm nights. This was one. Very silent too. He rearranged the screened light near the chronometer so that he could see the hands better.

Philadelphia went by carrying some hot water to the cabin, spilling a little as he passed. Anthony saw him return to the galley later. He was sitting there with his hands on his knees, shaking a little as if with a chill. A big fire was going. Two lanterns were burning. He was sorry for the darky. The captain was wicked enough in speech these days. The man looked positively yellow, Anthony thought. As he passed the cabin door he heard Mrs. Jorham crying monotonously; subdued. She had not done that before. Perhaps he had better take a look. But he would try not to disturb them. He went around and looked through the starboard light. No sounds came to him there, only movement below in the clear lamplight, a picture in a glow. There was something cosmic about this one, too.

The old man seemed to be up to some mischief. He was

going about looking for something. Evidently he could not find it. Mrs. Jorham slid into her bunk and closed the panel as if she were afraid. What was it all about? Mere drunken folly? Now he was rearranging the things in the cabin meticulously. All the plates on the rail. Exactly, just so. He stood back to admire the effect. Now he put the tea canister on the sideboard in front of the Virgin and bowed. "Was the drunken ass saying his prayers to her or making fun of her?" You could hardly tell which. He made sacerdotal gestures. It was funny and horrible at the same time. Now he was peeping over the Virgin's cloak. He was talking to the baby! Somehow he had recaptured the very look of a proud young father. His face had gone smooth. He snapped his fingers and bent down tenderly. It seemed terrible enough now, poor old devil! Better not spy on him. But just then the whole implication of the scene below shifted. Captain Jorham had lifted his face out of the big fold of the clay cloak with a look of preternatural cunning. This was the man who could sell Spaniards their own tombstones at a profit.

He looked about him like a cat about to jump on the table and lap cream.

Then with an elaborate drunken cunning that would have defeated itself if Mrs. Jorham had been peeping out of instead of crying in her bunk, he tiptoed over to "Elisha" and took out of that chest a long, narrow bottle of red wine. He grinned knowingly at its ruby flash as he crossed the cabin, reeling. Good Lord, he was going to smash the statue with it! No, he was going to give it to the baby! He slid the bottle down into the deep fold of the Virgin's cloak. It was completely concealed. Once again that evening Captain Jorham stepped back with his head on one side to admire his nice arrangements. Then his real motive emerged. With a look of grim triumph he turned and shook his fist at the closed panel of his wife's bunk.

Anthony could only laugh now. He wondered if Captain Jorham would remember that bottle when his wife began to cut down on his liquor after the spree. Hardly. Perhaps it was just drunken cunning? Then his grin suddenly faded. The observation!

He ran to the telescope and began to readjust it frantically. But it was too late. While he had been watching Captain Jorham hide a bottle in the bosom of the Virgin another equally important event in the cosmos had taken place. The inner satellite of Jupiter had immersed.

"You'll make a good first mate yet," said Collins with a touch of admiration in his voice as he listened to Anthony's remarks. "What was that last language, Portegee?"

Anthony closed up the telescope and reduced his meticulous preparations to debris. He did not deign to reply.

"As for immersion," Collins went on, conning the ship elaborately as a brief puff bellied out the sails, "I never did hold by it nohow. Nor feet washin' neither. My family was Antipoedabaptists and I sucked the milk o' pure doctrine from my mother's knee. Better not kick the chronometer, sir."

A loud crackling sound came from the cabin. The captain was evidently demolishing something brittle. They listened forebodingly.

"I expect tonight's the night," whispered Collins. "Na-ow I'll send the watch for'd and ye hold the cabin da-own, Mr. Adverse. 'Tain't helpful to discipline fer the crew to see the skipper bein' chased. Yep, I'll keep the wheel. Philly can help if he has to."

Anthony gathered his paraphernalia and went below. How important it had seemed, and how serious about it he had been! He could chuckle now.

Fragments of a chair were scattered about the cabin but the captain had disappeared. Anthony stood looking about him. The cabin was absolutely silent. The ship was just drifting before the lightest of airs. He heard the ripple along her keel as she picked up for a moment. Then it died away in subterranean gurgles. Suddenly his heart almost stopped. A growling beast was trying to bite his leg.

From between the legs of the table the captain's head projected and he was now barking like a dog. It was an eerily perfect performance. Captain Jorham *was* a dog. It went on for a while and ended in three long death howls.

Despite himself Anthony's flesh crept. With some ado he finally enticed the captain to his feet again. The commander of the *Wampanoag* now began to walk about shuffling and reeling, doing a nervous, spasmodic little clog each time he turned the corner of the table. He was trying to catch Anthony to see who he was. His face twitched and his limbs jerked. An endless stream of talk flowed from his mouth, now drawn to one side, as if all he said were an aside to someone invisible. Finally he captured his mate and insisted on shaking hands. The ugly gleam in his pupils vanished.

"Swan ef it ain't Captain Jorham's macaroni mate! Ye're a ri, ye a-a-a-*ri*." Anthony dodged the gargantuan fluke which was about to descend on his back. The captain staggered and reeled over into his bunk.

"Thank God for that," thought Anthony.

"Polly wants a cracker, polly wants, wants, polly—l'olly, dolly. Janie wants a dolly. Little Jane wants her dolly. Mrs. Jorham, do ye hear, do ye hear? Little Jane wants her dolly. She's comin' fer it, comin' *aboord!* Janie, baba!" He waved and then began to whisper. The hulk of him quivered and twitched.

"Listen!"

Something gurgled under the keel. The man's scalp crinkled up into a point pulling his forehead smooth.

Mrs. Jorham opened her panel. "Give him drink and get it over with tonight. Philly, Philly, some hot water!"

The darky descended warily. He took in the situation at one glance and scrambled out of the cabin as soon as he could.

"*Give* me that doll," said the captain making a sudden drunken dash at his wife. She closed the panel in his face. With some difficulty Anthony got him back to his bunk where he sat sweating. He mixed him some hot grog and got him to lie down. After a while he seemed to sleep uneasily. Anthony dimmed the light and crawled into his own bunk. He meant to stay awake. The light flickered and went out soon but he did not know it.

When he opened his eyes again it was absolutely dark and he was instantly aware of being bathed in an atmosphere of inexplicable terror. Someone had called Philly again, he thought. But no, it was Captain Jorham talking.

"Listen, do ye hear that?" he whispered.

"Hush!" said his wife's voice. "*Ssh!*"

The captain's voice was pleading now. "Give it to her, Jane. Let her have it."

A swift horrible scream tore the darkness. It was impossible to hear it and not to partake of a fear that went like cold to the marrow.

"Listen!"

No one did anything else.

Now for the first time Anthony began to understand that Mrs. Jorham might believe her child really was there. It was her breathing. He lay with eyes wide open in the dark, listening. He could hear now as he had never heard before. Furthermore, he gradually became sure himself that there was something at the door. Despite all he could do to reassure himself, he broke out in a sweat. Something *was* there. He could hear it.

"God!" said the captain.

They were evidently sitting together over there in the captain's bunk. Presently he heard one of them moving. It was Mrs. Jorham. She crept past him slowly on her hands and knees in her white night-dress. Now she was going up the little ladder. He heard her gasp. Something was tossed out onto the deck. Mrs. Jorham was lying prone there at the top of the cabin ladder.

Then Anthony had the shock of his life. In the darkness overhead he heard bare feet stirring very softly on the cabin roof. Immediately afterwards Mrs. Jorham fled back to her bunk and closed herself in.

This was more than he could stand. Jumping up he wrapped a blanket around him and went on deck. No one was there except Collins looking grim over the binnacle.

"Did you see anything?" asked Anthony.

Collins quietly pointed to the galley. In there a bright fire was still going. He went forward and looked through the door. The stove was glowing cherry-red under one lid. He lifted the grate and saw the remains of Mrs. Jorham's doll twisting in the flames. A smell of burning cloth and hair pervaded the place. Philadelphia was not there. As he came out again Anthony saw the outline of the darky's figure against the stars in the shrouds forward as far away from the galley as he could get. He sauntered forward and looked up at him a while. The cook was cowering there all hunched up. They kept looking at each other.

"Lil missee gone?" the man finally whispered.

"All gone," said Anthony.

Even then the negro came down slowly and sat on the bulwark for a while.

"Why did you burn it, Philly?" asked Anthony.

"She go way den." He ran his sleeve over his forehead. "Tell you I allus knows troubles comin', Mr. Adverse, when I see dat ooman gwine fer to dress a doll. She start 'bout a month ago now. Wish I didn't b'long to folks wid a baby hant. It jes' about done ruin my kidneys." He hitched himself uneasily.

"This is not the first time then?"

"No, *suh*. I done burn foh dollies!"

Anthony went aft and got the man a drink. It must have taken great courage, he thought, to creep up and get the doll. So it was real to them all. Not until long after the fire had completely burned out in the galley did Philadelphia return.

"I wouldn't mind a little myself, Mr. Adverse," said Collins. He looked at Anthony over the pannikin. "Well, what do ye think of it na-ow?" he asked.

"What do you stick by the ship for, Collins?" countered Anthony.

"Ye don't know the skipper, sir. He's a grand man," replied Collins wiping his lips. "He'll be himself na-ow, ye see if he ain't. Everybody has their own funny places ye know, in here." He tapped his head. "Ye can't tell how real they are neither. Na-ow . . ."

But Anthony did not care to listen, any more than he cared to return to the cabin. He flopped down on some spare canvas; smoked.

One thing—he was not going to be dressing any more dolls

himself! The madonna could stay in the chest. And he was glad he had taken the stand he had with Father Xavier. Toussaint had once laughed at him for being superstitious. And these people on board were Protestants, too. "Heretics." But what was he? A reasonable man, a man of facts and figures, a navigator! No more nonsense from now on—by God!—his pipe went out and he failed to relight it—no more childish nonsense! He would strangle his dreams, his dolls. A philosopher-scientist. Write Toussaint and tell him. These new ideas he had from looking at the stars, sailing the wide earth under the sky had opened up his mind. But mystery was there. Of course it was. Something to do with time—or was it space? He couldn't remember now. It was hard to think about that. You seemed to touch the bottom of things there—or the top. Oh, yes, that time on the masthead looking up, he had lost all sense of direction. What was that idea he had had then? Other things besides men, *things*. Yes, supposing I was a thing, or supposing a thing knew itself as "I." Oh, this is it. The "I" of a thing could have no sense of direction. Say, the sun. It would not know east or west or up or down. "I" felt that on the masthead looking at the stars. What of it? This is an essential thought, I am certain of it. It might lead to something—something, but not now, not now. I must rest. How long, how long life is! The end far off and I am sleepy now. Alone. Here . . . He saw the moon's disk again sweeping down dragon-toothed over a star. Alone here in this terrible vast desert of stars. This cold-and-fiery endless place! Where are you, living one? I am lost here. I cannot find you. I am cold.

He moved uneasily and began to murmur something on the verge of sleep. Philadelphia came out of the cabin and threw a blanket on him, seeing the dew on his face.

"Ah, warm again! In bed at last! Good night, then. Good night to you." From the wall above him her face was looking down. "Of course she was always there. I am glad. Now she is talking to me."

"What have you been doing all day, little boy?"

"Climbing the big tree. I am tired."

"Did you reach the top?"

"Yes."

"What did you see there?"

"The stars, Mother I-am, the stars."

"What of them, child?"

"I looked among them and dreamed I had lost you. I lost myself."

"But now that you are awake again you see I am here . . ."

What has become of the ship, the Atlantic Ocean and the stars above it? They, he, have vanished into something without space and time. What is it breathing under the blanket? . . .

The man in the lookout thought he saw some stars setting in the "west." They touched the water like lights and went under; disappeared. He was quite sure of it. In the "east" several more came up. He saw them with his own eyes. Presently they were followed by a great light. The man now saw a cloud before him on the horizon. It looked far away, very silvery and stood up from the sea like a cone. Suddenly he saw a forest and three little white houses in the middle of it. The cloud rent opened up and the land turned into a mountain with long scarves of mist trailing away from it. It certainly *was* a mountain.

"Land O," he roared.

"Belay that bellerin'," Collins roared back at him. "That's Nevis, and I seen it a half hour ago from the deck. Get a pillow, ye lubber, and turn over on yer other side. Come da-own out o' that. Philly, pass the word to the captain."

"Yes, suh," said that worthy delighted at the discomfiture of the lookout. "An' I'll jes' tote him a basin o' gruel." He winked.

A considerable stir now went on and Anthony woke up.

"Landfall sooner than we expected, Mr. Adverse," said Collins pointing. "Yer latitude was exact but ye're way out on your longitude. *I've* been expectin' it watchin' the landbirds for three days now. And I'm right glad, for I'm nigh tuckered out with double tricks at the wheel. The skipper ul carry on na-ow. He comes back marvellous."

Anthony climbed the shrouds and sat feasting his eyes on his first glimpse of tropical foliage. A beautiful mountain, gleaming, dark-green, strung with savannas and forests with here and there a bright flash from a waterfall lay some miles ahead off the port bow. A long scarf of mist perpetually dissolving to leeward trailed from the top. He could see a cluster of white houses in a town at its foot. The crew stood about or lined the bulwarks in small groups looking at it, too. Suddenly they scattered. Captain Jorham had come on deck.

He had a chair brought for him and sat on the quarter-deck with a blanket around his knees and a speaking trumpet in his hand. Philadelphia kept bringing him hot coffee every few minutes.

Mrs. Jorham emerged once from the cabin with her curl-papers still on, and going to the stern threw a lot of bottles into the sea. Captain Jorham did not turn his head. Anthony saw the bottles go bobbing astern. A large shark turned lazily on one side and swallowed one. Anthony laughed. He knew of another bottle in safe keeping. Forgotten, he felt sure. "On the knees of the gods!"

Nevis began to sink into the ocean astern. Only a few days now and they would be in Havana. The new world at last. He raised his right hand holding the palm open in expectation.

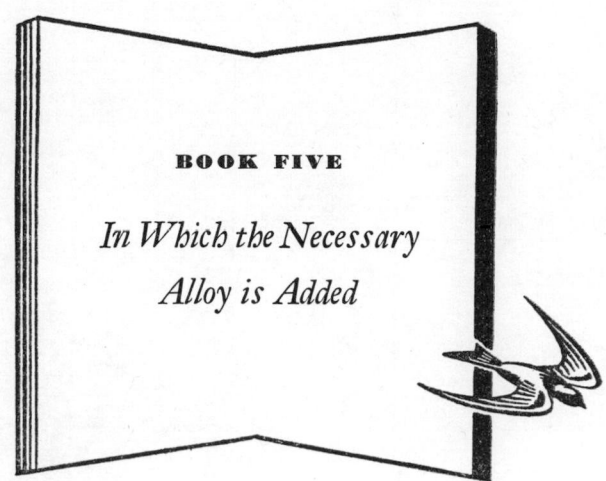

BOOK FIVE

In Which the Necessary
Alloy is Added

29. THE HOUSE OF SILENUS

Down the long, blue coasts of Cuba sailed the *Wampanoag* with her mate in the shrouds gazing inland as often and as long as the August sun on the Tropic of Cancer would permit.

In the mornings, when he first heard the men begin to holy-stone the decks and swish water about, he would go aloft with the small-glass sticking out of his coat pocket. Then crooking a knee about one of the stays and steadying himself, he took deep lungfuls of the rich land-breeze which lulled through the sails at that hour.

It was full of a thousand lush and exotic odours from the beeches, lagoons, and high plateaus; Sargasso weed, juniper and lantana; the fragrant quiebrahacha, tamarind, and rotting mastic leaves. A rank, musty sweetness rolled out from the sugar plantations and fermenting lowlands. His land-hungry nose seemed to taste rather than to smell it. In his mouth his tongue moved and became moister as if in anticipation of a feast.

By the last hours of starlight the brig would always have drifted close to the land. The sea-breeze lasted all night, but as the airs grew lighter she would make more and more leeway, until at last the distant whisper of beaches was audible on deck. It sounded as though the tropical night were about to reveal its secret; a softly sinister one. Then suddenly the sails would flutter, the yards would be braced around, and the land-breeze would fatten the canvas out on the starboard tack.

It was at this moment that the fish bit most frantically. A ferocious barracuda or two, or a young shark would always be slapping and slamming themselves on the wet deck. But after the first few mornings in the West Indies Anthony paid small attention to that, for by the miracle of dawn in those regions smell, hearing, and sight were in turn assaulted and overcome.

As soon as the warm odours of the land-breeze began to fan over the deck the wind also brought with it a distant and mysterious cry from the dark island beyond. It was continuous; strangely sustained. It seemed to come in waves out of the east and to scatter itself like spiritual rumours of good news discussed and re-echoed here and there faintly and more faintly down into the west. To Anthony hanging in the rigging, rapt, looking out over the dark ruffling water, it expressed perfectly his own deep and eery joy at being alive on this star.

The first time he heard this half-harmonic chorus he was nonplussed. No other song was like it. With a constant lyric stream, in which no individual notes could be distinguished, all the roosters in Cuba were blending their voices. The king-cock of them, he thought, with a million jubilant minions must be chanting somewhere in the as yet invisible island hills. This then was the characteristic sound of land—of all habitable land. He remembered it on those mornings in Italy in the cart with Angela. But this was a more magnificent chorus. It had the quality of laughter transposed into some unknown scale, musical, but non-human. At the first hint of grey the paean rose to a kind of harmonized scream of joy.

Then the parrots began, "*chat-chat, chat-chat, chatter-chatter.*" They seemed to wake an applause to accompany the cock-crow as if they had been startled somewhere by a single handclap. The half-heard thunder of billions of insects tuned in. The morning voice of Cuba swept into a crescendo. It reached a climax that maintained itself, a distant pandemonium that rapidly grew fainter as the ship drew out to sea.

Meanwhile his eyes must also be at work. The stars paled. The planets burned out like melting globes. In a white furnace-glow astern the morning star disappeared moltenly. At one leap the light climbed half-way to the zenith. The inevitable bank of low clouds along the eastern horizon, as if they were in rapid combustion, turned from black to dull red; to crimson; to transparent, white gold. Hot pencils of light thrust rods through them and they suddenly sublimed. A bright track of sea could be seen racing eastward toward an incandescent spot.

Then the incredible forehead of the sun lifted itself out of the water. Red globules of mist ran down his fat cheeks. The world glared from rim to rim. It was turning over. For an instant, as the sun's squat globe swam up from the water, the sea seemed to be drawn after him into a huge bloody bead. Then the black line of the horizon cut through it. It fell back, and you could no longer look that way. Already waves of heat were beating up into Anthony's face. After a while he would open his eyes again, after the blindness passed, and look at the long coasts marching either way into the intolerable, blue distance.

It was a mighty view. He was never tired of sweeping his little glass over it; now at some palm fronded headland or long reaching cayo; now at a purple shadowed vale in the mountains, or a little sunny patch with a peon's hut. He felt like some poor sailor standing in the rigging of the *Niña* or the *Pinta*, shading his eyes for a glimpse of gold-roofed temples on that first, memorable voyage.

They passed a hundred little, palm-lined rivers each with its savannaed delta and a bar creaming at its blue mouth. Where the bluffs came down to the sea these streams cut back into the hills mysteriously. A light mist hung over them in the morning till the sun looked directly at it. He could even see, with a very clear focus, a wilderness of ferns lining their gorges. Once there was a waterfall and a canoe under it fishing. From the woods near by rose a long feather of smoke. And this was the new world!

To him it was *his* new world. He had discovered it for himself. And he knew now how vast the earth was; how wide its oceans. Had he not crossed a sea of space to get here? Why must the ship always go creeping out to sea as soon as the sun rose? How long would it be till he was walking the groves of this island? "Use the glass, Anthony, use the glass—*Cuba, gloria mundi!*"

One step inland beyond the beaches salt-pans flashing like mirrors. Then a wide, low plain, sandy, grassy; then trees; then a glorious burst of palms and pines, plumed and festooned forest that swept up over the hills into the blue mountains, gentle, rolling from peak to peak with cloud shadows, feathered with giant royal palms standing in groves or lonely, perpendicular, looking down on everything else. Cuba and the royal palm, the tall, wide-blowing royal palm—he could imagine them rustling coolly in the trade wind. The sun burned his already brown face to black olive as he stood thus in the rigging, sweeping his glass inland a hundred and a thousand times to be rewarded at every trial by glows and glooms and vistas of what had once rightly been taken to be Paradise. The sun bleached the ends of his hairs and the roots where they rose out of his forehead until he looked like a grizzled, gilded youth with a bronze body.

"Although," said a book of travels he had in his chest, "Europeans have now pre-empted the soil of Cuba for three centuries, much of the interior of the island has never been mapped and its precise geography is vague." Looking day after day at the wilderness of hills and coastal islands that marched with the *Wampanoag*, he could believe that. Reluctantly, as the sun grew intolerable, he would climb down at last.

At noon the sails drooped. They ate under the shadow of a

tarpaulin in a sweat-provoking calm. Mrs. Jorham groaned and
began to talk about iced root-beer, and frost on cranberry bogs.
The captain said nothing. He was doing penance now. An hour
later the cool breeze came from the sea. Then they would begin
to tack out. For Captain Jorham had no desire to be boarded at
night by human caymans from some boca, or Cayo del Coco.
The number of "wrecks" even in calm weather along these
coasts was remarkable. It had already engaged the unfavourable
attention of the British Admiralty for many years.

"Expulsis piratus, restitutio commercia," said Captain Elisha
to himself, taking out his lucky pocket-piece and surreptitiously spitting on it. So by evening they would be ten miles
out, and the coast a long, undulating dream of blue. Then they
would slowly drift in again. Thus in long diagonal slants the
Wampanoag lazed along. One morning two breast-shaped hills
hove in sight.

"Do ye see them there, Mr. Adverse?" said Collins twiddling
the wheel a quarter over and back to nurse every cupful of the
fitful land airs, "them's the Tits of Havana, and ye'll see the
Morro before night."

A tower with a banner on it rose out of the sea as they lay
in the noon calm. Then the wind came shoreward and by
evening they were near enough to see the sulphur puff of the
sunset gun from El Morro. An incredibly ragged pilot with a
bouquet of flowers in hand for the captain, and his mouth full
of Spanish lies when he was not chewing a fat, black cigar,
rowed out and boarded them. He offered Anthony a cigar for
which he accepted one dollar.

"From the vuelta abajo, señor, the very darkest leaf. Now
we have exchanged gifts, bueno!"

Anthony lit the black torpedo expectantly. He had heard of
Havana tobacco. In a few minutes a light sweat burst out on his
forehead and the soles of his feet felt cold. He pressed adventure no further then, but tossed the thing overboard. After a
little he felt calm and soothed; in rather an enviable state of
mind. It was equivalent to strong wine but unique.

In the calmest of all lights, between a setting sun and a rising moon, they slipped into the great sack-shaped bay between the frowning batteries of La Punta and El Morro. He had never seen so many fortifications. The walled city lay to starboard, and the little Gibraltar of San Carlos, tier above tier of batteries with a vicious-looking bristling parapet, along the water front to port. Soon they were gliding along the bay front of the flat-roofed city that thrust out its long peninsula between them and the sunset. He could hear the horses now trotting along the Paseo Alameda de Paula and the noise of wheels.

What a welcome familiar sound was that, the striking of horseshoes on good solid earth! All these land noises were welcome. How he had missed them without knowing it! How silent the open sea really was! Its tones were variations of only one voice. The bay seemed to be full of different voices all calling to him; cries, laughter, carriages passing and repassing, the rumble of a town! The tremendous sour-sweet stench of a tropical city and a festering harbour overwhelmed him as the pilot dropped anchor in the Bay of Antares and demanded one hundred and twenty-five Mexican dollars for the astounding feat.

The twang of Captain Elisha's "God A'mighties," and other Biblical remarks to the pilot rolled up from the cabin to mix with curious hails from passing boats and the thudding of hard fists on canvas as the crew furled the sails and gossiped on the yards. Tomorrow, tomorrow they would be ashore, "Muchacha, muchacha" . . . An hour later the pilot left with ten dollars and buenas noches.

Mrs. Jorham came on deck to rock in the marvellous moonlight. She might have knitted, but the mosquitoes would not agree. Anthony climbed into the maintop above the pests and gazed inland at a circle of unearthly hills.

A few hundred yards across the water at Regla, a thriving little suburb with crowded docks and low, whitewashed houses, a lot of banjos and guitars were going strong. Some of the men started to clog on the deck till Mrs. Jorham snorted. They ceased. She gave a few vicious slaps at her wrists and went below. He was left alone with the banjos, guitars, and the moonlight.

And such mad, soft moonlight! God, what a rhythm was that on shore! The feet in the dance hall at Regla stamped it through an entire vacant interval of the *rumba* . . . now, *now* the frog-voiced guitars chimed in again. He waved his heels in the empty air and his throat swelled. "Habana, Llave del Nuevo Mundo y Ante Mural de los Indios Occidentales," *tunky, tunk tunk, plunk plunk-plunk*, the music went on.

The dew began to soak through his clothes. He jumped to a stay and slid down.

"Wall, ye wouldn't have come da-own that air way when ye come aboard at Leghorn," said Collins with a hint of pride in his voice as if he were responsible. He lowered his voice. "And na-ow she has her hook safe in the mud at Havaner. And I'll tell ye what, Mr. Adverse, we kna-ow who brought her acrost ta pond, eh?" He finally succeeded in closing only one eye and held the wink at last attained for some time. His eye opened. "Wall, ye'll be leavin' us na-ow I expect."

They were silent for a minute. A wave of homesickness at leaving the ship swept over Anthony. Collins looked grave. "I know," he said, "but barrin' the yellow jack and the stinks it's a fa-ine ta-own *tew-w-w*." The last syllable twanged and twinged like a taut preventer stay in a gale. It lingered musically, a sad nasal farewell. Anthony went into the cabin and began to pack. Captain Jorham, who was just drawing off his socks, watched him thoughtfully. So far he had never alluded to any of the events of the voyage. Anthony took his sextant, oiled it, and put it away.

"Ye done right well with that, mister," said the captain picking his toes. He cleared his throat. "We're all obleeged to ye." He went over to "Elisha" and taking out a bag counted out audibly seventy silver dollars. At the clink of coin Mrs. Jorham's night-cap appeared through the slide. She watched attentively. The captain arranged the coins in seven piles and stopped.

"There's five more comin'," said his wife.

He made another half pile a little regretfully.

"Them's yer wages, mister," he said. "No argument, ye've

arned 'em . . . from all I hear tell. Na-ow there's only one thing more I'm askin'. Even if ye're paid off, I'd like ye to try and help dispose o' these holy figures and figurines ra-ound to some o' the churches. Ye've got the hang o' the priestly lingo. You tell 'em for me, will yer?"

"Indeed, I will, sir," said Anthony. "You can count on me for anything as long as you lie in port. And I'll remember the marble, too."

"Na-ow that's right pert of ye," replied the captain. Mrs. Jorham nodded.

It was on the tip of Anthony's tongue to warn the captain about the hidden bottle. He wondered if the Virgin on the sideboard still had it. He strolled over that way. It was still there. But he did not want to bring up any embarrassing memories and refrained from mentioning it.

The captain leaned back in his bunk and lit a pipe. The mosquitoes hummed. He put the light out. The captain dozed and slapped automatically. A patch of moonlight flooded the floor. Presently Mrs. Jorham emerged in her night-cap and a long gown with a small vial in her hand. A strong aromatic odour filled the cabin. She came over and spilled some drops on Anthony's pillow.

"It's penny-riyal," she said. "Keeps the critters away." Then half hesitatingly she rubbed some on his forehead.

He was surprised to feel how soft and smooth her old fingers were. They lingered. She put some on his hair.

"Land sakes!" she sighed, "I ain't rubbed penny-riyal on sence Jane died." Her eyes glistened. He took her old fingers and kissed them.

"Good-bye," he said.

"We'll both hate to see ye go," she whispered. "Take yer pay. It's the old man's conscience money. He's turrible ashamed. Not that ye didn't arn it."

"Mrs. Jorham, how would you like to have me take you around to some of the churches and cemeteries here and translate the inscriptions for you some day?" he said impulsively.

"Na-ow that ud jes' be *lovely*," she sighed. "And we'll have a keeriage." She giggled. Then she spilled some of the penner oil on the captain's covers and went to bed.

Anthony got up and put the silver dollars into his chest. When he turned he saw the captain was looking on with satisfaction. He waved his hand generously in the moonlight.

"Sonny," said he, "let me tell ye suthin' about this ta-own. Don't ye patronize none of them places with stone benches they call latrinas here. Ye'll catch suthin' ul make ye think ye've been spanked with a curry comb. The muchachas air worse. Na-ow in 'ninety-three . . ." He lay back embarrassed.

Anthony waved his hand appreciatively and climbed back into his bunk. The penner oil was still cool on his forehead and the homely odour of it permeated his dreams. He felt very safe in the new world. Captain Jorham snored; Mrs. Jorham coughed softly. It was like having parents.

Very early next morning Collins came with a couple of sailors and loaded Anthony's dunnage in the whaleboat. Collins was taking the first liberty party ashore. The men were to be paid a quarter of their wages and lined up eagerly.

Mrs. Jorham came to the rail with her knitting to say good-bye. She and the captain looked down into the boat as it was lading, talking with Anthony.

"You'll find me through Carlo Cibo, the factor at Regla, sir," said Anthony. "He's Mr. Bonnyfeather's agent here—just across the bay. That pink house behind the stone dock, they say. You see?"

"Aye, aye," said Captain Jorham. "I've got my cabin supplies and groceries from him many's the time. Look out! He's a bit of a shark if he's not yer friend. Keeps a fa-ine house for officers boardin' on shore, or used to. Ye won't forget the stat-oo-airy, mister. I'll be seein' ye soon I calalate."

"I won't forget, sir," Anthony replied looking up and smiling, "and I have an appointment to keep with your wife, too. All the churches and graveyards."

"Oh-ho," chuckled the captain, "so ye *have*, have yer?" Both he and Mrs. Jorham looked pleased. "Wall, git along then."

"Shove off," roared Collins, "let fall! Give way together."

The boat slid over the oily water of the bay that still seemed to retain in its depths at that early hour the deep purple stain of night. A school of silver minnows rose and fell back like a shower of raindrops before it. Philadelphia stood in the shrouds waving his apron, his face shining with a warmth superinduced by the glow of five dollars in his pocket. "Bes' luck, suh, bes' luck in de world!"

Anthony stood up in the stern sheets and looked back at the *Wampanoag*, a delicate tracery of spars and rigging against the rosy city beyond. The jolt and rumble of huge, solid-wheeled carts drawn by oxen began to come to them from the alleys of Regla. The boat nosed into the stone jetty by the pink house and Anthony jumped out onto terra firma with a little cold shiver up his spine as his heels ground into the pebbles of the new world.

"I am going to collect what is owed to John Bonnyfeather," he said to himself, standing still for a minute. "Whatever comes, I am going to get that money." That he felt would constitute his success. His own eventual interest in the matter did not enter in, he told himself. It would all be for Mr. Bonnyfeather.

It pleased him to see that the men who piled his chests on the dock were merely casually respectful as they would be to any other mate going ashore. Sorry that he was leaving the ship? He wondered. The young Spaniard who had released the swallow offered to stay and watch his stuff on the dock. Collins raised his eyebrows but Anthony nodded. Collins touched his hat and the boat made off for Havana smartly. Suddenly it stopped. "Toss!" The oars all flashed into the air and stood upright. Collins was standing up waving his hat. It was a nice compliment. Anthony could have asked nothing more. The man on the chests grinned.

"You know Havana?" asked Anthony, turning to him as the boat sped away again.

"Sí, sí, señor, like a Rodriguez," the man replied grinning. "Like you I leave the cursèd ship of the heretics here. Sí, sí, it is a fine town. I am your servant, señor. I kiss your hands and feet."

Anthony laughed. There was something about the man that he liked. A lean, thin-faced young fellow, smooth-olive, and black-eyed, with an orange neckcloth running down his chest like a flame.

"Very well then," said he. "I will try you for a week at ship's wages. After that we shall see."

"Bueno!" cried the youth, "I am your hombre. By the swallow I swear it!" he cast an invisible bird loose with his hands, kicked his heels in the air, and lay back laughing. To be on land again!

◆◆

Leaving him with the chests, Anthony turned and began to walk toward the rambling, shell-pink edifice before him. Mr. Bonnyfeather's letter crinkled in his pocket. He swung his cane and beat a lively tattoo on the wide double doors. A stark naked, young negro boy, not at all embarrassed by a hearty morning erection, opened the gate. Beyond was a wide patio full of other naked children, mules, yellow curs, and a number of negro women moving about in bright-coloured turbans. An astonishing number of pouter pigeons ran cooing about their feet, fluttered, and lit on the shafts and spokes of several empty carts. He beckoned to one of the women and held up his letter with a small coin.

"For Il Signore Carlo Cibo," he said.

"The señor speaks Italian! The master will see him then. Wait." She rolled up a barrel for him to sit on.

"Go long, you dirty devil!" she cried, catching the young porter across the buttocks with a switch. "Madre de Dios!" and she was gone.

Anthony waited for half an hour. Several shameless cherubs of both sexes surrounded his barrel, looking at him with wide, brown eyes while gnawing sugar cane. He was finally offered some. A little girl swiftly swallowed the tiny coin he gave her in return. She was followed by the others regretfully.

"Doubtless," he reflected, "she will find it later on in safety."

123

A bull-like voice could now be heard bellowing from time to time in some distant part of the buildings. The women hustled and the pigeons fluttered at each throaty note. But they always settled down again. At last his messenger returned.

"This way, señor," she said, and led him out to the street again and around the corner of an alley to a small yellow door with a grille in it. She unlocked this and took him upstairs onto a veranda that overlooked another patio full of banana trees and palms. A huge man sat there in a hammock trying to comb out a mass of tightly curled black hair. A long, sweating, red clay jar swung from the rafters beside him. The woman drew up a cane chair and vanished. Presently the man in the hammock completed his toilet and came forward holding out two fat, white hands.

"I am Carlo Cibo, Signore Adverse. It is a pleasure indeed," said he in excellent Tuscan, "to be able to speak to a compatriot."

"I have written you letters several times, signore, about Brazilian coffee. So our acquaintance is already one of old standing, I believe," Anthony replied in his best professional manner.

"And will ripen into friendship I am sure," added Cibo.

They both laughed at the preciseness of it.

"Come, come," said the factor, "we are getting positively Castilian. 'I kiss your hands and feet.' But, aside from that, have you had breakfast yet? No?"

He did not wait for an answer but gave a roar that somehow included the world "almorzar." A parrot with a cloth thrown over it on a stand near by took its head out from under its wing and began to caw and cackle. Eventually it clawed off the cloth and began to cock its eye at Anthony. It was the most gorgeous thing he had ever seen.

"Almorzar solo, maestro?" said a soft feminine voice from the patio below.

"Por dos," roared the man.

"Dos, dos, dos," cawed the parrot, preening itself.

Some children, evidently half-castes, peeped out of a room across the veranda. A little boy stepped out.

"Put your clothes on for the gentleman, you bastard," said Cibo affectionately. The boy returned, but a baby girl also in a state of nature dashed out of the door and climbed onto the man's knees.

"Kiss my dolly, papa," she cried thrusting a costly doll dressed like a lady of the French court into her father's teeth. "Kiss her."

"Ah, ha, Chiquilla!" he chuckled, tossing her up and making a loud smack at the face of the doll. He danced off with the doll on one arm and the naked child on the other. She shrieked with joy, pulling his black curls awry and crooning over his shoulder at every fat skip.

"Daddy Carlo," she cried looking at Anthony. "Nice, bad daddy!" The little boy ran out now in a shirt.

Suddenly Anthony remembered where he had seen Carlo Cibo before. It was on an oval plaque over what had once been the door to the old wine cellar at the Casa da Bonnyfeather. Plump urchins were capering after a good-natured, fat god. A procession of them staggered after him bearing a huge bunch of grapes. And Carlo Cibo was the man. A naked child was laughing in his arm, too. And that fringed sash swishing over Cibo's fat buttocks cased in tight nankeen, the gross calibre of the white linen socks ending in small, black, varnished shoes that clicked on the veranda like hoofs—yes, he had seen him before.

"*Ha, ha,*" screamed the parrot, "*ha, ha, wheee-ooooo.*" It dragged itself up the cane chair by its beak and perching on the back of the settee looked into Anthony's face with a most knowing eye, making conversational noises and clicking its beak.

Cibo came back and sat down breathless. A purple cast slowly faded from his face. "Ah," he wheezed. "I am getting a little older, avejentado, avejentado! It is very sad." He fanned himself with one hand. The little girl still clung to him looking at Anthony. Finally he was rewarded by her with a glittering smile.

"Ah," said Cibo kissing her. "I like them this age. I have

many. When they grow up I have more. Always I have my babies to dance with me on the veranda. In the grocery business I can afford it." He put the little girl down and told her to run along.

"Cuba, it is a good place. I have done well here." He leaned forward and clapped Anthony on the knee. "You should set up here and try it, signore. Do you know?" He squirmed in his chair and managed to point with his entire body to a tall mulatto girl who was coming down the veranda with the breakfast. "See I am already giving you good advice."

Anthony looked up at the girl. Under his gaze her gait altered slightly. A ghost of a smile was born on the lips of both of them. He looked away telling himself it was nothing. But Carlo Cibo's "advice" had thrilled him. The nights on the *Wampanoag* had been lonely, he remembered. Those dreams—about "Miss Udney." That was strange. Florence, and not Angela had come to him. Yet he had made up his mind to be true to Angela, to remember her always. His eyes grew misty looking into green shadows of the banana leaves. Cibo smiled to himself.

Breakfast had come on a little mahogany wagon. There were two identical trays. On each was a brown jug of clear, black coffee, the heart of a ripe pineapple, white loaf-sugar, which Anthony had never seen before, and the saddle meat of some flaky, boneless fish fried in olive oil with green peppers. They took the trays upon their laps and ate comfortably, Cibo with a delicacy which Anthony could not help but notice. His fingers played with the bright, steel knife and the long, oval spoons skilfully. His hands were immaculate and white; ringless. They would have been dainty if the fingers had not been a little too stubby and luxurious. The pineapple was a dream of sunny flavour. They lay back in their chairs and lit mild, panetela cigars.

The sense of enjoying a delicious delusion overpowered Anthony. He seemed a thousand miles away from the *Wampanoag* and the blinding, blistering bay. Where was he? How had he come here? Cibo began to talk in a far-off, reminiscent voice while the wreaths of blue smoke drifted up to the ceiling from their cigars. He fingered Mr. Bonnyfeather's letter on the table beside him .

"You will pardon me, Signore Adverse, if I seem to have assumed too much intimacy in what I have just said. Your patron in this and other letters has been very explicit and full. He has explained to me that you are, as it were, the junior member of his firm. And I—for fifteen years now, I have been the honoured agent en Habana for the Casa da Bonnyfeather. In vain I have tried to collect this debt from the House of Gallego, for which I am responsible—in a way." He drummed on the table and faltered a little. "Perhaps I should begin at the beginning.

"We are both, as I understand it, under a peculiar debt to John Bonnyfeather. Of yours I have been told a little," he touched the letter, "and I can guess more. Many years ago I came here from Livorno a ruined man. I had been dismissed from the House of Franchetti there in disgrace. The chief clerk of that ancient establishment had engaged in speculations to a great sum. To cover his tracks he involved some of the minor employees under him, of whom I was but one. I was innocent, but I could not be convincing. With five others I was let go. I sold a little house that had come to me from my mother at Rosignano. I came to Havana where in a rash venture I soon involved what little I had. In desperation I wrote to Mr. Bonnyfeather, who had known me, and at whose memorable table I had sometimes sat. I told him my situation exactly, and that unless I could prevail on someone to consign me a cargo on commission I should soon perish of yellow fever in a Spanish prison. Signore, it was like a scene in a play. The corchete in his cocked hat had come for me when the news was brought that a ship consigned to me by Mr. Bonnyfeather was lying in the bay. I do not believe in miracles, but that one occurred. I disposed of the cargo to the House of Gallego at great profit. From that day to this I have greatly prospered." He knocked the long ash off his cigar and continued even more earnestly.

"As the agent for the Casa da Bonnyfeather my reputation was made. Other merchants from various places were also soon dealing with me. I was cautious, and careful to remember the authorities in other things than prayers. After some years I became a Spanish subject and went into the slave trade with old Señor Gallego. Five years of that made me richer than I have allowed anyone in Havana to suspect. But slaving is at best a risky business, and I have gradually ceased to have anything to do with it. I have cut down all merchandising also and have gone in for nothing but the importation of wines, table luxuries, and cabin groceries. It gives me a little something to do. For some years captains and ships' officers used to come and stay in this house, but even that grew to be a nuisance, and I have had none here now for a long time. In fact, except for the luxury trade in fine groceries and rare comestibles, the details of which a few trusted clerks manage, I have, as you see, practically retired. The only exception to this has been when our good patron in Livorno consigned me a cargo. That I have, of course, always disposed of as much to his advantage as possible, mostly to my former partners the Gallegos. The profit, as you know, on merchandise for the slave trade is large, although payment is sometimes delayed. For various reasons, which I shall explain to you later, the account with Gallego has become involved. But do not let us talk about that now. I would say something else.

"From what I have already said you will understand why it is that you will have every assistance that I can offer in collecting the sums due Mr. Bonnyfeather. Also," he added smiling, "why it is that *you* will stay here in my house in Regla as an honoured guest even if you remain in Cuba a lifetime. I should consider it as an implication that I am destitute of gratitude should you go any place else. A slur on my honour! Signore, we should have to meet! My benefactor, I see from his letter, regards you with affection. That is enough for me. Besides, do not mistake me—but I believe in first impressions—and I am disposed to be candid with you. I like you. Come, come, Signore Toni," he laughed. "Where are your things? Have you a servant? Have them sent up. Old Carlo does not often beg."

Anthony would have replied sooner, but he was somewhat

overwhelmed. But no one could refuse to melt under the enthusiastic candour of Cibo. "It would be ungracious of me, signore—" "Carlo," insisted the man. Anthony gulped a little. "Carlo," said he, "to pretend to refuse. I am sure I am more lucky than I know. I understand you. I also have a debt to Mr. Bonnyfeather—not only to collect but to repay. I am sure he would smile in his kindly way to know what you have just said. I shall write him that in Regla near Havana is to be found what he once told me was very rare, gratitude. Carlo, I accept your hospitality with the same rarity."

"Bravo," cried Cibo leaning back in his chair. "You are an orator, friend Toni. And a heartfelt one! You should get along well. I prophesy it this lucky morning which brought you."

"Cheecha," he roared, throwing his cigar into the patio. A quarrel over the stump began below.

"Come, do you want to see my establishment?" He rose suddenly from his chair with a grunt. "I have only one complaint with life you see. I am getting too fat. It is a little difficult for me to move one leg past the other. I chafe. Cheecha!" He took off his sash and hung it over the railing.

The girl made her appearance.

"Get me a dry sash and take these breakfast things away. You know they draw flies. Tell 'Fonso to send for the gentleman's things. From now on he lives here. By the way, Signore Toni, where are your chests?"

"On the dock where I landed them."

"Not unwatched, I hope. Caramba, they will be rifled by this time!"

"I have a man with them, a Spaniard off the ship whom I took on for a week, perhaps rashly."

"No, no, you did well. He can sleep below and look after you. I will have a look at him though. Hurry, girl, *my sash!*"

When it came he draped it once or twice around his waist, and then tucking a smooth fold of it between his legs, he tied the end into his belt. "Now I can walk in comfort," said he, "the silk is smooth and lets one fat chop pass the other." He swished slightly at every step as they walked down the long veranda.

"Yes, it is a sweaty climate. One perspires. Come, come, after all it is much too hot already to go over the establishment. See, we have been talking longer than I thought. The sun is coming into the patio." He leaned over the rail and began to unroll a split-cane awning that fell like a curtain leaving them in a kind of cool, green gloom.

"Cheecha!"

"Sí, sí, señor," replied the woman from below now a little breathlessly.

"Take the cigar-end away from little Juan, and bring me limes and sugar, and . . ." he collapsed into his chair again. A roar from the child below followed the woman's departure. Presently the two babies came up and began to play with the parrot. The boy had taken off his shirt again.

"Ah, it is best so," said his father peering down at him. "August in Havana, my friend! Do you know what that means? But, Dios, take off your own coat! You must forget that you have one. You must get linens. A dozen suits. You shall be measured immediately, mañana. No, you will not need a sash as I do—yet."

"I hope the debt will not take that long to collect, Carlo." Already the name came easily to Anthony.—"Before I wear out twelve linen suits . . ."

"Por Dios, you will use three suits a day or more. Today— today in that costume you will do nothing! I shall do nothing. We shall sit here and talk, and drink, and smoke. We shall eat and sleep. What will be accomplished? Much! We shall have lived another day comfortably. No one can do more. Have you ever spent a day like that? I bet you, not. Try it."

"I remember doing so when I was very little," said Anthony.

"Do not remember, it requires an effort," cried Cibo, "do not remember anything except that it is now. Here is my recipe for preserving the present."

By this time the girl had returned with the ingredients. He mixed some clear rum, sugar, and lime juice, and removing a small peg from the hanging jar drew water. "Here in the veranda the water keeps always cold," he said, and dropped into the pitcher a bowl of crushed fruit giving it a peculiar spiral shaking. A delicate barm appeared on the top, half effervescent. Pomegranate juice had tinged it red. In each waiting glass was a coil of orange peel. He covered this, and handing a glass to Anthony, poured a gobletful down his own throat. He poured it. His throat responded rippling. It was a drinker's throat pliable clear down to the chest and with a good bulge to it. Silenus, indeed, lacked only a few leaves in his hair.

Anthony sat turning over in his mouth small lumps of pineapple reminiscent of rum. When the breeze breathed through the veranda now even from the street beyond it felt cool. Safe behind the green blinds in the cool enclave of the porch, the fierce light and heat surrounded them, as the hours wore on, with a distinct menace. Action of any kind became more and more impossible. They dozed a little, awoke, talked quietly but eagerly, and dozed again. They were both at home.

For Cibo had about him a gift, a physical and mental quality of being that put you at your ease. It was not exercised, it existed. When it was exercised you grew merry, even hilarious. In his house it was impossible to be nervous or to worry about anything. All about you everything was quite obviously going well. The springs of abundance and fecundity seemed to have been tapped at some mysterious source. Nor did his abundance, or even a certain careless prodigality that accompanied Carlo like a rich music played with gusto, worry you. It was natural and instinctive. It was right and spontaneous.

Cibo was not only interested in himself but in what others had to say. He was the prince of listeners, and therefore bore the reputation of being a wit. When you related an anecdote to him a new quality was lent to memory. The events of the past seemed to have taken place in a halcyon glow of which, certainly up until the time you had met Cibo, you had not been aware. But now, as you were talking with him, you became fully conscious of their extraordinary significance and fine flavour. You felt that you had at last found the reflector of your own charming personality that you had long been in search of; one who enhanced your experiences without forcing you to exaggerate; one who could sympathize with you in your own delightful and hitherto unappreciated ironies. Yet, when you thought about it afterward, as you did when you stepped into the now banal and garish street, you wondered.

For if you looked at Cibo casually there was only a pleasant, curly-headed, middle-aged man with a sizable paunch seated in a comfortable chair, a man who wore a bright silk scarf like an Alguacil. Was it in the smooth eccentricity of the brilliant sash that the charm was concealed? Hardly. Yet every person from the Captain-General of Cuba to Cibo's latest slave just in from the Rio Pongo and having his horny feet fitted with sandals to keep them from blistering on the griddle stones of the patio, felt it and expanded under it.

Despite Carlo's toast to "the present," it was the past, Italy, Livorno, and Genoa, that they talked about after all. With the long pent-up eagerness of an exile there were a million things, a thousand people, and a hundred places that Cibo wanted to know about. Anthony found himself, under the keen and amusing probe of Cibo's questions, reconstructing the life of the community that he had lived in.

Indeed, it was under such a searching that Anthony talked best. He had lately become aware of a certain reticence in himself that frequently evoked confidences which he was not inclined to reciprocate. Perhaps it was the essential mystery of his own origin which impressed him with the fact that in the final analysis he could not convey who he was in any usual terms. So, for the most part, he listened and thought. Yet he loved to talk, too. And with Cibo he felt to the full the melody of his own favourite keys. It was—it was amusing.

Before the morning had passed he had found time to tell in full the curious story of Captain Elisha's purchase of holy statuary at Genoa and the queer events of the voyage out. Cibo's belly moved up and down at the thought of the big Madonna in the cabin clasping to her heart a bottle of red wine. The eery expression of a faun laughing lengthened his jaws. He sat up.

"Do you know," said he, "I shall have to help that skipper of yours in disposing of his holy wares. Between you and me, Toni, I am a sad skeptic. It is fortunate for me that since the occupation of Havana by the English the Palace of the Inquisition is closed. There are books on my shelves which even now I would not desire to have advertised. Did you know I was a great reader, a student even in a desultory way, and *of course* a philosopher? From what you say of him, I agree with your friend Toussaint, though we should differ sadly on politics.

"There is a Spanish priest in Regla who is a great friend of mine. We have many an argument. You must meet him. Tonight! It is only upon food that we agree. Like all Spaniards he is a provincial heretic himself when it comes to wine—but on food, oh, on food"—he smacked his lips—"we are both exquisitely orthodox. So we meet often in sweet agreement at the table. During the past five years we have buried our minor differences about the nature of the spiritual world under mountains of dishes. We understand each other, Father Juan and I. I call him Father Trajan. Do you happen to remember the busts of the Caesars, Toni? When you see Father Trajan you will understand. It is that gallant old rascal of a Spaniard come to life again. A case of metempsychosis I insist. It has even worried—Father Trajan. Do you know the Catholic doctrine of the soul? No? Well, it is too hot to go into it now," he took a long pull at the pitcher, "but it is essential. And Father Trajan comes from Segovia. It is a very ancient, an old Roman town. Take one good look at his head when he comes. But don't let him see you do it. And now where am I?—oh, yes—I will tell you. I shall buy that statue of the Madonna del Vino and present it to Father Trajan's chapel, bottle and all. It would be an excellent jest a few years from now to ask him to look behind her robe. Did you say it was port? All that time then he would have been incensing a wine which he particularly dislikes. Ha, by the shade of Voltaire, I shall do it! Let us ask your Yankee captain to dinner tonight with Father Trajan. All parties to the deal will then be present. What! Ask the captain's lady, too? Not so, my boy. Why not? A cause de la scandale, mon ami. No, I do not care if her face is hopeless. In Havana gossip deals with more basic considerations." With the prospect of some excitement ahead he burned up a full half inch on his fourth cigar. After that they slept.

Lunch came on the little wagon and was rolled away. They did not move much after eating it. Carlo mixed some more planter's punch. Outside the fierce heat threatened to sap its way into their shady retreat. Lime-white splotches of sunlight percolated through the blinds.

Anthony looked down once into the patio and saw his sailor asleep in a hammock under the dense shade of a palm. A pickaninny was fanning off the flies. The only sound in the patio was the hum of insects in the sun. His chests had been brought up, he saw.

It was curious to think of his madonna's being in this house. In the light of Carlo Cibo's proposed gift, for the first time in his life he thought of her humorously. How Cibo would laugh. The parrot gave him a wink and went on cracking seeds regularly. Like too long separated ticks of a clock they seemed to mark the passing of a more ample kind of time; to accentuate the somnolent leisure of the place. His eyes lost themselves in the cool green of the date and cocoa palms in the patio. The lizards streaked and flicked across the veranda. Carlo's two little bastards got up and went into a far corner and urinated. They came back again, curled up and went to sleep, the little girl with her head on her brother's stomach. Anthony lay back in his chair overpowered. Somewhere far away the huge carts were still jolting . . . somewhere . . .

At half past five the shadow of the patio wall suddenly seemed to engulf it. Almost instantly it was cool. They got up; bathed.

In a high-ceilinged room furnished with bamboo furniture and a mosquito net hanging ghostly from a suspended ring, Anthony dressed himself in a spotless linen suit that some former guest of Cibo's had left behind him. The very touch of it was refreshing, exhilarating. After the long sleep and floods of orange juice he felt light, very clear and cool, with a certain devil-may-care air and a penchant for the macabre in his mood.

Downstairs the voice of Captain Elisha could be heard rumbling true to form. A sonorous, clean Spanish that he took to be Father Trajan's rang through the halls. He heard Cibo laugh and hurried down.

They were already gathering about the table. In this place you seemed to do nothing but eat and sleep, and yet he was hungry. He found himself talking to, and at the same time half enthralled by Father Trajan. It was about fish. Father Trajan would take him fishing, mañana. Mañana the Virgin was to be installed in Father Trajan's chapel at Regla, the Chapel of St. Paul. Most of Father Trajan's parishioners were the wives of fishermen. "Quite early Christian in atmosphere," said Carlo, and sniffed. Captain Elisha did not see the point. But it was a question whether he or the priest was the more pleased over the affair of the Madonna.

"A good bargain for a heretic and a pious gift to the church by a pagan—was there ever such a combination of circumstances before!" laughed Cibo as his guests left late with everything arranged.

"Tomorrow you must certainly go fishing with the father," said Cibo yawning. "It will be an experience—for you. And we can take up that matter of the debt again. Mañana, mañana," he stretched himself and smiled.

"Good heavens," thought Anthony, "is the man going to sleep again?" They both were!

"Well, how did you like your first day in Cuba?" queried Cibo. "A fine life, eh?"

"J'en suis ravi, monsieur," said Anthony, and meant it.

He climbed into bed and looked through his mosquito netting that caught the broad moonlight in a silver gauze. Outside, the guitars and banjos were still going here and there. A strange, sickly, sweet odour of some blossom opening in the moonlight outside his window in the patio drifted in to him. He wished that Florence . . . that Angela were with him now. How it *would* be—both of them!

What had done this? Was it Havana? Or was it Carlo Cibo's wine? Mañana, mañana! Oh, rare new world!

30. THE MIRACLE IN THE CHAPEL OF ST. PAUL, REGLA

WRAPPED in one of Mrs. Jorham's patchwork quilts the Madonna del Vino, as Carlo persisted in calling her when Father Trajan was not around, was delivered early in the morning at the side door of the bare Chapel of St. Paul in the suburb of Regla.

Collins and some of his crew brought her and took the crazy quilt away again. Carlo, Father Trajan, and Anthony were on hand, each with a very different thought in his heart, as the Virgin was set on the stone floor and unveiled by the rough sailors.

A mason had already slung his scaffold and was preparing to install the statue in the niche behind the altar, where a poor little plaster figure without either beauty or prestige had long been the despair of Father Trajan.

Carlo was surprised by the serene beauty of the figure. In the shadows of the chapel the bright blue of her cloak was toned down until it fell in folds about her like memories of evening. He kept taking Father Trajan back a little distance "to give perspective"—and to prevent any chance of the priest's peering accidentally into the deep folds of the mantle.

The truth was, Cibo would have been ashamed to have had the wine bottle discovered now. It would look as if he had put it there.

Father Trajan was much touched by the gift; secretly mollified for many a remark of his table companion and sly dig at "the superstitions of the age." Now he would be able to obtain a grand indulgence from the bishop for Cibo. His friend's sins should be forgiven him. And there would be great joy amid the simple parishioners when their new Virgin was consecrated.

Perhaps it was a little irregular to have the mason put her in the niche this morning without notifying his superiors. But after all this was his parish. What possible objection could there be? And he would be able to beg a new cassock now for his acolyte. The present one was almost scandalous. Hey-ho! there would not be a more beautiful Madonna in Havana. He knelt down before her on the pavement and made a little prayer silently.

"Mother of God, we are very simple and poor people who come to the Chapel of the blessed apostle. We must serve thee with our hearts rather than with our gifts. Forgive, and be merciful, gracious Mary. The candles are not of the best. But thou livest in the light of the Father. Reflect his radiance upon us. Fill the nets of those who kneel before thee here with fish. And remember thy servant who is a fisher of men, and Brother François, who is digging roots now in my garden. Reward him for his merciful heart, as thou art merciful, santa Madre de Dios."

He crossed himself and rose.

"Come, come, Carlo," whispered Anthony. "You must never

say a word about that wine. Did you see the father's face as he prayed? You must promise me. It would be cruel. I should feel I had compounded at a sacrilege."

"Perhaps you are right," said Cibo.

"Perhaps!" said Anthony.

"Well, well, rest easy," retorted Cibo. "I shall not try to be funny by being cruel. The priest is my friend, you know. We are really fond of each other. My gift was kindly meant, too. We shall just forget that the bottle is there. After all that is nothing but a silly accident. *We* are not responsible for it. I might get the mason to remove it."

They were standing outside the little door by now talking in low voices.

"Let it go," said Anthony. "There would be awkward questions. Let well enough alone." Cibo nodded but a little whimsically.

"A hundred years from now some curious verger will find some remarkable port. I would like to come back and be that man." He smacked his lips.

Inside the chapel Father Trajan and the workman lifted the Madonna into her niche reverently.

"And mind you," said the priest, "I want the new stucco, where you have had to remove the old, smooth, and coloured like the rest of the walls. You can decorate the panel below, can't you—a little? I should like that."

"Sí, sí, padre, for two years now I have been working at the decorations in the cathedral." With the point of his heavy trowel he began to indent rapidly a deft little intaglio design of vines and flowers along the base. He leaned back, looking down from the scaffold for approval.

"You may go on," said the priest. "But *stop*—the cost!"

"I have been well paid by the generous señor grocer," the man admitted a little reluctantly. "A few more adobe flowers—" he shrugged his shoulders. "For a few prayers for my mother I will add the whole vine."

"One for each leaf," said the padre. "An acanthus. You know?"

"Sí," muttered the man. He began to mix.

"Do not forget to drop something in the box for the poor, my friend," said the father as he left to rejoin Carlo and Anthony.

"Ah! It is difficult to bargain with the clergy," muttered the mason to himself. "But I shall have the best of this bargain yet. Grow, vine! Burgeon my mother out of purgatory!" The point of his trowel and one finger flew. A delicate acanthus tendril with a thousand leaves began to unroll itself across the smooth face of the panel at the Virgin's feet. Outside, the voices of Father Trajan and his companions died away. The chapel was very close and still.

The mason worked diligently and fast. From time to time he laid down his trowel and wiped the sweat out of his eyes. At ten o'clock he got down from the scaffold and quenched his thirst at a cantina near by. He returned a little unsteady and went on. The tendril of leaves was almost done now.

He modelled the last fine spray of closed buds with his thumbnail and fingers. The scaffold shook slightly. The trowel which he had laid aside crept nearer the edge. Now—all but the last bud! He indented it in the stucco. Suddenly there was a clink, a tinkle, and the sound of gurgling fluid. The man looked about him uneasily, but he could see nothing amiss. Well, he would scrape up now and go. Caramba! His trowel was gone!

He hunted for it for some time. It was not on the floor. It was not on the altar, under it or beside it. It was not on the scaffold. He took that down. It had not fallen into the mortar bucket. He removed his dripping hand and sloshed it off in disgust.

"Madre de Dios!" And a nice, new little trowel well balanced with lead he had let into the handle himself! One would think those little sneak-thieves and naked gamins would stay out of a church. He had had a pious mother, thank God! A fine generation it was getting to be with the Inquisition suppressed!

He left, staggering away under a pile of buckets and scaffolding on his back.

In the meanwhile Father Trajan's little party had threaded

their way through the fishing quarter of Regla to his house on the water front. A small coral point projected into the bay, and there amid feathery trees at all angles, for the place was swept by winds at certain seasons, lay the priest's house bowered in green and surrounded by flowers and shrubs. Over the wall across the neck of land Anthony could see another priest hoeing vegetables in the garden, a spare, distinguished looking man in the robes and sandals of a Franciscan who evidently belonged to the Pauvres.

They walked into an alley of hibiscus mad with morning bloom, where the scarlet flowers seemed to hiss at them with their protruding, yellow-tipped tongues. They tramped through the gloom of the house and out of a blue square of doorway on the other side of it into Father Trajan's dooryard. Few who visited the priest were prepared for the pure loveliness of that little spot. It occupied the last few hundred yards, the very tip of the point of land. The house which lay directly across the narrow promontory screened it effectively from the town.

Here through the long years of undisturbed administration of his little parish Father Trajan had gradually brought back from his inland rambles every species of palm, fern, flowering bush, and vine that had pleased his vernal fancy as his eye had ranged over the estates and jungles of the Pearl of the Antilles. The gift of a rare flowering plant was to him more welcome than alms. Then too, his fishermen had brought him living shells for his beach and curious sponges and sea ferns for his coral caves. He had the gift of planting. Nearly everything he put down in either earth or water was soon at home.

Viewed from his bayside doorway, the result was what seemed to be a natural garden. The eye flattered itself and fell back tired with delight from the purple mass of a royal piñon to rest in a cool bed of ferns. Satiny lilies of plain and mottled colours looked at one from unexpected spots. There were smouldering clumps of anemones sprouting from cavities in the coral rock. Hanging from palms of unexpected shapes were orchids no one could have imagined, and against the faded coral-pink of the house itself bloomed four lusty trees of yellow, Moorish roses.

Yet, although every one of these things, except a few giant trees, had been planted by the padre, the place was still enchantingly wild. The glow of colour gradually ceased as the glance swept out to the point. Here was nothing but shadowy-green open spaces under wide-stretching date palms, waving ferns, and finally, grass; grass cut off clean and suddenly by the white circle of a tiny, moon-shaped cove.

"El paraíso del padre," said Cibo waving his hand.

"Ah, friend Carlo, you must let me praise this myself," cried Father Trajan, nevertheless colouring a little with pleasure at the compliment. "It is my one vanity.

"Come, señor," he continued, turning to Anthony, "I can see by your face that you will listen to me while I talk of my flowers. You have eyes to see, and you see! And there are some other things I must show you. We have an agreement to go fishing this morning, too. Carlo, will you join us?"

"What, broil myself for a basket of stupid fish I can buy for a peso!" exclaimed Cibo with genuine horror. "You know me better. I am for the veranda and my patio. But go along, my boy, do not let me prevent you. You had best take my palm leaf hat. Adios then," he cried doffing his hat with a wry face and exchanging it for Anthony's Leghorn which was too small for him. "And good luck. There will be turtle for luncheon," he called back. "Plenty for both of you. Never mind bringing the fish!"

"A heart of gold goes there," said the padre looking wistfully after Cibo. "What a pity that he injures his soul by the poor thoughts of his head. One should leave such matters to the church. But pardon, señor, you are of the true faith, I trust."

"I was raised in a convent, padre," said Anthony, secretly dodging the issue. What faith had he now? He wondered. He felt the key to his chest in his pocket—locked away there— safely?

"Oh, well then," said Father Trajan, as if there were a logical connection, "come, let me show you my fish ponds."

They walked down a narrow, wandering path toward the point.

"But look," cried the padre stopping suddenly at the top of a small knoll, "look! You can just see it from here."

A low cloud seemed to be spreading itself along and below the tidal bench that hid the beach from their eyes on the far side of the point. It looked as if a purple-tinged wisp of dawn mist had been blown loose from its cloud-bank and had caught on the tip of the little promontory that morning.

"I cannot imagine what it is," confessed Anthony. Father Trajan looked pleased.

"Hurry. It is really worth seeing," he said. "The most wonderful thing in the island, I believe."

Their path led through a reach of tropical bracken and suddenly emerged on the beach where a fishing boat was drawn up. Here along a low cliff for a surprising distance either way flaunted and burned a giant Bougainvillea vine. Where it had not climbed over the wind-carved pillars of coral rock and pre-empted the neighbouring trees and bushes, it was supported by the deck beams and ribs of an old hulk. This, stripped of its planks and half buried in the sand, had become a gorgeous pergola. There were seats here and there beneath it; even a low cairn on which nets were spread to be dried and mended. From the smooth, bleached sand of the natural floor below, the tremendous organ note of the vine's resounding mass of colour was reverberated back again in a deep imperial glow that harmonized ethereally with the body of bloom above.

Farther under the pergola were stained glooms of purple and magenta that shaded off near the front, where the glare of the beach penetrated, into dim violet shimmers to be seen only when you looked into the place directly. Sidewise they lost themselves beyond the range of vision into the colourless substance of the air. Yet even there Anthony felt them to be still going on. They might be faintly electric and account for something having raised his goose-flesh. Or they might have been transmuted into a rolling sound. For it was impossible to stand before this Bougainvillea and think of it as a purely silent experience. It had about it the quality of a muffled kettle drum; of continuous, distant, tropical thunder.

It was some moments before Anthony became aware of the fact that Father Trajan seemed to be looking at the vine through his own eyes. For the priest was gazing at Anthony as if lost in the expression of the young man who had gone a little pale under his tan. He stood wrapt in the vision.

"But who wouldn't be?" he thought. "It is all I have felt and dreamed about Cuba spoken in one word," he cried aloud.

"There are many ineffable thoughts like that in the forest, señor," said the padre quietly, "but none more beautiful. To think of it! I have been permitted to plant and tend this one with my own hands!" He held them up as if they did not belong to him but were mere tools that had been lent him. "Come under the leafy roof and look up. It makes even heaven more wonderful. Indeed, I cannot begin to say what I think about it. You will understand that."

They went under the pergola and immediately transfigured themselves. Anthony began to look about him half unbelieving. It was then, and in that place, that for the first time he saw Brother François face to face.

———◆———

Seated, leaning back against a pile of old fish nets in a far corner of the place, where he had at first escaped their notice, was a bare-footed monk in the brown garb of a Franciscan. The robe was brown in the sunlight, but in the light that filtered through the pergola it had about it the tinge of old blood. The man rose as soon as he saw himself discovered and came forward courteously. There was something distinguished and a little aloof about his carriage and walk, even an austerity. But no one could imagine being repulsed by him after a simple glance at his face. On it was stamped hauntingly the rare expression of one whose strong sweetness of character had turned the indubitable marks of great sorrow into a kind of holy joy. Sympathy with him was evidently both a wise and a strong passion.

"I would like to know how one can look like that," thought Anthony. "He is not happy like a fool."

"Ah, Brother François, we have disturbed you I fear," said the priest. "We have found you out."

"Neither, I assure you, padre," said Brother François smiling. "When I saw you were having visitors I slipped back here to my favourite retreat. It was my hour of contemplation, but that is over now. It is time again to commune with human friends. May I introduce myself?"

He stepped forward and did so with a charm that put even the padre, who was somewhat awkward about such things, at his ease. It was the "monsieur" instead of the "señor" which gave Anthony his cue, and he replied in French.

At the sound of that tongue a sombre delight smouldered in the monk's eyes . . . "And so it will be pleasant to chat a little in French, if you will," said Anthony. "The Spanish comes as yet only practically. The other world must be left out for me in that language as yet."

"This one?" asked the monk half seriously, touching his forehead.

Anthony nodded. "I am afraid so." He noticed Brother François continued to look at him keenly. It was a little embarrassing, for his eyes seemed full of a banked fire that might break into flame.

"You learned your French at Blois, didn't you? It is an excellent kind they speak there. At Blois, I am sure. Perhaps I have seen you before? Just now I felt certain of it."

"I have never been to France," said Anthony greatly pleased. "My master was, I believe, from some place on the Loire. I am from Livorno. At least I was born there."

"Then I could never have known you. Ah! I remember now what it is. Yes, that *is* curious! But, your pardon, monsieur, it is nothing but a remembrance I will not trouble you with. And so you are going fishing with the padre, I see. I envy you. He and I are both fishers."

The padre was indeed already beginning to gather together his tackle but several articles seemed missing. With some annoyance visible on his face he excused himself to return to the house for the missing things.

Anthony and Brother François sat down under the arbour.

Evidently the opportunity to converse in French was a precious one to the monk. In the familiar accents of his own tongue he became ardent and even confidential. They exchanged news. Anthony was soon comparing notes with Brother François while mentally composing a long pondered letter to Toussaint on the subject of the French Revolution. And here he found to his fascination was a man who had been in the thick of it, one who had actually seen Robespierre.

There was something almost occult about this monk. He stirred you strangely. He removed your reticences for he seemed to have none himself. It would be possible, very easy— there seemed to be a spiritual compulsion upon one to succumb to his spell. . . .

"So you see, monsieur, I am after all not an émigré in the usual meaning of the word. To preach the gospel and really to live like Christ—it was not more dangerous in Paris during the Terror than it is here and now. All of us who do that are exiles. We are merely passing through the strange countries of the world going home to our Father. In our souls is all of his kingdom that will ever be here. Yet just for that reason it might be everywhere and now.

"I am not making you a homily, monsieur, or talking about myself. You will pardon my excitement. It is the remembrance of the past few years in Paris that comes across my view. One cannot, if one knows, speak of them merely with the kitchen voice, 'Thérèse, a little more gumbo in the soup!'—no, no,— that will not do. That is worse than being exquisite or gay about it. Also I do not speak to crowds or in them, whether in the plaza or dans l'église. Always it is to the man, or to the woman or the child that I come, and not always with words. Man, mankind, the state, virtue, the people, justice, fraternity—what are they? Words that do not correspond to anything but philosophers' dreams. They are the worn out table-talk of Greece and Rome. Liberty?

"Monsieur Antoine, for two years I followed the tumbrils and I stood on the scaffold. I saw the keen knife of liberty fall and rise to fall again, and each time on an individual's neck. That is the way of the state. And those hundreds of eyes! They looked down into the basket at the eyes there that looked back. It was unthinkable that what lay in the basket was the end. Those who thought so died there, indeed. For those who turned to me for some confirmation of hope, I then shared what I had given me, the Comforter. Robespierre himself could not prevent it.

"Do you know I went to see that man. Mais oui! At the little house of the cabinet-maker in the Rue St. Honoré—in April only two years ago. It seems a century ago. It was the day after Danton, Camille Desmoulins, and the others had passed under his window in the carts.

"The two ruffians who guarded the tyrant came to the door when I knocked. I asked for Duplay, the furniture-maker, and got him to carry my name to the little man upstairs. Robespierre knew me. We both came from Arras. My family was a very great one. Monsieur would know its name. Robespierre knew that I might have been a bishop but that I went into the country instead as a parish priest. You see we had both read Rousseau together. I remembered when de Robespierre was a provincial dandy who read bad verses before the 'Rosati' at Arras. He had a sweet voice then, and he had resigned a criminal judgeship to avoid pronouncing a death sentence. Think of it! It was the same voice that I afterwards heard raised in the Convention, 'It is with regret that I pronounce the fatal truth, Louis must die that the country may live!' Ah, he was full of regrets like that. But anyway I was shown upstairs.

"He and Fleuriot-Lescaut were seated together. Robespierre looked very white. The great voice of Camille Desmoulins shouting the prophecy of his death under his window the day before had shaken him. I saw that he was afraid. He was still the little dandy in knee-breeches, silk socks, and powdered hair. He turned down a paper with a list of names on it that he and Lescaut were talking over and looked up.

" 'Well, citizen?' he said, 'what is it? Ah! I remember you now.' He tried to smile. That was terrible.

" 'I have a very simple proposition to make to you,' I replied. 'You must be very sick of all this blood-letting and of being the god of Catherine Théot. Is it not so? See where your philosophic virtue has led you! You will have to kill us all. You alone will remain, for soon you will be the only one who knows how to practise virtue. Another plan is needed. I speak to you, *for* you, not for France or any other dream, but for your own soul. You believe that is immortal?'

" 'What do you propose, citizen?' Robespierre said. He leaned forward and looked at me with hungry eyes and a thin smile.

" 'Simply that you leave this room now and come with me into the country. You can change your name and disappear. Then we can go about the world just as Christ would have done, doing good. We need nothing. We need make no speeches or sermons. Let us just go out and let things happen to us as they will, and try to help and comfort any man, woman or child who needs it. Let us be kind, a brother to this man and that. Let us persuade no one, but pass on taking whatever road lies before us and leaving a good deed done in Christ's name wherever and whenever we can. That is all. It is an old and simple plan, to do good to men with the spirit of God upon one. Do you not see by this time that it is the only plan that will work? *Leave everything and follow me.* You remember that?

" 'Why do you come here to me, and *today*, with a suggestion like this?' he asked. 'Do you not know that France is pressed down upon my shoulders, the hope of saving France, of the world!' He got up and moved about with Fleuriot-Lescaut gaping at him.

" 'But you are mad,' he flung at me. 'You have lost relatives. You are an aristocrat, a ci-devant Count.'

" 'That is not so, citizen. You know that even before the Revolution I became a parish priest. No, no, it is not I that am mad. I come to you because you are an idealist of sincerity. I can see that. And you are wrong, you have chosen the wrong way to help the world. You are working through the state and through institutions. You have made reason your divinity. See what it is doing to make men divine. You know. Still within you, *you know!*'

"He made a furious gesture but I kept on.

" 'You can disembarrass yourself of all this, citizen. There is a way to do good and to save yourself by forgetting yourself. I have found it. I am living it, and it is in me. Come! Let the Republic flourish as it may. The Kingdom of God is just beyond the door. Leave Robespierre here, my brother, and come with me.'

"Many that I have spoken to thus, monsieur, have been greatly surprised. Under all that they pretend to be and through all their bafflements I talk to *them*. They see the way opening before them. In truth most men have thought of it. But the world is too much for them. They keep their loss. Prudence insists on just a few chains to hold them fast to something tangible. So they remain anchored on their reef to be pounded to pieces on it when the tide of life ebbs. It was so with Robespierre. For a minute he saw, he remembered, he dared hope again. Then his face worked, and I thought he would spring at me.

"Monsieur, if Fleuriot-Lescaut had not given a great laugh just then I should have been guillotined. I believe in my heart he was a merciful man. His laugh saved me.

" 'Come, citizen,' he said, 'have this simple fool thrown out. *Disembarrass yourself*, as he says. We have not time here to argue with a mad parish saint. A cabbage head,' he roared, 'a green cabbage!' He pretended to kick me downstairs. I saw the tyrant standing at the top with the list still in his hand. It was the first time he had laughed in weeks, I suppose. I did make an unfortunate noise falling down the stairs. But do you know I still think—almost I won. 'Almost thou persuadest me,' his eyes seemed to say, and his hands shook. But God had another way. I only offered myself as an instrument. Did you see the padre when he held up his hands and said they had been *permitted* to tend this glorious vine? I heard that, too. Ah! the padre is a poet. A thought of God he called his vine. Well, it is best to think of all of yourself as the padre thinks of his hands. You will see then how thoughts of God flourish."

He looked up so that the violet tinge of the light filtering through the vine fell full on his face.

It would be impossible to exaggerate the impression which this narrative had made on Anthony. It seemed as if Brother François had been pleading with him. It was not so much what the monk had said as how he said it. Here was a man with an obviously complicated knowledge and experience who was living by and pleading for a great simplicity. The manner of an aristocrat and a courtier had been transmuted in him into a noble directness, a wise humility that was without fear. There was an ease about him that sprang from an assurance which did not annoy you. You simply understood that he was at one with himself and the world. Here was passion at rest and yet potential.

"Follow me!" Yes, follow along the way that child which the madonna held in her arms had followed into manhood, into something beyond, into the glory like the violet light on Brother François's face. Ah! what a way! That was what the madonna was holding out to you always in her arms—the child and his way. The most simple and direct one after all. Why had he never realized that before? What the monk had said had brought it home to him as a possible experience. Father Xavier had told him to think of the child. He saw what he meant now, he thought. To take up your cross and . . . *That* was not clear. Anthony had no cross. Life was delightful. Like the light under this arbour, beautiful, and colourful, and clear. Was not his private communion with the madonna enough for him? And yet she was holding forth something else to him, something that was very precious to her. Yet she would share it. It was a gift she seemed to hope you would take.

Yes, it meant that. Religion was not merely to refrain, and to worship, "to talk at night," as he used to call it. He smiled and he sighed too. No, it was a way. Had he really been travelling that way? Brother François had. By his overtones he seemed to make the music of that road clear. The road was life along which he went doing good. Had he been pleading for a companion? Why not join him, Anthony? It would all be simple and all very clear. The responsibility would be God's.

Simple things appeal sometimes even to complicated young men. Anthony sat with his head on his hand looking at Brother François.

"Thou knowest," said the priest very quietly, "to whom I have been talking. Hast thou heard me?"

"Yes, I have understood," said Anthony. But he could go no further.

Brother François waited a while. "Well, then—you have understood," he said. "That is the beginning. You must wait until you also feel. It is experience I mean. Then you will know, and then . . . then the answer will be yours to make and the road yours to take. But I see that it is not now. Only remember what I have said, if you can, when the time comes.

"Ma foi!" he looked up suddenly breaking the tension between them, "the sun is already overhead. You will not be going fishing *this* morning. This morning is no more. What can have detained the padre? He is—well, he is a fisherman, and there must have been a reason. Let us go and see."

They rose and sauntered down the path toward the house. It was very hot now. Even under Cibo's palm leaf hat Anthony could feel the exact spot of the sun. The little suburb of Regla that lay before them seemed extraordinarily quiet. It was already absorbed in its siesta. Not even a cart jolted. Suddenly with a startling clangour the bell in the chapel began to ring.

"What can it be?" said Brother François wonderingly, as the excited clangour continued. "It is like an alarm." They quickened their pace and entered the house. Father Trajan was leaning against the jamb of his street door listening in a puzzled way. He looked up when they came in.

"Pardon, señor, for my not returning. I will explain it shortly. I was detained. Mañana! What I cannot explain now is the ringing of my chapel bell. Possibly someone has been drowned."

Already they could hear the sound of running feet in the alleys beyond the hedge. "Ah, I am afraid that is what it is. See, here they come now to fetch me." A look of sadness overspread his features "I had best get the oil, I suppose. Who can it be this time?" He sighed.

Two women made their appearance at the gate breathless, and calling, "Padre, padre!"

"Ah, what is it, Juana, my poor soul?" said the padre from the next room with apprehensive sadness.

"Padre, padre," clamoured the two fisherwomen now at the door, "a miracle has occurred!"

"A what?" said the padre.

"A miracle," clamoured the woman.

"Yes, yes, by the blood of God it is true!" bawled the other.

"What is all this silly excitement about?" said the priest coming out of the room indignantly with the viaticum still in his hand. "What are they ringing the bell of my chapel for?"

"A miracle," shouted both of the women. "There is a new Madonna in the chapel and . . ."

"Foolish women, I know it," countered the priest. "Did I not see her brought there this morning myself? It is the pious gift of . . ."

"But she is bleeding! Her merciful heart is bleeding red blood drop by drop on the altar! We have seen it! A great crowd is already there watching. It is a blessed miracle from God!"

"Sí, sí, padre! Sí, sí, it is true! Come and see for yourself. Juana and I, we alone have remembered to come and tell you." They stood crossing themselves and trembling.

"Come, padre, let us see what this is all about," said Brother François. "I thank you, my friends." But the women had gone.

They hurried after them as fast as they could. The town was already alarmed by the bell. People dashed past them toward the chapel. A good deal of confused shouting could be heard here and there as the winds of rumour blew.

When they arrived at the door of the building it was already full and a crowd was seething about the entrance. With great difficulty a way was made for the padre and his friends. Inside the place was silent. Only the heavy breathing of the crowd and the clamour of the bell above was audible. Anthony could see that those near the altar were on their knees while those farther back were craning their heads and staring as if fascinated. All were looking in one direction.

He became separated from the others and finally found himself pressed back against the side wall. Only after some difficulty could he manage to get a glimpse of the front of the church. Father Trajan was already before the altar kneeling. Anthony saw there was a red stain upon it. The bell had stopped now. You could have heard a pin drop. Suddenly there was a *plop*, a distinct drip like falling water. The stain on the altar ran over and dripped onto the floor. A universal sigh went up from the whole place. He raised his eyes to the statue in the niche above. Some time passed. Then he saw it himself. Something trickled out of the cloak of the virgin and splashed onto the altar. In the candlelight it was red, and it did look like blood. The bell began to clamour again madly.

Father Trajan turned to face his chapel, now jammed from wall to wall. Here everybody who could was kneeling. He burst into the "Magnificat."

A great thrill of joy ran through the crowd. The simple faces of fishermen, labourers, and negroes looked up at the miraculous statue, filled with ecstasy and awe. The face of Father Trajan was glorified. It shone with a proud benignity and utter conviction.

"In his own chapel!" Anthony thought. "Poor man! I should have let Carlo take it away. I did not think *this* would happen."

He assured himself he was innocent, but his heart smote him sorely. There was not one unbelieving face present. "Now," he told himself, "no one must ever know. I will see to that. What a seed Captain Jorham planted that night! A miracle!"

Then, terrible as it was, he wanted to laugh. Struggling with himself in the intense excitement and the stifling atmosphere, for the first and last time in his life he felt hysterical. He wanted to laugh and cry as the women were already doing.

The bell burst forth again into a mad peal. Outside there was a renewed shouting. The whole town would soon be there. How could he get out? The side door! He looked across the chapel. Standing wedged helplessly against a pillar so that he seemed to tower above those who knelt around him was the tall frame of Brother François. He was looking with an expression of intense pity and sympathy at the hundreds of faces staring ecstatically at the magical clay breast of the Madonna del Vino.

An hour later Anthony finally gained the door. The "miracle" was still going on.

Wine seeps slowly through terra cotta.

31. A DECENT MAMMALIAN PHILOSOPHY

I T W A S about three o'clock when Anthony finally succeeded in returning to Carlo Cibo's. He had won his way out of the chapel literally inch by inch, and he was tired and exhausted. Whether the heat or the excitement were the more intense would be hard to say. Already the news had spread far and wide. Boats, carriages, and caballeros were coming in from Havana. The cantinas of Regla, he observed, were doing a roaring business. But in the patio all was shade and quiet. Carlo was asleep on the veranda in his chair, his short legs dangling.

"Wake up, Carlo," said Anthony. "A miracle has occurred. Aren't you ashamed, you old heathen, to be asleep while such things are going on?" It was some time before Carlo could be made to comprehend. When he did his belly moved up and down so fast as finally to stop his laughing from sheer physical discomfort. He lay back in his chair and continued to snort with his hands on his sash.

"Miracles should not be permitted to occur in the summer," he said at last. "They are dangerous to people like myself. It is hard on the heart. I shall take it up with the ecclesiastical authorities. Unfortunately the archbishop, who is a friend of mine, lives at Santiago.

"But," continued he sitting up and laying his hand on his lips, "seriously, let me tell you, my boy, you and I must keep a close mouth about this. If we are questioned we must know nothing. *Nothing*—do you understand?

"There will be a tremendous to-do over the affair. The bishop in Havana may even be annoyed with Father Trajan for being a little too up and coming. Or he may suspect me when he hears I am the donor of the miraculous image. He is no fool I can tell you, that old man. So mum's the word. There will undoubtedly be an official inquiry, depositions before notaries, and all that kind of thing. The whole town is a witness. But they won't press it too far I feel sure. It falls too pat into their hands. With the population on both sides of the bay stirred up it will be impossible, silly to deny it. There would be riots. No, no, it will be confirmed. As you say—'A miracle has occurred!'"
He lay back again breathless.

"Cheecha!"

"Sí, sí,"

"More limes and rum, mucha, mucha! Turtle soup for the señor. Hurry, delay not, haste! The soup hot, with much fat, and sliced limes. Go!

"Ah, Madre de Dios, what a day! Did I not say you were lucky, Señor Toni? See—you reek with luck!" He spread out his fat hands over the pitcher with utter conviction. Even the lime peel dangled from his fingers convincingly.

"And the curious thing about it is that this time all the depositions and witnesses will be honest. The poor bishop will really be confused by that. The miracle should have taken place at the cathedral in Havana which they are just now redecorating. The bones of Columbus were brought there only last January. But the Madonna bleeds at Regla, in 'the suburb across the bay'! All the rules for miracles are disregarded."

A leer came into his eye. "The future of Regla is made. Peons from Moron to Guanes will be making pilgrimages. My house is already twice as valuable as when you arrived . . . Signore, I thank you! You are a public benefactor. Por Dios, the rest of the holy cargo of El Capitan Jor-*ham* will now sell for ransoms! Even the black robes who are now lying low at Belén will scramble for it. A plain padre will have beaten them. It is—it is simply magnificent! I drink your illustrious health." He tilted an entire pitcher of drink down his throat. His voice came out of the deep receptacle like an echo from a cave.

"Are you sure," said he, "your friend the captain does not remember about his bottle?"

"I am certain," Anthony assured him.

The pitcher gurgled with a satisfied note. Its angle became more acute. "How do you suppose," continued its sepulchral tones, "that the bottle was broken?"

"A jar when the statue was put in place, perhaps," mused Anthony, "or possibly some carelessness on the part of the mason. But I really don't know. Do *you?*" cried he, suddenly suspicious.

"No, no," replied Carlo coming out of his eclipse with genuine solicitude—and the mark of the pitcher on his face. "I tell you I had nothing to do with it. I suspect it *was* the mason. I had already thought of that. But it must have been an accident as you say. He would not tell. I'll tell you what. To make this miracle beyond cavil you must again make sure of Captain Jorham. Leave the fragments of the bottle and the mason to me. Tonight, late, I will make sure of both. I know a way. They will examine the statue, of course, and within a day or two. Father Trajan—we are both thinking of him, I know—dear man, he shall have his miracle without a cloud. When the confirmation comes from the archbishop I shall give the finest dinner that Cuba has ever seen. It too will be a miracle. You are the first invited."

"An invitation is the best way to make a witness remember. I noticed that at Mr. Bonnyfeather's table. Invited guests never forget," said Anthony. He wondered if all events for Cibo inevitably resulted in more and better food.

"I have known even *un*invited guests to remember my dinners," smiled Cibo. "But that is really one of the greatest compliments a host can receive. I'll tell you what! We shall have you, and Captain Jorham, and Father Trajan—and myself . . ."

"And Brother François?" added Anthony impulsively.

"Ah, yes, the Frenchman! He *is* interesting. Did you know he is already in hot water with the authorities here for being a little too literal in his ideas of what Christ would have one do for slaves? He goes about nursing poor people with yellow fever and soothing the dying whether they are white or black. It is over the black that the trouble comes in, of course. It scarcely does, you know, after what has just happened in Santo Domingo, to have a man like that loose. The niggers might get the idea that God is sorry for them. Not in Cuba with a Spanish governor and garrison! Did you know the captain-general sent his aide to ask me to look the man up? Well, I did. He has an interesting story I can tell you! A little too interesting, and not regular enough. I don't think he'll be here long," said Cibo drawling a little. He began to mix more punch.

"Carlo, he is harmlessly extraordinary, isn't he? Brother François is a holy man if there ever was one," exclaimed Anthony. "What harm has he done?"

"Oh, he has been talking with you, I see," said Cibo. His face suddenly became quite serious.

"Yes, I agree with you, Toni. Brother François *is* a holy man. That is the trouble. He is not merely content to perform in the ritual of the church. He is one of your complicated primitives, a man who has penetrated behind the scenery of religion, one who intends to live the story which the ritual is supposed to illustrate. You see, he does not attack or interfere with the drama. That makes it a little difficult for his superiors. He does not provide them with an excuse to abolish him or thrust him out. On the contrary, as far as I can find out, he merely proposes to carry out their own precepts. That is, of course, profoundly embarrassing—to them."

Anthony tried to say something but Cibo went on.

"Brother François and his kind are the men who have always made Christianity a dangerous religion. Just when the church is about to be taken for a decorative and snugly-woven cocoon on a dead branch of the sacred tree, a place for a few fat slugs to hibernate where they have softly spun themselves in, *pouf!*— that cocoon bursts and the beautiful, living psyche of Christianity emerges. There is always a great running around then and waving of fine-meshed theological and political nets. The state is particularly anxious about such lepidoptera getting loose. Property! When the state can't kill a specimen quietly in a corner before its wings are dry, the church captures it and pins it on a card marked 'Saint Somebody.' Then the faithful come and see the body in a glass case, usually the glass is coloured. But there it is, catalogued, and belonging to its proper order. Now and then it may be permitted to work a few harmless miracles. A pile of crutches accumulates, or the story of the poor butterfly edifies the piously sentimental. They imitate its flutterings. Meanwhile the hard-working caterpillars keep making more Gothic or Romanesque cocoons for the slugs, always on the same closed pattern. They, of course, do not know yet what a Christian cocoon is really for." Cibo took another draw on the pitcher and ran on even a little more incoherently. "Now look at Jeanne d'Arc!

"The state is so frightfully careless and stupid about its executions. Executions, particularly the expunging of patriots or moral reformers, should be conducted in profound secrecy. To dramatize, or to allow news about such takings-off to circulate, whether the man is a criminal or a saint, is the best way for sovereigns to commit suicide. Yes, I often wonder at the politicos. They never seem to learn anything. Just about the time the world is getting bored by being asked by an enthusiast to adopt some kind of a life that no mammals could survive—Ha! the police descend! A great trial with all the implications of a Greek tragedy is staged. Soldiers parade, judges pontificate, women weep, priests snivel. After which the hero is then boiled in oil, or has his bowels let out, or is permitted to caper naked in the flames, or is hanged—or what you will. How can anybody forget him then?

"For saints I myself favour a dangerous foreign mission, transportation provided free. I have already suggested that to the captain-general. For people are already beginning to follow this Brother François about. His dramatic disappearance into the Morro would be embarrassing. He has friends. Whispers about him have already passed over the hills from plantation to plantation."

"How can you talk so, Carlo? It seemed to me just now that you spoke of him with affection. Don't you care? You are asking him to eat with you, too!" Anthony was now much in earnest and sitting up very straight.

"You do not understand me, Toni. I view all these matters from the outside, calmly. I am an unromantic Italian, a real Roman. I am purely practical. I am really the best friend Brother François has. Ah, you smile, but listen. If he stays here his end is certain. He is, I must tell you, of a great French noble family. He might have been a bishop under the old régime. He left all that and went into the country to be a parish priest. Then during the Revolution he drifted to Paris. He took a minor part as a peasant deputy in the beginning of the troubles there. I think he believed for a while that the state might help the people. Then he saw through all that and was horrified by the Terror. The last pink tinge of St. Jean-Jacques faded from his mind. He then became a literal follower of Christ. How? By joining the Franciscans, a Pauvre. He wandered begging into Spain. A troop ship brought him here. The men were dying on board of the plague, they say, and he swam out to nurse them at Cadiz. So you see even the garrison knows him. That worries the authorities. It is all frightfully irregular, of course, and could only happen in times like these. Now he is helping the slaves. No, he doesn't preach. He says nothing. But very shortly it will end in a tragedy for Brother François.

"Now I know all this. For years I have dealt among the natives and foreigners here and I have played carefully with the authorities, too. Always I play to avoid great trouble. The authorities have come to trust me. Yes, it has been profitable, but that is not all. You see, I like brave men. I don't want to see them die. I prevent it when I can. With Brother François it has gone like this: He has been ill. I prevailed on the good padre to take him in and nurse him in his garden. During that time his dangerous ministrations have ceased. In the meanwhile the captain-general has spoken to the bishop. Our good brother will soon be recognized for his work among the poor, and it will be arranged with the proper local authorities of his order that he shall go to Africa, to the field for which he has shown such aptitude! Even now they only await certain papers from Santiago. I have by just a few hints brought this about. If I had not, my friend, your holy man would have died before this of the yellow jack in a cell in the Morro waiting for instructions from Spain. They never come for people like him. Tell me now, *am* I so cruel? Or would you rather I should let him compose his own epitaph in some more romantic and heroic way?"

It was difficult for Anthony to reply. He found a large part of his emotions ready to applaud Brother François and yet he could not protest entirely what Cibo had said. He saw, too, that behind Carlo's somewhat cynical outline of policy there lay a well-meant human kindness.

"You do not intend to consult Brother François himself, I suppose?" he said at last.

"By no means," replied Cibo emphatically. "Your enthusiast who has a complete solution for everything on tap is always the last man to know what is good for himself. Indeed, with the millennium always just around the corner it is seldom that they take the trouble either to support or to protect themselves. They hook their chins on a cloud and then walk barefoot over all the broken bottles and old nails which those with a less lofty gaze easily avoid. A suggestion of shoes is hotly resented. In this case I am merely guiding the cloud-hooked gentleman out of a path, where a pit with a sharp stake is just around the next turn, into a road with perhaps a longer vista. Eventually, no doubt, he will find his own painful way to heaven. Several people will doubtless be impressed. Yes, speaking even as a disinterested pagan who wants all calvaries at a distance, I think I can see the stigmata on Brother François's hands."

Anthony's heart leaped strangely. Against all the assurances of Carlo there looked up at him as if out of a vision the face of Brother Francois as he had seen it under the violet light of the vine. "I think you are right about the stigmata, Carlo," he said after a while. "Perhaps I *am* romantic, but it did seem to me this morning that there was something about the man that was—well—shall I call it divine? I mean that the quality which saves men from being just animals has a greater share in him than in me. It seemed to dominate his body entirely. I am not sure they can kill that. Are you?"

Cibo passed his hand over his eyes. "No, I am not sure. But I do not want to watch anyone trying. Well, you touch me there, Toni, I will confess. In speaking of executions I should have added that ordinarily they get little attention, and for the most part do not deserve it. Men seem to have an instinct about them. There is seldom any vigorous protest over the mere slaying of so much meat. It is only when someone gets into the toils who possesses notably the quality of which you speak that the wrench is felt."

"It seems to me then you are not so pagan after all, Carlo."

The man stretched himself and laughed. "We are talking a great deal and it is getting late. Also I have now had my third pitcher today and that makes me voluble and illogical. But what does it matter what makes men talk if they convey their essential feeling? Brother François seems to have succeeded in doing that this morning to you. Confess—you are disturbed by him more than you would like to admit."

"Yes," said Anthony. "He stirred something in me of which I had not been aware."

"Exactly," said Cibo. "You have grown quite heated about him while we talked. You really care, and you are even ready to accuse me of being callous. But I repeat it is *not* so. Let me try to unfold my own philosophy a little. I think I see the basis of your feeling under all this. It is not merely a French priest we are discussing, is it? His unique personality, even briefly glimpsed this morning, touched you mysteriously. Didn't he?"

"I have already told you so. Why do you . . ." But Carlo was not to be interrupted.

"You should ask yourself, Toni mio—'*is* he really so unique?' You are young!" Cibo pointed his finger at him scornfully.

"When we are still young we think a great many people whom we meet are extraordinary. There is no one else in the world like them, we feel sure. Also our own precious selves are without parallel. We tell ourselves and each other, 'Neither we nor our friends, who are so unusual, are understood.' The world, we think, is not subtle enough to understand us. But we are wrong.

"The adult world is far too subtle to waste much time on us. It understands us instinctively by just remembering itself. It has thought through all our thoughts and is tired of our violent emotions. It does not need to care about youth because it knows youth will get older. Besides, it is too busy about the essentials of existence to go in for theories and feelings about them. Good old world! It is the young who do not understand it or themselves.

"From fifteen to twenty-five youth is busy talking about itself and trying to hatch doorknobs by brooding over them in a fever. Eggs—I mean events. They hatch themselves. Fate laid them pregnant on a warm beach. Everything that survives the process grows up according to the plan of its own egg. You can't do much about it. Not nearly as much as you think. No, really you can't!

"Fate is a wise old turtle. Imitate and accept her. Otherwise you will become feverish over the eggs you think you have hatched and go clucking and scratching about in the dust for chickens only to find that ducks must swim, and like it. When you learn that you are beginning to grow up. Grow up as soon as you can. It pays. The only time you really live fully is from thirty to sixty, provided of course you are healthy and don't die. No, the young are slaves to dreams; the old servants of regrets. Only the middle-aged have all their five senses in the keeping of their wits. I," said he, helping himself again to the pitcher, "am middle-aged; absolutely in my prime."

Anthony felt momentarily overpowered, almost an infant again. Then he saw how much Cibo was enjoying himself.

"My God!" continued Cibo lustily, taking another sustaining swig, "did you ever think what a terrible mess a young man really is? I mean a youth. That is—a kind of portable apparatus or attachment to three troublesome globes, one who has just stopped being a mad boy and has not yet been scared into being a decent man. One feels profoundly sorry for him. The only peace he can get is for a few hours after a girl has nearly killed him. The rest of the time he goes drifting about making a lot of noise like a ship upon which a perpetual mutiny is going on. He is always steered in the direction which his bowsprit indicates.

"Young men think life is a game, you know, an adventure. You hear them say so. Life is a mystery, not a game or an adventure. Birth and death are the only certain events in it. Eggs, eggs both of them! Maybe life is an egg? You can't tell what you're hatching. I'm getting drunk but never mind. (It's a wise man that knows how foolish he is when he's sober.) I'll tell you what wisdom is." He sat up earnestly and ponderously now.

"You now hear the most profound of all human oracles speaking. It alone holds the past and the future. Hearken to it, Toni."

Anthony had winced. It took him a few minutes to think of any reply to this unexpected and outrageous attack upon him.

"Your tongue and your oracle both sound alike to me," he said at last in desperation.

He was surprised and delighted to see that he had got home. "I always did think life was a mystery but not to be explained by a blast from the bowels," he continued making the most of his brief moment of victory.

"You underrate the guts," said Cibo at last. "What is even a wise book but a blast from the lungs made visible to the eyes? Man only makes foolish noises and smells in the face of mystery. No, Toni, do not get angry," he went on. "Forgive me for being a man . . . ."

"Forgive me for being a young man then," said Anthony.

"I do, I do! Believe me, I like you for it in spite of all I have said," cried Carlo. "I shall even pretend now to be sober.

"Toni, I have been watching you. You interest me. You see and feel things so vividly it is a pleasure. Why then don't you let it go at that? Enjoy the fascination life has for you. What more do you want? Why ask 'why'? Why let your mind always be demanding of you, 'Give me an understandable and valuable goal; explain to me why I am here'? That is dangerous. That will eventually spoil the fascination for you. That is why Brother François interested you this morning. You thought he could provide answers for those questions. Is not that so?"

"Yes," said Anthony, "I thought this morning when he was talking to me I saw a way open up to live by."

"The way to Calvary! Come, come, Toni mio, you are not going to try *that* way?" he laughed. "Nonsense, of course not! You are only dallying with a romantic idea. I know. You are going to live life, all of it, for the sake of living. It is worth while. Besides, you can't avoid it, being what you are. Listen, let us not devote more time to our Brother François. I want to talk to you about the most interesting thing in the world, with perhaps one exception. Yes, despite all I have said, a young man. One whom I know better than he supposes. For you see, as I was about to say some time ago, as one gets older with a much broader basis for judgment"—he patted his paunch —"every new person is no longer a surprise. Men and women fall into types.

"Now you are a type. You are very practical, and yet, you are always aware of the mystery of things. You have not yet made up your mind what the world is like or what you are. You are not quite sure what you would be, a mysterious or a practical man, and you therefore cannot foretell how you are going to act. Things happen to you, and then you are always surprised by your own possibilities and limitations. Now am I right so far?"

"Very much so," murmured Anthony. "I have sometimes thought so myself."

"Very well then, it will help you to have someone else say so who is not yourself. Here, have another drink. That is the least that a host who likes an audience can provide. I would like to hear you talk more. But, no, I know you will not. You would rather listen and think. Very well then. Now is your chance.

"What I meant to tell you is that unless you come to *some* conclusion about yourself and the world you will be a mere wanderer. Not finding any surety within, you will unconsciously go about the planet looking for yourself everywhere. You will get bored, or you will produce your own expelling explosions, and you will go on saying, 'In the next place, over there, I shall be happy. There I shall be myself. There I shall find the true Anthony.' But it will only be another small part of you in another small place, not the whole man. Or, worse than that, you will grow desperate and become extreme. You will try to pretend to yourself that you are all spirit and the world is only a dream, or that you are an animal only and the world is all real. Both are possible with you, for you will only believe things after you experience them. Ah! that is your trouble, a young man's trouble, the experiences of others do not persuade you. Nevertheless—take another drink, for I am going to give you some advice. If this talk were not all about you, you would be bored, wouldn't you?"

Anthony laughed and drank deep.

"For *so* much I can go on then," said Carlo, measuring the tumbler at the level of his eyes as he resumed.

"Practise then what I call a decent mammalian philosophy. Go in for the body, my boy, but remember you are a man. At one end of your spine is a brain and at the other end something that needs constant companionship. The two extremities are utterly dependent upon what is put into the vacancy. About one half of the time the brain is busy devising means to fill that hollow. The other half of the time is taken up with the matter of companionship—and the complications which result. The *remainder* of the time"—Cibo paused—"is given over to intellectual and spiritual affairs. Other minor manifestations of man I need scarcely mention. They are merely notorious.

"Now *my* ideal philosophy is one which admits what I have just briefly sketched to be the basis of human nature. I practise it constructively. For instance, my business is to distribute fine groceries and minor edible luxuries in and about Havana. But I do not regard this as an end. It simply provides me the means of filling my own cavity by filling others, with sufficient overplus to provide some amusement for my brain—and companionship for the other extreme—also the means of travelling a little, comfortably—but I don't want to. It is impossible to get more out of life. How can you? Add to this that I have the respect and fear of my fellow men in this vicinity, and you will see that my cup runs over. I do not interfere with them but I make trouble for them if they interfere with me. My code of honour consists of a few things that I will not do. There do not seem to be very many of them. Pagan you say? No! For you see I really love my neighbours as I love myself." He finished the last of the newly mixed tumbler, wiped his mouth with his hand, and went on.

"As for the peccadillo of the soul I leave that to the church; heroics to the military. I am fortunate, for I have no desire for fame. It appears to me to be a form of egoistic insanity. I prefer the mellow good-fellowship of the moment. It is much more real and infinitely more satisfactory. It exists when and where you are. What will anything matter fifty years from now to Carlo Cibo? I do not care to see through the bottom of my last pitcher," he chuckled, "and for those who would make the world over by using either religion or the state as an engine I have no use. No theories are sufficient to include life, and it is life and not theories that I want to see get on. It is difficult to live where any one idea has it all its own way. I don't want to see the priests, the politicos, the merchants, or the slaves completely on top. Any one of them would make it hard for a man—for me. I play them off one against the other and go my own way.

"Well, you can draw your own conclusions about me and some for yourself. My suggestion to you is that you drop all of these minor matters that have been troubling you and go in for being a decent, thinking mammal—a man. Thus you will avoid trying to live either as a pure spirit or a dirty, stupid animal. So you will get the most out of life. I do not know what your prospects are, but no matter! Take up some line of livelihood that will let you live, and settle down to it where you can live by it and not for it. Everything else you will find will eventually drop into its just place." Unconsciously he patted his paunch again.

There did not seem to be any ready reply to make to this. Anthony was surprised to find that while they were speaking both Brother François and Carlo sounded equally convincing.

"You seem very sure of yourself, Carlo," he said half aloud at last.

"I am," said Carlo, "you see I have tried it out."

On the basis of experience Anthony felt at a disadvantage.

"At least I am engaged in one very practical thing," he said finally. "I am determined whatever comes to collect that debt from Gallego. It is not only the money, but . . ."

"Good! And it may take you far," interrupted Cibo. "While you have been performing miracles today, I have found out the latest disposition of your own affairs. They might take you to Africa. How would you like that?"

"Carlo, are you trying to ship me off like Brother François?" asked Anthony half anxiously and half in fun. "I am no missionary."

"No, no," laughed Cibo, "but you may find it easier to convert your bills in Africa than in Havana. Most of Gallego's assets are now on the Rio Pongo. That is the only kind of conversion I had in mind. In any event we shall have to see the captain-general—tomorrow, perhaps. I will tell you about it then. It is, to be frank, a difficult mess. But no more of it now.

"It is late. Have your supper in your own room tonight. I have drunk enough to continue to talk you to death. But," said he, reaching up anxiously and laying hold of Anthony's arm, "do not think I did not mean what I have said. Think it over."

"Wait! Is there anything you want? Are you lonely? Sometimes the best way is to bury your trouble deep. It leaves you then—pleasantly." He smiled reminiscently still holding Anthony's arm. "There is for example—Cheecha."

"Not tonight I think, Carlo," said Anthony. He had hesitated a little.

"Ha, not tonight, *not tonight!* Adiós then, señor, at least I may wish you pleasant dreams." It was hard to tell whether Carlo's tone was mocking or really as regretful as it seemed.

Anthony went to his room, bathed, and lay down. Cheecha brought the supper. After he had eaten she rolled the little wagon into the corridor. Then she came back again.

"Is there anything else I can do for you, señor?" she asked.

He looked at her. She stood huddled back against the wall a little, but her intonation had been both submissive and hopeful. He looked at her for a long while. She giggled. Finally he shook his head.

"Adiós, Cheecha."

"Adiós, señor," she replied, her shoulders drooping disconsolately as she wheeled the empty dishes down the hall.

It was very hot. The mosquitoes droned outside the net. The day had excited him more than he thought. Although he was tired it was hard to relax. In what seemed to be a state of wakefulness rather than sleep he had a silly dream.

Captain Jorham's bottle of wine had fallen on his own madonna and smashed it. He felt unreasonably sorrowful. It seemed irreparable. He thought he got up and went to his chest to make sure. It was very hard to get the covers off the statue. Faith had put them on. They were tied up in intricate knots. Finally he came to the madonna herself. Yes, there she was. She was holding the child out to him, extending it through the folds of the cloth.

The child emerged alive and came toward him out of the chest. There was a violet light about it. But suddenly it was not the child. It was just Brother François with the light of the vine on his face. He was trying to say something and was pointing out a road they were both to travel together. Just then Father Trajan rushed in and bawled out, "A miracle, a miracle has occurred!" Father Trajan thrust his hands into the chest and pulled out the madonna proudly. It was broken and streaming with wine. The statue could never be put together again. It was full of pieces of Captain Jorham's wine bottle.

"It is your miracle that has done this," shouted Anthony. He was furious at Father Trajan.

Brother François was standing by looking very sad at all this. His face was full of pity. Then Anthony saw that Carlo Cibo was sitting on the chest laughing. "What difference does it make?" he asked. He was smoking a cigar.

"Brother François will mend it," Anthony heard himself exclaim, and started up to give him the madonna.

"I cannot help you," said the monk and pointed to Cibo. "He is sending me away."

Nevertheless, Cibo and the monk began to struggle for the madonna. She began to come apart in fragments. An overwhelming sorrow seized Anthony and he began to weep like a child.

Then, as is the way with dreams, the whole nature of the affair changed without apparent cause while remaining to itself perfectly rational.

The fragments of the madonna now scattered on the floor coalesced and became Mrs. Jorham's doll. Cibo and Brother François now seemed to be fighting over nothing important at all. A feeling of great relief swept over Anthony. The room appeared to be flooded suddenly with sunshine. Cibo and he and the monk were now on the deck of the *Wampanoag*. It was dawn and he could hear the noise of cock-crow, a joyous sound. "It is only a doll," he shouted. "Give it to Philadelphia and let him burn it." Brother François disappeared and left Cibo standing there whiffing his cigar.

"Only a doll?" said Cibo. "You are mistaken!"

Instantly darkness returned. The cock-crow was nearer now but frightfully ominous. Anthony was plunged into the full terror of a nightmare.

He struggled to his feet to get away. But he was back in the room again. Cibo and the terrible doll were there, too. "Look," said Cibo pointing with the glowing end of his cigar. He could not help but look.

The doll had become larger. She was towering against the wall, growing. In the deep gloom of the place she became gigantic. Only the end of Cibo's cigar showed now. It was going out. Complete darkness descended except where the doll stood in a kind of foul light. The doll was turning into Cheecha, huge, naked, with legs spread apart and rolling her stomach. "Bury your trouble," shouted Cibo, "bury it deep!" He pushed Anthony by the arm toward the black emanation in the corner. His grasp hurt. Anthony could smell her sweat now. He gave a stifled cry and struggled. It was too much to stand. It was loathing and terror unmitigated. He writhed, and awoke suddenly to find himself kneeling on his own sea-chest and leaning half-way out of the barred window into the patio.

All the roosters of Regla were crowing. It was the hour of false dawn. Under the window some shrub in the patio emitted a sickeningly sweet, musky scent. His arm was caught in the iron grille work. If it had not been for that he would have plunged out in his sleep into the garden below. Even that fall he thought would have been a relief from the dream. But he drew back at last cold and shuddering.

He cursed himself, and all the rest of them. The dream had been so vivid that he felt sure he had seen the actors in it as they really were. It was some time before he could shake it off. He lit a candle, drank a whole pitcher of water, and walked about.

Finally the mosquitoes drove him back to bed again, this time to an exhausted and dreamless slumber.

32. HONOR AMONG THIEVES

Wɪᴛʜ any important business in view the man Cibo shook off his lethargy completely and exhibited a native energy against which no climate could prevail. While it took several bowls of black coffee to clear Anthony's head of the wraiths of the night before, Carlo rattled on gayly at breakfast and exhibited triumphantly a mason's trowel and some pieces of a broken bottle.

"How did you get them?" exclaimed Anthony. The shards of broken glass seemed to have been retrieved from his dream.

"A few piastres in the right place also work miracles," replied Cibo, "as you will soon find, my boy, when you come to do business in Havana. But in your case it may take more than a few. By the way, we go to the intendant's this morning and perhaps to the Gallegos' later. You should call first for the clothes for which you were measured. You look hot and worn already. Let's be off while it's still early and cool. No business is done here after eleven o'clock."

They crossed the harbour swiftly. Cibo kept a smart cutter rowed by four blacks dressed in bright, cotton drawers. There was a polished copper strake around the boat under its brass gunwale. They both lolled back in cane seats in the stern in considerable style.

"This kind of thing pays here," explained Cibo. "Appearances count as much with Spaniards as with the Chinese. Even when I board a foreign man-o'-war I get attention. Mere bumboats are always told to sheer off by the officer of the deck. But all this, and my sash, look official. I have even been piped up the side. Why not have your man outfitted as an officer's servant? I see you have brought him along. Juan," said Cibo sharply, "sit up! Stop dragging your hands over the side. Your master is a rich man and we call upon exalted persons today. You must do him credit. It is the face we want."

The man dropped his handful of trailing gulf weed, squared his shoulders and looked pleased. "Sí, señor, I have noble blood. My mother . . ."

"Was a clever woman," said Cibo. "Act like her son." At the dock Juan leaped out and made fast with a flourish.

"You see," said Cibo quietly, as they mounted the broad steps to the Paseo. "Now keep him coming along that way."

The old city wall rose before them. Along it swept a broad, paved avenue skirting the palm-fringed contours of the bay. A number of pony-drawn hacks driven by black Jehus dashed up avid for fares. But Carlo would have none of them. He dispatched one of his own men on the run through the water gate near by. While they were waiting one of the disappointed ponies reached over and ripped Anthony's sleeve from elbow to shoulder.

"They are carnivorous," said Cibo and laughed heartily. "Do not laugh, Juan, it is not permitted."

In a few minutes an upholstered carriage with a fair-looking team rolled up.

"What do you mean, you rascal, by coming for me with rope traces?" said Cibo scowling at the black driver. "Go and return on your master's time. Pompons, buckles, and straw hats! Do you want to carry home a note with 'Six' in the corner?"

The man wheeled off to return in no time with his steeds in another set of harness and with sunbonnets. It gave them a smartly indecent aspect as if the two mares were disguised streetwalkers. Cibo motioned Juan onto the box and they drove off.

"There is a habit here when you are annoyed by a slave of simply writing his name on your card with the number of lashes in the corner and sending him home with it," remarked Carlo complacently. "The card is usually returned later with thanks. The custom imparts a certain tone and discipline to a tropical community. Remember it. You do not have to know the master. It is simply a local form of noblesse oblige." Cibo pointed to the now positively decorous coachman in a clean, white jacket, and grinned. A red ribbon had been added to the whip.

"Already we have assumed nobility," said Cibo and leaned back. "Voyez-vous, monseigneur!"

They rattled on through a labyrinth of narrow streets with endless, heavy, flat-roofed parapets, whitewashed fronts and heavily grilled windows; the inevitable patio. Most of the gates were still closed.

Havana discovered the same monotonous expression everywhere. It was a frown with a straight line over its eyebrows as if it had acquired it from staring at the sun. Behind the closed shutters one sensed the sombreness of high, toneless chambers nursing the shade. A few slaves carrying baskets on their heads and balancing from the hips passed each other miraculously on the narrow sidewalks. Women in black lace mantillas were still coming home from mass. Here and there a water carrier laid the dust before some more pretentious mansion boasting a wrought-iron gate. Yet every languid activity was merely a prophecy of the certain coming of the midday heat.

Suddenly they drew up before the tailor's. It was a kind of cavern in the street wall of a house. Huge wooden shutters, now propped up as awnings, closed it in at night. A small, brown man who had measured Anthony at Regla came out bowing.

"All is ready, señor, we have only delayed for your choice of buttons. That will take but a moment." He produced a case of wood and coral samples. "But the English cloth button, or plain silver, is now all the rage."

In this little spider-of-a-man Anthony thought he understood the word "obsequious" for the first time. He seemed to secrete thread from his mouth, and his shiny lapels flashed with needles as he bowed. Against the rear wall of the place on a long table six little men sat cross-legged, sewing valiantly. On every head was a black skull-cap. They were memorable. In all his stay in Havana they were the only men not slaves that Anthony saw doing any manual work. Almost alone these tailors clothed the fashionable Catholic town. Thus even in Havana Abraham flourished as usual on his natural monopoly of work.

The fitting took some time. Cibo was particular.

Anthony remembered afterwards that it was here he finally became a sans-culotte. The knee breeches and long silk stockings of the eighteenth century were done up in a bundle. Except upon a few formal and artificial occasions he never wore them again. He emerged from this hole in the wall in long, close-moulded, narrow-waisted trousers cut with a wide Spanish flare from the calves down. There was a V-shaped slit over each ankle through which peeped a crimson sock with a clock. There was a short round jacket with a high, rolled collar. In Cuba there were no tails. Your caballero there haunted the saddle. Underneath the coat was a tight, white shirt with an open breast and pleated ruffles. They must be starched and stand up. A wide, silk sash with fringed tassels hung just to the left knee. The tassels were a reminder of the sword. But even in Spanish America that was going out for street wear.

The sensation of new clothes, which eludes final analysis, metamorphosed Anthony. For him the nineteenth century really began four years ahead of that calendar in that hole in the wall in Havana where the six Jews sat sewing. He had literally shed his old skin. He stood up light, and trim, and airy in the new suit of white drill. His loins were girded with the grateful clasp of the slippery sash and his feet thrust into light pumps with silver buckles which his buttons matched. The sweaty and always bedraggled lace of the old cuff was gone. The new sleeve ended in a clean line. There were no garters at the knees. His calves felt protected. His trousers flapped a little when he walked and they pulled evenly. It gave him a physical feel of confidence in his lower extremities. They were no longer ornamental. This was a costume in which one could do things. No ribbons!

In all these details Cibo stood by taking a keen and sympathetic interest. It was pleasant to know someone who could understand how he felt, Anthony thought. It would take the profound simplicity of an Italian to do that. Here was an hour and a place where you adapted yourself and made visible a shift in time. Another mode and mood of things had fallen upon the world. You put it on and then you lived it, henceforth another man. He remembered a naked child in the vestibule of the Casa da Bonnyfeather. Clothes were, he felt, the most intimate and internal things in the world. How tall and keen he was now, how supple and light, how able in this armour to prevail!

"Ah! Carlo," he said turning himself about before a mirror—and Carlo knew it was not vanity—"I shall collect that debt!"

"Good, good, you understand why we came here. Flap your wings and crow, my fine cockerel!" cried Cibo.

The Jew clucked over the unexpected English gold out of Mr. Bonnyfeather's roll, and they all laughed. Anthony felt the talons of the little man touch him on the breast.

"White! white like a true caballero of the town," exclaimed the tailor bowing them out.

"He means you are not burnt black like a rider on the sugar plantations," said Cibo as they drove off. "There is a ring where your collar used to be. But that will soon correct itself in this glare." Cibo hummed a little and laughed as he chatted away. The tailor amused him. He kept talking about him.

"Your Jew sees everything and yet never draws a romantic inference. He only flatters you by telling you that he does. You are pleased in spite of yourself and yet you know that he understands. The Gentile is nakedly revealed in the fiction which he lives by and yet is truly flattered by the Jew. So your feeling toward Jews is one of soothed-irritation plus constant surprise. That is why many either pet or persecute them. Very simple people cannot deal with Abraham; they are either lured into his net or driven to seize the club. The complicated balance of emotions necessary to a prolonged traffic with Jews cannot persist in peasants. Peasants take one extreme or the other. So your Jew stays in towns. I have dealt with them a long time. Many came here some time ago from Portugal. Lisbon was too hot for them. Your friend the tailor was one. He and I have managed a number of little matters together. I trust him.

"In dealing with Jews you should find out what they laugh at. If it is only at matters that occur below the belt let them alone. Simply do not deal with them. Most of that type have a kind of rat's-eye view of life. They see nothing but legs and their appurtenances going by even when they look up. But there are some Hebrews who laugh at the way the world is made. They are humorous with God. Beware! They are wise. Make friends with them. They become powers in the state. Such men are wisely cruel and unbelievably kind. That is all included in the joke. I once saw the little man who just measured you driving in a closed carriage with his wife along the Alameda de Paula. He had introduced a new style into Havana and was watching all the aristocrats preening themselves along the Paseo. Through the curtains I saw him, sitting next to his moon-faced wife, laughing. Ah, Toni, it was terrible. You see, he knew. Most of the land-poor rich in Havana and Pinar del Rio are in debt to him, not only for clothes, but for jewels. He makes loans. If you want gold go to Moses of Cintra. He and I laugh together and we get along."

They turned into the Calle Obispo. Here were business

establishments and awnings over the sidewalks. A languid flow of traffic toward the Plaza de Armas was already under way. At one place they stopped and Cibo called the proprietor out to him, giving instructions as to the outfitting of Juan with great particularity.

"After you get yourself shaved," said Cibo to Juan, "wait for us here. Do not disappear in your new clothes, my friend. The convict quarries are always short-handed. Very well, we trust you then." They drove on to the *Caxa da Consolidación*.

Upstairs in the hall of the intendant, where that personage seldom if ever came, Cibo was at some pains to introduce Anthony to several of the clerks, managing to indicate that any papers which might pass through their hands with the señor's name upon them would be accompanied by double fees. "His business is my own," said Cibo and lifted his brows. Assurances of extreme solicitude over the señor's correspondence followed.

"They have annual cause to remember me," whispered Cibo crossing the room. "This is Herr Meyier, a Rhinelander, the only man not a complete rascal in the place. He is the chief clerk."

A pleasant conversation followed. Herr Meyier warmed to Anthony even over his bad German. Anthony supplied him with all the German news he could remember having overheard for some time past from Vincent Nolte while Cibo sat by greatly relieved at so promising a turn of affairs. Cibo even pretended to like the beer which Meyier sent out to have brought in from his own restaurant. It was the only beer in Havana, and it was warm.

The sympathy of Meyier having been aroused for the predicament of his countrymen in Livorno, it was not difficult for Anthony to enlist his interest in his own affairs. They dropped into Spanish so that Cibo could follow. . . .

"As I see it," said Meyier, "there are several people with whom you must deal. It would help greatly if you get an official admittance of the debt from Gallego. Without that it is a question, señor, if you can succeed. At least it would enormously hasten matters. Merchants here under the old laws of the Indies are supposed to import only from Spain. Of course, of late years that has been largely disregarded and winked at, and foreign bills must eventually be paid or commerce would cease. But there is no legal way here for a foreign merchant to press his claims. He must go through the form of transferring his claim to a Spanish firm when it is then presented as a domestic bill and payment allowed.

"Now it is a curious thing," said Herr Meyier smiling, "but there is only one firm here whose foreign claims are ever successful in court. It is the firm of *Cuesta and Santa María*. Señor Santa María is a great friend of the intendant. He has retired, but lives, I am told, quite magnificently in the suburb of the Salú. He is said to have remarked once to the bishop at a state dinner that he was not very anxious to go to paradise for awhile since only the pavements there are made of gold."

"We are not especially interested in improving the celestial landscape for the señor," murmured Cibo. "Is there no other way?"

Herr Meyier consumed very thoughtfully the last of his beer. It was very tepid. He looked down the long, cheerless stone room—where the sallow clerks sat in their shirt sleeves at heavily gilded desks—with a hint of nausea in his pale blue eyes.

"Ach Gott, Cuba!" he said suddenly, and spread out his palms in disgust. "I am sorry for you, Señor Adverse. What is the amount owed by *Gallego and Son* to the *Casa da Bonnyfeather?*"

"About forty-five thousand dollars in round numbers," replied Anthony.

Herr Meyier languidly calculated something and rang a small silver bell.

"Engross that for me," he said to one of the clerks.

"Old Señor Gallego has recently died, hasn't he?" continued Herr Meyier while waiting. Anthony nodded. "In that case there may be complications. You might have to levy on his estate." He shook his head. "I am afraid that will never be granted. Every merchant-planter in the island would protest. What is the son doing?"

"He is in Africa," answered Cibo. "Since the death of the father the transactions of the firm have been in slaves. Gallego's schooner, the *Ariostatica*, is now outfitting in the harbour for Africa."

"So," said Meyier, pursing his lips, "*so?*"

"Would it be possible to attach the ship?" asked Anthony. "In that case we might come to some agreement with them, possibly an assignment on the next cargo of slaves."

"Dunder!" exclaimed Meyier. "I begin to see light." He rang the bell sharply twice.

"Bring me the papers in the case of the ship *Black Angel*—and of the *Ariostatica*, Gallego, now fitting out." His heavy bureaucratic face grew suddenly animated.

"Now, señor," said he when all the papers had been brought, "come into the bureau of the intendant." He closed the door behind them, listened for a full minute, and then walked to the far end of the room.

They all sat down again about a magnificently furnished desk with dust upon it. Herr Meyier flicked it with his handkerchief and laughed. "It is not likely we shall be interrupted here," he said sardonically, and spread the papers out before him. "Now, gentlemen, your attention if you please. Let us see if we can't avoid drowning the cat in cream. El gato Santa María, you understand. Here is what my clerk has engrossed":

$45,000 *at* 18 *piastres local legal exchange is* 810,000 *piastres.*
$45,000 *at* 15 *piastres current foreign exchange is* 675,000 *piastres.*
Hence, the difference between the legal and foreign exchange is 135,000 *piastres.*
(½ *of* 135,000 *piastres is* 67,500 *piastres*)

"The import of this is extremely simple," continued Herr Meyier. "If you place your claim in the hands of Señor Santa

María he will collect it at eighteen piastres on the dollar, the legal rate, and pay you only at fifteen. That will place in his hands the difference of one hundred thirty-five thousand piastres which he and the intendant will divide. I understand they split evenly. For them, you see, a charming arrangement. But that will not be all. In order to engage the noble interest of these gentlemen a 'retaining fee' of eighteen thousand piastres is customary. Otherwise their valuable time might be wasted in ignoble pursuits. In addition to this you will, of course, have to meet all the legal fees. A jingling argument is the only one really convincing to the court. And on that too the masters of ceremonies here will also collect their percentage. If you leave Havana in a year's time with thirty-five thousand dollars you will be doing well. You can now see why sugar planting, for those who understand it, is so profitable. Very rich canes are usually crushed and squeezed twice in case any juice remains."

Carlo whistled whimsically and looked at Herr Meyier, shaking his head.

"You may well whistle, Cibo," said the German. "There is the possibility I think, however, of another way. Would you care to have me advise you, Señor Adverse? As it would be entirely extra-legal, a mere matter of policy as it were, perhaps you would care to—er, ah, make use of my humble services under the circumstances. I believe, if you saw fit to do so, you might not only collect the amount due you without the embarrassing deductions required by Señor Santa María, but finally emerge perhaps with a comfortable margin of profit. Call it interest on your long overdue account. What do you think?"

"You would not, of course, be averse to participating in the profits of so equitable an arrangement, Herr Meyier?" asked Anthony.

Cibo beamed with approval.

"As a silent, a very silent partner," said the German. "A reasonable percentage to be agreed upon, say five per cent on your claim, and ten per cent on any possible profits."

"And in any event two per cent on the claim," said Anthony.

"Did you say three?" murmured the German.

"Of course, how could you misunderstand me, Herr Meyier? And payable half in advance."

"Himmel! mein junger Herr, thou hast been nursed in the lap of Reason."

"I will be surety," added Cibo.

"We go on then!" cried Meyier. "Adiós, Señor Santa María! Will you condescend to look at these?

"They are the papers of the ship *Black Angel,* a slaver, which cleared for Sierra Leone it so happens exactly seven years ago today. Now notice," said Meyier rearranging the file, "that up until within three days of the time she sailed her papers are all in the regular form. Then what happens? On August thirtieth, seventeen-eighty-nine, an order of temporary sequestration of the ship by the captain-general of Cuba issues. A purser, sworn in as agent of the *Caxa da Consolidación,* is put in charge to collect certain sums due the colonial government by the owners. That is, you see, our purser accompanies the ship which is navigated by its captain still employed by the owners. *But* the cargo of slaves waiting for it in Africa is seized by the crown agent. Here, seven months later are the bills of sale for the entire cargo at public auction at Havana. That is the point of it all. The government agent being on board has prevented the cargo from being taken to a foreign colony, say Barbados or Jamaica, and quietly run on shore at night. The sale takes place here as of government property. The amount due the crown with all expenses is deducted, and the remainder returned to the owners along with the ship. Even at that, I see, the owners came off fairly well."

"Why didn't the government seize the ship to begin with and sell it?" asked Cibo.

"The answer is very simple, señor, for two reasons. The ship would not have satisfied the sum required, slavers are only worth a tithe of their cargo, and there is no ordinance for the captain-general to proceed upon an order to confiscate marine property. His maritime authority is limited. No, no, I remember the case well! It was when you spoke of the Gallegos being in the slave trade that it flashed into my mind. Old Señor Gallego has recently died and his son is in Africa. The estate is a huge one. Undoubtedly there will have been a lapse in inheritance fees and other dues and taxes with the heir absent. If not, trust me, I am a man of arithmetical imagination. Do you see my plan?"

"To use the case of the *Black Angel* as a precedent and seize the Gallegos' schooner *Ariostatica* now in the bay?" asked Cibo.

"Exactly!" cried Meyier. "An order will be issued of temporary sequestration for the *Ariostatica*. We shall swear in our young friend here as the government agent in charge. He will go to Africa as supercargo, receive for the crown the cargo which Gallego will have ready for his ship, and return to Havana where it will be sold. That sale, gentlemen, will be conducted by the *Caxa da Consolidación* of which I have the honour to be chief clerk. Señor Gallego will have nothing to say about it. After the sums due the, er—*government*—are deducted, any remainder will be scrupulously returned to him. I regret to say, however, that it looks to me as if the entire proceeds of this particular voyage will be swallowed up. After all, Gallego will only be having his hand forced a little to pay a just debt. If in that process a certain profit is realized, inadvertently as it were, only ourselves and the captain-general will ever know. I am sure, Señor Adverse, that if you received the sum due you together with reasonable interest, your curiosity at least would be satisfied. You, you see, will have done nothing but collect your debt plus, let us say, expenses. Your time is of course—valuable. Speaking frankly, I feel I am entitled under the peculiar circumstances of the case to the small premium we agreed upon."

"There can be no question about that, Herr Meyier. Set yourself at rest on that point. But speaking frankly myself, and not from mere curiosity, there are one or two points I do not quite understand yet," Anthony replied. Cibo leaned forward a little alarmed as Anthony continued.

"In the first place, how and why will the captain-general be interested enough to issue the order? And what is there to assure me, in case of your death, for instance, or your leaving here for any cause, that I shall not be sent on a wild goose chase to Africa? Suppose I am successful and return with the cargo. You are gone. It is sold, and the proceeds pocketed by—well, the 'government'—why not? Indeed, speaking absolutely candidly, I should feel much relieved if I thoroughly understood the real cause of your interest in my case."

"Herr Meyier and I are old friends," interrupted Cibo, "we play, I may say, very much into each other's hands. The scheme is a little more subtle than you suppose, Señor Toni. Things in Havana have ramifications all of which do not appear. His word and mine that you will receive the sum due you should be sufficient. Don't you think so?"

Anthony sat thinking for a moment. He was aware that the atmosphere was beginning to be a little tense.

"Yes," he said, "I shall accept either of your words, *of course*. But I must insist at least on knowing the reasons why you will not answer my questions."

Both Cibo and Meyier broke into a laugh.

"You might have been educated by the Jesuits, young man," said the latter.

"I was," said Anthony.

"Ah!" said Cibo. "To think of it! And how I have talked!"

"For the same reason you can rely on my discretion where my own interests are involved," interjected Anthony smiling.

Carlo snorted. "Tell him, Herman," he said to Meyier, "or he will find out for himself."

The German drummed on the desk for a minute.

"Ach Himmel! You are both against me. Then I shall a prophet be. It is modesty, you see, señor, which has kept me from speaking out. Carlo, is it for thee to laugh? I will tell you, sir, why the captain-general will issue the order. It is because I shall ask him. Carlo, is it not so?" The man puffed himself out.

"It is like this, Señor Toni," Meyier continued leaning forward and becoming familiar and convincing at the same time. "Have you ever heard of the Prince of the Peace? Yes! Well, he is the real ruler of Spain. By many he is said to be only the queen's favourite. He is that, but also much more. It is his desire to put vigour again into the government, to destroy where he can the worm of corruption."

"And to enjoy the increased revenues himself," interrupted Cibo.

Meyier made a deprecating gesture.

"Our friend is too cynical," he said. "Nevertheless it is true that in every part of the government some appointees of the Prince of the Peace are now to be found. They are put there for a purpose and they are feared, for they enjoy the confidence of this great minister at Madrid. That is why I, a German, an accountant, and an honest man, am now the head of the *Caxa da Consolidación en Habana*. I," he repeated, scrawling his own initials dramatically on a piece of paper, "am an appointee of the Prince of the Peace! Without these initials, no important government financial operation in Cuba is undertaken. With them much may be done. Is it not so, Carlo?"

"You scarcely ever exaggerate," said Cibo.

"But that is not all, my young friend. In Havana there are two parties. There is that of the captain-general and that of the intendant-general. It is a very curious situation. Some years ago the office of intendant-general was created over great protest to bring about a fiscal reform here. Most of the financial power of the captain-general was placed in the intendant's hands. Pouf! what happens? The second intendant-general who is sent out is a blood brother of Barabbas. Compared with his the clutch of a Turkish bashaw is like that of a gentle milkmaid. The cow—Mein Gott! she go dry! The intendant is a dangerous man, a successful politician, and he forms a powerful local party. He and Señor Santa María and the like had all but succeeded in diverting the revenues when I arrived. The poor old captain-general, he is alarmed. In me he sees an unexpected ally. He sends for me and weeps on my shoulder. 'Permit me,' he says, 'to draw my own salary. The intendant and Señor Santa María have consolidated the *Caxa da Consolidación*. They are patriots. I am only a viceroy.'

"That was seven years ago, my boy. The old captain-general goes home still a poor man. It is terrible. But a new one arrives. He also is comparatively poor, but he is a great hidalgo and a very cunning man. Very quietly we collaborate on undermining the intendant. The soldiers are now paid out of the revenues. I became head of the *Caxa da Consolidación*. Some money goes home to Spain. We entrench ourselves in, *ahem*, a comparative honesty, for we have to fight thieves and we intend to win. Then the grand reforms can take place. But in the meanwhile there is the intendant—and Señor Santa María. They are still very popular with certain merchants, with slave importers particularly. They protect them from foreign creditors. Do you see now? For this is where you, my young friend, come in!

"As I listened to you this morning I had suddenly the great idea inspired. I see instantly what has long perplexed me. I see how to frighten the friends of the intendant, provide an independent revenue for the captain-general, and permit foreign merchants to collect their debts. The mere threat of this will be sufficient. Señor Gallego shall be merely an example. It needed just your particular case to enable me to put two and two together, the *Black Angel* and the *Ariostatica*." He slapped the papers.

"Señor, I am grateful. The payment of your own debt is assured, for it is upon that pretext that we shall proceed. The authorities in Spain and my master can be made to understand the situation. Despite the old laws foreign merchants must be protected and rascals suppressed. Indeed, I shall regard the payment of your claims as a kind of premium for your going to Africa to collect them. In a case like this it is only someone whose own interests are vitally involved that we would care to trust. Do you see? Will you go? Much depends on it. Much!" Herr Meyier looked suddenly harassed.

"It may be a little dangerous, señor. Keep your own counsel —and ours. The knife is not unknown here as a method of cutting Gordian knots. I myself . . ." His mouth twitched a little —"Ja wohl! It is true that I may die at any moment!" He ended on a note of scorn.

"I will go," said Anthony.

Carlo patted him on the arm. "Men are not always such rascals as you think, my young Jesuit," he said.

"Oh, Carlo, you overdo that, believe me," said Anthony evidently annoyed. "I was right in asking Herr Meyier those questions!"

"What! what! Must the old dogs and young ones always be snapping at each other?" exclaimed Meyier. He tucked his papers under one arm and led them both toward the door with a certain air of triumph. "This is a lucky meeting, you know," he went on. "Now one thing more. Get that acknowledgment from Gallego's clerk if you have to garrote him. It is vital. If you have trouble let me know. Ach, my friend Carlo, I rely upon *you*. Let us work together in this as in old times. I myself will see the captain-general tonight and let you know his decision. I have small doubt about it. You must be prepared, Don Antonio, to visit the palace later on yourself. His Excellency insists upon knowing all his agents personally."

"Would it not be a good precaution to make sure the *Ariostatica* does not sail too soon, Herr Meyier?" asked Anthony.

"Ach, what a wise infant you have brought here today, Carlo!" exclaimed Meyier. "His words are dollars. Ja wohl, I shall see to it. An order to the port authorities, quietly! And now, auf wiedersehen." He opened the door and bowed them out past the clerks with a formal and distant courtesy as if some purely routine matter had been tritely disposed of.

Anthony walked down and climbed into the carriage with his heart on fire. "To Africa!" he said to the driver. Carlo exploded—and gave merely local directions.

On the way to the Gallegos' they picked up Juan. He was standing on the curb still in his sailor's garb but with a new, silver-mounted guitar under his arm. He looked foolish.

"What is the meaning of this?" inquired Cibo turning red. But the man addressed himself to Anthony.

"Pardon, Don Antonio, the money which you gave me to buy clothes—I have spent for a guitar." He ran his hands over its strings caressingly. "I do not know how I do such things. It is terrible. But I have a beautiful tenor voice. I lack accompaniment. Forgive!" He was white at the lips.

"You rascal!" said Anthony. Then he laughed. "Jump up, Juan. Driver, go on."

With the troubadour on the box they drove to the Gallegos'.

"You had better leave this to me," said Cibo, and went in.

It was sweltering sitting in the carriage under the leather top.

"Señor," said Juan looking around at Anthony with a dog-like affection in his eye, "shall I sing to you while we wait? I am your hombre. I would pour out my heart which is full of a passionate gratitude."

"Later on, Juan," said Anthony. "This is a respectable neighbourhood."

"Sí, sí," said the man and sighed.

Carlo finally emerged with a scared, middle-aged clerk who rode with them silently to the notary. The man made a declaration there setting forth that the sum demanded by Mr. Bonnyfeather was a just debt contracted by *Gallego & Son* for value received. He signed it as chief clerk of the firm, and an attested copy of his power of attorney to transact business during the absence of young Señor Gallego was attached. They left him still white about the gills.

"This paper has cost you five hundred dollars, Don Toni," said Carlo as they drove on toward the water gate, "but it is worth it. Never hire a chief clerk with a sombre past," he added. "It makes them too compliant with well-informed strangers."

A blue glimpse of the bay came in sight through the old water gate.

"Oh, I shall be glad to meet Cheecha with her little wagon on the veranda," said Cibo. "There is pompano today. The one fish I . . ."

He was interrupted by a scream of agony that made them both wilt. The thud of a whip, and the answering cries and moans of a number of black women gathered about a gate the carriage was just passing made a horrid chorus that accompanied spasmodically the whistling of a lash.

"Jesús!" whispered Juan. The strings of his guitar jangled faintly. The carriage stopped as if accosted by death. They looked through the gateway into the space beyond.

In the centre of a wide patio floored with blinding, white sand, a great, black grating seemed to erect its sinister gridiron malevolently from the top of a little platform. Lashed to this so that he was spread-eagled helplessly against the blue sky beyond was a black Hercules of a man. His muscles bulged in huge knots and his head hung back straining as if it would tear itself loose and be gone. Under each whistling blow he rippled from head to foot and screamed hoarsely.

"O God!" said Anthony standing up.

It was just then that they saw Brother François. He had emerged suddenly from a little door and was crossing the white, sunlit space to the gridiron in his bare feet and faded gown. He cried out and the sound of his voice filled the place with pity. The man with the whip turned. His large, jowled countenance fell flat with amazement. Nothing but the moans of the man on the gridiron could be heard.

"In the name of Christ," said the clear, quiet voice of Brother François, "this man is your brother." He took the whip from the man's hand. A dead silence followed.

Suddenly the man seemed to take in the situation. He gave a roar of astonished rage, and picking up Brother François like a child, rushed with him to the gateway. He hurled him into the gutter and started to return.

"Do not interfere, my son!" cried the monk getting up calmly out of filth. He caught Anthony by the coat and dragged him back against the wheel of the carriage. He put his cool hands on his cheeks. "This is for *me*. Remember, you do not understand yet."

When a kind of red darkness cleared from his eyes Anthony found Cibo holding him down in the carriage. Rage had loosened the caps of his knees till he shook.

Brother François was half across the yard again. He was

following the man and calling. The fellow turned sullenly. Brother François advanced smiling, holding out his hand. "My friend," he said. The man gave a confused bellow and rushed him. He threw him down on the sand and kicked him. Then he turned to go again.

"My friend," said Brother François rising. He advanced upon him again still holding out his hand. The performance repeated itself.

"Sit still, young ass," said Cibo holding Anthony. "Let God decide. Who are you?"

Brother François was getting up again, slowly now. He stood swaying a little but he still smiled. Suddenly he tottered forward to the man. He held up his little crucifix and pointed to the negro on the grating. Then he held out both his hands as if he would give shelter to the dew-lapped head of the tormentor on his own breast. The figure on the grating gave a great cry and went limp. The man in the courtyard looked about him as if appealing to the common sense of mankind and fled. The whip lay on the sand.

"Now," cried Cibo. "*Now!*" He laboured after Anthony and Juan who had dashed into the court where Brother François had fallen limp. The three of them picked him up and carried him limp as he was to the carriage.

"Go!" shouted Cibo. "Whip your horses, you black fool!"

Juan caught hold of the carriage from behind as it whirled off down the street. A shriek of despair from the women at the gate followed it as it wheeled around the next corner.

On the way back to Regla Brother François opened his eyes. They were pouring cool water on his face and hands. He said nothing. A great sorrow seemed to engulf them all. Ashamed of himself, Anthony cried out at the sight of the battered lips which hurt themselves to smile back at him. A tumult as of great waters had rushed through his soul. He sat and wept. Even Cibo was silent.

But at Regla Brother François insisted upon going home himself. He forbade them to come along. They watched him go down the little alley toward Father Trajan's, and as he turned the corner they saw him lift a basket of fish from the head of a small negro child whose legs wobbled under it. He took her by the hand. The negro boatmen grunted.

"I am afraid that this is the end of Brother François," said Cibo as they walked down the dock. "I hope we got him away without being recognized. Do you know what the penalty is for interfering with slaves who have been sent to the city-yard to be whipped? A monopoly of Señor Santa María, by the way. No! You do not know? Well, then so much the better," he said as he swung the little door into the cool green patio, "so much the better for your appetite for lunch. Cheecha!"

33. A MANTILLA INTRUDES

Hот countries, Anthony discovered, had a curious effect upon him. He had ebullitions of emotion; they passed, and left him much the same as before, dreamfully contented, merely existing comfortably. The crests did not disturb the form which was, after all, Cibo in his chair on the veranda with rum and lime juice. Then there was tobacco. He had begun to soak up a good deal of that into his system, the dark Cuban leaf. It made contentment easy and keenness uncomfortable. It prevented in a northerner the constant foolish necessity of doing something.

Despite the tremendous impression which Brother François's interference with the whipping had made upon him only a week ago—what was it now?—only an event of the extremely remote past, he thought as he sat smoking on the veranda with

Cibo, while a half-moon filtered into the patio and Juan fooled below on the strings of his new guitar. That lad *did* have a voice undoubtedly. A half-mocking song, no doubt addressed to Cheecha, mixed its soft chords with the moonlight and caused the parrot to shift sleepily on its perch. Tonight it was deliciously fragrant and cool. Pretty late though. Still you could not expect to sleep all the afternoon and all the night as well. The end of his cigar glowed revealing Anthony's face a little whiter than when he arrived, wrapt in a dreamful satisfaction. Cibo smiled to himself.

Yes, on the whole, as Cibo said, he had been lucky. His visit to Havana might so far be called a promising success. Brother François was doing very well. Getting about the garden again— that man! And as for Father Trajan—Anthony laughed as he thought of his crowded chapel. Carlo had certainly been most convincing with the bishop. It would take a long time, of course, to get the final confirmation from Santiago. Meyier seemed slow, too. But you couldn't hurry the captain-general. You couldn't hurry anybody here, not even yourself. And the *Ariostatica* had been detained.

He began to wonder how his clothes that he was to wear at the audience at the palace the next afternoon were coming on at the tailor's. Moses had promised them. Why couldn't Meyier settle all those details with the governor himself? Curious old dog that German! Able, and honest according to his own lights. Really trying to do a difficult job here. No one could live on a government salary in Havana. They weren't expected to. Ah, well, if Africa was like this it wouldn't be so bad.

"Good night, Carlo." The cigar streaked into the patio, and he went to bed.

Tomorrow morning he would have to take Mrs. Jorham to see the tombs. He wished now he hadn't promised her. Promises made in one mood could come back to haunt you in another. "Damn the beetles!" How they battered about the candle. "Puff!" In the darkness you were yourself again. No one on the wall . . . no, of course not . . . in the chest. And a good riddance . . . Yes? Mrs. Udney's sheets, ah-a-a . . .

But once on the *Wampanoag* again next morning it was not so hard to recapture the mood of only a few days before. It no longer seemed so far off. And both Captain Elisha and Mrs. Jorham were so glad to see him, and Collins dry as ever. That solemn face!

"So ye're harbourin' our desartar, Mr. Adverse."

Captain Jorham made small bones about Juan however. The prices which he had received for his miracle-working statuary had been miraculous.

"They're all gone but Jesus," he said. "St. Lawrence yesterday, fire and all, on an oxcart for some inland town. I'm holdin' out on the Saviour for eight hundred dollars with five hundred and thirty offered and a vacant niche in the cathedral biddin' against a new chapel at Cienfuegos." He rubbed his hands. "Say how *dew* ye suppose they fixed that Virgin at Regla? Pretty slick, eh! Got any idears, mister?"

"Not a single one, captain," said Anthony gravely.

"*Sa-ay!*" said the captain beating him on the back till he coughed. "But here comes the old lady all set for seein' the t-umes."

Mrs. Jorham was indeed dressed for the occasion. Long, fingerless, black gloves projected from her India shawl which was caught with a jet breast pin. A straw bonnet upon which rested a grey dove still glistened with camphor dust. A small sunshade, and a palm-leaf fan, as a slight concession to the climate, announced her upon pleasure bent. There was something eternal and widow-like in the droop of her shawl. But under her bonnet her face shone. A neatly bound copy of the Testament and four silver dollars distended her reticule.

Anthony handed her into Cibo's boat with great formality. She sat on the cane seats rather doubtfully and raised a doll-sized sunshade against the Cuban glare. From a strictly female point of view Mrs. Jorham was undoubtedly one of the most intriguing women who had ever landed at the water gate at Havana. The negro washerwomen gathered there to discuss her.

Anthony hailed one of the carnivorous ponies. In what appeared to Mrs. Jorham to be a recklessly extravagant mode of travel they set forth to do epitaphs. But the churches were a flat disappointment to the lady from Scituate. What few tombs they contained were to her sadly lacking in a sense of inevitable doom. The smooth pomp of marble and basalt conveyed a feeling of security in the hereafter, even an aristocratic contempt for it which outraged her. In the tone of the epitaphs she missed a single whine. *"Every hour wounded; the last slew me. I flinched not till I fell."* There were candles burning before that! She turned away, longing for some stone that recorded a snatch of thoroughly abject hymn that a Protestant woman could sing with fearful conviction. These churches seemed to have been built by superior beings for man. She longed for her white wooden chapels with a fanlight over the door and a cold, northern light inside. Chapels that man had built for God! One could make up one's own mind about religion there. Here, as she looked about from one church to the other, she saw that religion had long ago made up its mind about her. She snorted and waved her palm-leaf fan.

To Anthony, Mrs. Jorham was intensely interesting. He was curious to understand her sense of Protestant outrage. They went to Santa Catalina, San Agustín, and Santa Clara. They saw the curious oil paintings on the walls of La Merced. In the bare, grey limestone of old Santo Domingo they sat down on the floor and rested. Here for some reason or other Mrs. Jorham felt more at home.

"What was it made her so indignant?" he wondered, "and so grim?" He would like to take her to the cathedral. Poor soul, perhaps it was her idea of pleasure that made her so sad? He had a notion to try on a good time for her benefit. Havana with Mrs. Jorham!

He went out and hired a double carriage, only one of whose wheels was very oval. With her little mushroom sunshade projecting over the back like the small targe of a defiant warrior they left the churches and drove along the sea wall and the Alameda clear out to the Cortina de la Reina, and out the Paseo de Tacón to El Principe.

"My!" said Mrs. Jorham, semi-approvingly, as the incomparable gardens of Los Molinos burst on her view.

Good, she was thawing!

He himself felt like St. Lawrence and it was only ten o'clock. Under an awning in the old Parque de la India they had claret lemonade. He took her to a luxurious shop on San Rafael Street and bought her an expensive fan. He whirled her around the monastery of Belén at Luz and Compostela streets. Dashing as recklessly as he could prevail on the driver to dash, he finally wound up on O'Reilly where he bought her a black mantilla and made her put it on. Why he did all this he could not tell. Mrs. Jorham had touched off something of the devil in him. Mrs. Jorham in a mantilla was so gorgeous a solecism he almost began to make love to her. He finally bought her a chameleon on a chain.

"They live in cemeteries, Mrs. Jorham, and change colour," he explained. But she did not believe him. She put the chameleon in her bag with the Testament and the four silver dollars. He felt profoundly sorry for it. In the great heat he felt sorry for a chameleon in a reticule. O God! Here he was driving about in Havana with an old woman. He did not know any other woman in the whole place. Yes, Cheecha! He bought another chameleon for Cheecha.

"Mrs. Jorham, Mrs. Jorham," he hummed close by her ear as they drove off again.

"What is the matter with ye, young man?" said Mrs. Jorham through a mouthful of black lace. He looked at her. She was having a good time! He had a notion to let Cheecha's chameleon run up the back of the driver. The horses might run away then. No! Instead he would take Mrs. Jorham to the cathedral and show her the tomb of Columbus.

Mrs. Jorham sniffed disdainfully at the holy water from which the mosquitoes rose as Anthony dipped his fingers in it. The interior of the cathedral was still full of scaffolding. Some frescoers at work held her attention. She had never seen a painter at work before. She stood looking up till she was dizzy. They went over and sat down on unused stone blocks that had not yet been removed before the Admiral's new tomb. Several parties of fashionably dressed people began to arrive while Mrs. Jorham sat fanning herself. It was certainly cool and restful here after the scalding glare of the street. A verger came and uncovered the font.

"I alers did think Columbus was the bravest of them all. Crossin' the ocean fer the first time! It's bad enough now 'specially if yer husband can't navigate. Columbus believed in what he knew, of course. But it must have ban hard to get folks to do somethin' so new."

The distant wail of a baby interrupted Mrs. Jorham. She laid her fan spasmodically on her chest as if she had caught her breath. The organ started to play. Anthony looked up.

He was surprised to see the number of people who had come in. And the sound of more carriages arriving at the door could still be heard.

"There is going to be a christening, Mrs. Jorham, rather a fashionable one I think. Look, the bishop is here to bless the child. If we move over there in that corner we can see it all without disturbing them. Here by the big pillar."

"My! This *is* going to be worth while. Look at the jewels and laces and uniforms!" she exclaimed half to herself.

They drew back in their corner and waited while the family arranged itself about the font. The service began, evidently as long and complete a one as wealth and influence could obtain. Mrs. Jorham watched the small howling bundle of lace being passed from hand to hand, held up and waved about, sprinkled, and sung about in Latin. So much to-do over a baby made her think better of the Catholic Church. But that was not what Anthony was looking at.

Between the responses he had fallen helplessly in love.

The girl was standing directly opposite him just across the nave. And of such a witches' bundle and mad faggot of chances is fate composed that if he had not happened to move a little to clear himself of the pillar he might never have laid eyes on her at all. Or, if he had seen her otherwise he might not have fallen in love. He might only have admired or yearned over her a little. Or he might not have really seen her. Her image might only have fallen upon his eyes with no penetration. But he did move.

And as he stepped out from the pillar, at that instant, his pupils were opened upon the extremely delicate and mysterious living substance behind them. Looking inward he beheld a divine image within himself. He could not have imagined it in all its overpowering charm and living splendour. It was something which now drew upon reality and had its own independent vigour and validity although it was nourished within him. Looking into the outer world he saw a Spanish girl in a mantilla, with nearly black-blue eyes and pale gold-gleaming hair, regarding him over her fan. And the outward and inner images became one. The next instant their eyes met.

Exactly what happened then he could not tell. There was undoubtedly a current that passed between them. He had an irrefutable intuition that what was going on in his own eyes was also occurring in hers. The effect upon his body was a kind of relaxed and breathless suspense. Unconsciously he leaned back against the pillar for an instant and closed his lids. When he opened them again he saw that she was still studying his face. Then a wave of colour rushed up from her neck and shoulders and she disappeared behind her fan.

Heavens, would she never come out of that eclipse! At the font the sponsors were promising on behalf of the wailing baby impossible things. Several millenniums passed. The fan spread a little. It came down as far as her chin.

Splendour of Angels! Already he had forgotten how lovely she was. You could only remember it when you really saw her. He must always be able to see her. Always! Why, she was smiling at him! At *him!* Already there was a great secret between them. He straightened up and leaned forward a little. She shook her head. It was just the dream of a shake. Ah! She saw him now. Who was that dignitary beside her? Her father or an uncle, no doubt! Damn his soul! Surely that man could not be . . . But be careful. He would just answer her smile. He did so. The fan seemed to touch her lips. No? Well, he could not be sure. Now it made a graceful curve, opened out a little, and rested on her breast. She might have been fanning herself! He put his own hand under his coat and looked at her . . . Then he hastily managed to turn that heartfelt gesture into a trite continuation of removing his handkerchief from his left pocket. "Uncle's" eyes were taking him in coldly.

Everything that could be done for the baby was now completed. As an impeccable candidate for the communion of saints it and its family and friends departed, leaving Anthony leaning against the pillar hopelessly. Suddenly he realized he was being left in darkness. He rushed out just in time to see her driving away.

"Señorita Dolores de la Fuente," said the verger. He gave the man a gold piece and never knew it. Then he remembered Mrs. Jorham. He rushed back again. She was sitting again before the tomb of Columbus.

"Mrs. Jorham, Mrs. Jorham," cried Anthony seizing her by both hands and dragging her off a marble block. "Mrs. Jorham, I'm in love!"

"Now look here, young man, now look here," she said, snatching at her reticule. "Ye *behave* yourself. The idear! But air ye in love?" she said, "air ye?" peering out of her bonnet into his face. "Swan to man, I believe ye be!"

The verger, scandalized, looked at them and then went away. For short of arson the donors of a gold piece were, so far as he was concerned, invisible.

"You won't say anything, will you, Mrs. Jorham?" said Anthony as the sober light of day overwhelmed him at the door.

"We'll just cancel secrets, mister, and call it square," said she. "I never was one to talk much, except about sewing," she added, laying her black glove on his arm. "Na-ow," she gave a little sigh, "ye might take me home. Listenin' to that baby squallin' kind of made me anxious over 'Lisha. I guess ye know *our* secret."

They found the crew of the boat from the *Wampanoag* waiting with their jackets spread out on oars against the glare of the noon sun. Anthony was keeping Cibo's boat until later.

"I did have a good time," said Mrs. Jorham as she arranged herself in the stern sheets. She gayly waved her hand with the black glove on it. Collins grinned back at Anthony as they pulled away. Anthony saw her shawl fall out of its rigid folds into something more natural. At a little distance over the water she looked smaller, even frail. Suddenly he saw what Mrs. Jorham must have looked like as a young girl. That must be what was caught in Captain Jorham's eyes. Yes, he understood now. Mrs. Jorham was going home. That was what the *Wampanoag* was! Home! Whenever on sea or land, whenever . . .

"Dolores, I must find you!"

He ran up the steps again and jumped into a carriage. It was terrible to have business to do when he did not even know where she lived.

"Where, señor?"

"Ah, where indeed? Perhaps the driver would know!" But he could not bring himself to mention her name to him. Her name! He felt tears gathering behind his eyes.

"Señor?"

What the devil then! To the tailor's? His suit would not be quite done yet. But a last fitting before going to the captain-general's . . .

"Moses of Cintra in the Calle Obispo."

"Sí, sí! El judío." The man whipped up and drove off.

34. THROUGH A COPY OF VELASQUEZ

IF CARLO had not warned Anthony to pay strict attention to the advice of the little tailor he could scarcely have brought himself to wear the suit which he found waiting for him at the cubicle of Moses. It was dark, but gorgeous, and of the style Incroyable which the smart old Jew had just imported from Paris. Such a collar Anthony had never seen.

"I have made certain alterations," said Moses, "a concession to local taste. Those who go to an audience with His Excellency should bear in mind that he prides himself on being a very modern man. It is not only in clothes but in government, señor, that to a certain extent he admires the French taste. 'New times, new fashions, and new minds,' is a favourite saying of his. Permit me to pin the waist a little tighter. It is the Herculean bust, that which looks so well on the orator when he gestures from the rostrum with one hand in his breast, which has now come in. Ah! I am always breaking my chalk. More pins, Sabathio. But I would not advise you to orate to the governor. Let him do the talking.

"Great men always talk a great deal," continued Moses, despite his mouthful of pins. "They realize by a lifetime of conversational disappointments that others seldom have anything to say. Have you not found it so yourself, señor? Pardon, I slipped with that pin. And many are coming to believe here that Don Luis de las Casas is really a great man. In six years he has worked wonders. The Marqués de Someruelos who will shortly be sent out to succeed him is also of the modern cast of mind, they say. No, it would never do to go to the palace resembling an old hidalgo. They are out of date here. And the general will observe you keenly. He will question you without your knowing it. It has been his method here always to see personally those who are doing anything for him. All those who serve him must first be his friends. It is thus that he has made headway against the intendant. By his Junta as it is called, Señor Cibo, Herr Meyier, Mr. James Drake—even the bishop and the military are of his party. I myself have the honour of making his clothes! You can see you have been fortunate in Havana in having your ends shaped by powerful hands. There now! I think that will do. Some last stitching and the iron! Ah, the hot goose! What would tailors be without it?" He grinned and spat out the remaining pins. "A dangerous conversation, you see, señor. It would not do to swallow my words."

While the last touches were going on they went over and sat down, Anthony on a chair and Moses cross-legged on a table.

"Do you happen to know anything of a certain Señorita Dolores de la Fuente?" asked Anthony. "I should be glad of a little information about her." He was relieved to be able to say her name so casually.

"... *y Someruelos!* Do not forget that! Señorita Dolores de la Fuente *y* Someruelos, a niece of the incoming captain-general! Ah, the señor is to be congratulated on his eyesight. Yes, all Havana knows. She has preceded her uncle here with certain relatives and domestics to set up his establishment at Los Molinos. A lady with the true gracia of old Castile.

"It is because the present governor has permitted her to move into the palace that it is plain to all the world how the political wind blows. If the present and the newly-appointed captain-general were not both liberals the señorita would have to wait. As it is, the palace will now be all ready for her uncle when he comes. Extensive alterations are under way. All of the domestics are to have new liveries." Moses rubbed his hands.

"At the palace! I shall be under the same roof with her in a few hours," Anthony said half aloud.

"Pardon me, señor; but I do not think you will see her at Los Molinos," said Moses. "Don Luis has taken her under his wing like an eagle. It is not the custom here, you know, for young ladies ..."

Anthony held up his hand. "I understand," he said.

Nevertheless, as he put on his suit for the audience he felt fired with hope. "Dolores was at Los Molinos!"

Moses charged for advice as well as for his cloth, Anthony discovered when he paid the bill. But it was worth it, he felt, as he drove on to Herr Meyier's small establishment in a street just off the plaza. And he was enjoying himself. He wished Vincent were along. How he would gape at this raiment. What had become of Livorno, anyway? In the vividness of the present his old days seemed to belong to someone else. Old clothes—he would have to get into them again to remember what they felt like. Even one's contour changed. He kicked the bundle of the suit he had worn to the tailor's. Then he remembered he had left his watch in it! Well, he was already late for the appointment with Herr Meyier. He knew that.

Herr Meyier had a number of papers to go over carefully. The order for the temporary sequestration of the schooner was made out, Anthony's appointment as government agent, and an authorization to seize the slaves. All of these already bore the seal of the *Caxa da Consolidación* and lacked only the signature of the captain-general. Annexed to these were the long records of the process of the government in the case of the *Black Angel*, the rescript of the Council of the Indies confirming it, and a decision of the alcalde-major dated the day before called "Processional Confirmation of Precedent in Camera."

"All of these papers," said Meyier, "you will please notice, Don Antonio, are in triplicate. One set for you, one for my bureau, and copies for the captain-general. The last paper with the high-sounding title is the most important of all. It means that the highest court in Cuba has certified that the case of the *Black Angel* is a precedent upon which the executive government here can act. A 'procession' of other acts can now legally proceed from this first one. Do you see? 'In Camera' simply shows that the decision has been made at the private request of the captain-general and is confidential. No public notice of it is required. It is simply certified back to him as valid. Perhaps you do not fully appreciate the beauties of Roman Civil Law from the standpoint of a government official. From now on all that the executive has to do to seize any slaver is to—well, seize it—and certify that it is precedental with the case of the *Black Angel*. The viceroy's signature makes it so. It is then a fact in law. To re-establish possession for themselves the owners of slaves who have been subjected to the process must prove conclusively that the government is in error, that is, that the case is *not* a precedent. That is very difficult to do, and in the meantime the slaves must remain in the government's possession and may be sold. It is simply beautiful!

"I may say," said Herr Meyier getting up and walking about excitedly, "that this puts a weapon in our hands for which we have long been searching. The slave interests are powerful and have been the most active element behind the intendant and Señor Santa María, 'the patriots,' as they call themselves. Now they *belong* to us. Only one example will be needed. Señor Gallego is unfortunate. But that first example we must have.

"You must therefore thoroughly understand all of this when

you take the papers to the captain-general to be signed. He is a penetrating and exacting man. I have explained your mission here to him and I have also stretched a point by indicating that it was you to whom we should be grateful for suggesting this process. That in a sense is true." He waved his hand deprecatingly. "Naturally I worked out the details, but let that go. He will give you the credit. We shall all participate in the benefits."

"Are you sure the captain-general does want to see me?" asked Anthony.

"I am not exactly certain why he *insists* upon seeing you but I think I know. This case is a very important one. Out of it may proceed much revenue for the palace. Don Luis would assure himself that he is placing this matter in competent hands. It will be for you to convince him of that. If he feels you can carry this seizure through, your own reward, the matter of the Gallego debt, will be a trifle. But I am being frank. If he does *not* like you, he will find someone else and there will be nothing left for you to do but to make your suit to Señor Santa María. There is much risk in all this for you. I do not conceal that. You must, for instance, on the way to Africa avoid—well, avoid falling overboard. But I think I am right in feeling that you will not be prevented easily or cavil at small things. By God! señor, *make* the captain-general like you. Become a convincing young man! In that case it may be possible the governor will have a further proposition to make you. If he does I advise you to accept. If not—" he shrugged his shoulders—"there is one thing more. What is your nationality? Where were you born?"

"I do not know," said Anthony turning red.

"*So?*" said Meyier looking at him appraisingly. Then he laughed.

"Don Antonio Adverso, citizen of the Western Hemisphere, white, a subject of God? No, no, that will not do. It is a legal fiction you need in order to exist."

"I suppose I am English," said Anthony.

"Why, señor?"

"I cannot answer you, Herr Meyier, a matter of honour."

"Teufel! Englishmen are seldom mysterious about being

Englishmen. But, we cavil unnecessarily. Will you take an oath of allegiance to the King of Spain in order that the law may be able to see you favourably, and hence for your own protection?"

But Anthony hesitated visibly. He felt very much the same about this oath as he had felt about Father Xavier's wafer. As he looked at Herr Meyier he could see that he was both disgusted and surprised. He was losing ground with him—and there was the debt. Should he sell himself to collect that? But why put it that way? This was only an earthly affair, himself and the King of Spain. He could bargain there.

"I will take the oath if you do not register it," said Anthony.

"Good! I will only have it attested, to produce if necessary," grunted Meyier, and sent for a notary. So Anthony swore with his hand.

"It is," he told himself, "a compromise."

They packed the papers in one of Meyier's portfolios and put a lead seal on it. "Himmel!" Meyier had said at last, leaning into the carriage. "Do not let trivialities interfere with your success, Don Antonio, even a citizen of the Western Hemisphere must live. Yes! No?" Anthony had left Meyier grinning and waving good luck.

Incidents like these that threatened to uncover the merely vague grounds for the supposition of his own existence were terribly disconcerting. They left him melancholy. Herr Meyier's banter about the oath had gone deep. With Meyier the oath was a mere formality. Herr Meyier was a German. He was sure of himself. He had been born into and turned out of a mould. He was irrevocable to himself and to all men. He remained a German no matter what oaths he took. But Anthony— what of him? "Citizen of the Western Hemisphere, white!" How deep that cut! In all the inherited loyalties of men he had no part. At the table of the sun he drank to no king. He had no right to be there which was humanly visible. Perhaps Cibo was right and he should attach himself to something. But Mr. Bonnyfeather's legacy had made that difficult because it was unnecessary. He did not even need to go on playing at making a living. Life would be just a game with the means assured and no ends to play for except to win. Win what? Undoubtedly he must find something. Suppose—suppose a citizen of the Western Hemisphere proposed marriage to Señorita Dolores de la Fuente y Someruelos. What would he say, for instance, to the de la Fuentes and the Someruelos? He knew what he would say to Dolores. That would not be in the realm of logical argument —but to *them?* And he knew now that they would be there, too. The best he could now do would be to whisper something to Dolores in the moonlight—and go away. Someone like that baby this morning who had sponsors for himself must be the final accredited cavalier.

Well, he would go on. He would see. Perhaps the Western Hemisphere might be a mould. Feeling vaguely English because he looked it, and being sure himself that he was born, he would pour himself out into the mould. He would find out. Now that the madonna had gone she would also take his cradle of the pool in the convent with her. It was the only one he had had. That—and a certain face on a miniature which he must never speak of.

To hell with all that, then!

Here I am. I know that. I will try following up one practical thing, call my object all, and see where it leads to. Object, the debt. I *will* collect that. I make an oath to myself. The oath to the King of Spain is purely contributory. It is a means. Result so far: I have achieved nationality. Supposing the debt to be "x" I shall simply work out its value to me in the terms of what happens while I collect it thus:

$$y(\text{The } Wampanoag + \text{Havana} + \text{Africa}) = x$$

Now then, I make a note of that. *Memorandum for A. A.* He set it all down—and

$$y = the\ unknown\ factor\ of\ myself.$$

Let us see, are there any other factors? Luck? Oh, well, this is a non-human equation, not a logical one. To supply the value of luck would require a constant unknown factor operating throughout. To be able to know that would also imply being able to know "x" in advance.

He put his notebook into his pocket rather pleased with his fancy.

"Hence you see," he told himself, "it follows . . . what follows? That I am being drawn by two horses to see the Captain-General of Cuba at Los Molinos and Dolores is *there*. Very good, that!—Driver, a little faster please. I *must* be there by four o'clock. So this is what carriages are about. How reasonable!"

Yet what he really enjoyed, now that all the important business was set down in a "mathematical" memorandum, was the mysterious and easy pleasure of forward motion as he rolled along over the new military road toward Los Molinos. Having a constant series of impressions follow each other in rapid succession without doing anything to produce them gave him the sensation of having increased life. He was enjoying as a more powerful being might enjoy. The horses had accelerated fate and made the world change. In the collection of the debt, in solving "x," this would be one of the most enhancing experiences he felt.

"Driver, faster! Use your whip!" They flew along now.

The gardens of Los Molinos with the summer palace of the captains-general came in sight, a gleam of old ivory in a tossing sea of palms. In those living depths the wind blew the treetops back into white, glistening spots that shivered in the sea of green like the Caribbean lashing over a hidden reef. A sentry emerged from a gold-and-scarlet striped box and took his pass. Ten minutes later Anthony was ushered into the Hall of the Governors of Cuba.

———◆———

At first he could not see anyone there. The rather low room with grey stone walls and a moulded stucco ceiling looked more like a corridor than an apartment. It ran clear across the front of the main building with deep, recessed windows stretching from ceiling to floor. Through these, like reflections from the surface of a lake, fell the shuffling lights and shades of the waving palm fronds without which mirrored themselves and rippled aquidly upon the gleaming, ebony floor. Shifting spots of sunlight and half-lights flowed along the grey walls and lent an almost liquid aspect to the atmosphere of the room.

Indeed, it was no wonder that the eye at first lost itself in this ancient apartment. Had Anthony seen tropical fish come swimming through the windows he would not have been surprised. High, narrow teakwood chairs, set at stately intervals; chairs upholstered in faded red brocade shot through with tarnished silver threads died away into the water perspective as if all those who had sat on them were dead and this was the cabin of a foundered galleon. It was not until his eyes adjusted themselves to the somnolent and stealthy shifting of shadows that at last in the centre bay of the windows he discovered the captain-general himself.

He was standing with his back turned looking out into the garden and had evidently not heard the secretary announce him, for Anthony could still see his card lying on a silver tray before the governor's desk chair.

"Your Excellency," said Anthony.

General Las Casas turned with a slight twist of annoyance. Seeing it was not a lackey he hastily picked up the card, read it, and immediately broke into a quiet smile. Anthony could scarcely restrain a start of surprise. Here was the same gentleman who had been standing beside Dolores in the cathedral.

"Come over, Don Antonio, I am glad to see you. Have I kept you waiting long? Ah, I see. Well, you are not the first who has not been able to find me in this—aquarium."

He pointed Anthony to a chair by his escritoire, answering his bow with an easy and winning courtesy.

"You must really co-operate with me in helping to set aside the old formalities of a viceregal court," continued the general, leaning his head on one hand and looking at Anthony frankly and keenly. "Personally I find it impossible to get anything done in Cuba by insisting that this is the Escurial. It has shocked some of the old Castilians even here. But formalities are not the end of life any more. Things have been happening in Paris, you know. One must admit they exist. 'New times, new fashions, and new minds,' I often say. I see you believe at least in cutting your clothes to the year. You will not be shocked, I trust, if I do not permit you to kiss my hand?"

"Thank you, for breaking the ice of etiquette so thoroughly, sir," said Anthony. "I confess to coming here with considerable trepidation, despite the assurances of your many friends in Havana."

"I was not aware my friends in Havana were so numerous," said the governor. "But it is pleasant to hear you say so. You yourself, Don Antonio, seem to have fallen into excellent hands. Herr Meyier and our good Carlo Cibo have both been talking to me about you. I have been given to suppose that it will not be difficult for us to arrive at a conclusion about certain matters, and to our mutual advantage. You have already made a very happy suggestion, I am told." Anthony saw his eyes rest on him inquiringly.

"I shall be frank with Your Excellency. A very small part of the credit for that suggestion is due to me. It was only something I said inadvertently which enabled Herr Meyier to . . ."

"Tut, tut!" exclaimed the governor. "You dispraise yourself. But I see you are honest even in claiming credit and that is, to say the least, refreshing here. Your inadvertency was a very happy one. Go on, make some more. But Herr Meyier has entrusted you with some papers, I believe?"

"Here," said Anthony laying the sealed portfolio on his desk.

"You may gain some insight into the conditions of this business," remarked the general as he extracted the documents and spread them out, "when I tell you that it is only to a messenger whose own interests are inseparable from their safe delivery here that these papers would be entrusted. Do you realize, my young friend," continued he, opening his eyes a little wider, "that if certain gentlemen here in Havana had known of the contents of this portfolio neither you nor it would have arrived here this afternoon? As it is I have no doubt whatever that you are already being watched."

"I am prepared to take the risks which will inevitably be involved if Your Excellency sees fit to trust me," said Anthony.

"It is true my own interests are involved in this affair but that is not my main motive, sir. I want you to know that. No, there is something more." He hesitated.

"Go on," said the governor, "I am really curious now."

"It is the thing itself," Anthony burst out, "the difficulties that are in the way, what will happen, my own determination to go through with it. I would find out for myself how I shall cope with this affair. But I suppose that is not what I should have told *you*."

"On the contrary I am very glad you have said it, Don Antonio. It puts a new face on the matter. We shall not simply be using each other for so much cash. It encourages me, in fact, to propose to you something further since you are a caballero with whom gold is not all. What I shall say now is between us only, as men of honour. Is that agreeable?"

"You have my word, sir, but I reserve my decision as to your proposal."

"Naturally. Do not imagine I would inveigle you. Quite the contrary. In fact, as you shall see, to a certain extent I shall have to commit myself to your hands." He leaned forward and began to sand the papers for a minute. Then he looked up frankly and continued.

"Señor, in a few months I return to Spain. I return there a poorer man than when I arrived here six years ago. It might have been otherwise if I had cared to play the game here with the intendant and Señor Santa María. Meyier has told you of them? So! You understand then. But perhaps you do not understand fully. The 'game' is to separate Cuba from the crown of Spain. Troubled times are now with us and more ahead. With universal war brewing in Europe we shall soon be separated for months from Madrid. Insurrection gathers here. My successor, the Marqués de Someruelos, my cousin, will soon be left here alone to struggle with those who call themselves patriots. Need I add that their conception of patriotism is the concentration of revenue in their own hands? The intendant is not without influence at home. It has been only with the greatest difficulty that I have succeeded in having a loyal successor to myself appointed, a man of honour and ability, a liberal, but loyal. To smooth the way for himself he has sent his niece out in advance to set up his household here at Los Molinos. Social prestige is very important in Cuba among the great landholders. I am a widower and have been handicapped. But with the arrival of the Señorita Dolores we have been co-operating in building up the viceregal court. When my successor arrives there will be a court for the royalists to rally about. It has been very difficult for her. She has had to disregard many conservative customs. But—*as you seemed to observe this afternoon in the cathedral*—she is a señorita of singular charm."

He leaned back and laughed, enjoying Anthony's obvious confusion.

"I see to a certain extent you have already joined our party," he continued. "That is well. Much serenading now takes place on moonlit nights in the gardens of Molinos. All the voices are terrible so far, it is true. But we have gained a number of the influential young caballeros to our side, for the cult of Dolores must also, by her decree, be the policy of the King of Spain. There have been dinners—and duels. Several troublesome patriots have been removed—honourably. It is now fashionable to come to court on certain afternoons to kiss the hand of the captain-general and that of the señorita afterward. Her uncle when he arrives will already be enormously popular. Patriotism, which has only an intendant and a mustachioed Señor Santa María, will soon be left cold."

"Do you want me to come and join the choir in your park then, general?" laughed Anthony. "If so, you can count on me for *that*."

"Do so by all means," laughed Las Casas. "I shall instruct my sentries not to fire on the night when you arrive. Let your soul overflow. But we wander a little from the point.

"Under all of this, you know, I am really quite serious. Would you be interested, Don Antonio, for instance in being the agent for providing the somewhat embarrassed Captain-General of Cuba with an independent revenue? You might, *ahem, er*, participate—to a certain extent. I should add that you would deserve to do so for you would be providing the means for preserving intact the interests of the crown here."

"You mean," said Anthony doing some fast thinking, "that once in Africa you would like me to continue there for a while as your confidential agent."

"Your surmise has hit the mark very closely, señor."

"I could never consider engaging in slaving as a permanent business, sir, there is no need for me to do so, and besides I do not . . ."

"Certainly, of course not, that is for any length of time or in the usual way. My thought was this: once arrived in Africa establish yourself at Gallego's base and remain there long enough to ship me and my successor sufficient cargoes to permit us to get the upper hand here financially.

"We will undertake to provide you ships. They will be temporarily sequestrated from the friends of Señor Santa María. Thus the thing will work both ways to our benefit. It will hamstring them and provide us funds to pay the garrison and equip loyal colonial forces. I should say it would require some years to bring this about, provided you can keep sending slaves. It will not matter then if we are cut off from Spain. The commercial details of the matter will be handled by Herr Meyier through our good friend the rich grocer of Regla. Any reasonable arrangement which you and Cibo might care to make with the *Caxa da Consolidación* would, I am sure, be approved of at the palace." He smiled.

"You see the merit of the scheme is that the intendant and his friends will not be able to lay their hands on the root of the trouble at first. It will all be done quietly. You are not known here and it will be some time before they guess Cibo's connection, if at all. We shall take care to have the cargoes landed at Santiago, say, and marched overland if necessary. And slaves now are at a premium. I should hope for six or eight cargoes a year at least."

He paused looking at Anthony earnestly, again drumming on the desk. In the great room the sunlight was already beginning to fade.

"Can you give me a few men I can depend upon when the *Ariostatica* sails? It may be difficult to make this first seizure, in Africa," said Anthony. "Suppose that Señor Gallego objects."

"Ah," said the governor shrugging shoulders, "that I admit is the rub. Frankly I cannot help you there. To put a crew on the schooner and send them to Africa, I have no power. My authority ends three miles from these shores. If I carried it with a high hand and put men aboard, the cat would be out of the bag. The *first* move must be perfectly legal and unsuspected. I can arm you with papers and nothing more. Those papers give you authority to tell the captain what to do and to attach Señor Gallego's slaves. You must contrive to do that and to establish yourself in Africa if you can. If this first move is protested I can simply say I am carrying out the unofficial policy of the present ministry to permit the collection of a foreign merchant's debt. If you make use of your opportunity and establish yourself, ah, then—*then* I shall take some risks in seizing ships. Until then why should I? Apparently I should simply be compromising myself for you. No one would believe that.

"As it is now only four of us will know, and the marquis when he arrives. Indeed, I should not risk it with any Cuban. They all have local connections. I wished to see you myself before I broached the matter. I believe you can succeed in this, Don Antonio. If you do, in two or three years you will be a rich man. In any event you will be taking much the same risks just to collect your present debt."

"It will take several years out of my life," mused Anthony.

"True, and very interesting ones they may prove to be," continued the general. "But there—I would not press you. Either you will want to do this as you say for its own sake, or not at all. I can understand that. I see by these papers, however, we are both serving the same master now—your oath of allegiance. I have always served my king well. The profit has not always been great. One does the best one can—and goes home. You will forgive me for having pressed all this upon you. I am surrounded by rascals here or incompetents. It seemed our opportunity might be mutual in several ways. Well, let us seal these and go. The señorita receives informally in the garden this afternoon." He looked up a little sadly and gave the bell rope a pull.

At some distance the bell tinkled musically. The door opened.

"Lights, Pedro, for a sealing." Presently the lighted candles came.

"There is always something childishly fascinating about this," said the governor as he began to soften the wafers for the seals in a little pan. The pungent smell of lit wax made him cough.

Instantly before Anthony arose the library of Mr. Udney at Livorno. He saw himself moving about there a ragged, stammering orphan with a priest's hat under his arm. That was who he was! He remembered now. He must be making his own place in the world. And now—he was looking at the captain-general of Cuba sealing documents that concerned that same orphan. He had come for them half-way across the world from the library of Mr. Udney eleven years ago. Why not gather in all that the wax might seal? It was running now, as it were, through the general's hands. Soon they would be hardened, those seals, once and for all. Florence Udney . . . No pigtails now . . . Mrs. David Parish thank you! Dolores, how lovely you are. In three years I might . . . in three years, who knows?

"Your Excellency, I have joined your party," Anthony said quietly.

"Good!" said Las Casas, "all the better that you did not jump at the first glimmer of a golden hook. It is more than that, isn't it?"

"Much more," said Anthony. "*All* I think."

The governor smiled and pressed down on the last seal.

"Well," said he, "since you have joined *my* party, I suppose you will have no objection to joining the one going on downstairs. No!" He laughed and put Anthony's sealed copies back in the portfolio. "The rest of these papers remain here, and with Herr Meyier. I shall myself add a confidential memorandum for the marqués when he comes. Depend upon it he shall understand. Now we go down to the garden. Don Antonio—" he looked at Anthony fixedly.

"Your Excellency?"

"I congratulate you. Permit me to introduce you to the Friends of the King."

They walked across the room together. Anthony's heart beating fast. To his surprise, however, they did not turn toward the door.

"How do you think I do as a politician?" said the governor. "I have had to learn it here," he grimaced. "I am not the first captain-general who found himself alone in Cuba, however. Look here!" They had stopped before a full-length portrait of Don Philip IV just opposite the governor's desk across the hall.

"It might," said Las Casas, "be a portrait of the old days here. It is a copy of Velasquez. A predecessor of mine had it hung here almost a century ago."

From the deep shadows of a black velvet curtain behind him the pale and utterly weary countenance of Don Philip looked out at them as if they were not there. The gold ringlets over his narrow, austere brow shone with as cold a lustre as the fishy-blue of his eyes. Disdainfully, with a smile that had nothing human about it except a hint of cruelty, he was drawing on a pair of long, thin gloves.

"You see?" said Las Casas. "It is the same king who once had a soldier executed for catching him in his arms when he fell downstairs. High treason! He had impeded the sovereign." A look of keen enjoyment passed over the face of the governor not unmixed with regret. "The king did not have to be a politician," he went on. "But it has been otherwise with viceroys in Cuba. They have sometimes thought that even a way of falling downstairs without attracting attention might be convenient. Even a century ago . . . now . . ."

He put out his hand and pulled the picture toward him. It swung out like a door. A narrow flight of stairs dived into the wall behind it. They descended these in two turns in the darkness and came out suddenly into a tropical garden below.

The garden had been there so long that it had forgotten it was in a patio. The smooth, grey stems of giant palms sprang upwards to a green clerestory above, a luminous Gothic ceiling which swam rather than rested on the cleanly curved boles of its natural pillars below. The eye lost itself in the fronded arches of palm leaves or wandered away through a maze of living columns to be reluctantly halted at last by the time-darkened walls of the palace beyond. It was the old tiltyard of Los Molinos which the genius of some unknown architect had turned into a formal paradise for the viceroys of Spain.

A series of low terraces bordered with stone banisters and lined with ferns and giant cacti in green stone jars descended by regular degrees till they finally enclosed the centre of the garden. There was a level stretch of intensely green grass and ferns from the centre of which a fountain under great pressure lifted a constantly waving plume of spray. Water, indeed, was the secret of the place. The deep runnels of subterranean channels murmured with a constant moaning undertone as if the stream that had been diverted to refresh the place still softly complained. It was hard to tell whether it was the voice of the wind in the palms above or the rush of hidden water below that never ceased. It was a monotone that seemed to belong there and to be as natural as the cool shade of the giant palms themselves.

"An ancient tribe of peacocks once inhabited here," said Las Casas as they stood looking down a flight of broad Spanish steps that led to the fountain below. "The women's dresses moving about among the trees there remind me of them. It is a pity that hoops and brocade are now going out. We shall scarcely know what to do with places like this soon I am afraid. As for the peacocks—they had to go. They made a noise in the morning like filing glass. But come, I see they are waiting for us."

They were met at the bottom of the stair by a very old man of extreme Castilian gravity in a costume that might have done duty at the Escurial some decades before. Don Alonso de Guzman had been master of ceremonies at Los Molinos during the administrations of four preceding captains-general, and although he was now nearly eighty, he still contrived to impress even on a garden party a certain haughty air of mouldy etiquette that was only a memory even in Spain. To this personage Anthony was now delivered by Las Casas and a round of formal introductions began.

There was old Doña Mercedes, the captain-general's mother, who sat in a wheel-chair wrapped in heavy flaps of lace. A marmoset with a face like a bearded penny peeped out over her withered breasts. Above the low hum of conversation, the sound of water and of sere leaves, the dry, hacking cough of the old woman and the shrill whimpering of the monkey rang out disturbingly from time to time. As yet few of the younger generation had arrived. Everybody seemed to be waiting for the affair to begin.

In the meantime old Don Alonso struck his high, beribboned cane into the ground before the bishop, a sardonic, olive-faced old gentleman with a tight, churchly wig and a massive episcopal ring; before the Comandante of Police, Colonel Jesús Blejo; before Señor Gomez Calderón, a rich planter, and Mr. James Drake, an English merchant of much influence. The old courtier bowed with the exact degree of deference due to each while he introduced Anthony.

Several officers of the garrison now began to arrive dressed in wide-brimmed, straw hats with heavy, silver lace bands. These Anthony thought looked anything but military. Two or three of the foreign consuls came in with their wives. By the time Anthony had made his rounds with Don Alonso it was understood that another rich, young Englishman with letters was on his travels. This explanation of his presence seemed to have invented itself for him and he gladly acquiesced.

"I suffer greatly from the dreadful humidity of Cuba," said old Doña Mercedes, evidently touched that a young gentleman should have expressed sympathy for her cough. "How I shall survive the trip back to Spain with Don Luis only the blessed Virgin knows. His Lordship here has promised me a hair of the blessed St. Teresa in a bottle to take along. Ah, he is a comfort, that man. I am just saying what a comfort you are, Your Lordship," she called out. The bishop came strolling over looking both saturnine and bored. "You will not forget the blessed bottle, will you?" she reminded him.

"You shall have it tomorrow," he said, and made an elaborate note of it in a black notebook with a gold cross on it. The old woman looked at him dotingly while biting the pink ear of her marmoset with her gums.

"As an Englishman, Don Antonio will scarcely understand how much your kindness means to me," she said.

"Don Antonio is a good Catholic I hear," replied the bishop. "It was he who brought the miracle-working Madonna to Regla, I understand."

"Scarcely that, sir," said Anthony. "I merely arrived on the same ship."

The old woman looked at them both with a live interest now and began to chatter in an animated way about the happenings at Regla. Evidently it was the talk of the town. Through her pious exclamations of admiration, wonder, and surprise, the bishop kept trying to pump Anthony. He walked all around the subject of the miracle like a cat but he learned nothing beyond the facts that he already knew. He looked disappointed.

"You see, señor," said he after they had bowed and walked away from Doña Mercedes, "frankly, I am glad to meet you here. Let us sit down for a minute. Your name has been mentioned to me already—our friend Señor Cibo. Only this afternoon we have had a long talk. What you say about the remarkable event at Regla confirms in every way what he has just been telling me—" the bishop smiled blandly—"I am much gratified. I trust, however, that no more of the statues which were so thoughtfully imported will prove to be miraculous. It would be somewhat embarrassing if the age of miracles were to return by wholesale. The faith of this generation would scarcely be adequate to the occasion. I trust you appreciate my conservative attitude, señor. What do you think?" He leaned forward putting his long upper lip over the gold knob of his cane and stared out into the garden.

"I am sure Your Lordship has nothing more unusual to anticipate," said Anthony. "The rest of the statues which Captain Jorham is now disposing of are in no way remarkable except in price. Of course, I do not pretend to speak either with authority or inspiration, only a certain prophetic instinct as it were."

"Ah, you relieve me greatly," sighed the bishop taking his lip off the cane. "All the ecclesiastical authorities want to do with miracles is to be reasonable about them. As it is there has been a great deal of unauthorized religious enthusiasm in Havana now for some time. As the watchful shepherd of my flock I feel it should be allayed. By the way, señor, you were present at a recent occasion when a French monk, whom I believe you know, interfered with the punishment of a slave. A very serious business!"

"Your Lordship seems to be very well informed of everything that goes on in Havana!"

"*Very*," said the bishop. "It was also intimated to me this afternoon, with great discretion I might add, that you were expecting to travel to Africa shortly under somewhat favourable circumstances."

"Carlo should scarcely have spoken of it," said Anthony somewhat annoyed.

"Ah, do not say that, Don Antonio. You see he knew to whom he was speaking! After all we are all of one party here." He swept his stick around. "Under the circumstances I can even understand your sympathy for Brother François. You are very young yet after all. But you will also, I trust, understand my own great forbearance and the difficulty in which I find myself. The civil authorities are demanding I take some action about Brother François. Such things cannot go on." He paused significantly.

"My son, it occurs to me that if you could make things comfortable for Brother François on your approaching voyage you would be doing him a great favour. In fact I might add that I have arranged to have him, *er*, transferred to the African province. The captain-general and I have just had a little talk. He quite understands and has suggested that I inform you myself as the matter may be somewhat of a surprise to the good monk.

I understand you start soon. By the way, His Excellency would like to see you for a minute before you leave this afternoon." He rose. "This has been most gratifying, Don Antonio; you shall have my prayers for a smooth voyage, I assure you." Without waiting for any reply he walked away smiling.

"I shall warn Brother François tonight," thought Anthony and rose to greet Mr. Drake who passed just then with his wife on his arm. They talked for some time.

"You hail from about Dundee, do you not, Mr. Adverse?" said the Englishman. "I think I detect certain—ah—Dundeeisms in your accent."

But there was no time to reply. The company suddenly began to gather itself together on the lawn. Those who had been strolling about under the trees now suddenly appeared. Old Doña Mercedes broke into a violent fit of coughing to attract notice to herself. But no one paid any attention to her.

The brittle, snapping sound of the sudden opening of fans revealed several women advancing along a faint path through the ferns and palm trees. They seemed to appear suddenly out of the background of greenery and were now standing by the fountain fanning themselves, laughing and talking to those who crowded up to meet them eagerly.

From the remoter vistas of the garden, where they had evidently been concealing themselves and smoking to avoid the boring preliminaries with the bishop and Doña Mercedes, five or six young caballeros also hastened forward. Several little wisps of blue smoke amid the shrubbery discovered their former hiding places. But all this Anthony caught out of the side of his eye. For in the centre of the group of señoritas by the fountain was Dolores.

He lost no time in hurrying forward himself, and it seemed to him a particular act of grace on the part of Las Casas that he rescued him from the formal clutches of Don Alonso to present him to Dolores.

"Here, señorita," said he, "is a young gentleman whom I believe you have seen before." He seemed to be enjoying the slight evidence of confusion in both of them which marked his words. "Don Antonio has brought us letters from important friends." This was evidently for the benefit of the young Cubans who were standing near waiting their turn somewhat impatiently.

Anthony was aware of a sweetly modulated voice with a surprising depth of tone saying something to the effect that Cuba was honored by the presence of so distinguished a traveller. She was dressed in shimmering green with something in bright scarlet that fell down from her shoulders into long fringes. On account of the light which seemed to him to emanate from her garments their exact outline remained vague. He looked up to see her dark eyes smiling at him gravely while she manipulated her fan. A faint perfume slept in the lazy breeze she evoked.

"It is I who am greatly and unexpectedly honoured," he managed to reply not very happily. Then they both smiled at the immense gravity of this formal exchange—as if their meeting in the cathedral had already put them far beyond that. He saw the corners of her lips twitch a little with amusement.

"Have you brought along with you the charming lady who accompanied you this afternoon at the christening, Don Antonio, la inglesa?" She looked at him half mockingly over her fan.

"I regret, señorita," he began.

"Ah, *that* is a great disappointment," she said, "frankly my curiosity was aroused. None of us had any idea that young English caballeros were accompanied by duennas. Come, enlighten us, señor, who was she? I hope you have not trusted yourself alone here!" A titter ran through the group of girls behind her, some of whom Anthony now remembered having seen in the church. They looked at him archly awaiting his explanation.

"You do my moral character no great compliment, señorita, but you underrate the strength of the temptation it finds here. Can you blame me for needing protection? And besides it was I who was protecting the lady from the ardent caballeros of Cuba.

"As a matter of fact," he hurried on making the most of having turned the tables slightly, "I was merely showing the wife of a Yankee captain the epitaphs and tombs of Havana. She is a great authority on cemeteries and visits them all over the world."

The explanation aroused a gratifying interest. It was plain Mrs. Jorham and her cavalier had caused a good deal of comment. They had even been seen taking lemonade together. Anthony was presented to the other señoritas. The Cubans and several young officers now crowded up. The talk became general and extremely animated.

Evidently these garden parties of the Señorita Dolores were affairs of the younger generation. There could be no doubt that they belonged to her. She moved about here and there, always faithfully followed; the object of much ingenious attention, and with a dignity, a charm, and a serene enjoyment of her position which at once dominated everybody and yet put them at their ease.

Even Don Alonso recognized this. He withdrew quietly, accompanying the chair of Doña Mercedes which was wheeled off somewhere, leaving the light chatter and laughter of the group by the fountain uninterrupted by her cough. She and Don Alonso took coffee alone and exchanged the court gossip of previous reigns for hours at a time.

In the garden coffee and light confections were served by orderlies of the Andalusian regiment in the garrison. Anthony secured some cakes representing a Jew in the flames. He perched them on the back of a stone bench with coffee and a serviette and managed to catch the eyes of Dolores. She nodded and he came forward, bowing to her cavalier. He, however, still followed.

"May I not have the honour?" Anthony said to her, pointing to the bench. He smiled at her partner. "I hope, señor, you will permit me to intrude without offence. You have often the valued privilege of drinking coffee at Los Molinos, while I, I remain here for only a few days. I ask a great sacrifice I know, but imagine the memory you will be conferring."

"If the señorita permits," said the young cavalryman who was with her, half hopeful she would not.

"Tomorrow, Don Esteban, I promise you. Don Antonio departs so soon," she said. "You would not be cruel!" She tapped the young soldier with her fan.

The lieutenant bowed with more courtesy than enthusiasm and went off to light a cigarro philosophically. Dolores and Anthony sat down on the bench with only the Jewish martyr between them.

"I eat my cruel words, señor," she said. "You are decidedly *not* in need of a duenna. Don Esteban is not easy to put off. You see I know."

His hand shook as he poured out her coffee.

"Are you really so much moved, Don Antonio?" Her fan folded itself together softly on her lap. She sat back and watched him, studying his face.

"Thou seest, señorita," he said boldly, looking up. The blood rushed to his face as he looked at her. Her shoulders rose and fell deeply. At last she sipped her coffee, taking her eyes from his. He picked up the cup and drank from it where she had put her lips.

"He burns," said Dolores picking up one of the little cakes laughingly.

"Would you have no mercy for a poor devil in the fire then?" asked Anthony. "It is true I must go in a few days. Tell me, tell me at least that you are not glad of that. I believe you were glad to see me, that we did truly *see* each other when we first met this afternoon. All my life I have been looking for you and when I looked up, standing there by the pillar, I thought—I dared to think—that at last I was no longer alone. Just to have found you, just to know you are alive . . ."

"Be careful," she whispered, "the intendant is coming this way." They waited, sipping their coffee together while a dark, middle-aged man with a jewelled court sword passed close to the bench where they were sitting. He bowed deeply to Dolores and gave Anthony a keen glance.

"He knows he is not welcome here," she said. "Go on, Don Antonio, you were saying something, I believe."

"Was I, does it really interest you?" he asked. He leaned forward suddenly with his serviette drooped over the cake dish and took her hand from her lap under cover of it.

"Do not crush it," she said at last. Her eyes opened widely upon him. "Yes!—I shall keep this cake," she said. She took it from the plate with her other hand. "Now you must let me fan myself, señor! Remember where we are!"

He sat back reluctantly trying to clear his eyes of a dazzling golden light. The muscles in his throat relaxed again.

"Could I not see you somewhere else than here? Only for five minutes, but alone?"

She shook her head doubtfully. "It would be all but impossible."

"All *but?*" he said.

She laughed at him now. His disappointment was so grim.

"You are serenaded, señorita, I am told. Is it only the Cubans, 'the Friends of the King,' who are to be consoled? Ah! Sorrow of the Fountain, Dolores de la Fuente, por Dios, you are well named!"

He saw that she looked at him tenderly despite herself. She brought the fan up so that only her wide forehead with the pale, golden ringlets curling over the delicate hollows in her temples, and her eyes dark as violets at twilight looked at him like a vision. He remembered her that way; he remembered her always. It was like the forehead of the face in the miniature.

"Dolores," he said, "I do not burn. Do not think that. I love you with my soul."

He heard her gasp.

They sat for almost a minute and both were thinking the same thing. Across the garden they saw that General Las Casas and someone else were strolling toward them.

"It would be very difficult," she said suddenly. "There are many who come to serenade in the outer park but my windows open into this garden. No one could climb the patio wall . . ."

"But if they did," he said.

"Quién sabe!" she replied. "Here is the governor."

"Give me the rose in your hair, señorita, that at least to remember you by. I beg you . . ."

"Ah! your pardon, Don Antonio," said Las Casas. "It is really painful to interrupt under the circumstances," he bowed to Dolores, "but I must detain you a minute. How do you get on with Englishmen, señorita?" he said.

"Very well, Your Excellency. Indeed," said she, putting her hands behind her head, and looking up at him from the bench with her head thrown back in a charming defiance, while her fingers seemed to rearrange her high, silver comb—"indeed, I wish they did not have to leave Havana so soon."

"So!" said Las Casas, taking a pinch of snuff. "Iay, señorita, I am afraid we shall have to disappoint you."

"Adiós, then, Don Antonio," said Dolores with an exaggerated regret as she stood just finishing rearranging her hair. She gave him her hand to kiss. As he bent over it, in the folds of her fingers as they met, he felt the petals of a rose.

"But will I ever see her again?" he wondered.

35. THE TEMPORARY SEQUESTRATION
OF THE ARIOSTATICA

"Upon my word, señor, I am afraid I *have* some bad news for you," said Las Casas to Anthony as they watched Dolores walk away. She disappeared down a path which Anthony did not fail to mark. Now and then, before she vanished entirely, he could still catch sight of her black fan waving through the palms. He turned to find that he had kept the captain-general waiting.

"This is Don Jesús Blejo, el comandante de policia en Habana," continued Las Casas with a slight twist of amusement still visible in his smile. "The bad news, under the circumstances, is that you will be leaving Havana about sunrise tomorrow morning, Don Antonio."

Despite himself Anthony could not entirely conceal his surprise and disappointment. He stood crushing the rose in his fingers and biting his lips.

"Por Dios! It is high time you were on your way, I think," exclaimed the governor with a slight gesture of annoyance. "Still," said he softening, "I do not blame you. But we cannot even for so charming a reason delay. You may have noticed that the intendant was here this afternoon?"

Anthony nodded, trying to look as if he cared.

"He came to complain of the detention of the Gallegos' schooner by the port authorities. To preserve appearances I was forced to give poor Don Jesús here a thorough rating." He turned to the man who stood by rather uncomfortably with a look of surprised chagrin still on his face. "I trust you fully understand that now, colonel."

"Since Your Excellency has been pleased to explain," he said.

Las Casas looked extremely annoyed.

"You see what subterfuges I am put to," he said striking his sword. "So the *Ariostatica* has been released for tomorrow. I had to promise it, and even to pretend surprise that she had ever been held. We have only a few hours in which to act. It must be tonight or not at all. I have given orders to Don Jesús to have ten men and a boat in readiness at the Maestranza from midnight on. Fortunately, due to his loyalty and care, you can rely upon those he will pick for duty. As soon after midnight as possible you will row out and put yourself in possession of the schooner. Allow no one from her to return to shore. After you have once served your papers on the captain prevent all communication. You should be out of the harbour by sunrise. Make out to sea as soon as possible. The police will leave you and row in somewhere near Jibacoa. After that, señor, it depends on you. I wish you luck." He twirled his moustache and looked at Anthony a little doubtfully.

"You have my word, Your Excellency, to do all I can," said Anthony.

"Bueno!" said Las Casas. "This is a little more hurried than we had expected but it may turn out for the best. The intendant

when he inquires tomorrow will simply be informed that the
Ariostatica has been released as he demanded. He will suppose
that the captain has lost no time in getting under way. And in
that supposition he will be correct." He twirled his moustache
again with more assurance now.

"You will be wanting a few hours to make your personal
arrangements for the voyage, Don Antonio. Arm yourself," he
added significantly. "But you will also have to return to the
palace tonight to receive the final papers for the sequestration;
the release to the port authorities in due form. I shall have my
personal secretary make them out this evening. Return about
eleven o'clock if possible. They will be ready then and I shall
sign them. You will find Don Esteban at work in the big hall,
the 'aquarium'," he laughed. "Is there anything further you
can think of? Ah, sí! a pass for the palace tonight, of course!
What! There *is* something? I thought I had covered it all."

"Not quite all, sir," said Anthony hesitating a little.

"Ah, excuse us for a moment, Don Jesús," said Las Casas. He
and Anthony took a few turns up and down the path alone.
The comandante stood waiting by the bench.

The governor at last gave a relieved laugh. "I thought you
were going to withdraw at the last or make some final costly
stipulation," said he. "I am used to that."

"No, no," replied Anthony, "I would not bargain with you
for this. I appeal to you as a man of understanding and senti-
ment. I am going—who knows to what? A half hour only, Your
Excellency. Perhaps never again—quién sabe?"

"Ah, quién sabe?" echoed Las Casas. "But what would the
lady say? I am not in authority *there* you know, señor."

Anthony opened his hand and showed him the rose.

"Madre de Dios! you are a dangerous man. It is high time you
were on your way. But it shall be your pass. A half hour then—
fifteen minutes if you have a bad voice. My windows also look
into this patio."

Anthony spoke earnestly again for a turn or two. The governor broke out laughing aloud and finally nodded. "But I shall
give orders to search the guitar for lethal weapons," he said.

"That will at least save the comandante's face—and perhaps a quarrel between you. He is a man of literal duty you know, a Basque. By the way, you will treat him with marked courtesy. He is important here in the scheme of things."

"What is the least which will not insult him, sir?"

"Not less than a hundred dollars I hazard," smiled Las Casas, "but that is not all that I meant. He is somewhat nettled at having been transferred from his regiment to take over the police. Pride—you see?"

"It is a great pleasure to be associated in this enterprise with so gallant a soldier," said Anthony as they rejoined the comandante by the bench. "His Excellency has been speaking of your invaluable services here, Don Jesús, I am honoured."

The man's jacket bulged slightly about the breast as he bowed with a sudden and very marked cordiality. "I am at your disposal, señor. It is but for His Excellency—and you—to command."

Las Casas was secretly much pleased, too. The police were his chief reliance next to the garrison.

"I have passes made out to the palace for Don Antonio and his servant tonight," said the governor—"and a guitar." He smiled whimsically. "If the holders of the pass should be found during the evening in the patio . . . I trust you will not be alarmed, Don Jesús. The conspiracy is not aimed at me. In fact I have nothing to do with it."

"Except to bind me to your service with tender bonds," said Anthony bowing deeply.

"Ah! that remains to be seen," said the governor. "As you say, quién sabe? And now adiós, Don Antonio. I wish you well in several ways. Do not let the moonlight delay you too long. That is all. Don Jesús will accompany you now as far as Regla. Make what haste you can. *Do not forget that other matter, colonel,*" he called after them. The soldier turned and saluted again.

Looking back from the top of the steps as they left the garden Anthony saw the Captain-General of Cuba standing by the fountain smoking a cigar. An hour and a half later, after a

breathless drive and dash across the harbour, he broke in on
Carlo on the veranda with the news.

━━━━━━━◆◆━━━━━━━

But Carlo refused to be hurried. In the brief tropical twilight
he was comfortably having supper. A large tureen with char-
coal under it simmered audibly.

"Sit down and have some pompano," he said. "The most
delicious of fish. The only one I really care for. Some fried
yams? Yes! I insist! What is a mere voyage to Africa compared
to a supper like this? Ah! What you will miss! Tomorrow is
the dinner I have prepared for you and Father Trajan in cele-
bration of the miracle. And now you will be at sea instead!
Well, well, you must go well prepared. Now let me show you
something, since you are going to Africa, that land of servants.
Sit here and drink your wine. It is not necessary to move now
merely because you are going on a journey. Cheecha, send
Tambo, and Eunice, and three bright boys. Also rouse Señor
Rodríguez. Fly now!"

In a few minutes the various persons white and black who
had been sent for appeared. Leaning back in his chair with a
glass of Malaga in his hand Cibo gave his orders.

He had Anthony's chests brought out on the veranda and
repacked by the slave girls. He had several other receptacles,
iron-bound and provided with heavy locks, carried up by the
black boys. From a list which he wrote out by the light of a
candle he began to fill these with such a variety of articles,
clothing, food, private trading goods, luxuries and necessities,
that Anthony was amazed.

"When you have boarded the schooner tonight and taken
possession hang a green light in the shrouds and I shall see that
all this is sent out to you immediately. The boys will be waiting
with the boat laden at the wharf. Have these chests stowed
where you can watch them. Remember you are going to be
moving from now on in a world of thieves. You are going to
steal men, and in return you can expect them to steal everything
from you they can. Do not waste any time thinking about the

morality or philosophy of it. Use locks. I shall send you everything you can need for a year's stay. It will be the first charge on our trading account. It is fortunate that Moses has delivered all your linen suits. You will need them. The Rio Pongo alternates between a Turkish bath and a furnace. Sometimes the nights are cool."

For an hour Cibo continued to talk of nothing but slaving and Africa. He gave off a world of particulars and sound practical advice. He settled the last details of how he would act as agent for dispatching further ships if Anthony was successful. He drank two bottles of wine and described the Gallego establishment on the Rio Pongo near Bangalang, the tribes surrounding it, and the half-caste Mohammedans who came down in caravans from the interior to trade. He even touched on the rising opposition to slavery in the British House of Commons and its possible effect on the trade in general. At the end of his discourse, for it could be called nothing less, he presented Anthony with two cases both of English make. The large one contained a pair of splendidly mounted pistols and the smaller a set of razors, one for each day of the week.

"Use these," said he. "When you begin to look and act like a native it is time to leave Africa. I give you two, at the most three years. That is longer than usual. The blue medicine chest there is mostly full of cinchona bark for the fever. I will nail directions inside. Follow them or you will die. Did it ever occur to you that *you* can die? No? Well, you can. In fact you will. Delay it. Immortality should be shunned with intelligent forethought whether it is inevitable or not. Quién sabe! Cheecha, another bottle of wine."

In the meantime the moon was flooding the patio with a deeper and deeper light. All the ropes were on the chests. For good luck Anthony took a last look at his own with the sextant in it. He settled the little madonna deeper into some soft things under his great-coat and wedged her in. How curious that she was going to Africa, too! If it had not been that Cibo was sitting near he would have taken a peep at her. But he was in no mood for quips and raillery now. It had been hard enough to listen to Cibo at all with his own head dancing with Dolores, moonlight, and the adventure of the night yet before him. Only the man's immense kindness and the inherent wisdom of what he had to say had held him. And now—now it was time to go.

He sent for Juan who appeared grinning in his new servant's clothes. "Sí, sí, señor, I am all ready. Sí, I have the guitar." Anthony wrapped his boat-cloak about him and turned to Cibo to say good-bye. Then he remembered something.

He undid the bundle of soiled clothes he had worn to the tailor's that morning and from it took his watch. He gave Cheecha the chameleon on the little gold chain. It kept coming up between her breasts when she hung it about her neck, which was probably the reason that made her both laugh and cry out while at the same time she clutched a few coins he had given her. Her stream of blessings and thanks made him ashamed. After all she was not the woman he had seen in the dream. That was something else. Cibo laughed at his serious face.

"Leaving a chameleon at a girl's breast is nothing to worry about. Ha, Toni, what a tender conscience we have! A glass now. Something I have saved to the last."

He brushed some cobwebs off a small, green bottle with a reverential gesture and carefully filled two tumblers. It was a very old and mellow Montrachet.

"May whatever gods there be go with you," he said. They clinked.

Cibo walked down to the dock with Anthony. He was to cross again in the fast little boat. The dark bodies of the rowers glistened in the moonlight. Someone was patting a tune drowsily.

"Do you understand that I am grateful, Carlo?" asked Anthony. It was hard to tell now whether it was water or the men's hands slapping below the dock. Cibo drew in his sash very tight. He suddenly looked younger with his faun-like face smooth under the moon.

"All that is nothing," he said. "We could not help being friends. Remember me, your philosopher in exile."

"Adiós, Carlo. Farewell, farewell!"

"You should have waited for the supper tomorrow night, a great supper! I will send along some of the wine. Drink to . . ." Carlo's voice called after them as the boat flashed out from the dock. The swift click of the oars and the rush of water drowned his tones in the distance. The black rowers grinned and pulled together for the tip that was so soon due. Anthony turned around and waved his white hat.

It was a miraculous night. Havana harbour was one blaze of silver and the moon straight overhead. The city lay before them twinkling with a thousand little lights. Juan unslung his guitar. They fairly flashed by a ship where the heads of the watch lined the rail. The rollicking voice of the young Spaniard made the six negroes pull as one man. At every stroke Anthony felt the light, soft air cool against his cheeks. "Dolores, Dolores!" He had forgotten all about the *Ariostatica* for the moment.

Before his eyes burned a vision of the pale face of the Spanish girl. It was not merely a vague pictorial thought of her. As he looked across the molten silver of the bay toward Los Molinos an actual reflected image of her face seemed to be cast upon the water just ahead of the boat. The rich, full tones of her voice sounded in his ears. For a while she possessed him. When his brain cleared again he found himself still swinging to the rhythm of the oars and Juan's barcarole while Havana suddenly sprang up before him much nearer than it had been before. The lights in the harbour seemed to have shifted.

He took a deep breath of the warm salt air. Tonight belonged to him and to her. He was living fully and all for now. He was, he felt, the captain of events for the first time in his life. Things had come his way in Havana remarkably well. It would be his part to continue to make them behave that way in the future. His last monitor had disappeared; had been left, talking, on the dock at Regla.

He was glad to have left Cibo. He liked him. He was grateful. Yes, but he was glad to be sitting in this boat bound on his own affairs with the tiller in his hand. The only one with him now was a servant. Bueno, that was as it should be.

And he would take and drive the *Ariostatica* to Africa. How he did not know. But he felt sure of it, sure of himself as he sat there. Cibo's wine gave just enough of a tinge of madness to turn the city ahead and the harbour into something a little better than even the moonlight could confer. It was a slightly mad, transfigured world of Dolores and untold adventure, all marvellous, all good, all tinglingly vivid, that lay before him. It had no end. In it one was immortal. It was impossible to fail. The pleasures of it were as infinite as one's capacity to enjoy. It was hard, and youthful and real. And yet—it was beautiful and dreamful; it was moonlight and mad music over the water.

He sat up with an intense sureness and took active charge. The boat, which had been driving a little out of its course, he set directly on the water-gate lights. He stopped Juan and slowed the rowers to a steadier but more time devouring speed. The *Wampanoag*, he noticed, had slipped her mooring and was riding far down the harbour. So Captain Jorham was on his way. He must have sold all his statuary. Well, he had learned much from the *Wampanoag* he could use now. Adiós to her! Adiós to everything!

They glided into the slip by the water gate and he gave a gold piece to the stroke oar for the crew. A babble of African approval and well-wishes seemed to waft him up the steps of the quay. Two minutes later he was being whirled through the dim, narrow streets of the old city toward Los Molinos again.

Once beyond the walls of the town they began to trot swiftly and more swiftly along the straight, white road awash with mad shadows where the palm trees flaunted and rustled their lofty double row of seething plumes down an infinite avenue. There was a thin, gauzy mist blowing by here in the valley; there was a hint of northern coolness, the smell of heavy dew on grass and leaves, and a blurred-glistening of green things in the foggy moonlight. The horses broke into a gallop thinking they were going home. They bolted. To the expectation of happiness ahead was now added the exhilaration of speed. A divine recklessness rode with them. The tenor voice of Juan lifted itself in staves of some Andalusian love song that rang out over the vacant plantations like the chorus of an unearthly, lyrical hunt. A few dogs barked and howled in the distance. At the open doorways of huts dark figures outlined in the orange glow from within watched them streak past. The driver at last brought up his team beside a roadside fountain.

"He will founder them if he lets them drink now," said Juan.

"Let him," replied Anthony. "As long as we get to the gardens I do not care."

They sat listening to the beasts gulping and breathing and to the fall of the spout. A streak of moonlight fell full on a little slide of water that came down a steep slope of fern and moss-covered rocks just above the trough. In the shady nook by the road everything but the clear space by this spring was in shadow. Their eyes naturally came to rest on the brilliant little waterfall as if it were a piece of miniature landscape illuminated.

It was only for a few seconds, but as Anthony watched this weird little Niagara that seemed to be leaping forever out of a tropical elfland through a haze of maidenhair ferns, a gorgeous coral snake glided down to the brink of a still pool and began to drink. Under the moon its brilliant scarlet was turned to dark amber. It was so delicate in all its motions, so graceful, and so utterly wild that there was not the slightest hint of anything sinister about it. Its tongue like black, forked-lightning flickered into the silver water making all but invisible ripples, and the moon glinted on its small eye. Suddenly, when one of the horses blew loudly on the surface of the font just below, it was gone.

He had watched it without complications as Adam might have seen the first serpent in Paradise before the fall. It had, he felt, given an expression and a meaning to the tropical night in a language that lies behind words.

Juan proved to be no Cassandra. The tough little horses did not founder. Ten minutes later they were at Los Molinos.

A glare of candles in the centre bay of the front windows of the palace showed that the secretary was still at work, although it was now past eleven o'clock. In spite of the pass the sentinel on duty was obstinate. It was late, and he looked at them, but especially at the guitar, with profound suspicion. He insisted on searching the instrument. A sergeant came but he could not read. It was finally necessary to send for the comandante himself. While they waited Juan retuned his strings and groaned. He was afraid he had lost key. Finally Don Jesús appeared and the gates were opened.

As they went up the broad stairs to the Hall of the Governors Anthony took the occasion to press into the hand of the comandante "the least sum which would not insult his honour." Evidently Don Jesús carried about him some receptacle for such contingencies, for the roll of gold pieces disappeared, internally, as it were. It neither clinked nor bulged upon his person. Except for a slightly more familiar and affable manner, he remained exactly as he had been before. One eye-lid, one epaulette, and a shoulder, all on the left side, sagged. His moustache also drooped in that direction and he limped slightly. Anthony wondered if it was on that side that he carried gold. Don Jesús had evidently expected Juan to remain in the vestibule, but he made no protest at his not doing so.

"When you have finished, señor, you will find me waiting below," said he. "If possible we should be at the dockyard in two hours at least. Dawn is early still, and Don Esteban has already taken longer with those papers than we expected. I will, if necessary, arouse His Excellency to sign them, but I trust you will be through before he retires. All is ready at the water front. I made final arrangements on returning from Regla some hours ago." He threw open the great door for them, and excusing himself, went downstairs again.

The secretary in the alcove looked up and nodded as they came in. He introduced himself a little nervously.

"It will take at least half an hour longer, Don Antonio," he said. "It is the making of three copies which consumes so much time. They must all be original to take the seal. I am sorry to delay you. Will you be good enough to sit down for a while? The chairs are not very comfortable, I know." He made a grimace and shifted himself uneasily looking somewhat surprised at Juan and the guitar. Then he snuffed the candles and resumed hastily. Anthony thanked him and seated himself and Juan on two chairs flanking the large portrait of Don Philip IV.

The sound of the secretary's pen and the tread of the sentry below were the only sounds in the great apartment. Except for the bright lights on the desk, where Don Esteban bent over his papers intent on rapid and accurate copying, and a dim sconce by the door, the rest of the room was in a flux of moonlight and the black, moving shadows of the palms outside.

"To all officers, servants, and ships' commanders and to all loyal subjects whomsoever of the crown of Spain: Know that, inasmuch as the good ship Ariostatica *of our port of Havana in Cuba . . ."*

scraped the secretary's quill for the third time that evening.

Quietly opening the door which the portrait concealed, Anthony and Juan disappeared down the dark, little stairs behind it.

——◆——

Under the moon the shaded patio seemed to have suffered an unearthly change from the garden of the afternoon before. Long pencils of silver light stole down through its palm-fronded ceiling, turning the court into a kind of dream-forest where pools of white mist gathered in the hollows of its paths. Indeed, the fountain in the centre remained the only familiar landmark.

Anthony had hoped to find some windows with lights in them. But beyond the thicket of palms, on every side the dark walls of the palace loomed without a break of gleam. He thought he knew on which side her apartments lay—in the direction of the path which she had taken that afternoon. But he could not be sure. He and Juan went as far as the fountain. Anthony looked about him again. Not a human light. Only a few fireflies winking here and there. Well, he must risk it.

"Sing, Juan—your best now!"

"The lady is beautiful, señor, you say?"

"Lovely as the night," said Anthony with a catch in his voice and trembling with eagerness.

"This then!" said Juan.

The strings began a low prelude. Then the pleading tenor of the young sailor suddenly filled the old tilt-yard of Los Molinos with an even more ancient ballad.

In the middle of the second chorus Juan suddenly stopped. They both waited. A light in a double window above a balcony flashed out in the wall. Outside the tread of the sentry had stopped. They could feel the whole place listening. Someone, Anthony felt sure, had come out on the balcony. He ran back up the steps to look and caught the gleam of moonlight on gold epaulettes. Las Casas was standing on the balcony. Ah, he had thought that was the wrong direction for her room! Juan was singing again.

Suppose after all she should give no sign! How the governor would laugh at him! There was another light now. But not here, not so near the roof. Juan had stopped again. Anthony stood listening. Nothing but his own blood throbbing. Not a sound or a sign from her.

Then at the other end of the patio he heard a faint clapping of hands.

He dashed down the steps and taking the guitar from Juan tried to pick his way as nearly as he could along the path over which Dolores had vanished that afternoon. Presently he saw a light as if from one candle in a room on the second floor. He came out of the palms against the eastern wall of the patio abruptly. There was a dark gate with a heavy, wrought-iron grille just before him. Above that shone the dim glow of the window. Someone was standing there. He could just see her. She was in white with something dark over her hair. He looked up and stirred the strings of the guitar softly. The light tapping of a fan on the windowsill answered him.

"Señorita," he whispered, "I came to say good-bye and to thank you for the rose."

"Is it really yourself, Don Antonio? Where did you find your voice? I have another rose in my hair. Sing again and I will make a little snowstorm of the petals for you."

He came close under the wall and looking up saw her bare arm holding out something over his head. A few white petals

238

floated down like tired moths upon him. Like a beggar he held up his hat for more.

"You are already well paid," she whispered. "No more without another song." He heard her laugh again.

"Ah, Dolores, for the love of God, do not tease me now. Thou knowest I have left my singing voice by the fountain. Roses are not enough tonight."

"You despise my flowers then?" she said.

He came closer under the window and stretched up his arms to her.

"Come down!" whispered.

As if to mock him she let the flower fall onto his breast.

He caught it to him and began to plead with her. A hundred endearing names which he did not seem to have known before leapt from his lips. If she would only come down to him, come down, only for an instant!

"Dolores, Dolores! Do you not know the few minutes we might have with each other in this life are passing? I must go to the other side of the world tonight. Now! In only a few seconds, I must go. Will you only stand there? Come down, Sorrow of the Fountain, do not let my heart die when it is so young. Dolores, Dolores!" He kept whispering her name. Then his voice broke. In the silence that followed he heard her catch her breath sharply above him.

After all he would have to go then without . . . but she was speaking.

"Take the guitar back to your man and tell him to sing . . ."

God! was that all then? After all she . . . he leaned against the wall weakly.

". . . they will think you are still by the fountain then. That will give us a few moments . . ."

Reprieved then!

". . . when you come back I shall be at the little gate below. Hurry!"

The candle in the room above went out. He picked up the guitar and dashed back to Juan. As he stumbled back once more over the little path the voice by the fountain rang out again and went on. She was standing behind the grille in the gate. Her face was outlined in a frame of iron leaves. He put his hands through the tracery and clasped them behind her head, drawing her toward him softly. Only her weight resisted him. For a long minute he kissed her on the mouth. After a while she unclasped his hands. What moved him most was that he discovered she had tears on her cheeks.

His hands sought her through the grille again but she laughed a little and caught him by the wrists.

"Anthony!" she said, still holding him as if pleading for a respite—he could feel her trembling—"you are wearing the wrong kind of sleeve links. See they are pearls!" She held his wrists up in a ray of moonlight. "I should send you away."

"Is it so terrible then?" he asked anxiously. "Tell me, tell me what have I done?"

She came closer again as if she thought he might leave. Presently she was explaining to him with her cheek against his own.

"Don't you know that when a caballero's lady is away from him only carnelians are worn? It is a sign that his heart bleeds. Pearls mean that the innocent one is near." She giggled.

"Mine do not lie then."

"Were you so sure as that?" she exclaimed pretending to try to draw away from him.

"No, no, only my soul dared to hope. And now tell me, tell me for once and all. Was I wrong?"

"Thou knowest," she said and clung to him.

"Promise you will not forget me, Dolores. If I never see you again, even if you know that I am lost, if you are married and I can never even speak to you again, you will not forget that we love each other? If our lips can never say it again, still we shall know. Say it is so. Say, at least, that we can go on remembering. Tell me that if I ever can come to you, you will still be there." He kissed her passionately.

"If you *can*," she said, and looked up at him with the resignation of love in her face. She hid against his breast—"if you ever can."

They stood for a minute as close as they could, with the iron-work cold between them.

"Ah, I am afraid," she whispered, "I am afraid it will always be like this." She reached up and touched the grille that separated them. He cried out and caught her hands to him again, kissing them.

Just then they heard a warning whistle from the fountain.

"You must go!" She thrust his hands out.

"Dolores, I will never see you again!"

"No, no," she exclaimed, "my soul will come back to me!"

He heard a key grate in the lock. The grille swung open and she was on his breast. For a moment the world died to them conclusively. They had abandoned it and taken refuge in each other's arms.

The low, shrill whistle of Juan revived time again. They stood with it ringing in their ears—that keen doom! He cried out an incoherent protest. "Hush!" she said. She kissed him and broke away. He heard the gate clash softly behind her and found himself alone. When he rushed to the grille again she had gone.

"Señor," said the tense voice of Juan, "señor!"

Anthony groaned.

"The governor has sent for you twice. He is coming down the steps now himself. Hurry!"

They rushed back to the fountain. Someone was sitting on the bench smoking a cigar. But to Anthony's great relief it was not the governor but Don Jesús.

"His Excellency has signed the papers and has been waiting to see you," the man said a little grimly. "I trust you will be able to explain to him your presence here? I am responsible, you know, for seeing that no intrusion occurs even by favoured persons!" Don Jesús looked considerably chagrined and eyed Juan in particular with obvious doubt.

"I shall take the entire responsibility on myself," Anthony hastened to say. The man was obviously nettled. "On account of my immediate departure His Excellency has been particularly generous tonight. There were potent reasons. Surely, Don Jesús, as a gallant caballero you will not ask me to *explain!*"

Don Jesús bowed a little coldly but managed to smile. "Permit me to congratulate you on your remarkable voice," he said. He still looked puzzled about something. They mounted the stairs together with Juan behind them. Suddenly, from the direction in which they were going, it became evident that Don Jesús could know nothing of the private stairs.

"So that was why he was angry and perplexed," thought Anthony. Indeed, they went out by the big gate. The commandante glared at the sentry angrily.

"Your man had nothing to do with my entrance," said Anthony. "On my honour! Set your mind at rest." Don Jesús looked instantly much relieved and nodded.

"Very well then," said he. "Señor, I shall wait for you here. We should now be at the dockyard."

Anthony received the papers from Don Esteban who was waiting. He was somewhat more deferential than before.

"His Excellency requested me to wish you"—he looked at a paper methodically—"as good luck and as much favour elsewhere as you have found in Havana."

"Convey my profound gratitude and assurance of devotion to His Excellency," said Anthony. The formal little Spaniard wrote it down. Then he delivered the papers to Anthony, took a receipt and bowed.

"Buenas noches, señor."

"Buenas noches."

Now he was whirling back again along the road to the city beside Don Jesús with Juan on the box. The moon was far west now. It was after three o'clock when the hoofs of their horses echoed under the ancient stone arches of the Maestranza.

———◆———

Don Jesús was no romanticist. He had arrested Brother François in the garden at Regla some hours before with as little compunction as one removes a snail from a flower. He was a Basque, and could any other European have been introduced to what went on inside his head, he would have been amazed at how absolutely four-square and literal was the world which Don Jesús looked out upon. It was this which made him such a magnificent policeman. His arrangements were always *almost* perfect. They included and took into consideration everything "as is." Had he also been endowed with a little imagination he might possibly have become a dictator. But he was not so endowed. Hence, he was merely comandante of gendarmes for General Las Casas; hence, the unexpected was to him enormously puzzling. Why, for instance, had a peaceable parish priest like Father Trajan smitten four of his best bully boys full sore with the stump of an oar last evening when he had arrested Brother François in the garden? And why had Brother François taken the oar from Father Trajan and thrown it away? How silly! He had pondered upon this on the drive from Los Molinos sitting next to the young señor who had entered the patio at the palace apparently through the wall. Altogether it had been a confusing night. He would be glad when it was over. The governor, he thought, had laughed at him—quién sabe?—and even to Don Jesús the deserted dockyards of the Maestranza looked a bit weary under a sinking moon.

Indeed, no building in the New World is so heavy with the futility of the past as the Maestranza. With a wisp of harbour mist drifting through its squat belfry that had tolled the passing of the treasure flotas of Spain, it seemed now in the silence of the tropical night as if Fate were withdrawing her last skein of lucky thread from the eye of a broken needle. Only an occasional stray waif of the royal Spanish navy came here now to refit amid curses out of the doubtful pickings of the past.

The deserted dockyard sloped down to vacant quays piled high with pyramids of whitewashed cannonballs and verdigrised cannon cast long ago from moulds that no longer gave birth to anything. In these guns rats nested, squeaking in the sterile wombs of thunder. Silent rope walks, and towering erections for weaving cordage swung like tattered spider webs against the stars. The watchmen slumbered. Here and there the bow of some abandoned and despairing galleon thrust itself upward at a desperate angle. A reek of low tide, festering pitch, and rotting teak filled the nostrils of Anthony as they threaded the mazes of this nautical cemetery where the bones of a monarchy obtruded from the slime.

At the foot of a flight of broad, stone stairs glimmered a single lantern that marked the presence of their waiting boat. It proved to be a large one rowed by eight manacled negroes. Its passengers were six barefooted gendarmes in broad, cocked hats, and Brother François, who lay bound in the stern sheets.

Anthony exclaimed when he saw him, an exclamation half of indignant pity and half of self-reproach, for in the excitement of his departure and the absorbing events of the hours which had followed the garden party at Los Molinos he had forgotten all about Brother François. So the bishop had been as good as his word! And he, Anthony had forgotten to warn Brother François. He reproached himself bitterly. If it had not been for Dolores . . . ! Now it was too late. The best he could do was to prevail on Don Jesús to loosen the monk's bonds, and he would not even do that till they were well out from the dockyard and rowing down the harbour. Cock-crow had already begun. What a paean it was this morning! Brother François looked at him and smiled. There were red welts on his wrists.

The *Ariostatica* lay across the harbour about a mile away. The barge drifted down upon her easily, swept along by the fast ebbing tide.

"Señor," said Don Jesús, "from now on I am at your disposal. Those are my orders."

Anthony stood up and looked at the beautiful schooner that now loomed up before him like the vague outline of a great swan. His regrets vanished in excitement. He took command jubilantly and with assurance. They stopped rowing and drifted down upon the ship silently.

It was one of those breathless few minutes where much depends upon the simple negative of *not* being heard. The shadow of the graceful slaver stretched out monstrously in the dawn as if the black purpose of the ship with its vast consequences were mystically mirrored in the quiet harbour. Anthony looked down into the clear water and drew back again with a start which he could not entirely control.

Lying perfectly motionless scarcely a fathom beneath the surface with its sinister head pointed toward the stern of the *Ariostatica* was an immense hammerhead shark. It rose slowly toward them as if to see what of interest for it the drifting boat might contain. The sickle curve of its dorsal fin broke rippling from the water. It nosed the planks softly, sending a slight tremor through the barge so that all within it trembled as if the water of the bay itself had transferred to them the message of an earthquake. For a moment they could even see its long, grey flanks disappearing into the belly-pallor beneath. The brown, expressionless walnuts of its eyes on their protruding, transverse sticks looked at the boat and were satisfied. Some promising picture of sharkful hope must have mirrored itself in those black lozenges of pupils for the great fish sounded and turned with a slight phosphorescent glimmer to resume its station. As it did so they had one brief and sufficient glance into its utterly utilitarian mouth.

Don Jesús crossed himself automatically and nervously motioned to the crew to give way. The sound of the oars brought someone to the taffrail of the schooner. The man did not seem to realize at first that they intended to board. Only when they glided up and made fast to the small boat drifted against the schooner's stern did he suddenly straighten himself up.

"Hola, what do you want?" he said sleepily. Then for the first time he became aware of the armed men in the barge and half turned as if to give an alarm. Anthony rose in the stern sheets and covered him with a pistol. The man's jaw fell.

The fellow gaped stupefied at the little circle of the muzzle. The gendarmes swarmed in over the stern and secured the sleepy watch. Except for the pad of bare feet on the empty decks of the schooner there had been no sound. A few sparks were coming from the ship's galley. Brother François sat forgotten in the stern sheets of the barge with the shark just a few feet below and behind him. The slaves' manacles rattled a little as they passed about a single cigar. Anthony and Don Jesús stood on the quarter-deck with the scared individual who proved to be the mate. They looked about them laughing a little. It had been ridiculously easy. The growing dawn made the harbour metallic and the *Ariostatica* rosy. She was theirs— and without even a shout.

"Where's the captain?" asked Anthony of the now sullen mate.

"In the cabin."

"Have the kindness to introduce me, señor," said Anthony. "By the way, what is your own name?" He thrust the man before him down the ladder without ceremony.

"What's that to you?" snarled the mate shaking him off roughly.

"Nothing much to me," said Anthony, "but *this* to you." He gave him a resounding kick in the tail.

They were standing in a low passageway leading aft. A dirty lantern burned there dimly. As the man rubbed his posterior and whimpered, Anthony could hear the rats scuttling in the hold. The fellow was evidently a futile coward. His face was as yellow and undecided as an omelette. Anthony remembered how McNab had dealt with such cattle.

"I have not yet the honour of knowing your name, señor," he said, softly moving toward him again.

"María Magdalena Sóller," the fellow piped promptly enough now, clapping his hands over his derrière again.

"Listen, Mary Magdalen," said Anthony. "From now on I am in command of this ship. Do what I say instantly, and life will be easy for you; fail, and I will kick you loose from your stern. Do you, as it were, understand?" He smiled quietly.

"Sí, señor," whispered the man apathetically. There was nothing in him which even thought of resisting what lay behind the frosty look in his antagonist's blue-grey eyes. Besides, the tall frame, and shoulders of his new commander he now noticed almost filled the passage-way. On the deck he had looked slim and youthful, but not here. Por Dios, what a mule's foot! Under his trousers the mate felt sure he already resembled a pansy bed.

"El capitán está alla," he muttered.

"Captain who?"

"Ramón Lull."

"Bueno! Now go and hang a green light in the starboard shroud," said Anthony. "Have you one?"

"Sí."

"Sí, señor!" prompted Anthony. "And the green light quickly before it gets too light!"

"Sí, señor," repeated the man submissively, and scrambled up the ladder glancing hastily behind him.

Anthony went aft to the end of the passage and thumped on the door. He was amused to see that it was painted a cream-white and had a wreath of roses on its panel; a silver lock.

He looked about him. All the fittings were equally sumptuous. Evidently the *Ariostatica* had been built for a pleasure yacht. There was even an inlaid ebony deck. Christ, how elegant!—and filthy! Someone hummed a snatch of opera in a sleepy falsetto in the cabin. He banged on the door again with a will. A volley of shrill, Majorcan curses oozed through the panels like foul dew from a dirty rose. He gave the door the boot, springing the lady-like, silver lock clear out of kelter, and entered.

A small man in a silk skull-cap, who evidently owned the falsetto voice, for he was exhausting its abusive possibilities, sat up and arranged his night-shirt with the fluttered air of a startled canary. Seeing Anthony was a stranger he stopped and rested two white, smooth hands on the dirty sheet as if they had been paralysed. Behind him on the pillow Anthony could see the face of a quadroon girl with a wave of kinky, dark curls spread behind her like a fan. Save for the dark rosy-tan of her cheeks and the too-heavy lips, it might have been a face from a Greek coin that looked out at him. But the eyes ruined it. They drooped and were heavy-lidded as though tired with looking at a nightmare from which there was no escape. It was the countenance of a ruined angel. For an instant it made him so curiously uneasy that he forgot even the errand he had come upon. Then he laid his pistol and his papers on the table.

"You are the captain of the *Ariostatica*, Don Ramón Lull?" he asked.

The man slipped two thin legs from the covers and thrust his feet into a pair of ridiculously embroidered mules.

"Thou sayest it," he said managing to convey an insult.

"Do not '*thou*' me, thou little man," said Anthony. "Listen to this." He quietly read him the authorization for taking over the *Ariostatica*.

The captain took it very calmly, too calmly in fact. At first his only reply was to hum a few staves of a popular air from time to time. Then he asked a few keen questions.

. . . "I see, I see. I am still captain but you are in command. And the police are now on deck you say?"

"Six of them and the comandante," said Anthony.

"What does Your Magnificence command then? You see this is the first time I have ever been, *ahem*, temporarily sequestrated. I am still a little confused. I am sure Señor Gallego will be as charmed as I am. You will be *royally* received in Africa, señor, as the representative of the crown." He shifted the skullcap back on his head and grinned at Anthony in a way the latter did not like. Evidently Don Ramón would play a waiting game. Anthony determined to strike hard now.

"In the first place, my hospitable friend," said he, "I shall require your cabin for my own use. You will move out of it immediately. Also, even more immediately, you will go on deck and get your ship under way."

"Impossible," said the captain.

"It starts to happen now," said Anthony taking up the letter he had been reading and revealing his pistol under it. "Or—shall I call the comandante?"

The captain's face fell. He looked about him as if for some way out, shrugged his shoulders, and began to put on his clothes. With his shirt pulled half-way over his head he burst into another volley of shrill curses. An invisible little man swearing helplessly in falsetto through a starched frill made Anthony rock.

"Ah, for the love of Mary do not laugh at me, señor," said

Don Ramón reappearing at last with tears of rage in his eyes. "It is bad enough to lose one's ship and one's cabin without being laughed at too!" He whined on a little. "But you will permit me to keep my own cabin boy in the second room. I hope you will, señor," he added plaintively while drawing on his shoes slowly. The girl on the bed stirred uneasily. "You see I am much attached to him and he is my property. I cannot spare him."

"I have my own servant," said Anthony.

"It is a bargain then?" cried the man.

"Certainly," laughed Anthony, glad of peace at so cheap a concession.

The captain began to move about more cheerfully now as if he were well enough satisfied and had made his own terms. He even showed some alacrity and became voluble.

"In a minute, señor, in a minute. Three of the crew are still ashore. But we shall not delay. No, I assure you. I shall be on deck in a minute." He began to put on a pair of preposterous, green, satin breeches. "In five minutes we shall be under way." He put powder in his shoes. "Pollo, rouse yourself! My essence, the new scent bottle, where is it?"

The brown body of "Pollo" now emerged from the berth somewhat sullenly and without a change of countenance, walked over to a chest and after some bending over and rummaging gave the captain a small perfume bottle with a silver top. Anthony sat in astonished silence. If it had not been for the evidence of nature before his eyes he would still have thought that Pollo was a girl. Suddenly an overpowering odor of tuberoses filled the cabin. The captain had removed the stopper from the bottle and was anointing his hair. Anthony got up choking and drove the little man on deck with a hearty curse.

Don Jesús spat over the side and grinned at the apparition from a band box which now began to walk up and down the quarter-deck giving shrill orders and humming operatic airs. The order was repeated each time by a huge negro in a green turban. With much confusion the anchor was finally weighed. Pollo came on deck. Don Jesús spat again.

Anthony stood by the wheel taking it all in. He thought he

had never seen such a sorry crew. There were some truly vil-
lainous faces among them. The best were a few blacks who all
wore turbans.

"I do not envy you, Don Antonio," said the comandante.
Anthony agreed. But he was soon busy enough keeping one eye
on the deck and getting his own boxes on board. Cibo's boat had
arrived. How glad he was Juan was to be with him!

The sails went up by jerks one by one. There was no wind
yet but the tide was taking the ship out. In a few minutes they
would be passing the *Wampanoag* lower down. He climbed
into the shrouds and waited till they were abreast of her.

"Collins," he roared.

A familiar figure lounging by the *Wampanoag's* galley suddenly snapped to and looked about him with amazement.

"Here, Collins! On the schooner!" he cried. Collins ran to
the rail.

"Where be ye bound?" he shouted excitedly.

"Africa!"

"God help ye!"

Captain Elisha came up in his night-shirt. Anthony saw them
talking and getting smaller as the water between the ships widened. The captain cupped his hands.

"Wisht ye was aboard here."

Anthony waved helplessly.

"The Missus sends her regards. She says Lord love ye." He
tried to call something back to them but failed. The captain
waved his old night-cap. "And so say I," he roared.

It was too far to reply now. He could see them still watching
the schooner, and he knew what they were saying about her
sloppy sails. Oh, if Collins were only aboard the *Ariostatica*.
How it would go then!

He leaned over the taffrail and looked astern. Cibo's boat had
cast loose and was making back for Regla. Breakfast on the
veranda—how pleasant that was! He wondered if Dolores were
awake yet, and stood gazing back at the hills about Los Molinos.

The swift ebb at the harbour entrance took the ship and
drew her out to sea. The wind outside filled her sails as she

turned eastward, rising and falling slowly to the ground swell. The two boats that had drifted against her stern paid out behind and were towed along. The shackled rowers in the police barge were already sprawled out on the thwarts, belly down. Brother François was still sitting alone in the stern where he had been left an hour before. He was motionless. Anthony wondered if he was praying. He himself, he remembered, could no longer do so. He was alone now. There was absolutely nothing beyond for him to lean to. Cibo had put the last touch on that. Nothing was left but the world and Anthony. He had his own will and his wits to cope with coming events, and a bargain to keep. He looked back again toward Havana before turning to the deck and its business.

Following the ship a few lengths behind Brother François's barge he saw the black fin of the giant shark which had attached itself to the *Ariostatica*.

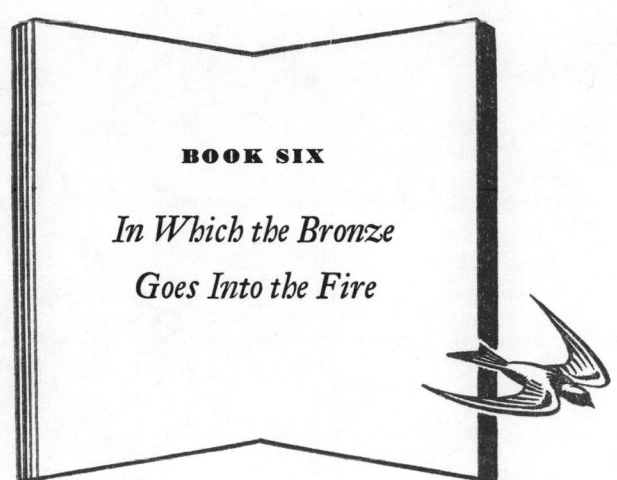

BOOK SIX

*In Which the Bronze
Goes Into the Fire*

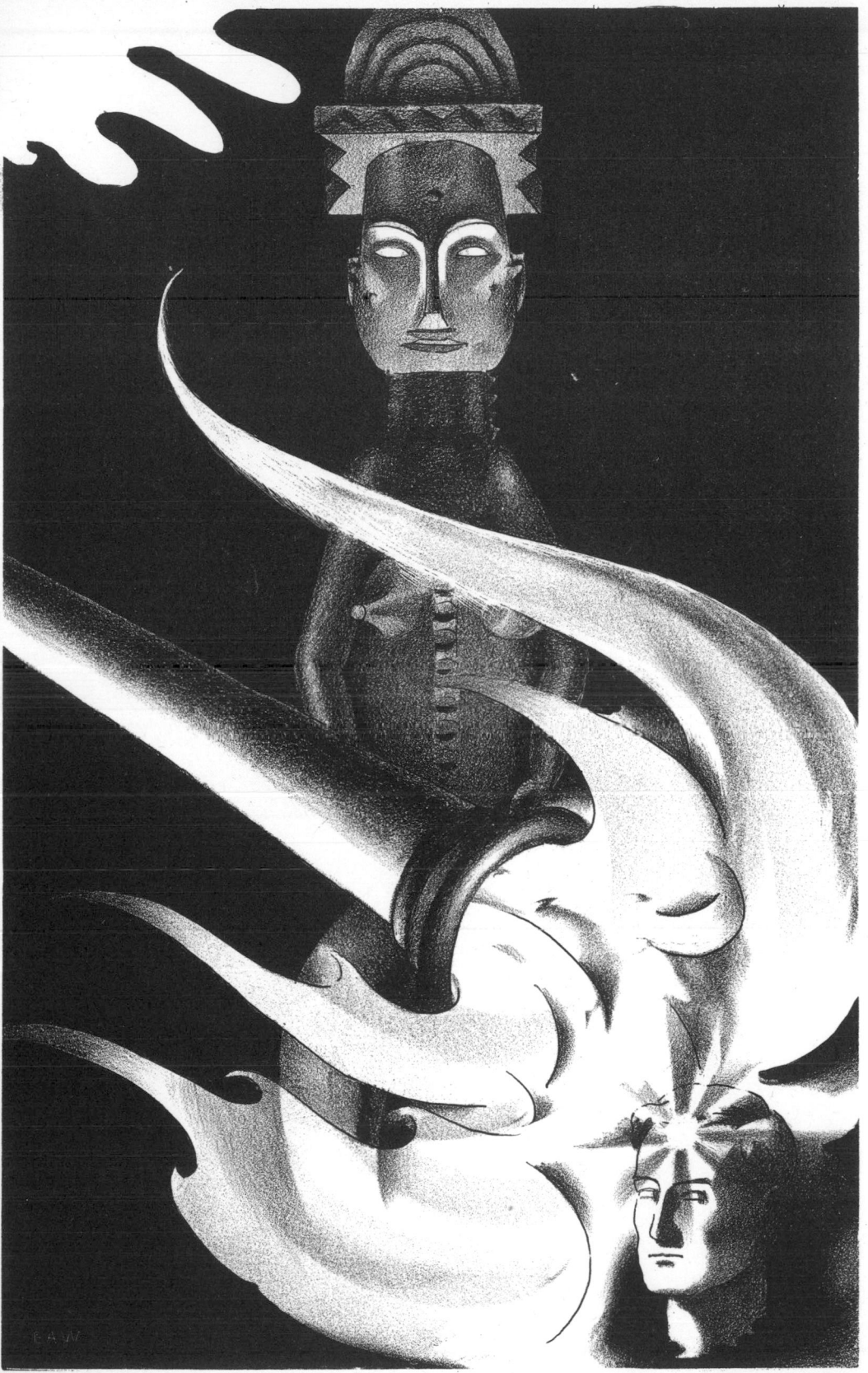

36. A GRADUAL APPROACH TO AFRICA

Nine weeks— and they were only a little south of the Cape Verdes. Much had happened in that time, although outwardly all was the same on the *Ariostatica*. She was a fast little topsail schooner with plenty of space below decks. It was only her dainty lines that made men apply a diminutive to her instinctively. But she had met light, baffling airs from the coast of Puerto Rico onward and had lazed across the broad belt of the world. Only constant showers had kept her crew from running short of water. Some of them were already showing the early symptoms of scurvy.

A thousand miles from land Brother François had come

down with the yellow fever. That and the persistent presence of the shark which had dogged them day and night were for some weeks the chief topics of conversation for the crew. Even the tense conflict which all on board felt to be going on between Anthony and the captain paled into insignificance before the persistence of the indomitable hammerhead who had been dubbed "Old Faithful." Every morning found his black fin in precisely the same relative position as the evening before. At night it moved a little closer. One attempt to hook the monster had all but ended in a catastrophe. After that they let the big fish alone. He seemed to know what he wanted when he followed a slaver.

"When he gets his belly full he'll go," said one of the old hands, "and not until then. But it's white meat he wants eastward ho. He knows. He's an old 'un."

Considerable humorous, but nevertheless nervous and superstitious speculation as to who might provide the tidbit was rife. Several youngsters who were persistently nominated as scapegoats were ready to fight. The sickening of Brother François was to them at least merely a providential designation of Jonah. But to Anthony and Juan, for the young sailor stood by manfully, it meant long hours of perilous nursing and the contemplation of the monk's patient agony.

Brother François had doubtless picked up the infection before leaving Havana, where he had secretly nursed many among those who were always being laid low by what amounted in that port to a perpetual epidemic. So when the headache and lassitude and the muscular pains began the priest was the first to diagnose his own symptoms. The only remedy available was common table salt in water and a purgative. He drank large quantities of the former, disregarding what effect it might have upon hastening the scurvy. Nevertheless, in a few days his condition was pitiable.

The news of the nature of the priest's illness, which could not be concealed, had a peculiar solvent effect upon the miniature world of the *Ariostatica*. Authority backed by a strong hand was the only thing that might have held it together. But in the noble captain, Don Ramón Lull, authority did not reside. He had neither the will nor the courage necessary to enforce it. On the same afternoon that Brother François took to his cabin with Yellow Jack as a bedmate, the realm *Ariostatica* divided into three distinct spheres of influence.

Don Ramón, El Pollo, and the estimable María Magdalena Sóller betook themselves to the quarter-deck where two hammocks swung under a piece of old sail sufficed temporarily for all three. Luckily for them the weather was calm and balmy. Only the shark disturbed their large view of things occasionally. But they did not look his way often. The captain's domestic arrangements might even be described as "nice." He and El Pollo had the double hammock. A small sea chest of the captain's provided with drawers was arranged near by with a silver mounted toilet set on the top. This contrived to confer on the little quarter-deck of the schooner a certain boudoir atmosphere unusual on the Atlantic to say the least. It wanted but one fresh breeze to ruin so fragile and dapper an aspect, but that brisk breeze was long lacking. Such was the first kingdom on the ship where in reality only a titular captain reigned.

The second kingdom was the fo'c'sle, the third was the cabin. The fo'c'sle quarantined both the cabin and the quarter-deck. The quarter-deck had already quarantined the cabin. Mortal fear of contagion, fear made physically visible by the genial presence of "Old Faithful" just astern, was the effective warden of the marches.

Anthony and Juan were left alone, strictly alone, with Brother François in the cabin. Indeed, they had now the entire suite of cabins to themselves and the hold beneath it, although that perhaps, together with the rest of the ship's lower regions, might have been described as the neutral empire of the rats.

In the fo'c'sle seventeen temporarily affable, man-stealing ruffians held forth and carried on in such manner as it pleased them best to do. Their reign of riot was aggravated rather than tempered by the overshadowing influence of one Polyphème, a Gold Coast Frenchman, possessed of one eye and one knife with either of which he could fix his victims suddenly even at a distance. This man was constantly begetting the twins Trouble and Confusion by a process of parthenogenesis.

So it was that in a few hours after it became news the illness of Brother François had produced on the *Ariostatica* a condition of static mutiny. As usual there was not lacking a logical reason. It was believed by all the Christians on the ship that the air, particularly the night air, communicated the contagion. Hence the more air they could place between themselves and him the better for their health. Thus far logic and Christianity. With the Mohammedans in the vessel it was different.

They, as good followers of the Prophet, believed that death would overtake them when Allah willed. For that reason they did not care into what portion of the ship they went, whether it was inhabited by the sick or well. All places were alike to them equally exposed to the unreasonable arrows of fate. Hence, as universal prisoners they remained free. The practical conduct of the ship soon fell almost entirely into their hands by pure force of circumstance. Captained by the giant Arab negro, Ali Bongo, they went where common sense and the occasional frantic voice of Don Ramón demanded. That the captain still delivered orders from the quarter-deck, some of which were still obeyed, either through necessity or caprice, was the chief reminder of the formal order of nautical life. Señor Sóller, the mate, made daily observations and marked his charts there. There the four Mohammedans also did their tricks at the wheel in regular succession, oblivious of everything but the double wages hastily promised them.

For this essential service they were despised by the free spirits of the fo'c'sle and carefully shunned as possible carriers of contagion. For in quarantining itself from the quarter-deck, the fo'c'sle had by no means been oblivious to certain privileges and exemptions which Polyphème had pointed out would ensue. These were now enjoyed to the uttermost. Any semblance of regular watches was given up. Cards, quarrelling, and boozy slumber were now the order of both day and night. The only systematic labour actually indulged in was the plundering of the ship's stores in the main hold. When the languid breeze shifted, a few of the crew sometimes condescended to trim the forward sails, but nothing more. The only exceptions to this delightful state of relaxation were the cook and his boy, who were reconsecrated to continue their usual labour by general acclamation and the violent laying on of hands.

Thus the drifting *Ariostatica* grew more and more a slattern day by day. Her standing rigging soon hung slack. Rubbish accumulated on her decks. Even primary sanitary suggestions from the quarter-deck were met by jeers. Food in wooden kids was shoved at the officers through the quarter-deck railing, and the cook retired. The same mess-kids were afterwards towed overboard in a bucket. Unfortunately the weather continued to favour this lax state of existence. Half the time it was dead calm or there were only fainthearted, little breezes interspersed with warm rains. About a hundred yards behind the ship "Old Faithful" battened on the unusually succulent garbage which now came his way. A small folding chair which Don Ramón hurled overboard in a rage went the same way and did not even produce a flurry.

Meanwhile, Brother François was tended by Anthony and Juan in the cabin. In the general state of affairs which had so unexpectedly developed Anthony felt himself temporarily helpless. The captain, indeed, did not fail to blame him for having weakened his authority. He frequently sat safely at the top of the hatch and expressed himself on the subject of divided authority with a laxative fluency. That there was some truth in Don Ramón's profane complaints Anthony recognized. But it was also evident to him that the captain was glad of the excuse and loaded upon its back all the blame for the trouble which the man's own weaknesses had brought about. And then there was another curious thing about Don Ramón; having once relieved his mind, he would return happily to the quarter-deck. There, despite his ridiculous position, he managed, as Anthony could tell from the noises that went on just over his head, to have a genuine good time.

For through the deck planks percolated into the cabin, where Brother François lay, the mild strumming of a guitar at night, the soft pad of the feet of El Pollo in some heathenish dance, and the falsetto of Don Ramón raised in song. Such lyric outbursts were often greeted from the fo'c'sle with an applause in which sarcasm and genuine appreciation were inextricably mixed. In the sound of that mixture of vivas, howls, and catcalls, Anthony recognized what was the real strength of his rival. He understood from that bad noise that while Don Ramón might be temporarily isolated, there was yet a certain sense of brotherhood between him and the fo'c'sle, a bad admiration for his open and unabashed enjoyment of an unmoral existence.

Don Ramón's, indeed, was a simplicity of evil which those who still suffered from dregs of conscience might well envy and admire. Between men who were ambitious to be abandoned and to prosper by it, it was a bond. In any crisis Anthony felt that the captain and the fo'c'sle would be found united against him. And he began to understand, too, that Don Ramón was cunning.

Perhaps his indulgence of the crew while the *Ariostatica* drifted to Africa through the doldrums was, under the circumstances, somewhat calculated. Don Ramón expected to reap his own advantage from it when the time came. It was a little plainer now why the owners had confided a ship to a man like Don Ramón. Perhaps they knew their own trade well enough to understand that the ideal captain of a slaver was one who had no squeamishness at all. At any rate the captain would find his advantage in confusion while Anthony could only prevail by bringing about an order in which legal authority would be recognized. That was the problem. Whether the crisis would arise during the voyage or upon their arrival at Gallego's slave barracoon at Bangalang, he could not tell. He must use his wits. That was all he had to depend upon. He had already taken precautions against purely sneaking violence. He and Juan went well armed and Don Ramón and Sóller knew it. That was that. Neither of them, he felt, would risk his own precious skin. Meanwhile, the captain and Sóller played cards on the quarter-deck, hoping that "yellow jack" would solve their difficulties by removing all the unwelcome intruders in the cabin.

That was another reason why the "quarantine" was so rigidly enforced.

"How do you like your temporary sequestration now?" grinned Señor María Magdalena Sóller down the hatchway. "It might be a permanent one, you know." He shrugged his shoulders. Ali Bongo was instructed to resist any possible émute from the cabin.

It certainly seemed likely that Brother François at least would leave the ship. There were small means at hand for detaining him. As the fever ran its inevitable gamut, Anthony sat by the priest's bunk doing the best he could. Compared with this trial his experience on the *Wampanoag* had been nothing.

"Certainly," he thought, "I have no reason to be in love with ships. I have strange luck there. It goes better with me on land." And for a time it went badly enough. He and Juan settled themselves as best they could to live through the state of siege. After that? . . . "But sufficient unto the day . . ." Anthony told himself. Certainly it was all weird enough. Temporarily shoving his own problem aside, which it was plain might wait while the good weather lasted, he and Juan devoted themselves day and night to Brother François.

They carried him out of the dark, little hole at the end of the passageway, where he had been contemptuously dumped by Don Ramón, into the big stern cabin from which the captain and his ami had been excluded. A large window of leaded bull's-eyes set in a kind of battened casement ran clear across the stern. After two o'clock the place was flooded with sunlight. There was still a vile, faded carpet with an obscure coat of arms on the floor. There was also a large stain in one corner, deeper than all the others, about which ugly stories were still told.

The *Ariostatica* was a woman with a past. She had been built at Marseilles for a rich and recently ennobled banker some years before the Revolution. She had been called *La Vénus du Midi* then. It was said that on a cruise to Naples her first owner had murdered his mistress—in proof of which there was the stain. The story had followed the ship persistently. She had soon ceased to be an instrument of luxury, and after several evil vicissitudes had fallen to the Spanish slave trade cheaply enough.

Hence there was something undoubtedly sinister about the now queasy luxury of her cabins in which those silver fittings which had not been wrenched loose or battered away still glimmered through a film of filth.

Anthony and Juan did their best to remedy this by such cleansing as they could contrive. But even in his misery when Brother François was first carried into the place he sensed its atmosphere.

The Gallic humour of a ci-devant man of the world glimmered in his eyes as he lay looking at the bourgeois cupids romping in sooty roses on the smudgy, blue ceiling. It amused him to think he was being brought to die in an apartment faintly reminiscent of Don Ramón's tuberose perfume, a cabin whose upholsterer must have had about him a touch of debased genius, for he had managed to relate in a series of damask panels the innocent story of *Paul and Virginia* in a highly interesting way. The story had even been given a happy ending.

Just over the ship's bed that Brother François now occupied, Paul and Virginia were to be seen in that full consummation of their love which the too-pure and tragic pencil of their author had originally denied them. That such art is universal, the smudges and prints of the dirty hands of the slaves who had been packed into the cabin on the *Ariostatica's* last voyage from Africa testified in a truly touching way.

The hand of one huge negro seemed to have striven to tear the body of Virginia from the panel. And through a hundred other wishful blotches wandered the traces of a pair of wistful and delicate finger tips which Anthony thought he recognized as those of the youthful El Pollo, the chicken. Anthony imagined he could see that arch youth locked in the cabin during his master's absence trying to seize from the panel what Don Ramón had denied him.

All this amused Brother François, for even in his approaching agony he still continued to be French. When he was carried into the cabin he managed to smile gallantly and to remark to Anthony that a happy ending to every story was what the multitude always desired.

"See," said he, pointing to the panel above him. "They have tried to tear love out of the panel of imagination and to make it real enough to handle with their poor dirty hands. Yet it remains apart. Comedy, you see, is what this unhappy age demands. Once I wrote about such things as that. It was long before the Revolution, before I had entered into real life. *Paul and Virginia* then was still thought to be charming." He sighed and settled back with an air of finality into the blowzy pillows.

"Well, I shall *try* to live up to my own criticism by making a proper end of it here. If not, pardon me for the trouble I am about to give you, mes amis."

Even then the fever was already upon him. He was talking in the accents of some former self. It seemed to be a soldier rather than a monk who lay there. But that was only momentary. He looked out of the stern windows along the wake of the drifting ship and at the tilting blue line of the horizon beyond. Through the bubbles a little behind the ship nosed the apocalyptic countenance of the shark like an obscene emanation from the bottomless deep. To the priest's now disordered imagination it seemed that the shark's mouth was so framed as to be able to utter only the word "Golgotha." He closed his eyes. Then he opened them at sunset, seeming to be able to gaze with a wide-pupilled, feverish glance out of his shadowed sockets into the red orb itself. The last thing he saw in the brief twilight was the shark which had moved a little nearer. He shivered.

"Men would be like that, my son, if God had not given them mercy."

They were the last words he addressed consciously to Anthony before the fever clutched his mind awry. He then seemed to be using his remaining conscious minutes to pray.

"If possible let this cup be taken from me . . . Nevertheless . . ." he muttered. He motioned to close the window and shut out the vision astern. They lit a dim lamp. "Let the Comforter be with us here, my Father. Where two or three are gathered together in Thy name . . . Thou rememberest . . ." After that he held converse only with unseen things.

Yet such was the vital and moving spirit of this man that even in the days of delirium which ensued his personality expanded and dominated by a kind of vibrant quality, not only Anthony and Juan, but the dowdy appurtenances of the cabin itself. Anthony found it impossible to explain this impression to himself by this and that or here and there. It was too subtle to isolate, but it was not too intangible to feel. The quality of the man's being, now strangely released, as if by the heat of the fever, evoked in those near him a continuous state of high emotion. In this condition they were able to glimpse and even to share to some extent in the exaltation in which it was now revealed to them Brother François must habitually dwell. Anthony, indeed, wondered now at the calm exterior of the man even when his health had endured.

For that which dwelt in Brother François seemed to be coloured like, and to move with the speed and force of the flame that jags from sky to earth. Yet there was nothing momentary about it. Like the vision of that flame seared upon the eyeballs it remained. It was not ephemeral. It was the natural state and condition of the man uncovered. Anthony could apprehend now why it was that the strong body of Brother François, despite its calm exterior, had seemed to be worn and emaciated from within. Recollecting him now as he had been at Regla, he found that his mental impression of him was that of something which emanated light. Perhaps he had been wrong in attributing all that quality to the vine alone.

How wonderful must be the strength of that gentleness which kept such vivid potentialities in control! Whence came the ability to poise and balance them? No wonder the world was afraid of such men! No wonder everyone from the captain-general to the philosophic Cibo had been disturbed! Had they felt a vesicle of lightning near? Suppose this force had been released to irradiate a community, what then? Anthony sat looking at him—where he lay apparently dying in the murdered harlot's bunk—lost in wonder, oblivious to all else.

For the drama of this spirit even in dissolution made all else seem trivial; ordinary life flaccid. Even though the light of this man was now dimmed by the dark heat of his dreadful fever, though the lightning motions of his thought were disordered by illness; while he lay thus revealed by the weakness of the body, stripped spiritually naked, no one near him could pay attention to anything else.

"I am thy lamp," he muttered once, "behold the flame consumes the oil of me. Let it be acceptable."

After that he no longer seemed to realize his own predicament. Through days of sustained delirium he tended only gradually toward a state of exhausted unconsciousness. Not until the third night was the crisis passed. Then the collapse came suddenly.

During this infernally and celestially illuminated period there were few niches of Brother François's past experience which a nursing listener was not forced to explore. From the total-recall which streamed incoherently from the monk's parching lips Anthony was eventually able to reconstruct for himself the order of time and place which the delirium ignored. To the parentless listener even the man's childish babble and talk with his mother was breathless with a mysterious sweetness.

At some château in Picardy the two walked through an orchard and spoke of the birds. In a field placed only in space he plucked flowers again with a shy little girl. "Laugh again, Adèle, laugh again," cried Brother François rising up to listen. "Here are daisies for your apron. I have never forgotten you. I knew you were not really dead. Here are the flowers. See, they are fresh still,"—and he plucked at the foul bedclothes. Then there was his gay but stern father, whose ridicule was smooth as polished adamant. "But it is here among our own people that I belong, mon père." In those days it seemed Brother François had besought God to assure him he was not mad. It had been revealed to him that he was more fully sane than those about him. This it seemed was the cross he found hardest to bear. He was always pleading with the "blind," always. Versailles had been horrible. They were all blind there.

On the second night in the midst of much vacant converse Brother François became almost lucid again. In a flood of semi-coherent eloquence he was once more accompanying the tumbrils on their way to the guillotine. Not a few of the blind eyes of which he had complained were then opened for a last look at life. The exhausting tension, the fierce ebullitions of frantic souls, the last tender confidences—words spoken to those who clung to him desperately for even a glint of hope—these were all fiercely renewed as the days of the Terror became incandescent again in the monk's fevered brain. Anthony seemed to feel the lean shadows of the buildings in the Paris streets falling across him as he rode in the carts with Brother François and the doomed.

In the chill lamplight of the cabin, silent except for the metallic cadences of the dying man's voice and the faint wash of the waves below, these scenes took on for Anthony far more than the vague outlines of a conversation. He participated in them fully and yet mystically as if at a distance. The endless monodrama went on interminably with all of the amazing detail of the mind which never forgets released again into life.

Clenched hands, weapons, impassioned faces tossed up in the words of the priest. Out of the sea of the streets came things which had long forgotten themselves. With Brother François Anthony overlooked the plains, the heights, and the abysses revealed by impassioned men and women about to vanish. He faced with them the thunder of drums, the prayers, pleadings, weeping; the laughter, the snarls, and the screams of the final act. "Ascend to heaven; son of St. Louis"—drums, and a tempest of jibes. One needed to have had faith, a true exaltation, to believe after that.

For the first time the desperate human necessity for hope beyond; the impossibility of rejecting it entirely when the whole being is really faced with the final riddle was flung into Anthony's face.

From such scenes the soul of Brother François seemed to turn with paternal fondness—as if on a visit to a beloved daughter and her children—to the people and the sylvan neighbourhood of his first beloved parish. For a while his spirit had found itself at home there as a pastor of peasants. His assumed patois itself was touching. His homely dialogues were compounded of a wise pathos, laughter, and tears. In all this, and in physical and mental intimacies beyond trace, intimacies which resided in the tones of his voice and the lines of his face—in all of them now poured out for hours on end like the seemingly rational talk of a madman, he seemed to be speaking only from the depths of some impersonal self.

Himself he did not remember, although he was occasionally vaguely aware of Anthony and of Juan. They bent over him giving him drink now and then. They rearranged his pillows and covers a thousand times. They plied him with a little food which he long refused. They even held him down. Once he caught Anthony's face between his burning palms and exclaimed:

"I have seen you before. Yes, I know who you are. It was in the face of that girl at the coach window that night at the inn that I first saw you. Do you know her? Her husband killed the young man in the courtyard. You remember? Surely you will remember what happened to yourself! That Spaniard with the virility of great evil about him who drove away with her into the night—he is still driving somewhere, I know. Driving! Such men go on and on. It is a great circle they move upon. Be careful, he will return! Remember! Tell him I buried the young man. He looked noble even in the pit. Only his horse missed him. No one ever came. Ah, do you know there is more in that than you can see! I am sure of it."

He rehearsed the scene again and again. A duel in some forgotten inn courtyard sprang into life. Swords clashed in the twilight while a woman looked on. Brother François bore witness to the saints against murder. "And don't you remember?" he kept asking Anthony—"and don't *you* remember?"

But Anthony did not remember. The tablets of the past were razed for him. Even Brother François could not recall what the doors of birth had closed upon. Death might reveal them again, perhaps.

Overhead the strings of Don Ramón's guitar sometimes purred softly. The eternal sound of water gurgling about the rudder washed in from astern. The long light of sunset after an interminable white afternoon lit the little cabin redly. From it, all that was banal and trivial now seemed to have been banished. Anthony saw nothing but the blue leagues astern marching to the horizon and the burning eyes of Brother François in his bed against the bulkhead.

The sick man had now slipped from all reminiscence and was conversing with someone whom he saw standing in the cabin. So strong was his own delusion that those who were nursing him could scarcely keep from sharing it. They no longer dared to cross where the last patch of sunlight slowly lessened about the centre of the cabin floor. From this presence the transported man derived an infinite comfort. An actual physical change for the better crept into his face. He no longer moaned as he talked in whispers but grew calmer. When Anthony brought him some water he drank it eagerly for the first time.

"Courage," he whispered, "courage! See! I can take the cup now. Yes, I will go. I will drink it all." He fell back again and spoke no more in words. The collapse had come. It would be some hours, Juan said, before they would know whether he would live or die.

From then on it was only the sick man's body that spoke. It seemed to have been left to conduct the fight alone. Its rumours of internal and external wars and troubles were terrible. The black throat and tongue bleated. The contorting muscles exacted from the breath which passed them with difficulty a continuous toll of unseemly sound. The nose, which was now growing peaked, collapsed flabbily about the nostrils, threatening to act as a fatal flutter valve unless the mouth gasped to relieve it. The bowels and stomach banished with bestial rumblings and hellishly humorous whistles from mouth and fundament gusts which all but overcame the two unwilling and horrified auditors imprisoned in the same cabin. It was necessary to rush again and again to the stern window to escape from a stench which anticipated the grave. And all this was only air.

At midnight what was now only the frame or case of Brother François, who had long been unconscious, rallied itself for a last essay. The fever mounted and became intolerable. Then from every possible vent of the body poured the liquids which discharged its disease—a clear vomit that finally became black, floods of urine darkly clouded and in unbelievable quantities, an irruption of bloody stools, a viscid stream from the nose.

With all this the two faithful nurses could not cope fast enough. They laid the discharging object on a succession of bedclothes on the floor and from time to time flung the clothes overboard. It was not the least of the trials of this night-of-nights that the shark ranged nearer and engulfed all that they threw into the sea. Terrified and sick, Anthony saw the indifference of nature.

It came upon him that the life of the shark was the same as that in the body of Brother François on the floor. Certainly what he knew as Brother François was in abeyance. He could not look upon the animated corpse of matter that now lay on the dirty carpet and still call it the man he had known. Something was withdrawn, he thought. What remained had only the life of the fleshly machine that laboured on. In the body of the man that animal life was weak and sickly; in the body of the fish it was horribly vigorous. But it was the same. One fed upon the other. Both bodies profited by the unspeakable exchange.

Early in the morning the body of the man seemed to deflate itself and collapse. It was the *stadium* of the fever, which now died away. They forced some wine through its lips. They wrapped the thing on the floor in blankets, for it now threatened to turn cold, and put it back in the bed. Nothing more could be done. The skin was smooth and dry and yellow, the eyes closed. They themselves, revolted and exhausted to the verge of staggering weariness, sat down in chairs and slept. When they wakened in the damp heat of the little cabin, Brother François had returned.

"Water, my friends," he whispered. "I am still with you again for a while!"

Anthony looked at him and wept. What now contained Brother François seemed like a parchment lantern in which only a feeble candle burned. Yet as days went on the light there grew stronger.

It had not been easy for Anthony and Juan to subsist themselves during this time. Without the negro Ali Bongo, and the chests which Cibo had contributed, they must have perished. From Ali Bongo, who was now the only person on the ship who would even hand them objects through the cabin hatch, they received water and occasional warm slops prepared by the cook. From the chests of Cibo came certain dainties, wines, and a few preserved delicacies that had probably saved the monk's life. Cibo had not been a fancy grocer in vain. Anthony now looked through these chests, which had been deposited in the hold beneath the cabin, and was amazed at the variety of useful articles and comfortable comestibles that they contained.

In this dark hold, while the monk's convalescence progressed, Anthony began to meet Ali Bongo who enjoyed pickles so much he would even risk his life for them. Here in the close atmosphere raw with bilge, over a candle, in the darkness of the ship's midriff where the beams and timbers obtruded internally in ribbed shadows, he and the black Mohammedan discussed the predicament of the *Ariostatica* and arrived after a week's time at a certain understanding.

Ali Bongo was a primal but sensible character. In the plan which Anthony proposed he saw certain advantages to himself and his fellow Foulah tribesmen which would not accrue to them by their merely remaining loyal to the ostensible captain of the ship. A present of one of Cibo's silver mounted pistols sealed the bargain and carried a fierce delight to the savage self-importance of Ali Bongo's practical soul. Here was a señor who knew better than to treat one who had been to Mecca like a slave. "By Allah, he would soon be a chieftain again!" He concealed the pistol in the folds of his sash and returned smiling to the deck. The only eye which noted the bulge at his waist, and drew its own conclusions, was the single one of Polyphème. That worthy concluded that objects of value were to be obtained by visiting the cabin hold.

The quarter-deck was somewhat nonplussed not to say disgruntled at the new aspect of affairs. Not only was it evident that neither Anthony nor Juan was going to be obliging enough to die; Brother François was actually getting well. He and his two companions now came on deck together. Their first appearance there gave rise to a violent altercation with the captain and the mate. The crew looked on afar-off with considerable interest, and did not fail to note that over the captain's bluster Anthony quietly carried his point. An appeal by Don Ramón to Ali Bongo, who was then at the wheel, found that tall heathen neutral. Brother François was carried up every day thereafter to sit in a cushioned chair near the stern. Anthony and Juan moved about as they liked, although constantly warned to leeward by the captain and mate who kept up their sanitary bluster.

Whether this bluster was sincere or fictitious now Anthony could not for a time be certain. Certainly both captain and mate were afraid of the yellow fever. But it was not long before it became pretty plain to everybody that Brother François's illness was being used as a thin excuse for a policy of isolation which had in view another end than that of health. What the fo'c'sle wanted, of course, was license. Why the captain also persisted in treating the cabin as if it were still a pesthouse was revealed strangely enough by the stars.

Anthony was now able to come on deck and renew his own observations. It was instantly clear to him that the position of the ship as marked on the navigating chart by Sóller did not correspond with fact. According to Sóller the *Ariostatica* was about one hundred leagues off the coast of Sierra Leone opposite Freetown. Anthony found her, after taking a lunar to check his longitude, at about 20 North and 30 West. A day's run further convinced him they were making for the Cape Verde Islands.

No doubt at Praia it was Don Ramón's plan to make port, hoist a signal of distress, and land those whom he would certify as convalescent to the authorities. There would certainly be a Lazar house at Praia. Who the "convalescents" would be, Anthony had small doubt. The schooner might have to lie in the roads for some days to accomplish this. But it would be too neat a way for Don Ramón to rid himself legally of his unwelcome passengers to be neglected. The Portuguese would pay small attention to Anthony's Spanish letters. It would be a fine thing to have all his high hopes end in quarantine in some filthy jail or dismal convent. The situation must be met instantly.

First making sure of Ali Bongo and his followers, who saw an end to their own expectations should the ship leave Anthony at the Cape Verdes, he approached the captain next morning on the quarterdeck as near as that nervous gentleman would permit. Don Ramón and Sóller were as usual playing cards. After some bluster they were forced to stop and listen while he pointed out to them the lamentable discrepancy between the ship's true position and the chart.

Anthony had now some time to study the captain. He had come to the conclusion that under almost any circumstance Don Ramón would do the easiest thing. It was a natural conclusion drawn from his cowardice and indolence. If one ruse was uncovered he would simply go on to another. "Anything to avoid bringing things to an issue," would be the captain's motto. In this case he therefore supplied him with an easy way out of the predicament.

He simply assumed that the calculations of Sóller had been in error. Nor did he neglect to salve that individual by mentioning that even an expert navigator and calculator frequently went astray through some fault in the instruments. That so accurate a mathematical mind as Señor Sóller's, an expert card player too, could have made an error of more than seven degrees in latitude was unthinkable. It was the instrument that was at fault! Perhaps it would be just as well hereafter to make use only of his own? At any rate, he himself intended to do so!

The captain and the mate turned a bit green at thus hearing their little plan dusted out. The mate was even inclined to argue. Armed with his data, however, Anthony was firm. He pointed out the imminent danger of shipwreck on the island reefs if the present course were continued. He assumed that it would not be, and laid out the correct one.

"The captain," he said after a little pause, "will be pleased to give the proper directions to the man at the wheel."

An interval of tense silence ensued. Don Ramón's hand remained trembling slightly upon a card which he had been about to play after a quarter of an hour's consideration. Anthony continued to look at him and smile.

"Don Ramón will recollect that by the letters issued under the seal of the captain-general I am empowered to direct the course of this ship. Through the captain if *possible*. It would be a pity if I were forced to take matters into my own hands." He leaned forward touching the pistol in his belt. The captain looked up and saw Ali Bongo grinning; Juan sauntering by.

Don Ramón scattered the cards from the board with an oath and gave the orders to Ali Bongo at the wheel. Sweeping almost a quarter circle down the horizon, the bow of the *Ariostatica* turned south.

For the rest of the morning the skipper and his mate muttered together pretending to be trying to reconstruct their game. Perhaps they were. What conclusions they arrived at Anthony did not know, nor did he much care. In the first crucial test he had come off triumphant. This was the ninth week out. The Rio Pongo, if the breeze held, could be only a few days away. In those few days he must get the ship into his own hands. It was the breeze, and Polyphème the single-eyed, that came unexpectedly to his aid.

A few hours after the interview with the captain, Polyphème was caught red-handed plundering the chests stowed in the cabin hold. Wine and fine biscuit being enjoyed by the fo'c'sle had aroused the suspicions of Ali Bongo. Hasty investigation showed that about half the wine and spirit from Cibo's precious little store in the hold had already gone. Anthony and Juan took turns at sentry-go there. The bulkheads in the schooner were only temporary and somewhat flimsy. On return voyages the entire space was given up to packing in the bodies of slaves. All barriers were then removed. The place was hot and stank of bilge, negroes, sulphur and vinegar, the last two having been used to cleanse it after a manner in Havana. Sitting there for three hours at a time was no joke. How the slaves endured it for weeks on end Anthony could not imagine. But he had his reward.

During his second trick as sentry he heard the sound of bare feet approaching the bulkhead on the far side. There were a few stealthy shufflings and a loose plank in the bulkhead was removed. A man's body came through the opening. Presently the fellow produced flint and steel, lit a candle—and found himself looking down the pistol of Señor Adverse. It was impossible not to admire Polyphème a little then. The expression on his face did not even change.

Anthony made him crawl ahead of him through the hatch into the cabin. That was a mistake, as he soon found. He should have called for Juan. He kept the man covered. But as he himself emerged from the drop which led into the little passage above, the fellow dodged like a lizard, and threw a knife. It had been aimed for the heart and it pinned the inner edge of Anthony's left sleeve to the combing. Seeing he had failed, and that the pistol still looked at him, the prisoner fell on his knees and began to plead. From the expression on his captor's face he was afraid his time had come. And in this he was not far wrong. If he had made one move to escape, the finger on the trigger would have squeezed. His one eye rolled now and he squealed.

Anthony locked him in an empty cabin and stood by a few minutes longer while Juan fitted him with irons from the ample supply provided for slaves. No one said anything. It had all been enormously easy, Anthony thought. Those on the quarter-deck had not even been disturbed in their siesta. Warning Polyphème that any noise on his part would bring Ali Bongo with a whip, Anthony pocketed the key and went on deck.

He was delighted with himself for several reasons. The capture of Polyphème in so ignominious a manner was an enormous stroke of luck. More important, however, was a discovery about himself. In situations of great danger he did not grow weak and tremble; he became strong from anger. Even better than that, he did not get confused. The nerves he had inherited were good ones. What an inestimable gift! He had actually been so much in command of himself even when the knife came as not to shoot.

How curious it was that things like this should be happening to *him!* A man had actually thrown a knife at him! He looked at Brother François sitting back weakly in his chair near the stern. He was lost in another world, poor man! But Anthony— Anthony was a part now of events. He felt he could not even afford to talk too much with Brother François. No, Anthony was doing things! Let them be done then. He felt suddenly sure of himself. He could bend those about him to his own ends. Don Ramón dozing, curled up in the shadow of a boat, filled him with contempt. Certainly he could outwit that man! He turned suddenly hearing Ali Bongo calling to him from the wheel. The man was pointing astern. Some miles away a white squall was tearing down upon them, lines of white caps racing before it.

Anthony began to shout warnings and orders to take in sail. Juan hustled Brother François below. Ali Bongo and his men stripped the mainmast while Anthony stood by at the wheel. He meant to bring the ship to, but the confusion in the fo'c'sle prevented him. Instead of lowering away there, an argument ensued and the foresail was reefed and set again. Ali Bongo danced with rage. A few confused people were fumbling on the topsail downhauls when Don Ramón sat up and confounded everything twice over by countermanding the orders already given. Missing Polyphème, the men forward were at hopeless odds among themselves. While she was in this state of provocative déshabille the squall romped down uproariously upon the *Ariostatica*. Luckily Anthony did not try to throw her up into the wind now. He let her drive.

Even under the reefed foresail the schooner keeled over so far as to ship combers down the hatches. The jibs and loose square-topsail beat about for a few seconds like the wings of a frantic roc and then literally leapt clear of the bolts to disappear ahead in a smother of foam. The rigging shrieked. Anthony saw the eyeballs of the entire ship's company bent upon him at the wheel. "Let go the foresheet," he roared. It was fouled! Ali Bongo crawled forward and hacked it with a knife. The boom swept around like a whip lash against the lee shrouds, knocking four of the gaping men cold. Ali Bongo rolled into the scuppers. For a minute the *Ariostatica* shivered.

Then she slowly rose righting herself and slipping off the tons of green water that had nearly foundered her. Amidships there was a lake where the cook and a large pot floated about with ashes and firewood. Then the bulwarks gave way there releasing the load. The ship bolted ahead like a whipped horse.

By some miracle the reefed foresail held. More surprising yet El Pollo ran forward and lashed the boom to the shrouds. Holding with all his might against the spokes Anthony was just able to keep the schooner from broaching to. With the aft sails and the jib gone, the drag of the foresail against the helm was terrific. Presently two of the Foulah tribesmen came and relieved him at the wheel which gave him a brief opportunity to look about.

He turned to find Don Ramón standing behind him with his legs spread apart and his hands behind his back. It looked as if through the whole crisis the captain had been coolly giving him orders. Thus it was that with most of the men on the fo'c'sle Don Ramón secured the credit for having saved the ship.

For an instant Anthony was overcome by rage. He felt himself losing control of his feet and hands. A mad impulse to kick the preposterous little hypocrite clear off the deck and down the hatchway all but mastered him. Then he determined to make use of the captain's cunning for his own ends.

Seeing the man was really at a loss what to do, he descended upon him and taking him unawares, half by threats in an undertone and by loud firm suggestions, forced him to continue in the false part which he had assumed. Before two hours passed Captain Ramón Lull had, as it were, been rushed off his feet into the command of his own ship again.

Anthony was greatly aided in this process by the reappearance of Ali Bongo who arose from under a chicken coop in the scuppers as if from the dead, but with a large cut over one eye. His countenance was rendered sufficiently ferocious by blood and swelling to work miracles by itself. If any had been washed overboard it yet remained to be seen. The crew at any rate thought that Polyphème had gone that way. Without a leader they were temporarily reduced to the condition of somewhat stubborn but confused sheep.

Under the inspired, piping falsetto of the captain, who by some miracle they did not understand was now issuing sensible orders, a new jib was broken out and bent on. The ship felt the relief sensibly and no longer threatened to lay to. Axes were produced and some wreckage on the fo'c'sle cleared away. Anthony took the risk of the tools' being turned to weapons. From the fo'c'sle the men were worked aft. Even the mate joined in and exerted his authority. "Under a decent captain he might have done well enough," thought Anthony. A small area of the mainsail was now shown to the wind and the crew assigned to the mainmast were put to work on the quarter-deck without further ado. The tempest, indeed, with its more pressing problems had banished the fear of plague from their minds.

The squall blew itself out rapidly. By twilight they were sweeping along under a fine following breeze. The regular watch was called and those who failed to answer were used roughly enough. With a few curses and some grumbling the crew found themselves somehow at their stations, and discipline was enforced through the remainder of the night. At dawn Don Ramón was roused too, to his vast disgust. It was a final test. Juan stood behind him with a pistol, hidden by the mast. The captain was forced to issue orders to clean decks. Some of the crew came forward at this unparalleled insult in an arrogant mood. The turbaned Foulahs descended upon them from the quarter-deck armed with the belaying pins and began to crack heads. It was enough.

When the sun rose it beheld the decks of the *Ariostatica* holystoned. The ropes were neatly coiled and the brass binnacle glittered. Anthony's ideal of the deck of the *Wampanoag* with Collins and a rope-end skipping about it was at least approached. If there had only been a little paint! The yachtishness of the *Ariostatica* emerged from years of grime. "Sacred blood of a sow," said a pimply-faced Frenchman spitting on the deck surreptitiously and looking at the stain with comfort, "and this is a slaver!"

Anthony sat in the cabin that morning immensely self-satisfied. In a few hours, through quick thinking and some luck he told himself, he had broken up the captain's little scheme of isolation and through him had assumed control of the ship. Don Ramón sat across the table too tired with rage to be angry any longer. The desertion of El Pollo to the fo'c'sle had, indeed, reduced him to tears. His favourite was now bunking with the rest of the crew. The shattered state of the highly nervous little captain was scarcely understood by those about him. His falsetto broke and ran a gamut when he spoke. The terrible Señor Adverso had threatened to put him to bed in the fever bunk which Brother François had occupied. He collapsed at the thought. He would do anything to avoid that. But he would also do anything to regain the solace of El Pollo. The boy was his slave in law but Don Ramón was the boy's slave in fact. So far had his passion now carried him that he really cared for little else. The command of the *Ariostatica* was to him merely the means of regaining Pollo. No one else in the cabin could imagine that. No one but the monk.

By long acquaintance and sad experience the passions of men were no longer much of a secret to Brother François. No excess of either good or evil could surprise him. The situation on the *Ariostatica* was to him painfully plain. Between the stalwart young man who had evidently suspended his ideals in order "to do things," what things, of course, he did not know, and Don Ramón who was mad with the excess of a single unnatural affection, the ship, he felt, and all the souls on her, was in a parlous way.

It might have surprised certain people to have known that in his heart Brother François felt there was little to choose between the baneful effects of obstinate, wrong human desires. Anthony's in fact he felt might in the end overwhelm more people than Don Ramón's. But he himself could do nothing. He was too weak. Scarcely able to move even in the chair in which he sat without dangerous exhaustion, he could only sit and think. What lay ahead he did not dare to dwell upon as yet. It would have stopped his heart. He lay and looked up at the bright colours of Spain that flaunted themselves from the peak where they had been hoisted at Havana. The gold and blood of them, he remembered, had always been associated with the banner of the cross. In the inextricable tangle of contradictions which this implied to him, for he believed in Providence, he sat back inert and benumbed. Only his own way was clear. But there was such a terrible light upon it that he could only face it now by closing his eyes. The body of him must sleep yet.

During the day both Anthony and the captain came to him; Anthony to try to make the invalid more comfortable, Don Ramón to obtain comfort from the priest.

"My son," said Brother François to Anthony after thanking him for some wine. "Has it not occurred to you already that you have made a bad bargain?"

Anthony went away angry. He did not care to think of that. Brother François was very sorrowful.

Don Ramón after much beating about the bush finally decided to risk his body by approaching the convalescent in order to save his soul. The monk's reassurances of all danger being past finally brought him to his knees near the priest in the shadow of a boat that hid them both from view. There he confessed himself and begged absolution. Brother François would grant it provided he would give up the youth. Don Ramón could not do that. He said so and wept. Brother François was again sorrowful.

The *Ariostatica* sailed on toward Africa. In a few hours Anthony knew she would raise the coast. At midnight she ran into an oily calm.

That calm endured for fearful days. Neither the water, the wind, nor the ship shifted. Only the lights of heaven had motion and a few birds that flew about the *Ariostatica* and went away again. Only they and the shark moved. The shark was still there. It ranged alongside from time to time expectantly. It nudged the ship and scraped itself against her barnacles sending a light tremor through her. The men swore now that it was waiting for someone. Half humorously they began again to throw dice and to draw lots. There was little else to do. The heat was intense. The shark was always there, by far the most interesting thing in their lives now. His persistence fascinated them. The lot one day fell for five consecutive times on El Pollo. That night he heard some of the men whispering about him. In the darkness he crept out of the fo'c'sle and fled back to Don Ramón. The days of utter calm in which the company of the *Ariostatica* seemed to have been condemned to the hell of their own society for the rest of eternity remained always a nightmare to Anthony. It was plain to him that what had been gained during the squall and the short time afterward was rapidly slipping out of his hands. By the fourth day of calm, with the glass still low but no change, no one could make believe to be in charge of the ship. The men separated themselves to the fo'c'sle again and no longer even pretended to pay attention to a hail from the quarter-deck. Only a half-pint a day of water could be allowed per man. And even that would soon exhaust the now depleted supply. A hundred miles over the horizon was land. But the crew did not know this. If they had been told they might have taken to the boats. Exactly what happened to the minds of those marooned on the idle slaver Anthony could not be sure. The changeless colour of the sea, a kind of breathlessness in the atmosphere, a perpetual expectation of something about to occur which never happened, the utter silence and the shark—produced the explosion that came.

There were a number of half-castes among the crew, all of whom, white or brown, were deeply tinged with Africa. What superstitious and fearful whisperings went on forward night after night and day after day as the wind failed to come, only those who put their heads together in the fo'c'sle and listened desperately might know.

On the eighth day a surly deputation came aft demanding that Brother François pray again for a breeze. He did so but nothing happened. On the ninth the liquid ration was halved.

That something had been resolved upon by the men was now patent to both Anthony and the mate Sóller as they served out the water and rum with Ali Bongo and his men standing by armed. On these Mohammedans Anthony now pinned his chief hope. They belonged to a tribe in the interior, the Foulahs, who frequently came to the coast in little groups under some leader and made a fortune sufficient for the rest of their lives by serving a few years at sea, usually on a slaver.

Anthony had, he thought, bound them to him by the present of two chests of scarlet cloth, the promise of much more when they arrived, and the cancelling of a year off their sea service. At the end of six months he had promised to dismiss them into the interior again with presents of powder and firearms. That was the understanding, and for the most part they had stood by him. But in the mystery which was now afoot they stood aloof, he felt. The most he could get out of Ali Bongo was that whatever was toward did not concern a good Mohammedan and he would not interfere. The outlook was by no means cheerful. The cabin retired on the tenth night thoroughly prepared, but not for sleep.

As the night wore on Anthony relieved Juan who was on watch on deck. He took his place in the shadow of the mast and leaned against it. No one was at the wheel. There was not a breath stirring. The helm, which had been lashed a week before, had remained so. Some distance astern a slight phosphorescent glimmer proclaimed the presence of "Old Faithful." All in the fo'c'sle seemed asleep. For a while he thought he was alone on the quarter-deck. In the moonlight he could hear the idle sails dripping dew. Then he saw the head and shoulders of El Pollo. He was lying back on some of Brother François's borrowed pillows in the stern sheets of the captain's boat where it rested in its cradle on the quarter-deck.

At first he thought the boy was asleep, but now he saw his eyes open. They closed slowly again. The expression on the lad's dark face held him spellbound. There could be no doubt what was happening. He lay looking up at the stars with a film of ecstasy on his lids. His delicately beautiful features were flat and strangely shrunken like some water-lily that had broken from its stem and decayed a little from its first early bloom while drifting helplessly downstream. This stupor persisted for a long time. Then the boy opened his mouth as if to bleat. But no sound came forth. The jaw merely relaxed and hung down. When a living expression finally returned it was one of extreme terror. He lay absolutely still for so long that it was evident he was afraid to move.

There was something Anthony could not understand about this. The boy lay with his hands behind his head. If it had not been for that Anthony would have put an end to the business. But the sight of so luxurious and self-hypnotized a dreamer had amazed and fascinated him. No other solution had occurred to him. The face alone had held him spellbound. Watching it, he had become aware of profound and hitherto unsuspected abysses in himself. He too had almost been hypnotized. When the captain suddenly appeared above the gunwale of the boat Anthony stood as if frozen. Indeed, his back grew cold.

Don Ramón looked about him and thinking the deck was clear stepped out of the boat and began to sneak forward. He was within a few feet of Anthony before he saw him. They stood looking at each other. Both of them knew instantly that the other was thinking of the shark. That was why the captain screamed.

Whether those who had planned what immediately followed that shrill cry thought they had been discovered and rushed the quarter-deck immediately, or whether the tone of it had merely shattered the ten-day tension of the unbearable calm, Anthony could never be sure. They must have been waiting, perhaps even creeping up during the minutes before the captain screamed. Scarcely was the sound past his lips when a half score of the crew were upon him. Anthony had just time to roll down the hatch. They had not seen him standing by the mast in the shadow. He caught himself on the ladder and drew his pistol aiming it at the moonlit square above. Whatever came he meant to hold the cabin. But no heads came into the bright square above. There was a hellish clamour on deck.

It was the falsetto voice of the captain. Doubtless they were going to murder him. At any rate he was begging them not to do something. Well, he would not interfere for *that* man! Not after what he had just seen. Certainly the agony was genuine now. Don Ramón could plead eloquently. Then Anthony went cold all over again. Don Ramón was screaming to them not to throw the boy overboard.

Anthony shouted to Juan desperately and started to climb up the ladder. A scream of terror beyond thought rang out above just as his head and shoulders came out of the hatch. The rest was over in two seconds.

Someone dragged the boy out of the boat to which he clung desperately, and clutching him about the waist raised him high in the air. The whole mad group precipitated itself toward the stern like an avalanche. For an instant he saw the still childish limbs thrash in the moonlight as the boy was tossed outward. There was a splash just as Anthony leaped aft. But he was met by a return rush toward the fo'c'sle. Rolling and milling about, his pistol went off.

Yet even in the mêlée while trying to clutch somebody he heard the voice from the water. No one could listen to that and not go mad. He started to club someone with his pistol but the man broke away.

When he rose to his feet again the grey decks of the sinister little yacht were empty. He stood there alone in the moonlight. He was clutching a bunch of black chicken feathers in one hand. That was all.

It must be a frightful dream. He would wake up soon. Yes, that was it. Chicken feathers! He knew it was a dream. Sailors do not wear feathers in their hair. He gave a weird laugh and found his chest and ribs hurt him horribly.

"*Ju-ju!*" said a wild falsetto voice in his ear. Don Ramón threw his hands up above his head. "No use," he cried. "All over." He staggered and was bleeding at the mouth.

Anthony went and leaned over the taffrail. Infinite miles of a pool of quicksilver seemed to lie astern. In all that glittering level not a thing moved. The shark had gone. He cried out into the night. Whether it was a prayer or a curse he did not know.

Next morning a faint breeze began to push the *Ariostatica* along toward Africa again. By noon she had gathered considerable way. They raised the low coast by evening and burned flares for a pilot all night. The red, funereal glare danced for miles over the black water. Finally a similar fire answered them from land.

37. THE CREW GO ASHORE

ALL night the *Ariostatica* gradually drew in toward the land. About dawn she was standing off-and-on just keeping under way. Nothing could be done until they picked up the pilot. Now and again the ship lifted sullenly to black hills of water that surged under and past her, marching in upon the coast. Half an hour after some unusual giant passed Anthony thought he could hear its cataclysmic roar as it staggered against the mysterious continent still hidden in darkness to leeward.

The sun rose suddenly out of a level, steaming jungle that stretched eastward as far as the eye could reach. While he watched, the straight clouds brooding over it wilted. Then, as the air grew hotter and clearer, a million foggy wisps exhaled into the morning as if the camp fires of night were going out. The sun licked the dampness up like a thirsty cat's tongue. In an hour the atmosphere was blue-white and quivering like the heart of a furnace.

This, he saw, was a flat, a sullen and silent land. No merry song streamed upward from that stagnant sea of treetops to eastward such as had risen from the gracious forests of Cuba to greet the sun. The only voice here was that of Ocean. Apparently quite calm, it advanced relentlessly upon the strips of islands stretching away over the long, flat horizon where endless miles of monotonous lagoons dazzled the eyes. As though balked of its prey by these thin barriers the sea continued to wrinkle its angry lips along their bone-white beaches, roaring with elemental appetite at the forest beyond.

Although the *Ariostatica* was still several miles out, the hungry crunch and smash of the breakers saluted her with a premonitory snarl.

Only at one point was there to be seen any break in the seemingly endless barrier reef that now lay directly before the ship. It was where the Rio Pongo, slipping silently out of the enormous forest, slid into the sea. Emerging from endless flats, the river was only a convenient funnel for the tides with scarcely any noticeable current of its own. A sharp dent in the façade of the forest beyond the lagoons and a surfless break in the barrier beaches indicated the river's whereabouts. This, and the blue dome of Cape Palmas which loomed up faintly to the south were the only distinct landmarks in the entire region. All else was a level sea either of green water or of even greener vegetation.

Sóller pointed out the river mouth to Anthony.

"A good landfall, señor!" He grinned a little sheepishly. "We ought to make Gallego's anchorage by noon. Well, you will certainly get a warm welcome *there!*" He strolled over to the rail and turned his back. Anthony felt sure the mate was laughing. He looked at the river gate ahead without enthusiasm. What awaited him there seemed as inscrutable as the dim arches from which the Rio Pongo emerged.

Some time after sunrise a black dot, which the restless ocean had been tilting into sight now and then for about an hour past, resolved itself into the expected pilot's canoe. It was paddled by two Kru boys stark except for breech-clouts. In the centre under a palm hat of Korean proportions sat the pilot in a ragged, military jacket, smoking a calabash pipe.

He knocked out this basin for tobacco as he came up the ship's side, and much to Anthony's surprise hailed the quarter-deck in English. Sóller seemed positively disgruntled by this. Evidently he had been expecting another man.

The trouserless emanation from the deep, dressed exclusively in a cast-off marine's jacket with four brass buttons over the tail, proved to be from the factory of one Thomas Ormond, better known up and down the slave coast and for many a mile inland as "Mongo Tom."

Sóller tried him persistently in both Spanish and Portuguese, but the pilot shook his head. For this he was heartily cursed at some length in both tongues, a warm welcome, which as a free man he resented.

"Me sabe go-go Bangalang alri'," he finally insisted, turning to Anthony who turned him over to the good offices of Ali Bongo. A bargain was soon struck for taking the ship up to Gallego's anchorage.

The mate grunted uneasily and went below, evidently to discuss this unexpected development with the captain who had not yet ventured to crawl on deck again.

The pilot took over the wheel without further ado and continued in active conversation with Ali Bongo in some unknown jargon. It appeared that they had known each other. After a while Anthony managed to join in. Ali Bongo did the honours. Berak-Jaumee, he assured Anthony, was one fine, fighting friend, honest-man.

Jaumee proved to be very proud of his "English." He had once made a voyage on a British whaler, it appeared. For that reason Mongo Tom, the Englishman, had taken him on. Jaumee was now not only the best but the only pilot on the river, Anthony learned. There were only two slave factories on the Rio

Pongo, Mongo Tom's and Gallego's. Both were near Banga-lang, a Kru village. Gallego's lay a little upstream beyond the native huts; Mongo Tom's below. Both slavers had once kept pilots, but—

"Gallego pie-*lot* no work no more."

"How come that?"

"Gallego no pay. Gallego no pay numbody. Him dade two moons. Feber! Gallego bery dade. Him hareem go-go big woods." Jaumee grinned.

Here was news indeed, news which it might be just as well to keep from the crew and the captain. If Gallego was dead, Anthony realized his only hope of getting matters in his own hands was a tight hold on the ship, instantly. Consequently he walked the deck doing some fast thinking.

The crew would be with the captain, he felt, when it came to a final showdown. If he could only break that combination! He sent for Juan, and did some intense talking with him and Ali Bongo. He was delighted to see how at the mere prospect of a clash the lean, black Mohammedan brightened up. It promised well, he thought. Ali Bongo had peculiar eyes with golden pupils like those of an eagle. Expressionless for the most part except of a constant fierce animal pride, as he and Anthony stood by the taffrail discussing calmly enough ways and means of taking over the schooner, Ali Bongo's eyes smouldered in the sun. It flashed upon Anthony for the first time how absorbing the business of killing might be. Nothing else could be compared to it for interest. It was the supreme gamble. In a ten-minute conversation with the big Mohammedan both of them had forgotten themselves entirely in the tense business at hand. Even lack of language had been no barrier. Where Ali Bongo's Spanish failed his expressive gestures went on like a more eloquent though silent tongue. They parted having reached a complete understanding.

The ship was now passing through the narrow cleft in the barrier beach. The tide here ran like a mill race. Thousands of square miles of salt lagoons and an entire river basin were to be filled in a few hours, and all through one lean nostril. It appeared to Anthony that the slight rise in the forest beyond was where the earth was expanding its chest in order to inhale the tide. The water about the schooner boiled with white sand. All sail had been stripped from the ship, which now glided forward rapidly and silently on the swiftly rising water floor. They crossed the wide lagoon behind the island in a few minutes and entered the boiling, sucking mouth of the Rio Pongo.

Instantly on both sides the great forest closed in upon the little ship. The roar of the beaches was cut off as if the soft oozy mouth of the river had closed its lips over her.

Anthony had never dreamed of a forest like this. Huge palms shot up to unbelievable heights overtopping the ship's masts, he could not guess how far. The *Ariostatica* seemed to be slipping down a throat lined with smooth, green vegetation into the mysterious maw of the continent. She swung around curves easily and majestically as if driven by some power within her, bubbling along on the advancing crest of the tide.

No one but an experienced pilot could have avoided the sandbars of the sluggish river's innumerable turns. Anthony glanced at Jaumee, glad to see that Ali Bongo was getting on so well with him. Evidently they were about to reach an agreement. In a few minutes he witnessed a curious ceremony. Each man produced a knife and after repeating some formula each pricked his own thumb. When a drop of blood appeared they then thrust them each into the other's mouth. Then they exchanged knives. Both spat upon the blades and saluted each other.

The pilot then walked over and kicked the two naked Kru boys who were stretched out asleep in the blinding sun. He began to say something to them . . .

"Time to serve out arms now, I think, señor." It was Ali Bongo who was speaking. Anthony turned to him startled, the man had come upon him so silently. "I have just made a blood brother of the pilot. He and his two boys there are now with us. You will have to provide the three rolls of red cloth I have promised. It is a great gift but their help is worth it. If the señor will act quickly now I think he can secure the ship. I will

bring my men aft. The rest of the crew are at morning mess."
He gave a keen whistle which brought the four other Mohammedans, who lived mostly on rice, and who ate and cooked by
themselves in the galley, running aft.

Anthony looked about him mentally mustering his forces.
Besides himself he had Juan, Ali Bongo and his four other
Foulahs, the pilot, and his two Kru boys. It was possible that
the cook and his boy might be counted on to stay with the ship.
Brother François was, of course, in event of any physical clash,
neutral. This was twelve at best, probably only ten in fact, that
could be counted on to act together against the rest of the ship's
company including the captain and mate. The odds were thus
about three to one. In Anthony's favour was the rather unusual
height of the schooner's quarter-deck, which had only one
narrow approach from the waist of the ship, and the fact that
most of the ammunition, although not all of the arms, was
stored in the cabin.

Anthony sent Juan and one of the Foulahs to bring up an
arms chest. Without attracting the notice of the crew weapons
were quietly served out to those on the quarter-deck. Several
loaded muskets were concealed in the bunt of the half-furled
mainsail. As luck would have it, just while this was going on
the head and shoulders of the mate Sóller appeared above the
hatch combing. He was about to come on deck. He took in the
situation at a glance and bellowed something down the hatch
to the captain. Just then Ali Bongo clapped a pistol to his ear
and hauled him on deck. He bound him to the mast and gagged
him. Anthony and Juan dived down the hatchway.

They were too late, however. A scuttling noise and the rattle
of irons in the cabin-hold told what was happening. They were
only in time to see the manacled leg of Polyphème disappear
through the loose board in the bulkhead. Leaving Juan to nail
up the loose plank, which he cursed himself for not having
attended to before, Anthony returned to the deck by way of
the cabin. The captain had gone, too. Evidently he had preceded Polyphème. The crisis was at hand then! He ran for the
deck.

As he poked his head up out of the hatch there was a deafening smack, and a bullet, which shattered the top of the combing, filled his cheek with wood splinters. He saw the captain standing on the fo'c'sle with a smoking pistol in his hand. The little man dodged behind the foremast and started to reload.

Everyone on the quarter-deck, including Ali Bongo, was now flat as a card. The pilot had let the wheel go and the bow of the *Ariostatica* was pointing toward the bank. The tide luckily enough drifted her sidewise upstream.

Anthony seized the wheel and turned the ship's head up the river again. The captain was having great trouble reloading. His hands and arms waggled out from behind the mast, working feverishly. Grabbing one of the muskets from the sail Anthony sent a bullet in the captain's direction that tore a long piece out of the mast behind which he stood. The shot was too much for the captain. He let out a wailing whoop and dived for the fo'c'sle. His appearance there, which was greeted by an encouraging roar from the crew, had been enormously accelerated by Ali Bongo's firing a pistol at him as he fled. All this had happened in less than two minutes.

Ali Bongo now came to life. He even persuaded his "blood brother" to return to the wheel. Seeing they had leaders who meant business, the rest of the men on the quarter-deck now ventured to raise their heads above the bulwarks and to handle their arms again. It was hurriedly explained to them that any further faltering on their part would result in their being hanged by the captain, if, and as soon as, he regained the quarter-deck. It was now win or die. This profound thought served to accelerate their zeal considerably. Even the Kru boys could understand it.

Indeed, their new flood of courage and enthusiasm over the success of the first blow went too far. The mere appearance of a head at the entrance to the fo'c'sle was the signal for an unauthorized hail of shots from the quarter-deck. Some of these, fired from behind Anthony, passed close to his ear. The fo'c'sle howled like a den of hyenas for a minute or two and then was quiet again. Now was the time to rush the quarter-deck if they had only known it. Every weapon aft was empty.

It gave Anthony an attack of goose-flesh to think of that. He exerted himself strenuously to put some discipline in his mob. The muskets and pistols were reloaded hastily. Some packing cases and bales were brought up and disposed as a breastwork along the forward rail of the quarter-deck. The four Foulahs who were used to muskets, to judge by the way they handled them, were placed behind this hastily constructed but effective enough barrier with instructions to shoot at anyone who appeared in the fo'c'sle door. Spare muskets were provided. One of the Kru boys was sent down to reinforce Juan at watch below at the loose bulkhead.

That bulkhead caused Anthony a good deal of worry. He did not want to have to meet a sudden rush from behind up the cabin stairs. The danger was thoroughly impressed upon Juan who began to make certain preparations. His ingenuity, Anthony found later, was considerable.

In the meantime, the ship, as if nothing extraordinary were going on, continued calmly enough to sweep on up the river with the tide. A babble of voices occasionally burst from the fo'c'sle where a kind of nautical town meeting continued to go on for several hours that morning. Considerable difference of opinion as to what should be done under the circumstances must have developed between the captain and the now thoroughly reckless Polyphème. That was as much as Anthony could make out. An intermittent pounding and smashing of glass, upon which Juan for some reason was engaged in the cabin below, drifted up the hatch.

Anthony was glad now that Sóller and the captain had freed Polyphème. Doubtless that was why the mate had stayed below so long that morning. It must have taken some time to file the locks on the Frenchman's irons. He discovered later that the man's leg chain had been cut through. Sóller had evidently meant to come on deck to make talk while the captain and Polyphème went forward to bring back the crew. What had been done, then, was just in the nick of time. Anthony had counted on the captain's waiting to act till they reached Gallego's. That had almost been a fatal mistake. He drew a deep breath. Where would he have been now if he had waited? A glance at the monster-haunted river did not reassure him.

They were now passing rapidly enough up a long, straight stretch of the stream. Except for the muddy shallows along the banks the Rio Pongo here resembled a broad canal rather than a river. This reach in particular was literally dragon-haunted. From time to time, disturbed by the passing of the ship, crocodiles launched themselves from the banks with a resounding splash that sent flocks of parrots screaming above the treetops. From a reedy shoal the pink, cavern mouth of a riverhorse opened suddenly and bellowed at them. A calf like a huge, fat grub appeared swimming at its mother's side. The smoke from the ship's galley had drifted into their nostrils. Monkeys let themselves down by the natural ropes of vines that dangled and looped for interminable miles along the vast living wall of trees. They dipped their hands in the muddy stream and drank, only to shrink back chattering as they saw the ship, or a pair of saurian eyes looking at them from what appeared to be a half-sunken log. There was not a breath or any movement in the leaves now. The damp heat vibrated above the stream with thousands of midges and living motes of things. Clouds of stinging flies made the men swear and stamp. Butterflies only to be matched by the cascades of bloom on the flowering vines that made the walls of the forest both magic and impenetrable, fluttered down on the deck and waved their wings slowly in the sun. The dark, festering swamp, from which this prototype of tropical forests drew gargantuan life, smoked under dim arches at midday with little wisps devoured by the sun.

Even in the midst of burning excitement Anthony looked at all this with amazement. To what place had he come? While the four Foulahs crouched ready behind their bales of cloth and packing cases he smiled to see that neither the battle which had gone on above his head nor the semi-infernal landscape through which the ship was passing had prevented the cook from preparing his usual meal. The galley smoked as peacefully as its imperturbable occupant. In the copper caldrons the salt pork bubbled and sang. At dinner time a pair of white trousers on a stick was waved from the fo'c'sle.

After some preliminary parley Polyphème's face and single eye appeared a little above the deck forward.

"You will not starve us, will you, señor?" he said taking off his red cap and bowing with elaborate irony. The four guns of the Foulahs were trained at his chest but he paid no attention to them. He stood there holding the ball and chain that was still attached to his leg, grinning, and looking at those on the quarter-deck with a malevolent eye. He succeeded in making them all uneasy.

"Send the captain up. I'll talk with him," said Anthony.

"*I* am the captain now," replied the man putting his hand on his heart and bobbing again while his chain clanked. "If you have any business to transact with the crew, monsieur, you must do it with me. Mais oui, you see I have just been elected." He swaggered a little, allowing the news to sink in.

"Put the captain on deck. I talk only with him," snapped Anthony in French.

"Ah, zat ees endeed unfortu-nate, Meester Adverse, ze cape-tain hav ches now, what you call eet hexpire. His noble heart hav stop beat. I tell you zat in your own goddam langweedge. It ees ze verity. Let me talk wiz you. I have ze bon pro-posal." He started to come aft.

"Careful, señor," whispered Ali Bongo.

Anthony halted the man just by the carronade amidships and kept him covered.

"You and me, we get togezzer now ze captain ees dade . . ." the sailor began.

"You're lying, of course," interrupted Anthony.

The single eye narrowed to a slit. "No! I swear eet, on my heart, monsieur." He bowed again slightly. His hand shot out of his chest. Anthony threw himself backward. His pistol went off in the air. It was the handle instead of the blade of Polyphème's knife which took him full in the chest. A number of muskets went off together like one gun.

The four Foulahs had fired straight into the fo'c'sle door. It had stopped the rush effectively. Forward someone could be heard screaming dismally. Despite a fusillade of shots which followed him, in the tense excitement Polyphème had dodged back again.

Anthony rose both bruised and foolish. To have had the same trick played on him twice! He picked up the knife and threw it into the sea.

It was just then that the noise broke out below. Evidently a scrimmage was going on in the hold. Suddenly it stopped. Then there was one shot. As he started down the ladder Anthony met Juan coming up. He was laughing.

"It's all over," Juan said. "I don't think they'll come back." He began to laugh again. "It was glass, señor. Broken bottles! I spread them in the hold in front of the bulkhead and waited. Dios! You should have heard the noise they made when I fired through the bulkhead. They all rolled over one another in the most fertile spot. Bare feet, too, Madre!"

"Was it indeed 'all over'?" thought Anthony. Unconsciously he found himself thanking the madonna, his own madonna, that it was not all over with him. His wishbone creaked where the knife handle had bruised him. A fine place he had brought himself—and the madonna to! Then he found himself laughing with Juan from sheer relief. A few minutes later the voice of the captain was heard begging for water for the wounded.

"They bleed down here badly, señor—for the love of Christ!" Anthony allowed this request. The return of the expedition from the hold had evidently sickened the fo'c'sle pretty thoroughly. He let the cook take some food down to them. Silence settled down upon the *Ariostatica* now. Her progress up the Rio Pongo was no longer marked by volleys and the screaming millions of parrots that rose in cloudy flocks. The tide was nearing the flood. The ship moved upstream more and more sluggishly.

They drifted slowly past the establishment of Mongo Tom. The forest opened out suddenly and a vista of rice fields, sugar cane, and plantains swept up to a large palisaded place, the slave pens. On a knoll was a comfortable-looking thatched house with a far-flung veranda. Anthony sent Juan for his glass. He could see a large figure, apparently that of a white man dressed in a loose garment of some kind, standing on the porch. The man was also looking at the ship with a hand telescope. Anthony made a gesture to him but he got no reply. Strangely enough no one else could be seen about. The place seemed deserted.

"Mongo Tom no like him people come say how-do Gallego ship. Many man's there alri'," replied the pilot to Anthony's questions.

Evidently there had been no love lost between Mongo Tom and Gallego.

"Him no like me bring up Gallego ship," continued Jaumee. "Jaumee free man," he added proudly. "Me *do!* Me work Gallego ship!"

Anthony nodded approval of these independent sentiments. "Me free man, me do!" he thought and smiled.

A canoe appeared at a turn ahead, waved a paddle, and turned back upstream. A few minutes later the pulsing throb of distant drumming seemed to emanate from the forest from all directions at once.

"Bangalang," said Jaumee.

The drums went on. The crew in the fo'c'sle began to call out. What was going to happen to the garrison on the quarter-deck, and Anthony in particular, when the ship reached Gallego's barracoon was not only described graphically but with obscene originality.

It was Anthony's intention to nurse this delusion of the approaching revenge of the defunct Señor Gallego. It fitted in with his plans for getting both the captain and the crew ashore without further deck fighting when they reached the Gallego establishment. It was no part of his scheme, however, to permit the crew to regain the deck before the ship anchored. As they approached Bangalang and several heads began to appear at the fo'c'sle hatch from time to time, he had one of the Foulahs fire another warning shot.

As the fo'c'sle hatch, a sliding door, was exactly opposite the quarter-deck, which faced it at an elevation of about ten feet due to the build of the ship, the effect of musketry from the quarter-deck only half a ship's length away was to plunge bullets directly into the fo'c'sle. They spattered against the forward bulkhead there with a devastating smack and a hail of oak splinters.

There was even a certain humour in this situation, provided one was on the quarter-deck. In order to protect themselves the crew had to keep the vertical, sliding hatch to the fo'c'sle closed; in order to sally forth or shoot back they had to open it. The opening of the hatch always announced itself by a loud screech of its ungreased rollers. By the time it was fully open, after several squalling jerks from within, five or six muskets were trained at the gaping door. Anyone who wanted to come up the fo'c'sle ladder then, and die at the top, was at liberty to do so.

Anthony reflected with a good deal of amusement and a curious chagrin that upon the combination of these very simple physical facts both his present and his future existence were entirely dependent. In several languages he could think of only one phrase adequate to describe the situation. "On les a."

When the drums began announcing the nearness of Bangalang and the end of the voyage, the forward hatch had been slid back in order to allow the profane advice of the fo'c'sle to reach the quarter-deck. As the loudness of the drums increased, showing the *Ariostatica* was nearly opposite the native town, the disposition of the crew to sally forth became imminent. A few heads were even risked above the level of the deck. At the same time a fleet of canoes making for the schooner appeared around the bend of the river just ahead. It was at this juncture that Anthony had caused the Foulahs to fire again. The demonstration was effective. Silence from the fo'c'sle and an outbreak of firing in the town around the bend greeted the volley.

The firing from the town was merely by way of a happy greeting to the long-expected ship. Bangalang, according to Ali Bongo and the pilot, was a village of Krus, a tribe of coastal negroes, mostly fishermen, who were of great service to both the slave establishments on the Rio Pongo. They had consequently been let alone. Slaves came from the interior. So there was nothing hostile in the approaching canoes, quite the contrary. Nevertheless, Anthony did not intend to permit natives to board the ship at this time. If necessary he intended to skip a few shots over the water to make the canoes sheer off. A happier idea was supplied by Ali Bongo, however. Several small kegs of rum were tied to a spare spar and set adrift. The canoes when they approached were warned off and the kegs pointed out. A few minutes later as the *Ariostatica* drifted past them, ten canoes were engaged somewhat violently in trying to divide four kegs between them. Muffled shouts from the fo'c'sle did not attract their attention.

The river now widened out into a series of lake-like tidal marshes. As the ship came in sight of the village, situated on an island knoll about a mile away over the flats, the drums in the place changed from a monotonous *tum-tum, tum-tum,* to a swift

> *Bonk, bonkty-bonk-bonk,*
> *Bonk, bonkty-bonk-bonk,*

endlessly repeated. Horns and screams of welcome joined in.

It was just at this point that Anthony felt a final crisis with the crew might occur. Everything depended on reaching Gallego's anchorage about four miles beyond the town. At her present rate of drifting it would take the ship an hour to do that, two hours perhaps. The tide was fast failing. He now sent two of the Foulahs forward to cover the fo'c'sle hatch point-blank and managed to slip Juan up the forward ladder to set the jibs. Over the miles of open flats breezes now and then rippled the water, while in the narrow river all had been dead calm. The ship increased her way considerably.

The rattle of the jib blocks on the deck and the drums of the village caused Polyphème to make another attempt. He raised his head above the deck level and found the single eye of a musket looking directly into his own. It was sufficient to convince even him utterly.

Nevertheless, the tension of that last hour was extreme. It was not until the schooner rounded a long, wooded point, and Anthony could look across another bay in the forest to the long barracoons of the late Señor Gallego, that he began to feel he might yet win.

A few minutes more, and he would have had to anchor below the point and hold the crew below all night. In the darkness almost anything might happen. As it was, assisted by some puffs that filled the jibs for several blessed moments at a time, he just made it.

The *Ariostatica* was brought to anchor about seven hundred yards from shore by a small anchor from the stern. With several possibilities in view Anthony was particular about this distance.

The tidal basin here was about a mile across. Gallego's place stretched along the water front where the stockaded barracoons stood. Various thatched houses attached to the establishment extended up a low, steep hill just behind. Many blacks, both men and women, could be seen running about greatly excited. On the porch of one of the houses farther up the hill Anthony's heart sank to see what was apparently the figure of a white man. Could Gallego be alive after all? If so . . .

"Him Ferdinando, Gallego factor," said Jaumee. "Him half-breed." He spat on the deck.

It was curious that no boats were putting out for the ship, Anthony thought. There was not even a canoe by the docks. Whatever the reason was, it made things much simpler. Without further ado he intended to act.

He had the two whaleboats slung in the schooner's waist lowered and towed up to the bow. Sóller, who since his appearance on deck that morning had been tied to the mast, was now unlashed. In the excitement of the past five hours he had been pretty well forgotten. He now staggered across the deck moaning for water. When he found Anthony intended to send him ashore with the crew he collapsed. His plight was pitiable. It was plain that he must know that Gallego was dead. He had heard Ali Bongo and the pilot talking, it seemed, and had put two and two together. He now pleaded earnestly to be allowed to remain on the schooner.

"You will not send me to die like a dog on shore, will you, señor? I see your game. To turn me and the captain loose on shore with those bastards below! Dios, we shall be murdered! I won't go! I will serve you now. I can be valuable to you. I will be your man . . ."

Anthony was forced to turn Sóller over to Brother François who tended him in the cabin below. The truth was the sun had nearly finished him. At any rate he was no good to negotiate with the crew. It must be either the captain or Polyphème. The captain would be easier to handle. After a hundred reassurances and seemingly helped by Polyphème from behind the little man was finally persuaded to come on deck.

He was nervously shaken by the events of the last forty-eight hours. All his swagger was gone. He stood blinking in the sun in a sweaty, silk suit in which the colours had run. Yet it was strange to see how soon the ghost of his naturally cocky attitude began to return when he found he was going to be sent ashore with his crew. Anthony could see that Don Ramón still thought him a fool and could scarcely believe his ears or refrain from boasting about what he was going to do when once ashore.

Anthony pretended to be driving a bargain.

"In return for letting you go I shall expect you to put my own situation before Señor Gallego as—well, *as pleasantly as possible*," said Anthony finally.

"Certainly, señor, of course, with absolute cordiality, depend upon it. Your generosity and tender treatment will be properly reported, have no doubt. I promise it on my honour."

"In this case I shall *have* to believe you. My situation, you see, makes me dependent upon you from now on, captain. I trust you understand my precarious position with Señor Gallego."

"Believe me I do," grinned the captain in spite of himself. "I wonder you did not think of it before. But I shall do my best," he added hastily, seeing Anthony scowl.

"Have your crew pile their arms on the deck then, as I said, and get into the boats one at a time. As a gentleman of honour you may keep your own sword." Since the captain had lost his scampering through the hold early that morning the last shot was between his wind and water. He winced, seemed about to reply, then thought better of it and went below.

Some time passed during which a few laughs hastily suppressed drifted up the hatch. In rather short order the crew then began to toss up on deck a heterogeneous collection of weapons. These were hastily gathered up and taken aft. There was some parley over a musket which had not yet appeared. Finally it was tossed up with a curse.

"One at a time now," said Anthony. "At the first move . . ."

A decidedly bedraggled departure now took place. As the men emerged one by one from the fo'c'sle they were sent alternately to one of the two boats and made to sit down on a thwart. Those who had bandaged and bloody feet from walking on Juan's broken bottles looked especially glum and foolish. Both the procession and the boats were kept well covered by pistols and muskets. As there were twenty-eight men in all it took nearly half an hour, thirty as tense minutes as Anthony ever lived through. Looking down in the boats, where the men were forced to sit with folded arms, he had no doubt that both of them were loaded with a cargo of pure hate. Polyphème and the captain came last. The former still carried his ball and chain, while the latter had found a cutlass far too long for him. He had taken Anthony at his word but tripped on the sword as he went over the side. Even his own men grinned at him.

The tide had turned during these proceedings and the bow of the ship was now downstream. The two boats, with the captain in charge of one and Polyphème of the other, were both at a signal suddenly cut loose. The ebb swept them clear of the schooner. They were carried fifty yards before the tired, dazed men realized what had happened. Then there was a great scramble for oars. A yell of derisive triumph went up from those on the schooner and a few wild shots which Anthony could not prevent spattered the water about the boats. Polyphème produced a pistol from somewhere and fired back. His bullet crashed through the stern windows. Yells, curses, and threats were hurled back from the boats, which, thrashing the water wildly, pulled out of range as fast as they could and made for the landing by the barracoons.

It was not likely they would attempt to return immediately, Anthony thought. He counted on the confusion which would follow when they learned that Gallego was no more. Above all he counted on trouble starting between the captain and Polyphème. There were gorgeous possibilities there. He himself would play a defensive game. He had the schooner now and could wait. He would consolidate his own gang and stand off the others. "Tomorrow," he thought, "—and almost anything may happen on shore tonight—perhaps the final move can be made."

How thankful he was the tide had served them to the last. Undoubtedly he owed much to Jaumee's skill. It would have been impossible to keep the situation in hand if he had had to anchor lower down and keep the crew below all night. Things had been too evenly balanced. As it was, they had just come through by the turn—of the tide.

But to wait was not necessarily to be apathetic. He must keep himself clear-minded and up to the mark, awake. And he must now be merciless, he felt. Above all he must supply the energy to drive things through. Already his little garrison was drowsing about the deck and dozing from heat and fatigue.

He stripped and poured several buckets of water over himself. He took a pull of brandy, and then lit a black cigar to quiet his nerves. He roused the men again by serving out some grub and a good tot of rum to each. Under Jaumee's supervision he set them to work getting up boarding nettings while he and Ali Bongo put the carronade amidships into working order. Powder, round shot, and grape were got up and placed handy. As the ebb increased the *Ariostatica* had dragged on her small stern anchor and increased her distance from shore. This was now brought up. The large starboard anchor was let go, and the ship's head brought upstream with only a short length of cable out. A few turns of the capstan would free her now, yet the heavier anchor held her fast.

By five o'clock all was shipshape again. The boarding nets were rigged, cutlasses, and loaded pistols and muskets ready at hand. A number of lanterns and flares were made ready, and a large kettle of boiling water kept steaming in the galley. Anthony and Ali Bongo had also spent some time training the carronade on various objects. It had very simple sights and one hand screw for elevation. They now recovered it, leaving the lashings off its tarpaulin and the gun loaded.

It was now time to think of his men again. He got up a ship's chest and served out new clothes. He gave the Kru boys their bolts of red cloth and the Foulahs the merchandise he had promised them. In addition he presented the Mohammedans with a small roll of lead and a bullet mould apiece. He gave Ali Bongo the captain's silver watch, which he had left behind, and from a chest of trinkets fished up a cuckoo clock for the pilot. Another round of rice and boiled meat followed.

While all now sat about on the deck with expressions for which "satisfaction" was too lean a word, the fortune to be made by sticking by the ship was made clear and the disasters of failure again pointed out in strong terms. A blatant dose of praise mixed with a few cold threats for those who might shirk, or go to sleep on watch, completed Anthony's first speech. A burst of cuckooing from the pilot's clock just at the end brought a roar of good-humoured laughter from all hands. The crew was divided into watches under Ali Bongo and Jaumee and went willingly to their stations.

So far nothing but distant shouts and the barking of a dog had come from the shore. The barking now reached a crescendo of excitement.

Leaving Juan in charge of the deck Anthony went below for his glass. He found Brother François attending Sóller who was now better but still with a rather bad touch of sun. Even the bullet through the cabin windows had not disturbed him. Brother François returned to the deck with Anthony. He showed no curiosity or surprise. He sat in his chair and looked out over the wide stretch of jungle-lined water which the sun was now flooding with level rays as it neared the western palm-tops. He offered no comment.

Anthony wondered what he was thinking about. How useless he seemed here! Perhaps the priest's seeming apathy was due to that; perhaps he sensed his helplessness here himself. The tremendous, brutal lushness of the tropical landscape all about seemed to oppose itself to Brother François. Against the scale of things here he seemed insignificant.

But when he had once focused the glass on the scene ashore Anthony soon forgot all about the man who sat beside him. The short distance between the ship and the shore was only sufficient to provide a dramatic perspective. Through the glass everything, even small objects, was very clear and apparently close at hand. But he could hear nothing except the dog barking. The animal was now frantic about something. He began to search for it, running his glass over the long barracoons along the water front and then up the hill. Now he was on it.

It was at the dwelling house half-way up. What was going on there was absorbing enough.

38. A WHIFF OF GRAPESHOT

The dog, a small, lean animal whose capacity for clamour seemed out of all proportion to its size, was tied to a pillar of the veranda, straining at its leash. The cause of its indignation and fury was the approach of the main body of the crew. They had now left the barracoons and stockade below and were climbing the hill toward what was evidently the master's quarters half-way up the first slope.

It was a thatched building of generous proportions. A number of blacks, both men and women, could be seen leaving the place from the rear carrying various belongings. The exodus was a general and hasty one. The figure of the man Ferdinando appeared at the main door once and then withdrew hastily again. Then the captain came out and stood with folded arms. He still wore his cutlass. The foremost of the crew now tore a small gate off its hinges, and followed by the rest rushed up a short garden path. They stopped short at the porch. The hound was baying frantically.

Some argument now took place with the captain. The little man waved his arms wildly. His words seemed to be having effect. He drew his sword. Several of the men clinched and started to roll over and over. Whether fists or knives were being used Anthony could not tell. Suddenly Polyphème stepped out from the crowd and drew his pistol. The captain dropped his sabre and turned for the door. There was a puff of smoke and the captain crumpled. Then the crack of the pistol reached the *Ariostatica*. The men swarmed like hornets into the house. The hound had apparently gone insane. Outside two figures lay in the little garden path before the porch.

The crack of the pistol on shore had brought all hands to the starboard rail of the schooner. Some few seconds later two figures dashed out of the house followed by some of the crew and made for the barracoons below. Anthony could not fix the glass on them, but in one he thought he recognized Ferdinando. The other seemed to be a woman, a young and active one it appeared, for she outdistanced her pursuers rapidly and disappeared into a clump of palms near the river front.

The man was not so lucky. He was headed off and hunted amid whoops and a great clamour for some time about the sheds near the slave pens. His hiding place was evidently discovered once, for the shouting broke out anew. Then it quieted down. Some of the crew kept looking about, but in about ten minutes they gave it up and trooped back to the house on the hill.

The cause of further lack of interest in their quarry was now apparent. A shed had been burst open and some barrels rolled out. A number of kegs loaded on the backs of slaves were soon seen ascending the hill to what was now quite patently the headquarters of Polyphème and his gang. That worthy soon appeared on the veranda and had the captain rolled away and the kegs rolled in. He then, to judge by the noise, devoted a full five minutes to kicking the hound to death.

It was curious, but the screams of the unfortunate animal did more to weld the crew of the *Ariostatica* into a unit against Polyphème and the men on shore than anything that had happened so far. None of the incidents of the fight coming up the river nor the miserable sights of wounds and blood which it had produced could be compared with it. Anthony remembered the cries of the child which had been trampled by the French cavalry at Livorno and their effect upon Toussaint. Evidently it was the voice and not the sight of suffering which most moved men. Ali Bongo who stood beside him at the rail listening, clutched the shrouds till the veins on his wrist stood out. And he was a Mohammedan who held dogs accursed. As the agonized voice finally ceased it now seemed to Anthony himself that he was engaged in a holy war, and that behind the taking of the schooner and the capture of the barracoon, which he planned as a final object, there was now a splendid moral urge. The cool murder of the captain seemed nothing in comparison with the nerve-shattering death of the dog. The captain had died silently so far as those on the schooner were concerned, and he was a man. Polyphème, in short, had now given notice to all concerned that he no longer kept even a sensible contract with nature. All *were* concerned.

"Señor," said Ali Bongo, "tomorrow we make One-eye go tell Allah about that. Allah can listen." He drew his finger across his throat significantly. They nodded to each other with complete understanding.

"Well, my son, how is your plan getting on with itself?" said Brother François to Anthony a minute or two later.

"Very well!" snapped Anthony, who was still leaning over the side looking shoreward. Something ironical in the priest's voice had aroused a host of questions in himself which he had thought were asleep. He was about to ask Brother François if he thought he could do any better himself, under the circumstances, when three men emerged from the shore sheds and started to make a bolt for it toward the landing where the two whaleboats from the schooner now lay without a guard.

A wild whoop from some of the crew on the hill gave notice that they were seen.

The distance from the sheds, and from the house on the hill to the dock was about the same. The three fugitives, whoever they were, had the advantage of a considerable start. Unfortunately, however, the two boats were not tied close together at the dock. They had only time to hurl themselves into the first and shove off before the crew was swarming out of the barracoon gate just behind them and making for the remaining boat farther down the dock.

The men in the boat pulled as rapidly for the ship as their desperation could contrive. They had already put a good stretch of water behind them when the craft manned by Polyphème and his gang shot out behind them pulling strong.

In the meantime, Anthony and Ali Bongo had snatched the tarpaulin off the carronade and were trying desperately to bring it to bear on the pursuing boat.

This was not so easy to do. They had left the carronade at too high an angle. The hand screw which controlled its elevation proved rusty and stiff. Before the elevation could be shifted to water level and the gun trained, the crew were gaining fast. The boat ahead, rowed awkwardly by only three oars, seemed about to be overtaken and captured before the eyes of those on the schooner. It was just at the moment when the gun finally came to bear full on Polyphème's boat that Anthony remembered they had no lighted match. He turned with a groan. Ali Bongo was gone.

Just then he emerged from the galley tossing a blazing coal from hand to hand.

"Keep her on!" he shrieked.

Anthony peered over the sights again. His target in those few seconds had rowed past. He slewed the gun desperately at a guess. Ali Bongo dropped the coal on the touch hole.

There was a terrific report and the carronade leaped back into the air against its tackles.

A million waterfowl rose screaming from the marshes. About

ten feet before Polyphème's boat a round shot struck the water a stunning blow, half drowning its crew with sheets of spray and caroming off into the wall of the barracoon beyond with a tremendous crash of splitting wood. For several minutes nothing could be heard but the screams of myriads of birds and the wail of women from the shattered building on shore.

Anthony could hear nothing at all. He was deaf but he was laughing. All of Polyphème's men had "caught a crab" at the same instant. Their oars seemed to stick in the water and fight with them. Then they had rowed all ways at once. Now they were making back for the shore thrashing frantically. If they could only get there before those on the ship could reload the terrible gun! They did so. Ali Bongo was dancing from the pain in his scorched fingers. Anthony was helpless. About the same time that Polyphème and his men raced back through the big gate of the barracoon the boat they had been pursuing made fast to the ship. Its three exhausted rowers proved to be the half-breed Ferdinando and two stout blacks.

Anthony welcomed them although he could just then hear nothing they had to say. Nevertheless, from the very first he liked Ferdinando. Gallego's chief clerk, or factor, as he was called, carried himself like a man. Despite his pale lemon complexion, small features, and dainty hands and feet, his main impression was one of intelligence and energy. His face was both refined and forceful and he evidently took great care of himself.

Somewhat bedraggled now, his first care when they descended to the cabin was to wash and put his dark curls in order. A clean white suit which Anthony lent him went far toward winning his heart. Anthony did not realize it then, but to have been received thus by the white man in charge of the ship with courtesy and solicitude had reached the half-breed factor where he lived. It had conquered his pride.

The sun had sunk. Darkness descended upon the forest-river lands as if a curtain had been lowered. A thousand mysterious noises arose of night birds, monkeys, and an occasional deep bellow from the river banks which drifted in through the cabin windows of the schooner where Anthony, Brother François, and Ferdinando now sat at their evening meal. Downstream over the low point Anthony could see the glow of the village fires waving in the sky and the monotonous but frantic drumming gradually became audible again as his ears cleared.

Juan kept a sharp lookout on deck and repeated that there was nothing to be seen ashore except a few lights and an occasional shout from the house on the hill.

Ferdinando joined genuinely in Brother François's brief grace. He regarded his own presence at that meal as little short of marvellous. A recital of events on shore that afternoon soon confirmed the others in this opinion.

The captain upon landing had left the crew in the sheds below while he had climbed the hill to Gallego's quarters. His disappointment, rage, and chagrin on learning that Gallego had been thoughtless enough to die two months before were indescribable. The factor said he had never seen anything quite like it.

"It was a curious thing to watch, señor. You can imagine my own state of mind, too, with that one-eyed dog and his sons-of-bitches hanging around about the sheds below—waiting. At any moment they might find out that Gallego was dead. Both of us knew what would happen without having to be told. I can tell you, you came in for some hearty cursing. We were caught like pigs in a pit by your little trick. I suggested arming some of the slaves and started some of the house servants hiding the valuables. There was Señor Gallego's big cash chest in which he kept the silver trade dollars. We started to smuggle it out the back.

"It was just then we heard them coming, señor. Either someone had told them about Gallego, or they saw the chest. I cannot understand Don Ramón. What kind of a man was he? When we heard them yell and the dog started to bark the captain was so frightened he turned green. 'It is death!' he said. Then he vomited all over the room. He had just had a bottle of red wine. He fell down. Then he got up again and took his sword. "I have my honour,' he shouted. I laughed at him then,

God forgive me! He went out on the porch and folded his arms. Señor, he made the crew a grand speech. Some of them fought for him. He died like a brave man. You know how." The factor crossed himself.

"As for me, I did not wait. No use. When I heard that pistol shot I called my sister from her room and we made for the little creek behind the palms. Since Señor Gallego died we have had great trouble here. A number of our people kept slipping away at night to the village. I had all the boats and canoes towed around to the creek and watched. That is the reason no boats came out to you. You see I have been much worried all along as to what would happen when the *Ariostatica* arrived. Well, it has been much worse than I thought!" He ran his slim fingers through his curls. "Much worse! Only the devil knows what that froth-of-hell will be up to tonight. It is trade rum they broke into, fourth proof—barrels of it. Madre!"

"Where is your sister now?"

"Well hidden, I trust, señor, Ah, she is a clever girl, do not worry! She will not be caught like a chicken in a coop. Besides there are plenty of women in the barracoons. It is fire that I am worried about. If it once gets started in the thatch!" He put down his glass, pausing at the thought. "But who are you, señor, and how did you come here?" He looked up now a little apprehensively.

With great care, for he saw how valuable an ally this man could be, Anthony explained his position and the events of the voyage. Ferdinando sat listening amazed. On the face of Brother François now and then Anthony thought he detected a faint flicker of amusement. It did take a great deal of explaining.

"So it is your plan then, señor, to assume charge of the factory here?" said Ferdinando at last.

"Since Senor Gallego is dead I can scarcely do anything else, can I? In fact I find myself in charge already, don't you think?" Anthony replied.

The factor laughed a little wryly. "Undoubtedly it is true," he said. Then he looked up turning a little white, but with determination enough. "And what of me?" he said.

"You will remain on as you are now," replied Anthony. "I had already made up my mind to that sometime ago. I see that you are—a gentleman!"

"You are the first that has ever said so!" said the half-breed leaning forward over the table and looking Anthony in the face. "I shall never forget it!"

Anthony went on deck and left Ferdinando talking with Brother François. He was glad to see that Juan had bountifully fed the two black boys who had come aboard with the factor. They squatted by the galley scooping rice out of a bucket with their own horn spoons which they habitually wore in their hair. They grinned at him and he nodded back. It was no small reinforcement he had gained. The odds against him were now only about two to one.

The night wore on quietly enough. Ali Bongo and his watch relieved Juan's. Ferdinando came on deck and they talked for hours. An enormous amount of information was to be culled from the factor. He was certainly a valuable man. Yes, he had been born here—at Bangalang. His father had been the captain of one of old Señor Gallego's ships. "A gentleman, señor, a Castilian." Of his mother he said nothing, nor of his sister. Anthony wondered how Ferdinando could be so sure that all was going well with her on shore. If it had been Anthony's sister, for instance . . . or was the half-breed merely indifferent? The moon came up very late, only a remnant of herself red and inflamed, looking through the fog that settled over the treetops. An increased roaring and howling of tribes of monkeys inundated the night. At Bangalang the tireless tom-tomers and drummers changed their rhythms again. Those drums! Not a sign on shore yet. Only the lights up at the residence and a few drunken shouts now and then. The barracoons lay miserably dark and silent.

Anthony went below and got his boat cloak and a thin blanket for Ferdinando. There was a certain damp-coolness from the river equivalent to cold. One felt it in the lungs. Ferdinando spoke of the ague. "You will probably die of that, señor. They all do who come here, sooner or later. Do you smell the forest?

I do only when I remember it. It is that miasma that gets in your bones. It is a very unusual season here, the rains have been delayed; intermittent. Usually it pours for weeks at a time."

"You seemed to have survived," murmured Anthony.

"Ah, that is different. A dash of . . ." Ferdinando bit off another cigar. He enjoyed the fresh Havana immensely.

Anthony also inhaled slowly. It kept him awake and soothed at the same time. He realized as he leaned back and began his fourth cigar that night how much tobacco had come to mean to him. Here he could see it might come to mean even more. One would need it. A little brandy was also helpful, he found—on a night like this—a very little of course. He passed the flask to his companion who agreed.

Brother François went forward with a light and disappeared into the fo'c'sle. He stayed there a long time. Finally he came aft again.

"Come," said he, flashing the lantern on the two leaning back in the chairs apparently asleep. "I want to show you something. No, *you*, my son." He motioned the half-breed back. Anthony followed Brother François into the fo'c'sle. The priest held up the lantern.

There was someone huddled up in the forward bunk. The blood on the blankets was of a peculiar, dark purple colour, almost black, and shiny. It seemed terrible that the man's hair was still dark and curly. It seemed to have a life of its own. The face was *so* dead—turned toward the wall and grey-ash coloured. It was one of the oldest of the crew. Yet he had somehow the expression of an infant now. It was also monkey-like. It needed life to make it bearable. Cold and only half awake as he was, Anthony felt the fear of it, a repulsion to the clay of it leapt up in him.

"Who has done this?" something asked. "This is really you—like you. It might happen to you. Run away! You will be overtaken by this fate. Beware"—and all the time he knew and tried to deny to himself that he had caused this. His mind to relieve him started to show him a map design in the bloodstains. There were the Cape Verdes and just east of it a large black-purple stain. A little *too* heart shaped for Africa, not perfect, nature scarcely ever did . . . The lantern moved and the shadow of the bunk swooped over the sleeper. Anthony saw Brother François was looking at him.

"One of the crew," he said mechanically. "I don't know. They must have left him here this afternoon. He may not have been dead then. They should have . . . Damn it! Do you think it is *my* fault?" he ripped out. The priest's gaze angered him. Brother François did not reply. . . .

"Well, what else *could* I do? You know the circumstances. Would you just have stood by and let them murder us? Would you?" He felt sorry and angry now at the same time.

"What is it you are trying to do?" said Brother François.

"Collect a debt," snapped Anthony. "Three shiploads of goods were . . ."

"Look at the ledger now," said the priest. He moved the lantern so that the light fell into the bunk again. Anthony looked. They stood silent for a moment. The lantern guttered.

"What is the use of talking about it?" said he, and stalked on deck again. He felt vastly annoyed at Brother François. Let him bury the dead. Now! Why keep on being reminded? He roused Ali Bongo and gave directions. "Put two shots in the shrouds . . . Before it gets light." He was glad to be back on deck again.

A great deal of shouting was going on on shore. He turned to watch that.

"They must all be very drunk now," said Ferdinando coming and leaning by him at the rail. They stood smoking for almost half an hour. The door at the high house on the hill finally opened and disgorged a yelling mob. Several torches flared up from one. Then a lot of them together started to come downhill. The shadows danced weirdly clear out over the water. A kind of Walpurgis procession accompanied by flaring pine knots borne by staggering and capering figures was streaming downhill. The crew stopped now and then to shout hoarsely and argue with one another. Something was up. They seemed to be pushing a cart. The lights glinted on metal. About half-way down they all stopped short. A shed room cut them off. By climbing the shrouds, half-way up you could still see them from the schooner over the top of one of the water-front sheds. It was hard to tell what they were up to at that distance and in the waving light.

Suddenly a streak of red fire dirked into the night. A round shot screamed through the rigging like a banshee. The loud slap of the report followed. On the hill a cloud of sulphur smoke drifted back redly through the frantic torches. A wild shout of glee went up.

"Madre de Dios," said Ferdinando, "it is the saluting cannon, a five-pounder. Gallego kept it dismounted in the warehouse."

They could hear a fierce clamour in the barracoons now. Above this the little gun spoke viciously again. A loud cracking started aloft followed by a dismal crash as the foretopmast tore loose and smashed along the deck. The hill clamoured with triumph. It was certainly the devil's luck of a shot.

"Get below," shouted Anthony. There was no use exposing the men now.

"The chances are in the darkness they won't hit us again," said he to Ferdinando as they came down from the shrouds.

"No, but on the other hand we can't reach them," replied the factor. "You see from the deck here they are hidden up the slope just behind the shed roof." Anthony, Ferdinando, and Ali Bongo gathered about the carronade. Nothing but the dim glow of torches showed over the shed on shore.

"Shoot through the roof, señor," suggested Ferdinando.

"No, that will carry clean over them I am afraid. You see they are down the hill a bit and dropping their shot on us over the shed roof. It would take a mortar to fetch them from here. This long gun will not give us the angle."

A shot plunged into the bay and ricocheted over the schooner.

"One mans on shore, him sober," said Jaumee, who just then came up to join the nonplussed group coolly enough.

They all laughed a little wryly.

"What do, Jaumee?"

"Wait morning-light," grunted the laconic pilot wrapping his blanket about him and sitting down in the lee of the bulwark.

The advice seemed good. They could drop the ship downstream at dawn if necessary. It was uncomfortable sitting still, but risking grounding on a flat in the darkness was worse.

The shooting continued for some time and then stopped.

"About an hour till dawn, I take it," said Anthony.

"A little longer I think, señor," replied Ferdinando.

Then he leaped to his feet. A waving orange light was irradiating the water front.

"They have fired the boat shed!" cried the factor. "The powder!"

A long yellow flame licked through the thatch illuminating the water and making the *Ariostatica* stand out darkly. On her deck the long shadows leaped to and fro. The shed suddenly began to burn fiercely as a tar barrel in it commenced to vomit flames. The whole bay danced with reflections now.

"Get the anchor up! Juan," shouted Anthony. The men began to tumble up. Strangely enough the shooting was not resumed yet from shore.

"They are waiting for more light," said Ferdinando. An explosion of the gun followed as if in answer.

A maddening delay occurred getting the bars in the capstan. Then the *clank-clank* of the schooner's anchor chain coming in sounded over the water. An answering roar of voices came from the hill. The flames from the burning shed at that instant leaped higher. A full half of it was on fire now. A roaring and crackling came over the bay. Showers of sparks fled up into the stars. A white light beat along the water front. The dock and the barracoons behind it projected themselves clear as midday in a frame of blue darkness.

Suddenly the big timber gate at the water front was flung open and some of the crew rushed out and started to shoot muskets at the schooner. They were gunning for the men about the capstan. The bullets splashed about. A beam in the shed fell sending up a fountain of sparks.

"Help, señor," shouted Ali Bongo. "See!"

Anthony left the capstan and rushed to aid Ali Bongo at the carronade. Racing aft he glanced over his shoulder. Through the gate of the barracoon the rest of the crew was emerging rolling the little five-pounder before them.

"Allah, Allah," shouted Ali Bongo. He was stuffing the contents of a trader's chest of notions into the carronade; copper bangles, brass beads, knives, a small music box. It began to play "Richard, O mon roi."

"Out of the way, man, bring fire!" Anthony laid the sight square on the gate. The crew were bunched there, swarming about the little gun, a black writhing mass of men in the fatal glare. This time the match was ready. He blew on it. "Richard, Richard, O mon . . ."

The two guns from the ship and shore spoke at the same instant. Splinters ripped from the bulwark of the schooner. Anthony felt the wind of the ball. But he had eyes for nothing but the fiery scene ashore.

In the gateway of the barracoon a wave of chains, toys, and slugs had mowed the crew down like the blade of a whistling scythe.

Not a sound could be heard except the crackling of the flames. Everyone stood rooted gazing shoreward. A red arm leaped up out of the shed into the sky; a thunder-clap; a long roar. The whole shed vaulted into heaven bellowing.

In the intense glare of the powder explosion Anthony saw the whole of Gallego's place stand out like a landscape in a thunder-storm; the long sheds with the solemn dark palms drooping over them, the residence with its wide porches, the black jungle-covered hills.

"Mine!" he cried.

Darkness swooped; sparks and hissing timbers rained into the bay. He took a long, deep breath. The air felt cool just before dawn. He filled his lungs again to their usual rhythm. That had been disturbed only temporarily. Life in this new place was going to go on again. What were swift events? Merely an interlude. As long as the lungs and heart went on one went on with them. That is, one resumed. And now at last he was master. Let the new day come quickly. He leaned over the rail looking shoreward.

From the forward deck of the *Ariostatica* came the voice of Brother François saying the office for the dead. Presently there was a splash. Anthony turned and went below. No matter what happened a man had to sleep. Tomorrow and tomorrow and tomorrow?

39. VIEWED FROM GALLEGOS

Fᴙᴏᴍ the porch of the "Residence" at Gallegos there was a sweeping view. The establishment lay on the first rise of ground inland. It was quite high enough to overlook the tallest treetops of the coastal jungle on the plain below it. At evening the sun could be seen flashing on the distant silver of the Atlantic that bounded its horizon westward. Also, Gallegos was high enough to catch the sea breeze at night. That was what made Gallegos possible for white men.

Southward, you looked out over Gallegos Reach, a kind of tidal lake in the forest about a mile across, where the Rio Pongo widened out swirling slowly when the tide changed. You kept on looking—if it was not midday and the waters below turned into an intolerable blinding flash—over the mangroves on the long, low point where the hawks nested to the wider reaches of the tidal flats and swampy islands about Bangalang lower down.

The huts of the Kru settlement were built along a brief stretch of sandy beach on a low island. By day the long fisher canoes could be seen drawn up on the sand in regular rows, and by night the native fires wavered and twinkled through the river mists. Over the roofs of Bangalang, five or six miles away, the long slave pens of Mongo Tom's establishment and the whitewashed house just above them stood out boldly from the clearing on the river bank which it occupied. Indeed, with a small glass, from Gallegos the slaves working in the manioc rows of the Mongo's fields could be seen quite plainly.

All the rest of the world to be seen from Gallegos was forest.

A vast, flat sea of treetops marched northward hundreds of miles toward the doubtful boundary of Sierra Leone, and Freetown. The same boundless ocean swept without an undulation southward toward Cape Palmas far over the horizon. Over this the eye ranged monotonously, the only breaks in the flat roof of the forest below were a few loops of the river west of Mongo Tom's where it suddenly narrowed again and twisted tortuously to the sea. Known to traders as the "Rio Pongo" from early Portuguese times, the river was called the *Kavalli* or *Cavala* by the various Kru peoples who inhabited the coast.

Gallegos was in a great many ways a pleasant place at which to live. It was situated in a nest of low hills just where the river finally emerged from the plateau behind it and debouched into the lowlands.

The ground here rose in three distinct steps from the stream.

Along the river bank, on a flat a few hundred yards wide, were situated the dock with the various stores and sheds attached to it, and the long barracoons or slave pens, which occupied considerable space. From these the hill rose fairly steeply to a level horseshoe-shaped inset containing some fifty or sixty acres of rich, black soil. Behind that again the crest of the little range of hillocks was reached by a rather easy ascent.

There the upland jungle began and stretched away eastward towards the unknown—or the "Mountains of the Moon"—if one preferred to take on faith the first object besides elephants and lions marked on the maps. At any rate, it was at this point that the trail from the interior emerged from the forest over which every year came Arab caravans with their human and other merchandise, which supplied the reason for Gallegos' being a place at all.

Not long after taking over the establishment Anthony had built himself a new residence. The old one, which Ferdinando now occupied, lay near the top of the lower rise and was constructed with wattled clay walls and a palm-thatch roof. One rainy season spent beneath its dripping cover, and many harrowing experiences with both white and red ants, had convinced Anthony of the necessity of a better abode.

During the endless, dreary days when the rain fell for weeks at a time he had amused himself by drawing elaborate and careful plans, not only for his new "castle," as he called it, but for the rehabilitation of the whole establishment which the last Gallego, not much of a man he soon learned, had allowed to fall into considerable disarray.

Labour was no consideration on the Grain Coast. The slaves who would otherwise have been confined to the barracoons were set to work as soon as the dry season returned the first November after Anthony's arrival. In the meantime experience had taught him a good deal about the country, and, as he sat late one afternoon on the porch of the new residence overlooking his domain, he felt justified in feeling that on the whole, for a new arrival, he had then planned well.

Not that in the light of what he knew now, after longer familiarity, he would not do some things differently. The slave pens should have been further enlarged, for instance, and the dock extended. It would save a great deal of time and worry to have the ships tie up to the dock directly instead of anchoring in midstream as they still had to do. But who could have foreseen that things would go as well with him at Gallegos as they had?

Indeed, there had been that anxious four months the first year when he had not been sure that any ships would ever anchor at Gallegos at all. Old Mongo Tom, too, had certainly made all the trouble he could. Thank the stars that was over with, the old dog! Well, he was brought to heel now, and probably for good and all. For all practical purposes the entire landscape Anthony now looked over, from the new veranda at Gallegos to the Mongo's fields six miles away across the bay, was a very—well, a very Adverse one. Yes, on the whole, a great deal had been accomplished since the *Ariostatica* had pulled in three years before—a great deal!

He leaned back in the ample cane chair and threw his palm hat on the floor. It had been a hot day and he had been all over the plantation. It was two months till the autumn rains yet and things were pretty dry. But that was to be expected. Also the irrigation helped. Now for a bath and a drink!—or a drink. Why wait? The house servants brought back from Cuba had it too easy anyway. They needed a mistress.

"Cheecha."

"Sí, sí, señor."

"Rum, and limes!"

"Sí, sí."

It was like Cibo to have sent him that girl. Well, he could well afford to as far as that went. Cibo had had his pick now out of many a shipload. Fourteen ships in three years! And the fifteenth swinging at anchor below there now, *La Fortuna*, a new one to the trade. He hoped Cibo had not forgotten to send the right kind of trade goods. Another caravan was due soon, despite the nearness of the rainy season, and the stock in the warehouse was low. Not a slave in the pens and Mongo Tom had less than fifty, all old ones, too! The neighbouring country was pretty well worked out.

He lit a fresh Havana that had just come on *La Fortuna*—and enjoyed it greatly. The mould here did play the mischief with tobacco. The smoke drifted straight up to the ceiling. The sea-breeze would not be in for an hour yet. Twenty minutes after the sun went down the wind changed, by the clock. Gad, how well he knew the ways of the place now; the seasons, the clouds, and the winds; their rhythm; the very look and smell of things!

In a few weeks the cloudless sky would commence to become a little hazy. Already the river mists were thicker at night. Then the clouds would begin to pile themselves up higher day by day. Great cliffs and mountains of them would finally tower up height beyond height till it was dizzying to look up into them. The sunsets were beyond thought then. Soon there would be lightning at night; far-off thunder muttering. Then nights of a long battle-roll of it and on into the day, and then— the clouds would approach each other and exchange broad- sides. They would dissolve into one grey pall, a few drops would fall, a shower, and—as if spigots had been turned on above—one long month by month downpour. It did not seem to rain by drops. For three months it slanted past and furiously down, as if each slant were an individual and perpetual jet from a hole in the sky. But it would be better this rainy season, the first in the new house since it was finished. It might even be comfortable, and there would be a let-up in the perpetual man- hunt. There would be time to put things in order, to go over the accounts, and to make plans for next year.

There would also be time to devote to Neleta! No more sur- reptitious meetings because of Ferdinando's pride. That half- breed! So was his sister! What of it? No, they would live to- gether now in the same house! Brother François could look as sad as he wanted to. Neleta would be housekeeper now. House- keeper! He smiled, and drifted away on a vision that relaxed him in the chair.

Ferdinando could not expect him to marry her. Marry her? He laughed.

Ferdinando was making too good a thing of it as it was. He was sorry now he had allowed him head-money on every cargo. It was enough for Ferdinando to have the run of the place as factor—and his sister was the mistress of the big house on the hill. What a fool he had been to wait so long to bring her up from her brother's. It had got to be like acting. Let her come and live with him. He was master here. Master—a rich one, too.

To think that only three years ago he had been trying to collect a debt for Mr. Bonnyfeather—and now . . .

He let his eye wander over the ample plantation that lay just below the house.

He had built the house well below the crest. The shadow of the hill behind it gave two extra hours of coolness in the morning. All his planting was doing well; the coffee, the rows of cassava; cocoa, maize, yams, rice and eleusine; pumpkins, gourds, cabbages, sweet potatoes, and okra. They flourished, and with only a little tending. Next year he would increase the acreage and put in indigo, cotton, sugar cane, and ginger; enough manioc to supply the whole establishment. It would take a few more field hands but he was not going to ship every last man, woman, and child that came down with the caravans to Havana any more.

No, he was in a position to hold back now and dictate a little. He would build up a permanent establishment here and he would make it self-supporting. If anything happened to cut him off from Cuba he would be able to go along then on his own account. About twenty field hands, ten Foulahs for a garrison, and a few more house servants, well-trained ones, would do. This year would see the whole place stockaded. It had been a big job, ten-foot tree trunks from the crocodile creek behind the hill to the river front. They swept clear around the place in a convincing horseshoe. With the next gang that came down he would stockade the creek bank, too. The thorn boma there was only good to keep out the chimpanzees.

It was a relief to get rid of those rascals and the monkeys. Watching big Diana monkeys with the orange behinds ransack the new fruit orchards had been a trial. Shooting them from the front porch was all right by day—but in the morning! Well, he was pretty well enclosed now, and by next summer he would have quantities of oranges, limes, and lemons. The papayas were already prodigious and there were shiploads of bananas. The cocoanuts, avocado pears, and figs one had to wait for. But not long. Now that the little zebra-goats couldn't get in and girdle the trees any more! They *were* devils. He wondered if Cibo had sent him the pineapple cuttings. They ought to do well here.

Next spring, the wonderful spring after the rains, when the air grew clear and the sun seemed to pull things up out of the earth by their tips—spring would see Gallegos the little paradise he had planned. No place on the whole Grain Coast would be like it. And he would live here with Neleta and keep on accumulating. Neleta would look after the house as it should be looked after. Some day he would go back, rich. He would settle in London or Paris, and live! He would invite Mr. and Mrs. David Parish to dinner—to a very formal dinner under very fine chandeliers, a splendid place, butlers and lackeys, the Bonnyfeather arms. Why not? Perhaps Dolores would be at the other end of the table. But to give all this up now; Neleta, the house; not to see the growth next spring; not to go up-country after being here three years! Unthinkable! Yes, it would be very lovely next spring, and it would pay, pay highly, to stay. After all, what would he be doing in Europe? Really he couldn't imagine that. One dinner with Florence was not a life.

The wild fowl were going now, going south. As he watched a great flight of them lifted from the reach below and made off over Cape Palmas way. The handsome little sparrow-hawks that lived on the rocky point above the mangroves seemed excited about it, too. But they stayed. In the spring all the ducks would come back, and the great black swans. The rains certainly could not be far off.

He had forgotten the Christian calendar here. He told time only by the rhythms of the seasons. The swinging back and forth over the sky of the vast flocks of birds just before and after the rains, the slow ranging and rearrangement of the clouds, the shifting of the winds, and the gradual dying out of the intense green of the forest below him as the dry season advanced marked the passing of the year. Even the stars failed him in these latitudes. They were all strange, and much inferior, he thought, to the northern constellations. Only the wandering planets and the moon came back like old friends. The sun was so fierce it seemed another sun. Gradually one learned things about the tropical sun; how friendly and how deadly it could be.

Yes, he acknowledged to himself, he loved it all. Gallegos had become home. This month—he knew it was February from the manifest of *La Fortuna*—this month it had all, rather suddenly, become "home." He knew he was going to be here a long time now. Perhaps Neleta's coming to the house had something to do with it, but he was not sure. Perhaps?

He finished his drink, the early evening drink, that he had to admit now he depended upon. It made him feel himself again after the day in the sun. His face lost something of a certain mask-like quality it had taken on. The yellow tinge that had grown under his tan faded. His eyes grew bright and the small red veins at the corners of them stood out a little.

He felt now, after the rum and lime juice and sugar had taken hold of him, he felt as he had when he first came from Havana three years ago. Why was it though, he could no longer get as much done in the day as he always planned to do the evening before—after the drink? By noon it did not seem to matter. Last year it had not been that way. But, pshaw! how could he feel better than he did now? All bronze, not an ounce of fat on him! He put down the glass to watch the sunset. A drowsiness overcame him. The darkening blue dome of the sky with the black lines of birds streaming across it down to the lower range of the horizon beyond the two lakes slowly faded. The birds seemed to be going downhill from the top of a bowl. He closed his eyes.

Half an hour later he wakened chilled by the sea-breeze and went in to change into dry clothes. He shivered slightly. Sitting in sweaty clothes in the cool wind was the one thing you should not do. It was almost dark now; stars. He looked out of the window at the dank river mists gathering below. Fever lurked there. He took his drench of cinchona bark. Horrible stuff, bitter! He killed the taste with a good swallow of brandy. Then he felt warm again. His feet lightened under him. He hustled into a heavy cotton evening suit and put on a cravat. The captain of *La Fortuna* was coming up to dinner tonight. Ferdinando would be up too to go over the ship's manifests with him. It would be the first dinner when Neleta would sit at the table. How would Ferdinando take it—and Brother François? Well, they could—*take it*.

He shrugged his shoulders and went into the eating room.

40. THE MASTER OF GALLEGOS

Don Ruiz de la Matanza, the captain of *La Fortuna*, which now lay anchored in Gallegos Reach, was a Toledan of ancient family who had seen better days. There was a decided but a native hauteur about him. Only in a way was he glad to find himself in the merchant service—via a naval court-martial which could only be said to have been lenient.

Even in the Spanish navy the practice of selling the cannon out of king's ships for old bronze had to be discouraged, and the wrinkles in the official forehead had frowned Don Ruiz into the streets without even his sword left to protect his outraged honour. The terrible dilemma of begging for work had made even a Matanza pliable, however, and after some years Don Ruiz wriggled himself onto a merchantman's quarter-deck.

A fine full-rigged ship was now his, *La Fortuna*. Originally built for the Manila run, she had splendid cabins and great hold space like the galleons on whose track she had followed. As a balm to his hurt pride Don Ruiz ran her like a king's ship in all ways—except selling her cannon for about half what they cost. He had only consented to enter the slave trade on account of the very high profits, and by the clever solicitations of Carlo Cibo at Havana.

Anthony could see as soon as he entered the eating room that Captain Matanza was inclined to hold himself aloof. Mere slavers were evidently not his usual company. The very way he emphasized the "de la" in presenting himself showed that. And he was evidently nettled that only the factor Ferdinando had greeted his distinguished arrival.

Anthony, however, had taken a leaf from the excellent book of John Bonnyfeather in how to receive and entertain ship captains. He no longer met the ships as soon as they anchored but sent out Ferdinando. He then received a report as to the nature of the ship's commander, read personal mail which the vessel brought him, and with all necessary human and business details thus thoroughly in mind sent an invitation to dine to the captain.

All this had its effect. If it did nothing else, it induced the more surly rascals among ship's officers to recollect what decent manners their memories might still retain. And it impressed all newcomers with the fact that in dealing with the Master of Gallegos familiarity was not in order, for as long as they lay at his anchorage, he held not only the whip hand, but the face cards in every little deal. To be invited to dinner at the new residence was therefore something to remember, and to talk about afterwards in Havana.

Indeed, the approach to the new house had been planned somewhat for its "diplomatic" effect. A flight of broad steps hewn out of the living rock of the hill led up from the sheds and barracoons on the flat to a loopholed palisade on the level of the plantations. From this a straight road of beaten clay lined with giant funtumas already twenty feet high, so rapid was their growth, gave a clear vista to the house itself situated about an eighth of a mile across the cultivated fields of the little plateau and half-way up the final rise beyond. Beyond that the pointed posts of the palisade could be seen against the sky, crossing the hill in a bristling arc.

The house itself was built of large, native brick made from the same clayey soil in which coffee flourished so well. It was absolutely four-square and surrounded on all sides by a veranda of noble proportions set on natural pillars of dracaena trees. These had been stripped of their bark, leaving the smooth, oily surface beneath to harden and glisten in the sun. The rafters of the roof and the porch were the same, making one sheer start from the peak of the roof to the eaves of the veranda. Anthony had covered them with red tiles which had been brought as ballast in an empty slaver from Cuba. Not only was this the only tile roof on the West coast, it was also the only rain- and snake-proof house-cover in that part of Africa. The outer walls of the place were whitewashed.

Seen from the anchorage, this house had the appearance of a large white tent with a red roof, the flag pole projecting from the centre court and the shadows under the poles of the veranda completing the illusion. It was only when it was approached closely that its essential solidity and capabilities for defence became apparent. A small trench supplied with flowing water, that was really only a defence against ants and other pests, completely surrounded it and gave it somewhat the look of a moated grange. The heavy shutters of the few outside windows might be seen by an observing person to be loopholed, set at commanding angles in the wall, and few and far between. The door was small and would have taken a cannon to dislodge it. Indeed, the outer openings were scarcely more than holes for ventilation, and the house depended for both air and sunlight upon the large and beautifully planted central patio, where a spring bubbled up, and to which the house was open internally on all sides.

All these details had by no means been lost upon the ex-naval eye of Don Ruiz de la Matanza as he ascended the hill with Ferdinando. Nor did he fail to note the Foulah sentry protecting the stockade parapet with an elephant gun, nor two heavy culverins in concealed enclosures where a man kept watch night and day with a match burning. From their emplacement just a little below the house round shot could be plunged onto the deck on any vessel below. In fact the whole establishment and the river bays for several miles were subject to the muzzles of those guns. Whatever else he might be, Don Ruiz had already decided before he entered the house that its owner was no fool. His experience at supper that night strengthened this opinion.

His impression of Anthony when he entered the room was that of a tall and powerfully slender young man, the quiet assurance of whose bearing was rendered attractive and rather remarkable by his extreme ease of movement. A certain polished aloofness of manner, which to anyone but a Spaniard would have seemed a trifle old-fashioned, gave him a dignity that scarcely coincided with his years. This precocious gravity was really a projection of John Bonnyfeather rather than Anthony's inward conviction of pride, but it had the effect of making others feel at first a little puzzled and uncomfortable and so constituted for Anthony at once a means of attack and a hidden but powerful reserve.

His voice, when he spoke, which was not often, had now greatly deepened. It ranged when he was angry or scornful into the bass. Ordinarily it remained quiet, mellow, and clear. But he enunciated his words now with a certain assurance and precision not altogether pleasant. In two years the master of Gallegos had acquired the easy habit of command, but he had also lost a certain natural persuasiveness which had once been a positive charm. This, to tell the truth, he was not at all aware of.

At first there seemed something hard-bitten about his face to a new-comer like Don Ruiz. It was very—almost too regular in feature. The finely chiselled nose would have been too sensitive and feminine if it had not been for the hard chin beneath it and for the nervous but firmly set mouth. No one could tell what his complexion had been, he was now burnt so black. His eyebrows were bleached white and his lids slightly puckered. The whites of his eyes were no longer boyishly clear but tinged slightly yellow. His large pupils seemed to veil themselves as if they had something to conceal. It was this quality of the eyes, always directed somewhere else even when looking at you, that lent Anthony a certain mystery which few who saw him failed to feel. In the final analysis it was hard to tell to whom you were talking. It even seemed as you came to know him better as though the gracefully directed precision of the young man before you was somehow controlled from otherwhere.

All the negroes noticed it. Even the wide and pleasant forehead, the now closely cropped but still wavy and sunny hair could not overcome the impression. Ferdinando had once mentioned it jokingly.

"The niggers say a wizard has stolen your soul, señor."

Anthony's unexpected and electric outburst of fury had left the half-breed a paler and a wiser man.

To Anthony it seemed that he was at last finding himself; at least he told himself that. Or perhaps he was creating a new self out of the vivid incidents and the cruel, stark realities of the life about him. He was "doing things"; he was being a very practical and a successful man in a situation that had required courage, finesse, adaptability, and grim determination to carry through. In three years he had not only "collected" the debt due to Mr. Bonnyfeather but he had also put himself in the way of being a fairly rich man. What had happened to the firm of *Gallego & Son* in the process he did not know and he did not much care. That some payment as a sort of rental for the place on the Rio Pongo was made to the Gallego heirs he had finally elicited from Cibo after several inquiries. "Herr Meyier is taking care of that out of head-money, and the forced lease has been declared legal. I advise you to drop the matter forthwith as it annoys His Excellency. You have nothing to fear." That was all there was to that. He was master of what the blast from the *Ariostatica* had won, and he did not intend to go out by the same way he had come in.

Yet in growing into the kind of mammal which Cibo had so strongly advised, there was a part of Anthony which seemed to be withering by the way. It was the part of him which lay locked up with the past in the fireproof storeroom he had built, where the chest which had come from Livorno reposed with Mr. Bonnyfeather's books, the sextant, some smaller, more youthful clothes, and his old madonna. Not since he had arrived at Gallegos and buried fourteen of the crew of the *Ariostatica* in Brother François's new graveyard had he once opened it.

Yet it was upon this part of him that his eyes looked when they turned inward. And it was the refusal to listen to certain old promptings that turned his pupils stony and had given him a fixed mask-like cast of countenance. It was all that which turned him white with fury when it had been suggested to him by his half-breed factor that what lay locked up in the fireproof storeroom might be his soul.

He had jumped the doubts as to which was the better man of the two, the old self or the new Master of Gallegos. His will was now all on the side of the latter and it took less and less willing, he thought, to keep himself the Master of Gallegos from day to day. As that man he was devoid of visions. There was no doubt what was real and what was unreal to the newer man. The things of the body were now no longer merely on a par with dreams. They already mostly were, and might soon come to be altogether the whole world in themselves. It was difficult for him to have achieved this. Two things above all helped him to maintain it; intercourse with Neleta and what he poured into himself from a glass. With only a little stimulant, so far, he could attain for the time being what seemed at least to be a solid basis of personality. Indeed, it was more than that, it was the sensation of a complete unity, of being absolutely physical. Tobacco soothed and allayed; wine stimulated and completed. Neleta was beyond all this, Neleta was indescribable consummation of the flesh alone. He did not need to think about her. He consumed with her. Neleta was fire.

———◆———

On the evening upon which the captain of *La Fortuna* had been bidden to dine Anthony had finally decided to bring this fire to burn openly as it were upon his own hearth. The girl had so far lived, ostensibly at least, with her brother Ferdinando in the factor's house below. She was now to be the mistress of the new residence, and of its master, to run the domestic side of the establishment, and to provide what Anthony had found only she could provide. It was not the nice moral code of the Grain Coast which had hitherto prevented this arrangement from being consummated openly. It was only the hope on the part of Ferdinando that his sister might marry a ship's captain and leave Africa, and a certain lingering reluctance in Anthony to take on any open obligations when there was no necessity for doing so. But Neleta had become necessary and he was now about to admit it. He shook off the recollection of Angela's "marriage breakfast" which occurred to him as they sat down to Neleta's supper. It had taken several glasses of Constantia to effect that.

"It is a 'wyn' which the Dutch raise on the Cape, captain, better I think than Malaga. Certainly it is stronger," he remarked as they sat down to supper. "I secured a whole legger of the Drakenstein of ninety-five for thirty pounds!" and he filled the captain's glass for the third time before the meal from a squat, marble-coloured magnum.

Under the urge of the sunny spirit imprisoned there, which was now released around the whole table, the captain's reservations vanished. The manner of the strange señor inglés became more cordial, he observed, as the meal advanced. His host, as it were, became more and more at home in his own house.

"You see, Don Ruiz, we manage to be fairly comfortable here on the Rio Pongo. We are not such terrible people as rumour, I hear, sometimes paints us."

"I have already discerned that," replied the captain. "Green turtles are not the only attraction on the Grain Coast. Other things also go into making one's soup palatable here, I observe." He smiled, looking at Neleta at the table's end, with more admiration than respect.

"A great deal of sherry," murmured Anthony. "It gives a certain dryness which I mightily like."

The captain somewhat hastily returned to the former subject. "I am really better prepared to find things as they are than you might suspect, señor. Our friend Carlo Cibo was quite glowing in his accounts of your establishment here. Under ordinary circumstances I would not put *La Fortuna* into the slave trade. She is a very fine ship . . ."

"So I am informed," Anthony interrupted. "Carlo was equally glowing in his accounts of *La Fortuna*. I might add that we are both grateful, captain, at having a ship like *La Fortuna*, and a responsible and understanding man like yourself, come out to Gallegos. When we began here we had to put up with what we could get. At that time, about three years ago, the captain-general seized what ships he could at Havana and sent them along. Some of the specimens of both human and naval architecture which came to the Rio Pongo then would make your eyes hang out on your shirt. As soon as I could I protested vigorously. Most of the losses in this business are through stupidity. Brutality and dirt! There is no need for either. 'Send me fast ships with intelligent officers and I will double your profits,' I wrote home. 'Charter them if necessary. What is the use of throwing your cargoes into the sea?' It was a long time, however, before they could understand my arithmetic. So I can honestly say, that it is very gratifying to see a ship like *La Fortuna* riding at anchor here and to be able to entertain her captain as a gentleman deserves. I trust you will find your errand thoroughly worth while. *To your return*, Captain Matanza."

Don Ruiz clicked glasses and with evident satisfaction.

"To you, señor, and—to the lady," he replied rising to the occasion.

They all drank to Neleta, standing, Brother François and Ferdinando, too. Anthony was thankful to them and Neleta radiant. Across the table her sibilant monosyllables came bidding the captain welcome to Gallegos graciously enough.

"Thou art a Catalan! . . . señorita?" he exclaimed.

Anthony overlooked his familiar address. It would not do to press things too far—probably no harm was meant.

"My father was from Barcelona, señor."

"Ah, then you know the Rambla there, perhaps?"

"Very well, indeed, I have played along it often. When I was five years old my father took me and my brother to live there. We *lived* for five years."

"You are dark for a Catalan, señorita. There are many blondes in Barcelona, but mostly the plump, sleepy kind," he laughed. "Perhaps your mother was from Sevilla? It is there the honey-coloured señoritas are found at their best. Pardon, but I admire them greatly. And you wear the shawl thrown over your arms, too. Ah, it is my admiration which has carried me away. Sí, the women of Valencia are beautiful. But let us talk of Barcelona sometime again, señorita. With the señor's permission, of course!" He added that hastily, having become aware of a sudden drop in the temperature. Ferdinando sat looking into his plate as if there were worms in it. He hated his negro blood.

Neleta murmured some politeness in reply and turned to Brother François. "How were his orphans coming on to-day?" . . .

"As I was saying, captain," continued Anthony, engaging that gentleman's somewhat reluctant attention again, "we shall look forward to your returning here often. Now if you will follow my method of storing your cargoes and taking care of them on the voyage home, you will find them in better health when you arrive than when you leave here. It will also keep your ship sweet and clean and I have persuaded Cibo to offer a higher bounty for a healthy shipment delivered in prime shape. He can well afford to do that out of the higher price they will bring. Due to the invention of a cotton-picking machine I hear there is now a great demand in North America for sturdy field hands."

The captain now began to prick up his ears.

"The hunters up-country have been instructed this time to bring down as many Gora warriors as they can round up. I should tell you that we gather our cargoes here in three or four ways. I depend still for the most part on the caravans of slaves which the Mohammedans bring down from the interior about the end of the dry season. You get all kinds from them, good and bad. But you can never be sure. So this year I have also organized some raids of my own under an Arab by the name of Ali Bongo, who is an excellent man. They are working now in virgin country north of the St. Pauls among the Gora forest people. They are a very fine race, totally unlike these ugly coast niggers, the Krus and Gubos, Putus, Sikons and whatnot. The Gora are lighter in colour, of pleasing, almost European features. The lips, of course! They make excellent servants and respond to good treatment. I hope to make up your cargo for the most part from them. My friend Mongo Tom across the bay there works all the local country about here and up and down the coast. By a special arrangement I take them off his hands. Between us we control all the trade on the river. There are also other ways of gathering slaves as you shall see before you go. You will probably have to lie here two or three weeks as the barracoons are practically empty now and you have arrived before the caravans. In that time, if you will, you can pick up a good deal of information about the best method of handling your people on the return voyage. It would be to our mutual advantage, certainly greatly to your own, if you will condescend to profit by our experience. A dirty ship and silly crowding, for instance, can cut profits in half.

"Your able factor has already been telling me things, señor," said the captain. "I can well believe there are tricks in this trade as in any other."

"Ferdinando *is* an excellent man," said Anthony in a low tone. "I back him to the limit. At the same time, captain, if you feel obliged to come to me about anything, please be at liberty to do so. You will find me reasonable, and close-mouthed. I run the place and no one else."

"Thank you for that, señor. You know the chief difficulty a ship master has is with agents and subordinates from whom there is no appeal except . . ." He made a coin-counting motion.

"You do not need to fear that here, Don Ruiz."

The captain raised his brows a little and smiled. "At least you can count on me to follow out your suggestions and learn what

I can," he continued. "I am genuinely anxious to do so. My great pride, señor, is my ship. *La Fortuna*, ah, she is *beautiful!*" His face lit up as when he had been speaking of the women of Seville a few minutes before. "I would not have her filthy, have her smell, her beautiful feathers all smeared, fah!" He held his nose. "I have seen slavers that way. But cargoes are hard to come by now with this cursed war on. I come here only because I must. Ah, pardon me, I forget, but I do not criticize, señor. Not you! We all make our living as we must in this world, not as we should like. It is my ship! I . . ."

Anthony laid his hand on the man's arm. He had found out what the man honoured most. "A ship is not the worst God in the world," he thought, "especially when she is a goddess."

"Come," said he. "You are from Toledo I am told—of the family Matanza! Do you remember this? It is luck that we have it—the last ship in . . ." he drew the cork carefully and filled the captain's glass. The captain sipped.

"Peralta, señor, Dios de Dios! You will be offering me trout from the Tagus next. Ah, that tinge like a remembrance of muscat, the smell of it! It *is* Toledo." He closed his eyes. "I can see the Puerto del Sol! Did you ever see the women of Toledo? They walk in black satin slippers over the sharp, sharp little paving stones there. And their arches never touch them. Firm little bridges over a million sharp diamonds! Toledo!" He opened his eyes looking a little foolish. The wine was gone.

Anthony filled his glass again.

"Gracia, gracia."

"A La Fortuna, sí?" said Anthony.

"Ah, Madre de Dios, señor," murmured the captain draining the second glass of Peralta. "Thou understandest!"

Anthony laughed and the captain hastened to explain.

"It is a relief to find things so." He spread out his hands in a gesture of glad acceptance. "Of Africa and the trade I have heard terrible things. True, your Cibo was persuasive, and *La Fortuna* was lying idle. But I would scarcely have risked her, no, I am sure I would not have come if I had not been asked by Cibo to see the last cargo you sent landed. Madre! The ship, that little *San Pablo* was clean and the niggers all well and dancing. It made me laugh to see them. They were so glad to be in Cuba. You should have been there. They were each given a red cap and a blanket. They forgot all about their friends and country, dancing about like monkeys and putting on new clothes wrong side before. Imagine it! When a cart came they were overwhelmed by the horses. They did not know beasts could be made to work. Then a black postilion in a silver laced hat, sky-blue coat, and white breeches came riding up. They could never get through feeling his polished jack-boots, and watching him leap on and off his prancing horse while his spurs rang. He cracked his whip and told them what a fine thing it was to be a slave of the white man. And they believed him. It was better than anything they had ever known. They all ran to snap fingers with their lucky brother. And the prices they brought next day at the sale! Ah! but in some ways that was *not* so good. The women will cry for their children." He ended looking a little grave.

"I have no doubt what you say is true," said Anthony. "I have never seen any of my cargoes landed in Havana but I know what kind of a life they leave here, captain, and there is no doubt that they go to a better place in Cuba. You see what most people forget is that these people are already slaves in Africa. They have been captured in war, or seized for debts, or condemned as criminals or for witchcraft. Any excuse is enough to make a man or woman a slave here. The powerful chiefs regard the weak or unfortunate as just so much walking capital and they draw their interest by putting them to work. It is the way that this part of the world not only does business but exists and it always has been that way. On the whole, the life they go to on any plantation run by Europeans in America is better than what they leave here. They are safer, more comfortable. Even their hardships are comparative luxuries. The English, I believe, are the worst masters. Jamaica, they say, is a bad place to go, even worse for a slave than Africa."

Anthony looked up to catch a smile on Ferdinando's face.

"Señor Adverse is eloquent sometimes, captain," said the

factor. "He should add that there would not be nearly so many slaves captured if it were not for the temptations the white man brings in the way of goods."

"Yes," said Anthony a little reluctantly, "that is true. It is curious to think that after all it is the desire of the European merchants to sell cloth, firearms, rum, and various manufactured articles that makes men slavers here. That, and the necessity for cheap labour in America and the West Indies. That is what makes the New World go."

"Go where?" interrupted Brother François who had been talking to Neleta.

"Ah, father, I will not argue with you tonight," laughed Anthony. "You are not a trader. The father is opposed to all this," he explained. "He spends his time here making it as easy as he can for those who are gathered in by the raiders. I will show you his good works tomorrow. They are, well—remarkable. I co-operate, you know. That is all I *can* do." He frowned a little. "Try some of this Arab stew, captain. It is curried lamb with rice balls seethed in milk. Do!" He heaped Don Ruiz's plate for him and refilled his glass.

The captain and Ferdinando now devoted themselves to their plates and sundry items of commercial news. Brother François had fallen silent, Anthony observed. Neleta ate quietly. Only in her eating did she betray her native origin, everything was managed with a spoon and two fingers. With apparently no effort she simply made her food disappear as if by sleight of hand.

Anthony sat looking at her at the other end of the table momentarily forgetful of everything but the coming night that they would spend together. It had been a long time now! Occasionally her eyes, that shone in the candles with a greenish flare, looked out at him from under her long black lashes. From time to time they lightened like a leopard's half concealed in moonlight. The spidery-silk fringes of a Manila shawl drooped from her tawny arms and its embroidered magenta roses seemed to clamber over her breast and shoulders as if a tropical vine had found a strong, lithe young tree to flaunt itself upon in some open glade of the jungle. Under the shadow of her yellow bodice her breast rose and fell slowly with a deep visible motion that timed with a slight widening of her keen nostrils or a flash of her large white teeth.

The colours that the girl wore would have overpowered most European women; they would have been bizarre. But there was something so vivid about Neleta, so brilliantly passionate and virile without a hint of nervousness, that the magenta roses in the gleaming white shawl and the golden yellow of her dress were reduced by her to the equivalent of more sombre tones. What she put on, she made a part of her. Yet she triumphed over what she wore, for through the folds of her shawl and the yellow silk of her dress her body shone with even more luminous curves and lines.

Neleta was the crown of all this new life Anthony had carved out of the forest and seized for himself. She was the walking answer—and how she could walk!—to the objections expressed and understood which Brother François—that the mere presence of Brother François—constantly posed.

It was still a puzzle to Anthony how Brother François could still disapprove of him and yet be affectionate and kindly. Indeed, it was the affection in his disapproval that was hardest to stand. But he would forget all that—tonight! After he had gone over the ship's mail and the invoices with Ferdinando—then—then he would give himself to Neleta. It was like that. He would give himself to her. She would be waiting.

He leaned his head on his hand looking at her with the strong, calm glow of wine thoroughly upon him. In the light of the candles and of the palm-oil lamps, where cotton wicks floated throwing a mellow glow through the calabash rinds, the room swam with a soft suffused pallor while Cheecha and her assistant girls came and went silently on bare feet like ministering shadows. One side of the place was screened from the court by long strips of white muslin sewn together and on this he could see the shadows of palm fronds moving in the moonlight. The spring gurgled in its stone basin beyond. The red-striped native pottery stood out above the table-cloth in startling patterns, and the faces and voices of his guests seemed hazy and distant as he lost himself inwardly in a dream of contented approval, wordless, and imageless except for what lay vaguely before him. It was a feeling of satisfaction and equilibrium that he would allow no thoughts to mar.

It was Neleta who finally motioned to him. The others had finished. She and Brother François left. Ferdinando dumped the mail pouch on the table. With a bundle of black cigars before them they spread out various papers and got down to the business of the evening.

Anthony set aside the bundles of newspapers in various languages which Cibo assiduously collected for him from ships' captains at Havana. They would serve to while away many a tedious afternoon during the rainy season, although some of them were nearly a year old.

The business of being a slaver, Don Ruiz could see, was an intricate one. Indeed, Anthony's long hours spent with accounts, correspondence, and invoices at the Casa da Bonnyfeather now stood him in good stead. Most of the slavers on the Coast, he discovered, had failed largely because they kept no books. They were always in debt when they closed out, or they got careless and turned over the warehouses to clerks who robbed them. Gallego had left his keys to the old woman in charge of his harem. Ferdinando had been helpless under her pilfering. Anthony had shipped her off to Cuba as he did not wish to be poisoned. She had gone aboard ship foaming. The rest of the seraglio had departed with her. It had been a memorable day. He grinned remembering it, while he ran his eye over the statement of the last voyage which Cibo had sent him.

Carlo Cibo, Agent, Regla, Havana, Cuba, to the Master of Gallegos on the Rio Pongo of the Grain Coast, Africa.

Voyage Statement of the Schooner *San Pablo*, 90 tons burthen, Miguel Gomez, Master

1. Out Costs

Fitting Out:

New sails and extras .... 956.43$

Carpenter's bill	1,005.00
Cooper's bill	684.22
Provisions:	
For crew	784.90
For slaves (on return trip)	560.21
Wages Advanced:	
18 men before the mast at 50$	900.00
To captain, mate, boatswain, cook, and steward	440.00
Trade Goods:	
Muslins, muskets, powder, lead, cigars, copper wire, beads, trinkets, mirrors, rum and 500 Maria Teresa dollars, etc.	9,849.60
Gratifications:	
To Port Officials	150.00
Clergy for blessing the ship	25.00
Police	200.00
Governor's Secretary	50.00
To owners for use of ship during temporary sequestration	1,200.00
	16,805.36$
Commission to Señor Carlo Cibo at 10 %	1,680.54
Total for voyage out	18,485.90$

2. Costs Return Voyage

Wages:	
Captain	225.00$
First Mates	175.00
Second Mates	125.00
Boatswains	90.00
Cooks' and Stewards'	257.00
17 men before the mast	1,872.00
Head-Money:	
Captain's at 3$ a head	681.00
Mate's at 2$ a head	454.00
Other ship's officers at 1$ a head	454.00

Water casks and medicines purchased from ship
Mercedes at sea on return voyage 83.50

Total for voyage home . . . .   4,416.50$

3. Charges at Havana

Captain-General's honorarium . . . .   1,000.00$
Gratification Herr Herman Meyier 500.00
Gratification Clerks at Caxa da Consolidación 155.00
Havana pilot 10.00
Wharfage 25.00
Subsistence of slaves on shore before sale 136.00
227 slave dresses at 2$ 454.00
Mid-wife's fee at lazeretto (twins) 2.00
Coffin for mother 5.00
Hire of wench for wet nurse 1.50
Sundries, purser's cash disbursements, and all extras   984.60
Sale announcements and barkers-up 32.00
Auctioneer's fee at 2 % 1,422.92

Total charges at Havana . . . .   4,728.02$
Total all expenses . . . .   27,630.42$

4. Returns

Proceeds of 221 slaves at auction . . . .   71,146.00$
Proceeds of 5 female slaves by private view sales . .   2,730.00
Proceeds twin infants born Havana 20.00
Proceeds gold dust, ivory, and palm oil 18,124.00

92,020.00$

RÉSUMÉ

Total proceeds slaves and cargo . . . .   92,020.00$
Total all expenses 27,630.42

Net profit on voyage . . . .   64,389.58$
J. Garvin, Clerk.

. . . You will see by this [Cibo's letter ran on] *that business is not half bad. There is a great dearth here of slaves due to the disturbed state of commerce since hostilities began, and healthy ones especially bring large prices. The Yankee brush with France has blown over and there has been an influx of Yankee bidders for the Carolina rice plantations and the Virginia cotton and tobacco fields. Bueno! What do you think—your Jew tailor bought the twins and is raising them in his back patio. All Havana is laughing at him. Like most Shylocks he has a soft spot in a hard heart. His Excellency is also in a seventh heaven over additions to his revenue. I have, mon vieux, arranged to split with the government on this cargo, their share three-quarters net proceeds on the slaves. In other words, you receive 11,566.40$ as all expenses are charged against the slaves, and the government gets the remainder. This does not, of course, touch the proceeds from the gold, ivory, etc., as that is disposed of quietly on the side and is no one's business but our own. You will therefore get a total of 29,690.40$, less my 10 % consignment commission which you must admit, as a fellow mammalian, I deserve. I am forwarding by a sure carrier your share of these cargoes to Messers Baring Bros. Co., as you requested a year ago, and I enclose the bills of exchange on London. I suggest that you write them to put part of your now snug little fortune at interest. Not all of it. The world sometimes turns upside down and only those with light, liquid assets float to the top again. Now as to "La Fortuna"—I have chartered her. She is not sequestrated.*

An excellent large ship with a decent captain whom experience has educated. Trust him—distrustfully. I told you of him elsewhere but I am glad to have secured him. His ship is large and fast, which cuts costs in the end, and will make fewer voyages necessary. You can load twice as many niggers as on a small schooner. I have laid out heavily in the trade goods "La Fortuna" brings you, and followed your advice carefully. You should find everything you requested except the muskets which are now at premium in Europe. I send you instead brandy, rum, and blankets. You will have to do as best you can with the Mexi-

can silver dollars; no Austrian are to be had. Blame Buonaparte.
You will also find your pineapple cuttings. Let me know how
they thrive. I prophesy that the chief monument of your ex-
istence will in a few years be pineapples in Africa. A sugary
epitaph shall be thine—but who will remember even if it is in
every mouth? The only lasting good we accomplish is when
we play with nature. All else is vanity. I have another baby, the
nineteenth. According to Father Trajan God never runs out of
souls, and I am built like a bull. Happy, happy world!

By the way, do not neglect to look in the little satin box in
the purser's pouch. A lady at the palace was most particular
about it. *She has asked me twice about you. Why don't you*
write her? You neglect your opportunities, I swear. Or are you
comforted? How did you find Cheecha? You do not say. When
do you come to Havana again? Never? Your chair on the veran-
da yawns for you. Send me some words of affection, my boy, I
grow old—and lonely. It is the fate of old bulls. Adiós then till
anon, thine.

CARLO.

Regla, the 7th of January, A. D. 1799.

As he leaned back reading this he could almost feel Carlo's
warm, fat hand grasping his own. But the date chilled him. Two
months ago now! How far away it all was! No, he had never
written Dolores. Somehow he couldn't. He undid the little box
Cibo had spoken of and sprung back the lid. A pair of carnelian
cuff links, nothing else; no writing. He closed the box again
and after a while put it aside. He would send her an ivory comb.

Ferdinando and the captain were busy checking invoices. A
discrepancy had arisen over two kegs of biscuit. Bother!
"Charge it to my account, Ferdinando." The factor did so,
saying nothing. "A curious man," thought Anthony. His negro
blood made no difference. He was an accountant. All he cared
for was to balance his accounts. His sister was not that way,
thank God! Neleta! It was too heavy a mail to finish tonight.
He would only read a few more letters, some from Livorno.
The rest could be finished—mañana.

He bade the captain and Ferdinando good night.

"Tomorrow we can go over the place together. It has been a pleasure, Don Ruiz. Let me know if there is anything you need. Call on me! The factor will see you aboard. Certainly, I shall be glad to convey your compliments to the señorita . . . Ah! thank you! I heartily agree." The ass, if he only knew! Would he never go?

The house seemed silent as their voices died away down the hill. From a beam overhead a little wood dust trickled down on the table. White ants again! They must have been in the wood. He would have to remove that. The devil! He shook the dust off a letter a little savagely and opened it. McNab's writing.

. . . the maister canna hold the pen the noo. His hands be sair twisted and he walks seldom. It gars him sair ye dinna come hame. He says to me—"write and say—'There is plenty for you here. Do not tarry too long. I would see you again, my son. That would be better than the monies you send. I commend you nevertheless for your care in that. Come home. The house is dark without you'."

I say amen to that, Maister Anthony. We (mysel', Mr. Toussaint, and that faithful woman) are still here. I draw salary for Nothing. Mr. B. is lying in the great bed as I write. He spends much time there. All of it soon. Do ye ken what I mean? Captain Bittern of the "Unicorn" has taken many prizes. We keep that quiet. My accounts await your return. Young Mr. Vincent Nolte calls for news of you oftener than we have it. I trust your health continues as mine does, and will last you home.

Your humble obd't servant,

WILLIAM McNAB.

"Home, come home!" Would they never cease? Where is home? Italy and the Casa da Bonnyfeather? All Europe was like the Casa da Bonnyfeather, he thought, a building with frescoes of old, lovely dreamful things fading and flaking off its walls, where forgotten gods feasted on oblivion overhead, and little men crawled underneath keeping accounts and writing letters about things; where Toussaints sat forever at desks and dreamed hopelessly of love, and mumbled of freedom and of golden savages, and ate their hearts out and were afraid of themselves. Go back to that? Go back to the Villa Brignole and Father Xavier; to the dead gardens under the moon and the music of the crazy woman; that opera that would never be sung?

He did not belong to all that. He belonged to a different and better time, something that he remembered had brooded in the court of the convent about the fountain; something that the bronze boy was remembering as he looked at the water, that the leaves of the great tree and the pigeons had spoken of before Father Xavier came and explained it away as only a reflection in the fountain, a dream.

It had been real once. In the villages of Italy on those morning drives with Angela he had caught glimpses of it, a world that remained in fragments; that let itself be seen by segments out of the corner of a wise young eye. It was the world he had found once with Angela; once, too late, a lost world. He could not "go back" to it. He would have to find it, or make it here. Here in the forest where the germens of it remained.

He leaned forward a little over the table, seeing nothing but light, and resting his chin on his hands. It seemed to him that he understood at last what the bronze boy by the fountain had gone blind looking for in the ceaseless, monotonous changefulness of the water that flowed past him like time.

It was what he himself was going blind looking for in the waters of change that flowed past him forever and forever, the mysterious fluid of events that looked so clear as it dashed for a moment into the sunshine, streaming from some mysterious source and flowing ever in one direction on into the unknown. Yes, it was *like* that.

He himself might be the other bronze boy, the missing twin who had disappeared from his brother's side by the fountain ages ago. Perhaps he was? Perhaps, he had only come back again to watch the water for a while. Perhaps, that bright vision of the beautiful playmate, the boy whose face was in the fountain, the child who had lain amid the branches and talked with him was real. Perhaps he had been talking with himself then after all. Who knows who I am? What knows? And who cares! . . .

The lovely madonna that had visited him that night with Angela, she might have cared, would have . . . but no more. In his being he knew he would never find her again. With Neleta all was dark as he lay—nothing there but his frame. But that remained! That *remained!* He would enjoy all he had left; prove to himself he was still alive . . . feel. Wine! He poured himself another glass.

———◆———

The candles had long burned out now, even the palm-oil lamp was waning. He rose and swept aside the letters—from the world of cobwebs. Mañana! What did they matter? He blew out the light. The distant howling-boom from the forests seemed to fill the chamber. It was always stronger on moonlight nights. He breathed heavily in the darkness, listening. The little owls in the orchard below kept bubbling. Somewhere a mouse shrieked. But beyond these shrill, near noises constantly rose and fell, now in high chorus and now in shattered undertones, the voice of the fathomless jungles that surrounded Gallegos; the roaring of crocodiles in the valley below, the far-off trumpeting of herds of elephants, the howling of monkeys hurling themselves along their treetop avenues through the moonlight, going nowhere. At Bangalang someone was comforting himself with a tom-tom. The throb of it rather than the sound came, a dim pulsation in the wind. The stridulous cry of quadrillions of insects made the night quiver. He stood and trembled with it. Like a dancer lending himself to irresistible music he gave himself to what seemed to be a tune remembered by his bones and muscles rather than his mind. The frame of him swayed to it. The warm air from the patio bathed him luxuriously and wandered under his loose clothes. He let them fall to the floor listlessly and enjoyed the stimulating, soft freshness of it caressing him from head to foot where he stood. The rank, male flowers of hundreds of papayas in the plantations below imparted a tang to the breeze as if lemon blossoms were being crushed by his feet.

He kicked the clothes under the table, and enjoyed the silent tread of his bare feet while gliding down the corridor to his room at the end of it. There was not a sound in the house now. Cheecha and her girls slept in the wing on the other side of the court. The main door locked itself and closed by a weight. Surprises in this country might be final and fatal. He had tried to eliminate surprises by insects, animals, and men. Only the terrible or ingenious succeeded in finding privacy in Africa. There was a certain fascination in having attained it against the entire scheme of things; in maintaining a successful defence against a perpetual siege. When he entered the room, completely at ease about his understood isolation with the woman who shared it with him, Neleta was asleep.

She lay on a light couch which she had pulled out from a corner and placed for coolness close to the rush screen that formed the wall of the apartment where it opened upon the court. Through this the moonlight penetrated covering part of the floor with a carpet of small parallels of light and shade and the walls with a dim pallor. She lay breast down, coverless, with her head resting lightly on one arm flung easily before her as if she had been swimming in the river of night and had paused in her stroke to dream a while and float down its tide. The curious effect of parallel black stripes and silver fell obliquely across her honey-coloured hips.

Although he was already tense with the certainty and anticipation of finding her awaiting him, this peculiar pattern of light and shadow with its background assumed for Anthony—as soon as it arranged itself before his eyes where he stood naked in the dim centre of the room—that supreme importance which the state of fire always has everywhere in the universe. All that he was, in the world about him, seemed to be drawn on a hurrying wind into the living symbol before him and to be sublimed there.

The meaning of that symbol was to be understood only in terms of feeling. With it the individual mind of Anthony had little or nothing to do. For him the gears of existence were shifted automatically by the signal of Neleta's naked hips from the secondary and rational order of existence into the primary and material. To it his own part of the alphabet of the eternal word answered convincingly. Matter was about to get the necessary business of its preservation in a certain form accomplished, and the means to this end now violently emanated heat as a preliminary to the process. Anthony was aware of all this. He did not think of it in so many sentences as he stood for a minute looking upon Neleta asleep in the barred moonlight; he apprehended it all as though it were expressible in one deep-breathed word, the exquisite hieroglyphic of which was the form of the woman before him with all her secrets bare.

The meaning of it was action, the supreme action upon which all other acts depend. Perhaps the only thought he had as he moved through the moony twilight to consummation was a realization that only by the addition of his own body to hers could the letter of the word be made complete. But this realization could scarcely be termed a thought, for the primal knowledge of it was accompanied by so intense a glow of pleasure that it was completely resolved in feeling alone.

He shifted her head slightly and she awoke looking up at him half dreamfully, contentedly settling herself in her nest face down. He put his arms about her, locking his hands on her breasts and letting his weight come upon her. She sighed fondly, and locked her legs about his own.

The union of Anthony and Neleta was physically a complete one. It was that of a mature man and woman who were together often; who knew what was to be expected of each other, and how to act. Neither had any doubt of self and each was wholly absorbed for the time being in the other. In this way they were able for considerable intervals of time to escape completely from themselves and to become another which was both of them. Theirs was not that ghastly wraith of love summoned forth from the grave of the body by friction to die feebly with nervous gasps and hatred, nor was it the spasmodic wriggling of curious younglings interested in experimenting with themselves. They were not furtively surprised at last by a really intense, final throb of pleasure. Nor was one completed suddenly and the other left desperate. Once having given themselves to each other, everything else was taken care of for them by forces over which they had, and desired to have, no control. Indeed, the supreme contentment of it all was that once locked together all that followed was involuntary. They participated in and became one in another impersonal self. The reward of obedience to the will of that self beyond them was a long continued and increasing ecstasy that just upon the verge of becoming unbearable blessedly relieved itself and left them to rest in each other's arms.

In the morning they would wake to see that the sun was making a golden pattern through the screen where that of the moon had been silver the night before. They would hear Cheecha and her maids moving about in the courtyard beyond with that peculiar rippling quality of sunlight in the tones of their talk and laughter that only the morning voices of Africans can convey. They would get up quietly without saying much, and giving each other a kiss of peace and happiness, would put on some light clothes and go out to breakfast in the courtyard.

After that the housegate was unbarred, the bridge of steps let down over the little "ant-moat" before the veranda, and the work of the day began. Neleta busied herself with the house and its keeping, in all the generously supplied details of which she took an immense and efficient pleasure. Anthony found himself pleasantly overwhelmed by a thousand details that in the voluble persons of blacks, whites, and yellows clambered for immediate attention and decisions of considerable moment to many souls. He used the cool morning hours diligently.

On the morning after the supper with Captain Matanza of *La Fortuna* the "barkers" came in from the hill country, saying they had persuaded a large Arab caravan to come and trade at Gallegos. All was instantly in rapid preparation for its advent. To give certain direction to the guides, and to honour the approaching Arab mongo, or chieftain, one of the cannons began to fire at regular intervals.

41. A GLIMPSE INTO THE FURNACE

"IT IS quite unusual for a caravan to be coming to us at this time of year," Anthony remarked to the captain as they sat smoking together on the dock, watching *La Fortuna*'s cargo being whipped out of her hatches under the active superintendence of Juan. The squall of the winches and the shouts of the crew working block-and-tackle came over the water. Several large boats and rafts plied back and forth. The morning was sticky-hot and the river valley breathless. In the brown water the velvet shadows of the barracoons wavered sullenly as the boats passed. Anthony removed his wide palm hat from time to time to mop his face.

"Like bronze beginning to sweat in the fire," thought Don Ruiz, who had seen cannon melted, "just when the first drops begin to run. After a while the metal collapses—suddenly." He was feeling like a rag himself this morning; inclined to be weakly reminiscent. He found it hard to be interested in anything.

"Oh," said he, "I thought caravans just kept coming." He looked faint. Anthony laughed and passed him a flask . . . They both felt brighter now . . .

"No, usually they get here in November when the dry season begins. *La Fortuna* is the magnet now. You see some time ago I sent barkers with special inducements to one of the chief Foulah mongos back in the hill-country, the Ali Mami of Futa-Jaloon. He is an Arab ruler who lords it over a great reach of territory stretching, I do not know how far, north-and-east up toward Timbo. The boys who returned this morning tell me the old scoundrel has been raiding far-and-wide and has sent down his nephew, one Amah-de-bellah, in charge of a big caravan.

"Amah, by the way, is a very intelligent and pleasant young Mussulman; black, but a gentleman according to his lights. I have had some amicable and profitable dealings with him before. Indeed, he is anxious to convert me to his own faith and has even invited me to visit his uncle's capital. I may do it yet.

"But come, they will not be here for several hours yet—have another pull at this—helps, eh? . . . Well, we might as well see what is going on and get you familiar with Gallegos. I make it a habit to go over the place every morning." He shoved his hat back on his head. They rose, and chatting together, strolled down the dock into the big warehouse.

"We rebuilt this after a fire when I first came," Anthony explained. "The smaller buildings up the slope are for storage, too. It is a good idea not to have all of one's cocoanuts on one tree, you know. This shed is where the actual trading goes on, however."

In the grateful shadow of the place the captain now looked about him with considerable interest.

The building was a long barn-like structure with lofts. The ceiling was provided with trap doors. These were now hanging open, and various bulky packages of trade-goods were being lowered in preparation for the approaching caravan. A bolt of striped cloth suddenly escaped from someone's hands in the loft above and streamed down out of the darkness like a flapping serpent. Cries and shrieks of raucous laughter arose. Half the Kru boys on the floor stopped trundling bales to help rewind the cloth. They got tangled in it. It took Ferdinando with a cane to restore order.

Nevertheless, the shed continued to hum with excitement, loud talk, songs, whistling, and a rhythmic stamping as the luxuriant cargo of *La Fortuna* rolled in from the dock and was hoisted into the lofts or trundled to the opposite end of the building. There was an air of triumph about it; the sheer joy of the Ethiopian at being surrounded by plenty and largesse permeated the place. The Kru boys whooped. A trolley on a travelling pulley ran from one end of the shed to the other and was whisking back and forth, dangling a net full of bales and clinging black boys who screamed with delight at the spinal thrill of an aerial ride. Like large liver-coloured flies their bodies seemed struggling in a vast spider web as they passed through the grotesque shadows of the beams and windows that barred the place with transverse shadows and shafts of light. The air danced with dust in a thousand sun pencils, and the captain now saw rather than heard the sound that permeated the whole atmosphere, for the very motes in the air were leaping to the low but swift and nervous lilt of drums. Gay and humorous greetings met the two as they continued along the warehouse floor, the captain's brass buttons, fat legs and skin-tight trousers causing many an eye to roll back till it showed as white as the grin beneath it.

"Merry enough!" said Don Ruiz who was now feeling the effects of a half-pint of brandy.

"It is the only way to get things done in a hurry here," replied Anthony, "songs and excitement. If you get the right beat going you can move mountains." He pointed to two youngsters at the door working away delightedly at small hand-drums. A blue-black Mandingo buck shuffled by doing a slide-and-slap under a mountainous bale. Don Ruiz burst into a laugh. In the fellowship of humour the man roared back like a gorilla.

"These stevedores and boatmen are all Mohammedans hired from near-by coastal villages; mostly Krus," continued Anthony. "It pays. Their wages are less than what slaves would manage to steal."

They stopped for a moment at the extreme end of the shed in a railed-off space. Here under the eyes of Ferdinando chests were being opened; bale covers were being ripped off and the contents spread out for display or heaped in convenient piles while two armed Foulahs watched every move.

"Samples, here," said Anthony. "The chief traders, and petty chiefs make their choice out of this stuff. But we can't linger too long now. Come this way."

They stepped out of the factor's office, already brilliant with striped cloths, brass jewelry, and rolls of copper wire, into a long porch covered by half-transparent tarpaulins slushed with beeswax. The place basked in a kind of amber glow. There was a wide, beaten-clay floor under the awning, several stone blocks with rings in them, an X-shaped whipping post. A low bench provided with mats for squatting extended the whole length of the place.

"The slaves are stood up and examined here before the goods are paid over. I watch that myself."

"Do you use the post much?" asked Don Ruiz.

"Not often, but now and again," said Anthony. "The captured witch-doctors sometimes need a little nine-tailed magic to convince them. I leave that to Ferdinando. He knows." He passed the black post rather hurriedly. The tarpaulin-covered porch led directly into the first of the barracoons that lined the water front for some distance beyond it.

The barracoons were long sheds built of heavy, hardwood timbers flat on two sides and driven into the ground so closely together that not even a knife-blade could be inserted between them. A wide opening in the roof for air and sunlight extended down the centre. The space for each slave was marked off with whitewashed lines on the stone so that the floor in its semi-gloom looked like a board upon which some giant game might be played with pieces six feet by four. Each space was provided with shackles to keep a pawn from moving itself, however, and there was a wooden pillow, a stool, and two earthen pots in every "square." A more lavishly furnished corner screened by mats with small, round windows in them marked where the two overseers kept watch.

Four of these barracoons, each with its number given in red strokes on the door, lay separated by about a twenty-yard interval. But they were so disposed that each formed one side of a square. The intervals between were heavily barricaded. At Gallegos there were two of these enclosed squares or slave pens.

"For the most part we shackle the slaves only at night," said Anthony. "In the day they exercise in these yards if the weather permits. That keeps the barracoons from getting musty. We feed them up well, make them bathe often, and get them fattened up for the voyage."

"Why, you could house a regiment here!" exclaimed Don Ruiz.

"Yes? Well, as a matter of fact, in the last three or four years several regiments have passed through them. Did it ever strike you, captain, that a large part of the New World will inevitably be rather African? Hundreds of shiploads of these black people have been going west now for hundreds of years. And Africa is now being poured out into America and the islands faster than ever before. Yet they are still calling for more from Boston to Buenos Aires. This war between England and Spain has only put up the price."

"Niggers don't count in America," said the captain tossing away a cigar stump indifferently.

"Each counts one, and they might possibly have children," mused Anthony.

"What the devil do we care?" grunted Don Ruiz. "Isn't it profitable? You yourself seem to be making a pretty good thing out of them. What are you worrying about? And yet, pardon me, but it did seem strange to me, señor—last night I thought of it—that a man like you should be slaving. No offence, of course," he hastened to add. "It was merely a passing thought."

"It *is* strange," replied Anthony laconically, looking about him for a moment as if he found himself in a curiously unexpected place.

The captain grinned. "My mother intended *me* for the priesthood," he said.

"Perhaps mine did, too. Quién sabe? But after all it is what we do that makes us what we are, isn't it?" queried Anthony half to himself.

"Quién sabe?" re-echoed the captain. His eyes also for a moment had become bleak. Suddenly they both recognized each other's look and laughed.

"Exiled, eh," thought Don Ruiz. "Regretful," thought Anthony.

"Try one of these, amigo mío," said the captain producing his cigar case. "These long, black fellows from Havana make one forget. The real leaf! I smoke ten a day. By evening the ground under one's feet becomes velvety. It seems to give a little when you step out. Even the prodding fingers of destiny are made blunt by tobacco. It was discovered just in time. Think what we should be without it! This age is like a busy mother-in-law to a man of feeling. We can no longer marry the world and be happy with it. Madre!" He struck fire like a craftsman, and they ascended the hill together in a cloud of blue smoke.

The little gun near the residence was still faithfully banging away at intervals. There was so little breeze even half-way up the slope that the yellow powder-smoke drifted slowly in long ribbons through the plantations. After each explosion the parrots settled back into the trees again. Anthony paused suddenly beside a small foot-path leading down from the road into a wooded hollow.

"Turn aside here with me for a moment and I'll show you what you have forgotten," he said. "It is more interesting than the barracoons, I think."

◆

They threaded a small thicket of date palms and fig trees, and soon disappeared from the road amid the dense shade of an ever-more luxuriant little oasis as the ground grew lower and damper. Already it was getting cool. Suddenly they came out into an open, palm-lined, grassy place about an acre in extent. A small stream rushed down it babbling fondly.

The water gushed out from under a low cliff; raced for a few hundreds yards as though frightened by the sunlight, and then disappeared into the hill again with a surprised gurgle through a rock that parted its sandy lips to drink it in. They both stooped and drank eagerly of water so evidently pure from a manless world. Refreshed, they rose and looked about them.

Before them half a dozen beehive huts were scattered about the oval, green levels in a rough semi-circle, like straw dwellings of enormous honey-gatherers. At the upper end of the glade was a Lilliputian chapel built into the rocky outcrop from which the stream itself sprang. There was a rude wooden cross before it, large, out of all proportion. There was even a miniature belfry in which hung an old ship's bell upon which the sun struck with a single brassy glint in the surrounding ocean of green.

Seated on a stool at the foot of his rood was Brother François in his now much-faded gown, sandals, and a large planter's hat. There were nearly a score of young darkies about him. They were repeating in unison something he was teaching them and the high murmur of their voices came to the two unobserved onlookers, where they stood in the shadow of the palms at the edge of the clearing, faintly and mixed with the responses of the stream—yet with the universal accent of happy childhood. It instantly reminded Anthony of the fresh gales of young voices which had sometimes come through the school windows at the convent while the pigeons and fountain talked together. in the court below. It was a sound like the leaves in that lost valley of the Moselle stirred long ago by a cool morning breeze. He remembered it. For a while both he and the captain forgot their cigars which accumulated a long ash while they stood watching and listening. Don Ruiz felt he might wake up at any moment as a boy again in his room at Toledo with the vocative Tagus gossiping a hundred feet below.

Both men, in fact, found something peculiarly affecting in the little scene before them.

Yet the sheer reality of it, drenched as it was in the stark, equatorial sunshine, the vividness of the black children dressed in white cast-off rice bags lying about their master like so many animated handkerchiefs on the glassy green of the grass conveyed its own meaning in a deep and natural tone. It was a bass note in which there was not even the suggestion of a sentimental tremolo.

On account of the noisy stream neither Anthony nor Don Ruiz could hear what Brother François was saying nor the children's replies. But from time the time the man's face shone out from under his hat when he looked up to speak, and the effect of his words could be seen by the ripples and wriggles of his small congregation. What he had to say was evidently something they were glad to hear. But more than that—it was because he was saying it that they listened.

No one—Anthony felt sure—no one who had not seen the tenderness, that strong and vivid look of affection upon Brother François's face, could have imagined its gentle strength. When he looked up and spoke, his features succeeded in their own particular way in giving a personal and living meaning to the general abstraction called "mercy."

"Do not disturb him, señor," muttered the captain in a changed voice. "It is a saint we have seen." He turned as if to go and then stopped to look back again. They both stood watching farther withdrawn now under the airy groins of some date palms, like cathedral sightseers, who, blundering upon a service in a side-chapel, had shrunk back at the thought of disturbing prayers.

It did not seem to Anthony now that Brother François appeared impotent against the world which surrounded him. What the man was doing there, what he was, looked permanent. Because his work was so invincibly humble as to escape notice, it seemed likely that it might prevail. It had, he thought, the delicate strength of flowers that perish easily and are constantly being trampled upon, but which succeed nevertheless in transmitting their unchanging pattern of beauty through aeons of seasons. Suddenly he thought of Father Xavier, too—

And was instantly reminded of a fossil water-lily that he had once seen in a cabinet somewhere; the cabinet was dark. Oh, yes—he had seen it at Maddalena Strozzi's. But he always thought of Brother François and light . . .

What was it he had been thinking about light that day on the *Wampanoag* while Mrs. Jorham had been showing him her sewing? What was it, now? Oh! . . . *said let there be light and there was . . . The Word . . .* or something. Well, well— at least the captain too was touched by this scene today, and he was no softy, God knows . . . stole cannon, Cibo said . . .

Now in these dense forests all about Gallegos trees fell but the light beat down and the forest went on. The light healed wounds and scars and nourished seedlings to fill up the places of trees that fell in the forest . . . that fell there and rotted. And all the seedlings struggled up toward the light. Those that couldn't get out of the shade died. But strange things lived in that perpetual shade; their forms were nightmares, horrible . . . no light! "How is it, Anthony, you have been so long a lurker in darkness, a mighty bringer down of trees—and men? Brother François has hidden these children from you." Yes, he always begs for the very young and sickly—"And now look! Why are you crouching here in the shadows . . . afraid of the light?"

"O Mother of . . . !"

"Stop! You must remember you cannot say it. Carlo said . . . And I know."

The *boom* of the little gun on the hill above shattered his reverie and the captain's simultaneously.

They turned without saying anything further and took a short-cut up the hill. Their path now led them directly to the foot of the low cliff that hid the small valley from both the road and the residence. Indeed, from the house veranda the valley might not have existed. It might have been merely a dip in the hill over which the eye shot directly to the barracoons below. But just from the top of the rocky outcrop, which otherwise hid it so well, all of it was visible at one glance. The cliff was not high but steep. They stood breathing a moment after the climb and looked down.

They saw the small chapel again and a graveyard with white crosses hidden in the trees, which they had not seen before. There was a surprising number of crosses—considering. Women were moving about the beehive huts with children hanging on their breasts. From rows of banana trees purple blossoms and ripe clusters also depended heavily. It was all intensely green, silent, fruitful. The place seemed to have dropped out of the world into a hollow. For an instant the spell of it clutched at them again. There were no shadows there. High noon . . .

Just then the little bell rang out softly and clearly.

They watched it turn on its wheel. Its clear notes fell out of the silence like quicksilver dropping out of darkness into sheer light. The captain crossed himself automatically. Anthony stopped his own hand just in time. He saw all the children and people below there kneel down. From the chapel came a distant voice. He knew what that man in there was saying—those words—

"God have mercy upon us . . ."

he thought . . .

Suddenly from the hill above came a great shout and the crackle of musketry.

A nasal singing and the mad beating of tom-toms could now be heard emerging from the forest beyond the stockade and getting louder. The little gun began to answer as rapidly as it could.

"Well, captain, your slave caravan has arrived," Anthony said.

"Mine?" laughed Don Ruiz looking a little startled. "You are *too* generous, señor!" They went up again without looking behind them. Anthony thought once that he could still hear the bell. Yet it must have stopped. And hell was to pay about the stockade gate. What a waste of powder!

At the residence all was now in final frantic activity, although Neleta had been actively preparing for the advent of the caravan since early dawn. A portion of the veranda had been screened off with mats and a huge cocoanut rug spread on the floor. Chairs for Anthony and the captain of *La Fortuna*, a prayer rug and a sheepskin for the approaching mongo of the caravan completed the arrangements, except for a half dozen Foulahs armed with flintlocks and cutlasses who now disposed themselves as a guard of honour. Behind the door Neleta stood ready to receive her guests, with Cheecha and the other women slaves. As the honourable mistress of the house, she wore a long embroidered veil over her face and shoulders.

Anthony and the captain had scarcely had time to snatch a cooling drink and seat themselves on the veranda before the battery on the slope below began to fire smoky salvos and the caravan was seen filing through the stockade gate on the hill above. As the nephew of the Ali Mami of Futa-Jaloon, Amah-de-bellah was to be received as a prince of the blood. At the same time the ample defences of Gallegos were also made sufficiently plain.

The procession which now began to unroll itself through the gate and to advance down the slope toward the residence seemed to the unaccustomed eyes of the captain bizarre if not positively weird. So strange were the aspects of the men and beasts who walked and stalked in it that it might have been an embassy from another planet, he thought.

A crowd of painted Mandingo barkers preceded it. They were dressed only in breech-clouts, but armed with the deadliest weapons of noise; enormous oboes that shrieked and grunted like pigs in the flames, cymbals, tom-toms, jar-drums, bull whistles, and gourd rattles on long sticks. These, and fifty other hellish devices, produced an atmospheric disturbance that, added to the salvos from the cannon, raised the wild-fowl from the marshes for miles around. And out of this immense volume of sibilant, wheezy, roaring, and brassy noises combined throbbed a continuous syncopated undertone of drumming and rattling to which the mob of naked heralds advanced shuffling and stamping; meanwhile howling out like a pack of lyrical hyenas the surpassing power and generosity of their approaching chief. Those who could no longer howl, droned.

Amah-de-bellah himself now appeared mounted on a fly-bitten but stalwart grey barb reduced to its own skeleton by having dined for two weeks past on nothing but tropical moss. The chief was followed by a fat, black dervish on a vicious mule. The holy man held a whip in one hand and a huge Koran wrapped in a prayer rug in the other. Three of Amah-de-bellah's wives in long white veils in which there were only eyeholes appeared next like ghosts riding upon diminutive donkeys. These little asses, which continually brayed and sobbed, were driven forward by thorn whips in the hands of the harem attendants who took turns at beating them, although themselves loaded down with great-pots, mats, vast umbrellas, bundles of apparel, and hut furniture.

Commerce having thus at once advertised itself with its usual modesty and exhibited its veiled cause, its inevitable and necessary armed escort followed.

In this case it consisted of a guard of some fifty or more fanatical Foulahs dressed in the white robes of peace and their own skinny, black legs. They rushed through the gate in a body, firing matchlocks, whirling, shrieking, capering, and waving bright scimitars in the air. The hair of this jungle militia was in each case frizzed-up into a kind of cock's comb dyed purple-red by a delicate solution of iron, urine, and lime. As they streamed after their leader in a mimic mêlée they managed to confer on the word "ferocious" a new and more sinister meaning.

All of them, however, and the people who had just preceded them, were now brought together half-way down the slope, where Amah-de-bellah had halted to await the rest of his caravan before advancing in state to the veranda. An interval of unexpected and consequently dramatic silence ensued.

In the midst of this, without any prelude whatever, a long, dark, glistening body commenced to crawl through the gateway as though a legendary serpent were sliding into the stockade. It really seemed at some distance to be one body. As it came nearer, however, it was seen to be composed of hundreds of naked, human bodies rubbed shiny for their approaching sale with palm oil and rancid butter. In the sun they glittered like ebony scales. Bamboo withes stretched from one tight neck-fork to another bound them together into one interminable, twisting line. Soon the small forms of children could be made out darkening the intervals between the passing legs of this huge millepede as it wound down the slope. Hovering about it, and along its flanks, were white-robed Arabs with rhinoceros-hide whips. An occasional report like a pistol-shot from one of these instruments helped to keep the worm crawling fairly rapidly.

Although the best of all his merchandise had thus arrived on its own legs, Amah-de-bellah did not at once advance to the veranda. He delayed for nearly half an hour while various minor chiefs and forest traders, each accompanied by his own slaves, native wares, and pandemonium, came through the gate. The bulk of the caravan, indeed, consisted of these people.

In the meantime Anthony and Captain Matanza sat solemnly and quietly smoking cigars.

"It would, of course," remarked Anthony, lighting another, "be far beneath the dignity of such potentates as ourselves even to notice the fact that so small a thing as a caravan of a thousand souls has arrived in our backyard. It is like having a policy toward an earthquake. It is not even to be thought about till it announces itself."

"The best people at home treat a revolution in the same way," said Don Ruiz. "Until it sets fire to their houses, or cuts off their heads, it does not exist."

"Precisely. In the same way we should lose caste if we seemed to notice that Amah's people are here. As yet he is only 'about to arrive.' Nevertheless, there is no objection to my men distributing the gifts of welcome in advance—as I see you have noticed. These 'gifts' are carefully calculated. They are really part of the trading and will later on be returned in kind. I leave this part of the preliminaries to some of my own Arabs, who estimate carefully what each one of these small traders has to offer and welcome him accordingly. The liberality of the trader is judged by this earnest of his desire to trade. Amah and I have not exchanged gifts yet. We will do that at the big dantica, or trade-talk, that will shortly take place here. But here they come!"

A renewed outburst of mind-sickening noise now shattered the silence. Aided by men with bull-whips, Amah could be seen riding along the flank of his motley host licking it into what might pass in Africa for a semblance of order. A large cock-ostrich at the rear of the column gave the most trouble and dodged about with such garguantuan effeminacy and nervousness in his mincing strides that Anthony and the captain were hard put to it to remain solemn. At last having settled all to his liking, including the ostrich, Amah rode to the head of the procession and tossed his cloak in the air. At this signal the whole howling host precipitated itself toward the residence like a dark flood.

The space before the veranda on the far side of the little moat was soon dense with a hustling, black mob. The numerous petty chiefs thrust and elbowed one another trying to press forward. Fights and jabbering ensued. But for a few minutes nothing could be heard on the porch except the thunderous chanting of Amah-de-bellah's barkers answered by Anthony's men; each side trying to outpraise their respective masters till wind was exhausted. Presently the armed Foulahs in the centre faced outward, and by beating on the bare ground with their musket butts succeeded finally in clearing a semi-circle at the expense of numerous sore toes. Silence, except for the braying of donkeys and the squalls of babies, was at length restored. Amah and his dervish now advanced into the centre of the cleared space, where a prayer rug was spread by the latter. On this the chief knelt facing Mecca and returned thanks for the safe arrival of his caravan. As he rose hundreds of voices insisted in bastard Arabic that there was only one God and Mohammed was his prophet.

The captain was now more than ever amazed by a scene

which had become somewhat familiar to Anthony. Behind the thin line of red-combed, white-robed Foulahs clustered a forest of dark faces made monstrous by lip disks and rings in their noses and ears; rose a mountainous landscape, tier upon tier of grass-wrapped elephant tusks, roped boxes, bundles, and mat-covered bales. A shimmer of copper bracelets, torques, and arm bands together with spearheads and polished muskets caught the sun and tossed it from point to point. Long, cigar-shaped bundles of damp banana leaves smoked wispily upon the heads of the fire-bearers. On the hillside beyond, rows of yoked and shackled captives looked on apathetically. A fetid smell like that of a neglected monkey cage mixed with the pungent odour of burning leaves caused Don Ruiz to cough and puff hastily at his cigar. Weaving back and forth over the fuzzy heads of the multitude, the chinless face of the ostrich peered insanely, blinking with pink and inflamed lids.

Prayers finished, Amah-de-bellah took the Koran from its bearer and held it to his forehead in token that all he was about to say was true. Gifts were now exchanged between him and Anthony. The Mohammedan received a fine Mexican saddle with evident pleasure; Anthony a small goat's horn filled with gold dust. He was amused to note, as he hefted it, that what it contained was worth almost exactly what the saddle had cost.

The preliminaries having been settled Anthony came forward, and bidding Amah welcome with much ceremony, conducted him to his sheepskin on the veranda. Here the captain was introduced and cordially met, for with a happy impulse he took his watch out of his vest pocket and presented it to the mongo. A heavy, gold bracelet from the chief's arm left both parties extremely satisfied. Neleta now appeared with a small silver dish and from this before the whole assembly the three men on the veranda ate dried rice cakes dipped in salt.

One of Anthony's Foulahs now advanced to the edge of the porch and announced that the powerful Master of Gallegos and the mighty Mongo having eaten salt together—as all might see —Gallegos bade the servants of the Mongo welcome. Five bullocks and innumerable sheep had been slaughtered and were roasting at the fires below, where ample camping space for all was to be had. By the blessing of Allah, trade would begin this afternoon—at the firing of a gun. In the meantime let all depart, find quarters, and refresh themselves at the superb feast provided by the matchless generosity of the Master of Gallegos. The usual tribute to monotheism and its prophet proclaimed that the dantica was over.

The crowd broke and raced down the slope, every petty trader trying to outdistance the others to a choice camping place. These had been so arranged as to lie under the muzzles of the cannon on the hill and the guns of the ship. The armed Arabs, the bearers, and slaves followed at a more leisurely pace, leaving the three on the veranda alone. Neleta had already conducted the wives of Amah to a hut in the court-yard, nicely furnished, and erected that morning out of new mats. Neither Anthony nor the captain looked at the three veiled apparitions which passed them. Presumably they did not exist.

It was amusing to Don Ruiz to see—once all ceremonies were concluded—how easily Anthony and Amah conducted themselves. They fell into a long and friendly talk assisted by one of the Foulahs who acted interpreter. Anthony's "Arabic" was by no means satisfactory yet. The trade jargon of the Grain Coast, indeed, was a compound of Arabic, Portuguese, Spanish, and Mandingo in which the first predominated. Fingers, knuckles, and toes supplied arithmetic.

This was the third caravan which Amah had led to Gallegos. Anthony and he had entered into what amounted to a partnership based on a general admiration for each other's resourcefulness and the mutual advantages of co-operation. Amah watched the inland trails constantly and swept into his net all the small traders going to the coast, in the meanwhile carrying on a holy war against the heathen upon his uncle's borders. In this way he was able to gather together large caravans of both slaves and traders, offering to the latter his "protection," and incidentally watching that they did not skip off to trade at the establishments on the Grand Sestris, Timbo, or elsewhere. For this "protection" he levied a tax. But unlike other leaders of caravans he collected the tax and no more. On the whole everybody was satisfied.

Amah was very anxious to have Anthony come inland with trade goods to Futa-Jaloon in order to supply his uncle with arms, ammunition and European merchandise directly. He had promised Anthony protection and an ample supply of slaves at home-prices, and he had been pressing in his invitation on his last visit a year before. On the present occasion he now renewed this request with the information that his uncle had promised to proclaim an annual market at his capital and not to invite any other European traders for a period of three years.

After an hour's talk, in which all the details for the journey were settled and an ample escort promised to Anthony whenever he should ask for it, Anthony in turn promised Amah to visit him at Futa-Jaloon when the next dry season should set in. Greatly pleased at having obtained consent to his cherished project and at the account of the fine cargo of *La Fortuna*, Amah retired to his mat hut in the courtyard. The separate shelter prevented him from living under the same roof with slaves and Christian dogs. Here he partook of his own rations and solaced himself in retirement with his wives. The little court was full of his furniture, animals, and servants, and Neleta was consternated for her flowers.

At half past two the boom of the gun announced that trade had begun. Anthony, Don Ruiz, and Amah-de-bellah betook themselves to the water front below.

—◆—

The swiftness and orderliness of trade had been considerably accelerated at Gallegos by reaching an agreement beforehand with the leaders of caravans as to the prices to be paid for various kinds of goods. This did away with endless chaffering and making dantica with swarms of small traders over every ox hide and piece of ivory. Slaves were another matter.

As a caravan must be entertained at the expense of the establishment until trade was over, time was dollars.

The barkers now went about among the fires and camp huts announcing prices. Ferdinando threw open the small trade-

window of his storeroom while Amah and Anthony sat just
outside with a scales between them. Several Foulahs armed with
whips kept back the half-frantic mob that now pressed forward. The province of Amah was, ostensibly, to see that none
of his followers suffered short weight or measure, but at the
same time he took care to deduct the caravan tax from each
trader's return as it was paid out. The storeroom now began
both to fill and to empty itself rapidly.

Hides, beeswax, palm oil; ivory in large tusks, lumps, and
small teeth; gold dust, and baskets of rice were weighed or measured and disappeared into Ferdinando's window while barkers
distributed in return cotton cloth, bars of tobacco, powder, salt,
rum, trade dollars, and great quantities of copper wire which
would later appear on the arms and legs of forest belles in massive coils and ornaments. Meanwhile the purchase of bullocks,
sheep, goats, and poultry went on about the fires.

Profitable as this petty trade was, it was minor compared to
the trade in man himself which was to follow. It was soon disposed of and the examination and barter for slaves began.

Under the porch-like structure covered by tarpaulins the
small slave traders—who as men of some importance and property assumed a dignified mien—had squatted along the low
bench provided for that purpose like so many dark, heavy-
lidded Buddhas. A beverage concocted of goat's milk, eggs,
sugar and rum was now served out in great quantities, to which,
despite religion, the Mohammedans were partial, calling it
"milk-sweet." A gong was struck, loiterers were cleared away,
and Ferdinando threw open his sample-room where the best of
his goods were now arranged in tempting display. The crowd
of traders then filed through the room to see what was on hand
and to receive a customary good-will gift. A large bale of London "beavers," which had been included in *La Fortuna's* cargo
by error or chance, proved to be unexpectedly popular. The
majority of the traders returned to their places under the tarpaulin in high hats. Even Brother François, who was always
present at these sales of human bodies, went aside with Captain
Matanza to laugh.

Amah-de-bellah designated the turn of each trader, and as he did so the man had his merchandise walked-in and lined-up before the block. Every slave as his turn came was cut loose from his fellows and stepped up onto the big square stone. The examination and appraisal was carried on by two expert Foulahs under the eyes of Anthony and Amah.

The inspections proceeded rapidly but meticulously. The slaves were stark naked, and from the crown of their head to their toe-nails they were thoroughly appraised. They were made to squat, to get up, to lean over; to dance and to walk about. They were asked a few swift questions and the tones and intelligence of their replies noted. Their mouths were pulled open and their teeth examined; the whites of their eyes; their pulses, and the colour and texture of their skins.

The two Foulahs had reduced the proceeding to a swift and efficient but varied ritual. They were alert for every possible symptom of disease. A swelling, an unsoundness or a malformation was spotted by them off-hand. In particular they were on the watch for slaves who had been doctored up for the occasion. And there were a hundred clever tricks in that black art.

The number of those rejected was small. By this time it was known that "painted horses" could not be sold at Gallegos. Both the unerring rejection of the unfit and the exposure of tricks by the examiners were now the occasions for derisive laughter. The traders enjoyed it particularly when some well-known old rascal of their number, or a newcomer, was nicely shown-up.

The plight of the rejected slave, however, was terrible. The rage and chagrin of his luckless owner was usually extreme, and, as the property had been officially pronounced worthless, it had been found necessary to take care of such cases after a special manner at Gallegos to prevent sickening tragedies. Unfortunately, this arrangement was peculiar to Gallegos.

Indeed, the very worst that could happen to a slave was to be rejected as unfit; the best, since he had already suffered the huge misfortune of being sold or captured, was to please both his old and new owners by being valuable. For that reason nearly all of those who had wit enough to appreciate their own predicament tried to appear attractive on the block.

———◆———

To Brother François, who, seated on a stool, viewed these sales from the crack behind Ferdinando's door—since his presence in the sales-porch gave mortal offence to the pious Mohammedans—the barter of human bodies for the goods piled just behind him in the sample-room was an experience of inexpressible pathos and agony.

It was not only that he believed that his Master had given His body for these dark children of the forests and that they were truly the sheep of His fold, but having been born where and when he had been, Brother François understood the meaning of the word "liberty" in both its practical and abstract sense. It was, in fact the favourite word of his age. Consequently, every one of these scenes was, for him at least, a Calvary. The perspiration ran down in his sleeves. Occasionally he wiped his palms on his now almost transparent robe. If it had not been that he also believed that violence was always both wrong and futile he would have rushed out as his ancestors had once done to die fighting in the midst of overwhelming numbers of paynims. But this belief and the glimpse of a certain face before him kept him temporarily inactive. The face was Anthony's.

To most of the others present, including the slaves themselves, the occasion of their barter was merely one of more than usual emotional interest. But not much more. Passions of all kinds, especially the passion of greed, were unleashed, it is true, and everyone participated to some extent even if unconsciously in the drama of the occasion. For even the fate of a slave is the fate of a man or woman, and therefore potentially dramatic. Hence, there was even among some of the traders themselves a dim, half-conscious sense of the tragedy of it all. A note of relief in their jovial and too-hearty laughter showed this when some trivial comic incident cropped up; when some fat man tripped ascending the block, or a black houri wriggled under an appraising slap on the buttocks. They proved to themselves how funny, how very humorous it was. "How they have to laugh together," thought Brother François, "the laughter of merchants—where everything is for sale in a sad, bad, merry world—and 'we' are getting our little profit out of the joke. 'We,' who know that men and women can be traded for things, we practical men. Laugh, brothers, laugh! For laughter shows we are such good-fellows after all. Who better than we when we get together? Who shall impugn 'Us'? Is it not custom, commerce, and therefore fate immutable?

"How shall I explain my plan to those who believe in trading men for things to call it profitable. Yet even these savage traders have some dim feeling that something is wrong somewhere. They laugh to balance the depressed inner scales. Is there no one here to whom I can appeal? That young man there with the rigid face—Anthony?"—thus Brother François sweating on his stool.

—◆—

At first Anthony had also smiled; had tried to. But he could no longer do that. At this game of human barter his features registered what he wished he could feel about it, nothing at all. In the final analysis he did not really care for the goods which trade brought him. He told himself he only cared for the mode of living trade made possible. There was something in that. A great deal, he insisted—but not so much after all, he knew. Otherwise he would not have insisted upon it to himself. For even a mode of life was only living, doing. And it was action and not gain which was his profit. Perhaps, it was the sense of power, then? Yes, that was the masculine secret, deeper than love of women, or friendship—or God. That was what women were always curious about and would like to have—and lost it in getting it. Power is what a man keeps for its own sake and not for what it will do for him. Power he was determined he would trade for nothing at all, but he would trade all things even men for it. That was what he meant by "getting things done." Let them be done then! He would identify himself with the power that can act—anyhow in all directions. It was that kind of man he would be. Having was only incidental to doing.

Therefore, his expression was much the same whether the slaves wept or the traders laughed—the same no matter what went on. As the cause of both tragedy and comedy he remained calm in the centre of both. His words were fewer than ever now; only necessary ones to get things done. Consequently he was respected as a strong, silent man by nearly everyone about him—who also feared him because they did not know what he wanted for himself or how he thought or felt. The nature instead of the amount of his price was unknown. How could they alter his will—what bribe? None apparently. Hence, he made the rules for, and directed the game of life on the Rio Pongo as the one who was mysteriously best fitted to do so, and would and could.

Not that he stated all this to himself as so much philosophy. It was rather more largely a program of instinctive action into which he had drifted after being launched in that direction as a "citizen of the Western Hemisphere," where so many of the world currents and the tides in the affairs of men between Europe, Africa, and America were carrying him along. His association with Brother François had so far tended to confirm him in the opinion that even the "subjects of God" could do nothing about it. And one had to live as—to be a man. That was what Cibo had insisted upon. Be practical. And Anthony had felt that Cibo was right. There was only one thing which kept Anthony from feeling entirely successful, practical,—he could not entirely stifle his feelings. During a slave-barter he always became peculiarly aware of that. Somehow this trading in men in the sales-porch seemed to be the whole crux of the mattter.

"If what I be depends upon what I do—and this is what is being done! Then?"

His feelings rose up against him. It was all he could do even to conceal them outwardly on the days of slave-barter. He therefore looked more than usually self-possessed and grim, calm and determined. Yet what a dry, fiery oven was heating within him.

For as the afternoon advanced, adding incident after incident, as one purchased body after another stepped from the stone block to the barracoons—Anthony's state of feeling became all but unbearable. He was now beholding, he knew very well, the inmost core, the essence of doing things in order to get them done. The process was as naked to him as the slaves who stepped onto the block. Each one of them in fact personified it, and the effect of the afternoon's procession was cumulative. He was at once fascinated and tortured. What if his state of feeling should prevail over his will and become his whole state of being? What would he *do* then? What would become of Gallegos?

The slow friction of his determination and his emotions turning in different directions, turning, as it were, on the pivot of his personality, twisted it, threatened to tear it apart; generated a slowly mounting heat. That heat was of necessity kept smothered within from the time the trade-gun fired till the porch was emptied. The irritation of it crept slowly along his nerves out to the ends of his toes and fingers. His hands and feet felt dry, and his mouth parched. He would sometimes send for a drink. Nevertheless, he would feel a mounting impulse to discharge this nervous pressure in outbursts of anger at trivial mishaps; to wreak vengeance on something or somebody outside him for his own miserable state within. But policy forbade that. He must remain calm and sober, the Master of Gallegos, beginning with himself. By evening he would have dark circles under his eyes where the lower lids had set up a minute twitching. Then suddenly something would collapse within him; give way. Even tobacco was no help now. It rather sickened him. Going home up the hill he would suddenly feel small, and cold. A slight shaking as of a weak ague made his steps a little uncertain. And how tired he was! The climate would get him yet, damn it! Neleta would be waiting too, damn her!

While a caravan was at Gallegos, on those nights, even Neleta was no solace. After a day of burning he was left cold with her at night. Last time Amah had been here it was worse than ever. He had dreamed his old madonna was smothering in that chest where she was locked up. Somehow he was in there too and struggling desperately with her to get out. The bed covers had slipped over his head and Neleta had wakened him, still struggling. It infuriated him to be going back to dreams like that again. Great God!

To Brother François, watching from the crack behind Ferdinando's door, the expression on Anthony's face and the scenes on the block were complementary to each other. He understood the cause of that expression. He had seen the will and the emotions at war before, turning men either into jovial pigs or iron masks. It was, he felt, one of the commonest symptoms of the moral disease of the world he knew. How to make both the will and the feelings of a man work together so they shall both feel at ease at what he is doing—how to be a whole man? "What to do, and what not to do, in order to be?" That was his question. "Or it might be—it might also be, what not to have in order to be," he told himself. There was only one to whom he could look for perfect direction in how to be a whole man, he had found. And because he had found abundant life in that direction, despite what might happen to the carcass of him, he desired to share it and re-explain it by living it. Seemingly the most passive person at Gallegos, Brother François was in reality one of the few people in the Western World who had positively identified himself with the power to be.

The truth was that this extraordinary man did not feel that through the crack of the door in Africa he was looking on at anything unusual. The slice of life he saw there seemed to him, although presented in primitive and uncomplicated terms, to be quite an ordinary one. It was merely another case where sympathy between men had become inoperative because greed for the possession of things and profit at the expense of others had reduced part of the population to slavery. In a place where things were valued more than men it was inevitable, he saw, that men should be reduced to the state of being less valuable than things. In that case, what more natural than that some men, those who could not help themselves, should actually be traded for things? "Sambo for three kegs of rum and an ell of cloth," he thought, imagining himself to be a trader. "My helpless brother for my own happiness! And certainly with three kegs of rum—and an ell of cloth, certainly I shall be happy. Shall I not be rich and envied? . . .

"But how does this differ from the universal commerce of the world for personal profit? Is it not all a trading of my brother for an ell of cloth or some more intoxicating substance? Did not my own father trade the bodies of his serfs for his ease, for his fine clothes and court career, his library and his château?"

And how many merchants and bankers and statesmen were doing the same thing. Because their system was more complex was it essentially different? No. What he saw here, if it differed at all, differed in degree and not in kind, he told himself.

Perhaps, this door slit in Africa gave a really more penetrating and genuine view of the system than if the door had been slightly ajar and he seated on a stool behind it somewhere else. For here the slaves were called "slaves" and the things for which they were expended were piled up in Ferdinando's sample-room all about him. It was naked men for naked things, and the traders out there bidding openly.

The cure for all this Brother François believed was only to be brought about by awakening sympathy in the hearts of men, man by man. And there was only one way of doing that, he thought—by presenting them with the opposite example of the way of his Master and letting them see it work. Words would not do; a billion sermons had been preached since St. Paul began. Theories and philosophic concepts died because men could not or did not embody them. Only the example itself, the way of his Master embodied in a man's life might avail.

In his humble and often faltering way, by the help of prayer and by a hard-won sense of communion in which he sometimes seemed to touch the fingers of Christ himself, Brother François stumbled blindly, sometimes mistakenly, but always sincerely and constantly, along the ineffably difficult way of being an exemplar.

If he sweated and sometimes wept as he looked through the crack of the door at the world working for its own undoing, while at the same time he felt the cold and faintly puzzled, but hostile eyes of Ferdinando fixed upon the middle of his back, it was nothing new and surprising to him. Nothing was here which by the unexpected shock of it could cause him to deliver himself over to his emotion and nerves and break out in a desperate but futile demonstration. The body-changers he knew could not be driven from the temple with their own whips—if at all. He had simply come to regard Gallegos, and his own little garden-valley in particular, as a kind of Gethsemane. It was a place where after much agony he prayed and waited, sure of the glory of failure—meanwhile doing what good he might according to his plan.

At Gallegos this plan consisted in buying up, for whatever he could get together or beg, the slaves rejected on the block; nursing the sick ones till they died; or keeping the crippled and maimed in his garden where their light labours sufficed in that climate to support the little community. A few of these unfortunates he had even been able to rehabilitate completely, but not many. Most of them soon came to rest in the ever-growing graveyard. In particular, however, Brother François concerned himself with children.

Many an exhausted black child, unable to follow the caravan any longer, who had seen the long file in which its mother was yoked disappear into the shades of the forest, now owed its existence to him. Lying in the forest waiting for darkness and the inevitable end, dumb with exhaustion and fear, it had heard the leaves rustle, screamed—and found itself in the arms of the good shepherd of Gallegos.

"For I also," said Brother François, "hunt like a lion, and do seek my meat from God."

He was followed upon these not infrequent man-hunts along the trails of caravans by an old Susu warrior wise in forest ways whom he had cared for till he could wield a spear again, and by a woman he had once come across in a raided village with her breasts cut off. Yet because of that she was now the best of several nurses in the cluster of beehive huts in the little valley; fierce and fearless in her work of mercy. On her expeditions into the forest with Brother François and his guide she bore a basket on her back to carry back the living meat which the leopards had not yet found.

What extra goods and help he needed to carry out his plans in the valley Brother François had always asked from Anthony. It was given to him without question, usually by a written order on Ferdinando.

The little settlement attracted small notice and few visitors of any kind. There was nothing to be had by going there. There were orders against anyone's disturbing it, and it remained a kind of enclave of peace, an *imperium in inferno,* for the rescued unfortunates and children who dwelt there. In a few years by a kind of natural evolution it had developed a self-sufficient economy which was at once primitive, native, early Christian and communistic. Beyond a few iron tools, some wine for himself and his sacrament, a little cloth, flour, and medicines, Brother François asked nothing more than the privilege of being let alone. The only opposition he met with was from Ferdinando, and this was latent rather than active.

The truth is, that small as was the charity the priest required, the method of charging it on the books puzzled Ferdinando. The half-breed, although he had acquired most of the outward manners of civilization as a youth in Spain, had in reality only one vital touch with it. It was the very primitive and unemotional one of commercial bookkeeping. Except for his clothes, his European manners, and his always perfectly kept books, Ferdinando was a savage. He did not know to what account to charge the small sundries issued from time to time to Brother François. It worried him greatly. He was enormously chagrined at finally having to ask Anthony about it. The latter's ironical suggestion that he should start a new page headed "Losses by Acts of God and the Public Enemy" only confused him the more. When he came to balance his books he had no idea how to handle a comparatively small but ever-growing account which seemed to be a debit with no possible credit to balance it. How could one liquidate something which was perpetually suspensory and ever increasing? An element of confusion was thus introduced into the fatuous order of Ferdinando's confused mental world. It finally became a rough pebble in his mental shoe. Shift it as he might, he could not get rid of it. By the spring of 1799 it had grown to the lump size of 126 pounds three shillings and sixpence. The factor determined that he would some time balance his books and show profit. He had a scheme. As yet he had not said anything about it to Anthony. It could wait. The charge went into "Accounts Temporarily Suspended." It was impossible for even Brother François to guess that in so simple a fact as that lay the Nemesis of his quiet valley. He continued to receive from time to time certain small benefits.

Small as this help was it had, nevertheless, enabled the monk to accomplish much more than would otherwise have been possible. And it was a constant indication to him that Anthony had not altogether succeeded in suppressing a part of himself which Brother François still had hopes of resurrecting as the whole man. During the three years he had spent with Anthony at Gallegos he had become intensely aware of the bitter struggle going on in the soul of a young friend over whom from their first meeting his own spirit had yearned. In that time their intimacy, for the most part a rather silent one, had, despite the frequent pain of it, deepened. Nor could Brother François forget the cabin of the *Ariostatica*.

There were a thousand little things that showed that this was so. The priest could not make up his mind to abandon Anthony. If he left Gallegos, as he had often considered doing, it seemed to him that he would be writing over its gate the hopeless inscription. And within those gates dwelt a beloved friend. "Not lost, not lost," he whispered, watching him.

Alone among the many Europeans who now came and went on the Rio Pongo, the monk was the only one cultivated and sensitive enough to understand the tragic irony in Anthony's fate—that tendency in affairs to enrich with things men who do not care for them. Anthony, he saw, might well become one of those characters abandoned by God and insulated from man who must find in the mere conduct of business at once their rich material reward and their utter spiritual poverty.

The face of Anthony reminded him now, while he stood by watching the proceedings on the slave-block, of the features of several other hopeful young men he had once known. Men whom he had seen in later manhood metamorphosed, or disguised to be great merchants, financiers, subtle priests, or ministers of state. What was once living and mobile in their expressions had become firm and fixed; what was formerly the strength of sweetness had become the power of sternness. Even now he felt that an appeal for mercy might be answered from Anthony's lips by a negative good reason or put off for expediency's dear sake. The unconscious smile that had once lurked on his mouth like sunlight striking through an open door had vanished. The door was tightly shut. Such faces Brother François knew could only be relaxed by a stroke of God—or the guillotine. He prayed for the stroke, and yet, because he loved the man for whom he prayed, he would avert it. He closed his eyes.

But despite many memories and the thoughts which thronged upon him out of the past, there was in this present scene before him a purely incidental and very human fascination to which the monk was thoroughly alive. He would open his eyes again and lean forward peering through the crack of the door.

Just over the block a section of the tarpaulin had been removed and the light streamed down in a brilliant slant of white radiance on the black bodies of the slaves as they stepped up one after another while the afternoon wore on. It was curious to see how under the necessity of selling themselves for as high a price as possible basic types of character emerged and all else vanished. The coquettish woman was now all smiles, even her muscles flinched under the prodding fingers of the indifferent appraisers in an alluring and half-playful way. The frightened young girl seemed to know now that virginity was her chief asset and trembled for her modesty as touchingly as she could. Youths and boys danced and shouted to show how gay and active they were. The notoriously fecund Gbandi women stood huge and cow-like, as if ready to receive whatever burdens were about to be laid within or upon them. Mandingos, who made the most prized house servants in Havana, were already compliant, a little furtive and too obsequious; ready to answer even a painful whack with a laugh. Mothers clung to their babies apprehensively. It was found easier to let them hold them while they mounted the block where they were indifferent to all but the child on the breast. Even the Foulahs hesitated to waken the tiger in them by handling the baby. The very young trembled, scared by something new. The naked, sullen warrior looked about him still using his last weapon, silent contempt. In Africa, as elsewhere maternity and martial honour were the only things which would not sell themselves, which rose supreme to all personal misfortune. Warriors Anthony occasionally secured for his personal force on the plantation. He bound them to him by giving them weapons and their freedom. When he spoke with them he felt at ease again.

As the sun neared the edge of the western jungle and its level rays struck with sudden revelation along the line of squatting traders still waiting for their turns under the tarpaulin, Brother François rose, and gathering up two unfortunates who were his for a little tobacco and powder, led them uphill to his valley. One of them was an oldish man who had proved to be nearly blind and the other an emaciated girl tottering with weakness. The mercy which had overtaken them they could not as yet comprehend. The sounds of twilight happiness in the little valley only bewildered them, for they had forgotten the kind of sound that accompanies peace and contentment. What the bell meant they had yet to learn.

* *

In the sales-porch the last batches for the day were being rapidly worked off. The amount due a trader was written on a chit by Anthony and given to him. A duplicate went to Ferdinando. His store-room was kept open till late at night paying off in goods. Already the lanterns were lit there and the bales coming down from the lofts. A sunset gun put an end to the day's proceedings. The last slaves were led off to the barracoons and the merchants returned to their tents and huts. Anthony and Amah-de-bellah climbed to the house on the hill as twilight was falling.

While he stood alone on the veranda that night after supper, Anthony told himself he had no cause to be dissatisfied. The trade had gone well. He had also struck a good bargain with Amah for the bulk of the slaves in the caravan. *La Fortuna* could sail soon now, loaded down. From the courtyard came the weird wailing of some outlandish wind instrument in Amah's huts. It irritated him greatly. He could also hear the wild rejoicings about the camp fires below. They were just over the edge of the hill but the red light of them beat up into the sky. The fog-wraith over the river reflected it back in a pulsing glow. If the drumming could only be stopped for tonight! Tonight he was tired.

He was always tired after a day like this; depressed. He hated himself. His face which had been so stern and fixed all day worked in the darkness. He was glad there was no one there to see him. He shivered. He felt as if he had been listening to a perfect babble of reproachful voices for hours, and that they were right. Perhaps after all he could not become what he had set out to be. He leaned on the railing gazing at the lights on the ship in the harbour. The red light in the fog flickered as the fires waned and leaped. The hill fell away so steeply at night! It seemed suddenly as if he stood close to an abyss, the edge of the world. Pandemonium was at the bottom. The drums drummed and drummed and drummed. He was going to fall and he was right on the edge now. "God . . . I *am* falling. Ah —eeee . . ."

"Neleta!"

Twice before she had heard him cry out that way. She was with him in an instant, soothing him and reassuring him. She felt sure someone had bewitched him and was trying to steal his soul. The witch-doctors often did that. She had seen the blacks dying when their souls were stolen. They looked strong but they just went out and died in a few days for no reason at all. She would see her old aunt at Bangalang about this although Ferdinando had long forbidden her to go there.

Perhaps it was only a touch of the fever!

But he looked so different tonight as she mixed him a strong drink that she felt uneasy. She put her arms around him and held him closely to her in bed. Yet she did not seem to possess him. When the moon rose she raised the net a little to look at him. His face was much younger now. It was not like the face of the Master of Gallegos. It was not the face of the man she knew at all!

"Madre!" Ferdinando or not, she would certainly see Aunt Ungah about this. After all her mother's people did know a thing or two!

Outside in the courtyard the wailing oboe still went on as if someone had charmed a snake out of its basket and was afraid to leave-off playing.

42. THE VISION OF LIGHT

FERDINANDO's books promised to show a startling profit in the exchange of *La Fortuna*'s cargo for the merchandise of Amah's caravan. There were three hundred and twenty-eight slaves in the barracoons at Gallegos, and down-river Mongo Tom had unexpectedly kicked in with forty more. The ship was to pick them up on her way out. But she could not carry all of these people at once without undue risk from plague and British privateers. Anthony therefore determined to split her cargo, leaving about a third of the number to wait for the *Ariostatica*, which was expected back again in a month or so.

Don Ruiz grumbled a good deal at seeing his profits cut but was too well satisfied on the whole to be angry.

Still, all this was embarrassment of riches at worst, and the entirely unsentimental Ferdinando could not understand why the Master of Gallegos continued to look disgruntled while he studied his factor's statement showing the flourishing state of their tangible affairs. The half-breed took a profound satisfaction in it. He had, in fact, done not a little toward bringing it about. Besides, his own profit on head-money was considerable.

"Three hundred twenty-eight plus forty equals three hundred sixty-eight dollars," he told himself. He wished Anthony would ship the whole batch on *La Fortuna*.

"When this cargo is turned into gold and bills of exchange at Havana, señor . . ." he pointed out. But he received only a lack-lustre look.

"You have done very well, Ferdinando—I suppose," Anthony said finally—and closed the big ledger with a bang.

"As Amah is always saying, 'It is written'," he thought. "Mohammedans seem to get both justification and comfort in that. 'It is written!' " He glanced at the columns of Ferdinando's meticulous figures again, and stalked out of the warehouse office in a cloudy mood.

For Anthony found no comfort in the statement of his "profit." This time, even after the departure of the caravan, his fit of glumness had lasted.

The various small traders had departed early, disappearing into the fathomless forest on the far-side of the stockade, silently, and with no farewells. In the morning their fires would be ashes and they were gone. Now they had all left but it made little difference. By day the heat and the silence that lay on the place seemed intolerable. Yet the wailing of the flute in Amah's hut at night was even worse.

Amah and his three wives had lingered on in the courtyard. At last he left with a final "feu de joie" from all fifty of his Foulahs' muskets; with gifts, and an urgent reminder to Anthony of his promise to visit Futa-Jaloon. At least it was a relief to get rid of the flute, Anthony felt. Neleta had the courtyard replanted. She invited Don Ruiz up to dinner every night now in order to cheer up Anthony about whom she was much worried. He had somehow slipped away from her. Finally, she suggested a fishing expedition to the barrier reefs.

He caught at the idea eagerly. He was tired of Gallegos, he told himself. Neleta was right. What he wanted was a change. He would arrange to go down-river on *La Fortuna* and stay at the out-islands till the rains began—a week or two at most. Some of the Krus could come with him. The clean sand and open sea were just what he needed. And it would soon be clouding up now. A good drench of fresh air untainted by the forest—sunlight! Bueno!

Now that it seemed as if he too were going with the ship Anthony began to press *La Fortuna's* departure with something of his old zeal. Ten days in barracoons had already done wonders for the slaves in resting them up after their long march to the coast. Most of them had begun to look sleek and even contented. There was not only lots of food but Ferdinando saw to it that there was also drumming and dancing. He held a dantica and told them about the happy lot ahead of them in Cuba. There was a great snapping of fingers over that. No sickness had developed. So far so good.

On the day before the ship's departure, which was always one of great feasting, the head of every man, woman, and child was shaved smooth. Finger-nails were pared down to the quick to prevent scratching when the inevitable fights for sleeping room should take place aboard ship. *La Fortuna* took in her last water cask. Lights were doused early in the barracoons and silence rigidly enforced. At the first grey of dawn the transfer to the ship began.

The slaves were taken out by batches of ten in boats and canoes. As they stepped on the deck they were stripped of every rag; of even the smallest article they might still possess. Every bead and the tiniest fetish and charm went overboard. Buckets of water were then dashed over them and they were mercilessly scrubbed by a gang of Mandingo boys who enjoyed their job immensely and who were more vigorous than gentle.

The gangs were now marched forward and their shackles struck from them while they dried off and shivered. Cries and lamentations whether from children or adults were ruthlessly suppressed. The work proceeded with the greatest order and dispatch.

Every slave was made to wash his mouth out with vinegar. As each approached the hatchway he was seized by a gang of tattooers, thrown over a spare spar and had three white dots tattooed on his back. This was the Gallegos mark which had been substituted for branding with a hot iron. It was also, as a matter of fact, indelible, and the ancient way of marking slaves on the Grain Coast. But there was more trouble over this proceeding than anything else. Many of the people as they were stretched over the spar thought the end had come. It required the attention of a stripling armed with a large paddle both to stimulate and to quiet them. At this task the boy was an artist.

The slaves were next separated and led below. Whip in hand the mates and boatswains superintended the stowing of the cargo. The women were stowed on the starboard side of the ship facing forward; the men on the port side facing aft. All lay with their heads in each other's laps and on their right sides as this was supposed to favour the action of the heart. A clear space along the centre of the deck was kept open for the guards and for other necessary passing to and fro.

Between-decks the ship had been scrupulously cleared of every loose article from stem to stern. Wherever possible even the bulkheads had been removed. Short of pulling up a plank or ripping out one of the ship's timbers from its bolts, there was literally not a single article in the hold of *La Fortuna* that could serve the slaves as a weapon of any kind. Small reed canes were served out to certain chosen trusties, each one of whom was put in charge of a gang of ten and held responsible for their discipline. The reward for this service was a little tobacco and an old, white shirt that served to distinguish these "mess-leaders," as they were called, from the black, naked mass of their fellows; a mass that now rapidly filled the long decks of the ship from end to end.

Into the dark cavern of the ship's hold fell here and there streams of pale daylight down the open hatches, each barred with a heavy iron grating against which a lion might have hurled himself in vain.

About these apertures, that served for both egress and ventilation, black faces and forms stood out in startling silhouette and ranged back, growing dimmer row after row until ebony blent with the darkness. In the remoter parts of this floating cave only the flash of eyeballs and white teeth could be seen or it was flecked here and there by the light shirts of the mess-leaders. Between-decks the slaves squatted by day or lay by night during the entire voyage until they wore the planks smooth and greasy. When the weather permitted, and if they seemed docile, meals and certain periods of exercise on deck were allowed.

Outbursts, or infractions of sanitary rules, quarrels or lamentations were promptly visited either by the canes of the mess-leaders or by the whips of the overseers. For the furiously recalcitrant or rebelliously sullen there were irons, and the deep, solitary darkness of the regions of rats and bilge-water below. It was an absolute rule that no fire whether for lantern or tobacco could ever be taken below. So their nights were spent in pitch darkness when not even the overseers ventured amongst them, and their days in deep gloom.

Thus even before she left the anchorage at Bangalang the 'tween-decks of *La Fortuna*, like every other slaver, had taken on for her unwilling passengers all the aspects of a troubled, grotesque dream in the darkness from which is no escape even by waking.

The first effect upon coming aboard was to reduce even the African temperament to silence. A few women sat rocking on their hunkers and crooning. Here and there a deep guttural in some forest dialect disturbed the gloom among the men.

Presently the ship cast off from her buoy and began to slip down-stream with the ebb tide. The angles of light streaming down the hatches shifted slightly. The helm creaked. The shock of the saluting cannon jarred the ship and made everybody start. One at a time dark shadows began to slip forward to the latrines at the bow and to return. This traffic of nature was an incessant one. It was both enforced and restrained by the negro overseers with a cat-o'-nine-tails lashed to their wrists, men who were known as the "masters-of-the-hold." Two of these were always on watch and were regularly relieved.

Anthony stood on the quarter-deck with the captain while the transfer was taking place, explaining and hastening the process. Matters had gone very smoothly. It was just after sunrise when the ship cast loose and began to drift down the river, slowly at first, but gathering way as the drag of the ebb became heavier. Juan was acting as pilot. He knew every trick of the Rio Pongo now. As they doubled the long point that jutted out between Gallegos and Bangalang, and *La Fortuna* was swept along by the full force of the midstream current, Anthony could no longer conceal his elation that seemed to grow in proportion as Gallegos was left behind.

When at last the palms on the point finally shut out the barracoons and the residence a load seemed to have dropped from a basket that had been pressing his head down between his shoulders. He was amazed at his own cheerfulness. Don Ruiz also looked at him with surprise. He had not up until then met the free-and-easy young man to whom he now found himself talking.

They went into the stern cabin of the ship and discussed an excellent breakfast. The stern windows of this high, Spanish-built vessel were thrown wide open. It was like floating along in a wide, glass house well above the water. They could look for miles over the low islands and flat brown-coiling reaches of the river. The morning sun touched the brass cabin lamps and the captain's silver table-plate till it glittered. Don Ruiz had a good steward and drank a mixture of Java and Mocha that was heartening. The cabin was cool and airy. Anthony looked about him at the neat panelling and ship's furniture. It was pleasant to be in touch with civilization again. In the forms of things in the cabin all of Europe seemed to be concentrated. Suddenly he was at home again.

Don Ruiz enjoyed being host. He talked engagingly of the dangers and fascination of travelling in Spain. With Anthony he forgot *La Fortuna*—and her cargo. Caramba! This señor inglés was a caballero! One could afford to know him. "More coffee, Pedro." Anthony wished he too were going on to Havana and said so. In the grand Castilian manner he found himself presented with the ship and entreated to remain on board as a perpetual passenger and owner. It was hard not to accept.

They were passing Bangalang now. From the beach below the little fisher huts on stilts half a dozen canoes put off and raced past the ship making for Mongo Tom's. They were going to bring the rest of the slaves aboard there. Half an hour later the ship was lying-to off the Mongo's establishment while the canoes plied back and forth rapidly. A noise like a porpoise breathing announced that Mongo Tom was ascending the ship's side. Loud, complaining rumbles in a husky voice went on for some time on deck.

"He wants a salute fired," said Anthony listening. The voice was curiously exasperating.

"Come down," shouted Don Ruiz at last impatiently.

He was answered by an elephantine grunt. Something not entirely human appeared at the cabin door. The presence which there heaved itself into view was, in every sense of the word, overpowering.

Two large, negroid feet with projecting heels and long yellow toenails, only one of which extremities was wrapped in a frayed rice-straw sandal, provided a seemingly insufficient support for the majestic belly that projected above and beyond them in a cosmic periphery. From this hung down in indescribably greasy and yellow folds what had once (*circa* 1780) been a pair of white canvas trousers. But the action of time had long ago reduced these *bracae* to a state of filthy fluidity that Lazarus himself might have been shy to own. Furthermore, they were suspended from a startlingly clean and brand-new piece of shiny Manila hemp tied in the middle with a bud-like knot.

There was something shocking about this sartorial item. It seemed to mark the too cute, imaginary equatorial belt of a

Jovian planet that might laugh and discard it at any moment. It was artificial and unnatural. To those who had to talk with its owner for any length of time it was an irritation rather than a comfort that the implied catastrophe which was always imminent never finally occurred.

Indeed, it was difficult for the eye to pass much above the central boundary of this human mass, for immediately above the small belt-knot, as if put there to remind the onlooker of what it had once been like in infancy, was the navel of Mongo Tom now expanded by the general distortion of his girth into the exact semblance of a large, alert-looking ear.

It was to this, much to Anthony's amusement and his own dismay, that Captain Matanza found himself addressing his remarks in too-loud a voice while the Mongo lowered himself into a well-stayed chair. A wrinkling of the man's paunch in the vicinity of its ear seemed to reply.

"Dios," said Captain Matanza looking at Anthony as if to ask, "Can this be possible?"—"Have a cigar?"

"Carried *nem con*," said the presence whose portliness seemed already to have made him the chairman of the little meeting in the cabin. He banged his fist on the table so that all the dishes jumped . . .

"That is to say in Spanish señor captain, 'there is no dissent from your not unexpected proposal.'"

Don Ruiz bowed—to the ear apparently—and Anthony burst into a roar of laughter. Both of the others looked at him in surprise. The captain's face flushed. What might have been meant either for a scowl or a smile wrinkled the fat, moonlike countenance of the slaver as if a gelatin pastry had registered an earth-tremor that had passed on leaving the pie intact.

He stuck the cigar in his mouth and lit it, exhaling smoke in a series of whirling rings. Out of this half-invisible megaphone the voice of an habitual drunkard issued as though at a considerable distance.

"Now he looks like a ham with a single clove driven into it," thought Anthony. The voice continued in curiously correct English as if it were wound up and running down.

"My father, sir, had two ambitions: the first was to circulate the scriptures amongst the natives of these coasts, and the second to introduce them to the noble amenities of parliamentary procedure. It was he who once described their internecine bickerings as both unreasonable and unnecessary. In order to further his laudable ambitions he allied himself with a princess of the Susus. I am the offspring of that union. My father, sir, was an English doctor of divinity."

"So I have heard some thirty times before," interrupted Anthony. The Mongo emitted a number of rings. Having recreated his speaking trumpet he paid no attention to Anthony but went on.

"I have devoted myself to more concrete and practicable things," the voice did not seem now to belong to anyone at all. It was both debauched and cultivated—"With the exception of four years spent in England in clerical company, as the pet of bishops in fact, during which time I translated the Gospel according to St. Luke into Susu, I have busied myself here with transferring the benighted denizens of these forests to Christian lands where the light of the Gospel could shine with unadulterated fervour upon 'm. This, in my very humble estimation, is preferable to sowing seed among the tares *in partibus infidelium*."

Anthony had had to listen to this talk a number of times before. Even the cadences he knew had been inherited from the Mongo's father, a renegade missionary. It was now only a fine formula, a kind of dantica by which the Mongo felt he established himself with white men as a respectable character. One corner of the mouth now lapsed and a succession of smoke rings emerged travelling at great speed.

"The Society for the Propagation of the Gospel in Foreign Parts and His Grace of Canterbury have honoured me . . ."

"The captain does not understand English, Tommy," shouted Anthony.

The face with the cigar suddenly smoothed out and collapsed into a kind of indeterminate human landscape down which the sweat poured in copious streams.

"For Christ's sake, then, give me a glass of grog," it said.

The request having been complied with, and the bottle left on the table, the rest of the interview went on in Spanish for the benefit of the captain.

Don Ruiz thought he had never seen such a man as the Mongo. His coat, evidently donned for the occasion, stretched only half-way across his shirtless chest. But in the middle area between, nature had supplied a frill in the form of a hirsute ridge that stretched from just above the umbilical ear to the region below the neck. Here the hair became exceedingly luxuriant and very red. It was also hard to tell whether the man suffered from elephantiasis or was just enormously fat. Even the top of his head was fat. The hair there had retreated into a number of puffy places like small, wooded islands, and the inhabitants of this curious archipelago could occasionally be glimpsed passing in a leisurely manner from one island covert to another. Mongo Tom stunk like a dead fish in August, and no one on the Rio Pongo could recall what his colour had been in early youth. It was now a sort of yellow-mahogany darkened by tobacco smoke.

His mind, however, when not totally obscured by drink, was exceedingly clear about his personal affairs. This obscene mountain could both boast and bargain. It took as keen a half-hour of dickering as Don Ruiz, who was a sharp man himself, had ever listened to, before Anthony could complete the bargain for the forty slaves which the Mongo had brought aboard. In the process of this they went on deck again and looked over the new arrivals.

"Sink me if they ain't as likely a flock of bucks and lasses as you're likely to find," insisted the Mongo. " 'Ary a one over twenty-five. The pick of three villages up the Sestris. Fine gels! I'd like to try 'em out myself." He gave a throaty chuckle. "Now what do you give for the lot? What d-ye offer, Mr. Adverse? What!"

He was finally lowered over the side clutching the price in his huge, fat paw. Anthony and the captain watched him being ferried ashore as the ship again cast loose and began drifting toward the sea.

"How long do you suppose you have to be in Africa to get like that?" said Anthony.

Don Ruiz laughed. "Don't worry, señor. Several thousand generations on your mother's side at least, it seems."

Anthony shook his head. He had already thought of *that*.

"I must get out of this soon," he muttered. He looked forward to a glimpse of the open sea eagerly. He hoped Neleta would not have any children. It was curious that she didn't. He wondered about it. For three hours they twisted and drifted around the curves through the jungle where the *Ariostatica* had once battled her way going up. It was all sadly familiar now.

This was his fourth trip to the coast. The crocodiles did not seem to have moved. He shot at one from the deck and missed. The women with babies who were kept on deck in the bows cried out. Suddenly it began to get cooler; suddenly he could hear the whisper of the sea. *La Fortuna* slid down the last, straight, canal-like reach of the Rio Pongo in the grip of the strong ebb and flung herself free of the forest.

Across the beautiful, blue lagoons between the islands gulls were flying. Green and white glints with fiery opal hearts gleamed far and near in the water as the clouds shifted. There was a low mist on the other side of the islands where the surf pounded, a stiff salt breeze, white caps far out. Look at the huge roller coming in over the bar! Oh, what a glorious clean-washed world! Life again, life!

He gave a glad cry that brought Juan running from the wheel. He raced back again before the ship could yaw, having caught the infection of joy himself from Anthony. He set his hat on his head jauntily like the Juan of old times and gayly gave orders to set the jibs. The sound of the surf grew louder and louder as they drew slowly across the broad lagoon.

The first batches of slaves came on deck and sat down about a kettle to eat. It was just ten o'clock then. They were made to say a brief Latin grace. They would learn it soon. A bucket of salt water was passed into which they dipped their hands. A kid of farina and beans was placed before each gang. At a motion from a leader they dipped their hands into the food together; at another signal they swallowed. Attempts to snatch or to avoid eating brought the canes into use. All appetites were assumed to be the same. Both men and women were now given a whiff or two on a pipe passed about rapidly. They clapped hands, shouted "Viva la Habana," and having received a pint of water apiece were sent back into the hold again.

"Do not let too many at a time come on deck, captain," advised Anthony. "Wait till you find out their temper."

Don Ruiz nodded. He was anxious now as the ship was rapidly approaching the narrow inlet. Anthony turned to hasten the preparations of the Kru boys who were going to take him and Juan ashore. His light boat which could be paddled was slung out ready to lower. As usual a great moiling and bubbling of sand and muddy water was going on in the cut through the barrier reef. The pace of the ship increased. Suddenly *La Fortuna* was seized by the violent current whirling through the tidal gulf and spewed out into the open sea beyond. She stood shivering a moment. Then her jibs filled again.

"You have her, captain," shouted Anthony. "Adiós. Come on, Juan!"

The boat was lowered with a rush and cast loose. For a moment the black bulk of the ship with her blind ports loomed hugely above them. Then came a great whispering mound of green water. As the boat rose the ship seemed to sink. Through her wooden walls Anthony heard a long muffled groan, the crack of whips . . . then he was swept landward, boiling in on the crest of the mile-long roller with the backs of the Kru boys before him bending frantically to the paddles. Juan lay back on the stern looking up at the sky ecstatically. The pace was terrific now. Suddenly they were hurled forward into a smother of foam. The boys leaped out and raced the boat up the shelving beach. They all leapt out onto the firm, clean sand. He watched them carry the boat into the sand dunes as if they were still impelled by the last wave. And out there—

La Fortuna hurried westward a glimmering mountain of sail with a daylight moon looking at her wanly.

There is the fellowship and aid of human companionship, the consolation and sustenance of religion, the healing and health-giving power of certain land and seascapes. All of these have balms with which to poultice the slowly bleeding bruises and contusions of life. But they can rarely be invoked or singled out like some chemical drug in the *materia medica*. They occur like wild, healing herbs sown accidentally and reaped by chance. It is a mistake to suppose them to be panaceas. They are at best palliatives or restoratives, but often excellent ones for the time being, particularly if they are imbibed without the patient's being fully aware that they are being administered. His trip to the coastal reefs long remained in Anthony's memory as one of those curative experiences, an episode which, without being able to explain, he regarded as having both prolonged and enhanced his existence.

And there *was* something enormously clean and invigorating about these islands washed by the tides and scoured by the sea winds; there was nothing mysterious or shadowy. They lay drenched and soaked, quivering in eternal, tropical light. He felt this as soon as he stepped ashore.

For unknown miles before him the virgin beach of the narrow, barren strip streamed northward. It finally hid itself in the white surf-mist that at some distance ahead glowed with rainbow patches now and then when a league-long roller crackled and smashed. Gulls darted along under the curl of these translucent green combers and miraculously escaped to go lilting off over the surface again. The wind blew keen and fresh, warm, but robbed of its dank forest languor and the odour of rotting vegetation. The salty tang of it cleared the head.

Above all there was an overpowering sensation of the downpouring of white light on the sand and water; of the upbeating of blue rays again; of immense wastes and spaces of cobalt sea and robin's-egg sky. Beyond and beyond stretched the taut, black thread of the horizon. Here was boundary. Otherwise it might have been eternity.

Seaward, soapy flounces of green water wavered along the beach in ever shifting patterns of melting curves. Landward, marched a mimic mountain range of dazzling white sand dunes crowned by a miniature tropical table-land. There was not even the memory of man here. Nothing living accompanied Anthony but flocks of sandpipers that always flew a little ahead, alighted, and waited for him to catch up with them again. Then they would take wing with a whirr and faint, shrill cries that only accentuated the solitude. They left dainty tracks fading into the wet marge. And there was a species of beach crab to be discerned only by its shadow flitting across the sand. In the glare their bodies were invisible. Thus to the sound of wings and waves, and in the midst of a perpetually dissolving net of milky shadows that flowed away before him he walked all that afternoon.

The hollower boom of the surf as it broke against the more abrupt prism of the beach uncovered by the ebb at last warned him that it was time to return. He faced south and began to retrace his footsteps. He had covered two leagues or more. Yet his elation on landing was not yet expended. He swung his arms and legs joyfully. One could walk forever on the smooth silver of these firm sands.

The sun sank. The brief, tropical afterglow faded leaving a bitten remnant of the waning moon to pour grey glory along the strand where castles of foam bubbled and flecked away like piles of melting opals. The white surf-mist became suddenly ghostly and magical. The returning tide began to sound a slowly ascending scale. Soft voices seemed to cry to him from the surf from time to time. His eyes widened and felt comfortable again. Suddenly it seemed as if his whole scalp had loosened. In the first cool of the evening he bathed in the beach pools and trotted along the edge of the sea with the stinging salt water racing around his calves.

What a relief it was not to have the roaring and the howling of the forests suddenly begin at twilight! Here there was no sound except the rhythmic boom of the breakers and the whisper and lisp of the waves as they swished up the beach. They seemed to wash his mind as clean of memories and forebodings as they did sand and seaweed from the interstices of protruding lumps of brain-coral that rose here and there above the sand.

Yes, it was a timeless place.

Here he could live again for a while the untroubled life of a healthy body using its mind for nothing but the needs of the instant. He was trotting along over the sand in the present only. Even the thud of his feet no longer bothered him. He seemed to skim lightly, without an effort, shoved along as if he were on vanes by the light, tingling thrust of his bare toes.

A mile ahead of him a yellow glow sprang up a little way inland among the dunes where Juan and the four Kru boys had made camp. Supper would be ready! He was suddenly very hungry. He took a final plunge in the surf opposite the bivouac and came in hand-over-hand in a glorious smother of foam. He followed the men's tracks up into the dunes.

There it was pleasantly warm again where the sand still gave off the stored heat of the day. From a little sand ridge he looked down upon the camp. A forked, orange flame kept the shadows dancing in the hollow amid the scrub-palm thickets where they had pitched for the night. The five men lay sprawled about the fire, their assegais thrust into the sand with the broad blades twinkling in the firelight. The sound of their murmuring voices and a low laugh drifted up to him with the odour of roasting meat. Thank heaven there were no women here! What need of them? Here for a while, here it would be like the garden before Eve and her daughters came. But it would not be lonely. There would be the strong, friendly, passionless existence of males with all the million details that women were always bothering about left out, dropped and forgotten. Here they would kill and eat, sleep and swim, talk when they listed or remain silent. Here they would live alone and clean in a brief, happy brotherhood of fishers and hunters till the rains came.

Good then were these long, barren islands with the ocean on one side and the wide, blue lagoon on the other; good the golden net of unknown stars above and the peerings of the sun and moon in their majestic transits. Here the eternal sweep of the salt winds had reduced the scrub thickets to something tame and manageable. The mischievous monkeys and the huge, hungry swallowers were absent. Only beach rabbits and a tiny species of deer; only the sea-birds haunted these coral rocks and pleasant groves. On the landward side the cocoanuts grew down to the border of mangroves. Little arms of the sea penetrated this ancient reef of time and ended in coves bordered by silver, sickle-shaped beaches; strands untrodden, unknown, strewn with glorious shells, secret and beautiful. And it would all be understood, it would not have to be put into words and explained. Down there by the firelight where his fellow Adams awaited him—they knew already. They waited for him with their spears thrust into the sand.

He threw his useless clothes in the bushes and stepping out into the moonlight gave them a hail. Loud shouts of greeting came up to him and the figures about the fire leaped into sudden, vigorous life.

From a barrel sunk in the sand that afternoon Juan gave him a clear, tasteless drink. It was a freely-flowing fisherman's well he now looked into. They dined on beach birds, and the roasted carcass of one of the small deer speared that afternoon. They roasted some yams in the fire and ate them with a little salt. Pipes were passed around. One of the Kru boys told of adventures spearing sharks. They wrapped their blankets about them and dropped off to sleep.

In the morning the place seemed to be washed and scoured by light. It grew brighter, fiercer. The blue sea through a dip in the dunes became opalescent and luminous. The shadows of hawks passed over them. The palm leaves clicked together in the breeze.

But they no longer heard the incessant voice of the ocean or the clack of the little forest. They had blent themselves with that tune and had become a part of it. It was eternal. It was always now. They existed in warmth, health, infinite leisure and a universal bath of light. The mind of Anthony which had become a place of gloomy shadows signalled to his body that all was well again. Suddenly he had become young and at peace with himself.

Juan looked up at him that morning while he plied the fire

with dry palm leaves. The flame, which was invisible in the white light that engulfed it, could be seen only by its orange tips and the heat shadows streaming over the sand. It was merely a part of the burning day itself. Light going back to light. The dry leaves returned to light in the process. They returned to that from which they had come. There were no ashes. It was quite an obvious process. You saw it without having to think about it, just as you saw the water from tidal pools running back into the ocean again, leaving perhaps a little sediment.

Juan had grown into a powerful man. There was something a little gypsy-like about him. He was intensely sensitive to the moods of others, yet he himself was perennially gay. He lay back now, as he had lain that day on the dock at Regla, and kicked his naked heels in the air. A gay challenge to heaven it was, a kind of triumph in the light over the silly shadows of things.

"What is gloom, my master?" he seemed to say. "Do I not also live in the eternal light in which I know, and knew from that morning when you watched me send the swallow back, that your own being is also bathed." Pretending to strum a guitar he sang in his clear tenor,

> *"Wild, wild is the child*
> *In the vale of Bembibre*
> *As he leads his white flock*
> *Where the low willows grow.*
> *Where the steep river calls*
> *I have heard him at noonday*
> *Go down by the pools*
> *Of dark waters below.*

> *"And I heard him again*
> *When the glory of evening*
> *Beat red on the heights*
> *Where the wolf is his foe.*
> *Mad, mad are the songs*
> *Of the vale of Bembibre;*
> *Wild, wild is the voice*
> *Of the child of Minho."*

That day they fished a little, swam, slept,—and when evening came they slept again. Anthony wakened once to watch the meteors falling like tears of light down the dark cheeks of the sky. The moon had set. That most mysterious of the constellations, the Southern Cross, smouldered and winked. Over the dunes the chant of the surf sounded like deep basses intoning an elegy for a world beautiful but forgotten ages ago.

At first Juan had kept a calendar by nicking a log every day with an axe, but he forgot to do so after a while and the log was used for firewood. They knew, if they cared to know, what time of day it was by the height of the source of glory, by the length of the shadows of the dunes. Yet night constantly surprised them as morning always did. To Anthony the nights and days had already flowed into one thing that was a mere sense of continuance. Something refreshed but not interrupted by sleep.

They took the boat out and chased great fish in the lagoons. The shadows of them could be seen through the colourless water, stealing along against the white sand banks. They would drift down quietly and dart the harpoons into the blue mottled shade that had suddenly resolved itself into a shark basking in the warmth. A terrific battle would begin. They would play these great fish for hours. The boat would be towed along by them, with the water being dyed behind by the dark banner of the monster's blood. Sometimes they would have to cut loose to avoid shipwreck. Or, at long last, the terrific face of the thing would be brought to the gunwale and heaved up. Then the assegais would plunge and hack. It was sheer, mad butchery. Great and little fish would rush in from all sides as the trail of blood seeped along the reefs. From a hundred holes in the coral, blunt, and parrot-nosed beings rushed forth to eat and be eaten. The snapping and tearing and the whirling would rapidly become universal. Then they would cut the still twisting mass loose and watch it turning over and over, sinking in a great whorl of feasting things, flashing, tearing, stabbing and writhing.

Once they pursued an apparition like a giant water-bird that waved its way with wide, black wings through the liquid atmosphere. It was a large whipray and nearly proved their undoing. They lanced it and it started. After one tremendous burst of speed that nearly swamped them it turned and attacked the boat. Its great liver-coloured flukes came rushing up out of the water lifting the boat half-way out of the element when it struck. Then it sounded and turned on them again. But they did not wait. They made at top speed for the beach and watched the dark cloud dart into the shallows after them. There it floundered about for some time and finally made off. Juan spent the next day caulking the boat.

But all this was incidental, a sort of punctuation of the long, dateless flow of days in the white dream of light. Anthony liked best to spend hours angling off a rock with sand fleas for a little rainbow-coloured fish that would seldom strike, or to wait patiently with one of the Kru boys in a small sandy valley among the dunes where the tiny deer, not much larger than great rabbits, would finally approach the lure of a scarlet rag waving on a stick. It would take them hours sometimes, but they would always come at last. Then the bow would twang, and supper transfixed by an arrow would be kicking in the sand. One of the boys could kill these little fawn-coloured animals with his assegai. It was the last test of skill with the spear, for they ran like lightning in zigzags. Yet the spear guessed right nearly every time.

With four such Nimrods there was no use for firearms. The single musket they had brought was never used. Food was no worry. They would drain a beach pool and fill a basket with mullet. The rest they left for the gulls and fish hawks which became absurdly tame. And there were cocoanuts, groves of them, meat and drink. And no ants! Only a few exhausted butterflies blown over from the mainland reached the barren reefs across the protecting moat of the far-flung, wind-swept lagoons.

There was one cove in particular which Anthony regarded as peculiarly his own. It was understood when he went there he was not to be disturbed. It was closed from the sea by a reef through which nothing but small fish and water could penetrate. It was a clean, white basin with a few cocoa palms hanging over it from a bank that curved inward overlooking a narrow beach just above the reach of the ordinary tide. Here he swam for hours and slept in the shade of the bank. Here he indulged an endless glowing day-dream, peopling the beach with bright god-like figures that seemed to come to him like visions of a forgotten world of light and song. He was filled with an infinite, happy regret for this lost world, the world which the antiphonal voices of the surf lamented at night, singing together in sad, liquid basses as if they would have it back again with the morning.

Even in the daytime the strange, far-off echoes of those watery voices sounded incessantly in the hollow of the shell-like cove. At last he thought about nothing. He listened. He saw the light striking down through the limpid water, where, on the bottom, the shadows of the waves moved in faint, grey etchings of the movement of motion itself. A few shells lay down there, twisted whorls of things. At first he thought they were dead and empty. But as the days passed and the utmost minutiae of his surroundings burnt into his brain by the incessant stream of light he saw that they also moved. Their triangular relations to one another changed.

And it was light, light, light!—the perpetual tropical beat and shimmer of it, the overpowering glare and the living, burning glory of it in all its colours and angles and shades and airy and watery prisms and essences that now at last saturated him until his very blood ran with it; and the farthest, darkest chamber of his mind admitted the effect of it. The light was in him now. He understood one day, as he lay on the beach timelessly gazing into the water of the cove where the light seemed to concentrate, that he was like and one with the rocks and the trees and plants about; one with the creatures that moved only a little down there on the sand-floor under the water. He saw that the whorls of their shells, which now glimmered up to him greatly magnified, and the whorls on the trunks of palm trees that marked the ascending helix of their seasons were of the same signature, nature's tellurion, the writing of the name of light.

And all that he had been thinking about light for years past, all that had been going on in his mind about it when he did not know it, coalesced. As on that day on the *Wampanoag* when Mrs. Jorham had interrupted his vision, he ceased again to think in progressions. He apprehended. He thought all at once. He saw. He closed his eyes to see better. . . .

He was floating now in a boundless place without direction. It was absolutely dark. He could no longer open his eyes. Only his mind existed in the gloom. In his thought was stored the quality of light. "Let there be light!" Instantly a flower of light bloomed furiously in the void. It was a day stream beautiful beyond expression that spread outward in all ways at once, a sphere that instantaneously pre-empted all of space and yet was forever spreading. Where it was not was nothing. Where it reached was light. All things with bodies were part of and existed only in this flower of light. To watch the shifting of its endless petals of things from stars to seashells was to peep at time. To see the whole flower itself ever expanding through the nothing of darkness was to see all of time and to see it as one flash. For though the flower existed for eternity, that which looked at it as from a great distance and apart from it saw it as one outgoing flash. Instantaneously everything from the beginning to the end had happened.

He opened his eyes and realized that he had closed them only an instant before. He was in his body again. He moved his arms and legs. He felt painlessly exhausted; happy. It was some time before he could tell the difference between the voices of the surf and the blood whispering in his own ears. He began to play aimlessly with a small palm-nut smooth to his fingers. He started tucking it into the sand. "A tree will spring from it," he thought. "It is alive . . ."

The thing came out of the ground like a snake. It put out a leaf, another. Its leaves whirled around with the sun in a great ascending spiral. For an instant it waved its green hands fully-grown against the light. Then it dropped seeds. The tree withered to its base again. It was gone. He was still holding the seed in his hand. He finished tucking it into the ground. "So that is the way trees grow! They and the seed are one. To the master of the flower-of-light they too are a flash. I am. All things are. 'A thousand years in his sight are but a day.' Aye, a million aeons of ages—one swift flash."

He thought no longer now. He lay on the sand utterly quiet in spirit and still in mind. The feeling in his body was equivalent to a long wordless prayer. Without an image or mediator he worshipped his maker, the creator of light. Finally the tide came up and lapped over his hands. He left then and went home to the fire.

That night a brief spatter of rain fell on them. But Anthony did not feel it. He slept as if he had exhausted himself by a ten-mile run.

Juan was worried. The rainy season with its first storms must be close at hand. But he would say nothing about it, he decided. What if they did get wet—mañana. He pulled the blanket closer while looking up at the hazy stars and hummed a soft, lilting tune. Life was very pleasant here on these barrier beaches. After a while they would go back again. The tune died away in his throat. The voices in the surf sang on.

43. THE IMAGE BEGINS TO MELT

To an epicure in odours the village of Bangalang just before the rainy season closed down would have been an adventure without illusions. At that time even the native canoes plying between Mongo Tom's and Gallegos passed it to windward. There were great piles of drying and putrefying fish on the beach, the kettles were busy trying-out palm oil,—and the combination of fish-guts, grease-wood, and rancid vegetable-butter was something that only the inured inhabitants and the delighted buzzards of the vicinage could stand. Great clouds of these birds continued to arrive daily, attracted by a place which advertised itself so well to Buzzardom. As a consequence, the palm thatch of the fishers' huts showed, even at a distance, as if covered with melting patches of snow.

The hut of Ungah-gola, Neleta's maternal aunt, occupied the most salubrious site in the redolent town. That is not to insist that its environs suggested the jasmine in full bloom. But the house was built over the water, and what was thrown through the floor-door, its only entrance, was regularly removed by the diurnal besom of the tide instead of decomposing leisurely in a more normal manner. To a woman of eighty,—by far the oldest woman on the Grain Coast, where the female life-span was usually brief—the absence of flies was something, as was also the exclusion of both rain and sunlight which the rather superior construction of the hut afforded.

Ungah-gola, indeed, according to the standards of her neighbourhood, was well-off. In one corner of the hut she had an old ship's chest full of cowrie shells. Her battery of earthen pottery was luxurious. She had several large mirrors, one of which was suspended from her neck, and the amount of copper wire wound about her fat arms and legs was prodigious. All this, and the ample furnishings of her hut, she had accumulated slowly by the simple process of outliving three husbands and telling fortunes. For many miles up and down the coast there were few Kru fishermen, whether Mohammedan or pagan, who ventured upon any important undertaking without first consulting the wise widow of Bangalang.

On a stifling afternoon toward the end of the dry season— which was now so unusually protracted as to have caused the old woman to mistake the droppings of buzzard dung on her roof for the first spatter of the long-expected rains—Ungah-gola was awakened from her half-comatose siesta by the sound of paddles rattling in a canoe, which was evidently being moored to the piles beneath her hut.

Some young fisherman in trouble, she supposed.

She sat up, and glancing in her mirror renewed the circles of white paint about her eyes. Presently the shaft of light in which she was working was obscured, and the head of her niece Neleta appeared coming through the trap in the floor.

A series of excited greetings and inquiries passed between the two women, who had not seen each other for over two years. Neleta was made welcome with an unusually prolonged finger-snapping, which the loose joints of old Ungah contrived to accentuate as if a skeleton were acting host. Neleta deposited her presents of food, cloth, and brass jewelry at the old woman's feet, and while Ungah discussed a soft pork pie with succulent sounds in the darkness, the young mistress of Gallegos unfolded the secrets of her troubled bosom to her invisible but highly audible aunt.

"Art thou not with child yet?" croaked the crone at last, choking on a pig's knuckle.

"No," said Neleta, "that is one of the things I have come to talk with thee about."

Her aunt grunted and sucked the marrow out of a bone with a loud *plop*. Neleta could see nothing but the white rings about her eyes.

"Is the white man without seed, then?" the crone queried disdainfully.

"Nay," said Neleta. "He is copious, and I am replenished often. But he does not burgeon within me."

"Thou art like thy mother," said Ungah. "Though her strong husband strove with her nightly, she brought him only two children in ten years. We come of a rather barren race, you know. I myself with three husbands had only four children— but we live long," she added. "We live long! *Um-m-m.*"

She grunted, and threw the wooden base of the demolished pork pie through the door. They heard it splash in the water below.

"I have thought," said Neleta after a long silence, "that it is because someone steals my husband's soul at night that we have no children. His body is perfect but his seed gives no life."

"And thou?" said Ungah, holding up a brand which she blew upon while peering at her niece.

"I?—*I* am a woman!" said Neleta proudly, standing up and dropping her robe. Her aunt peered at her and grunted.

"Come here," she said.

Under the fingers of the old woman the girl trembled.

"Tell me of all this," said Ungah, who appeared to be satisfied with her niece and began a rice pastry soothing to her gums.

A long talk followed. Neleta elaborated her theory: In his sleep, it seemed, Anthony became another person. Brother François would pay no attention to her fears. And Neleta was alarmed. Before Anthony returned from the islands she was resolved to do something about him. Her mother's people, she felt, would understand. Aunty Ungah would give her a charm —or a drench. Would she not? Everyone knew witchcraft could only be fought with witchcraft.

Ungah grunted sympathetically and spat at the name of the Christian priest.

It had been hard enough to slip away from Ferdinando, Neleta went on. He would have no further dealing with his mother's people. Aunt Ungah softly cursed him. "He would beat me," insisted Neleta, "if he knew I was here now." She appealed again to her aunt. "Thou knowest from whom the rice and presents come. Not from Ferdinando," she said. "And I am now mistress in the great house. If I had a child. Only just one!" She started to moan like a savage woman bereaved. Her aunt determined to call in help.

She blew several toots on a conch shell and a few minutes later the form of Mnombibi, the local wizard, her collaborator in many a mysterious mischief, thrust through the floor-door. The shells on his ankles, filled with dried peas, rattled as he drew his feet into the hut and he squatted peering into the darkness. There were now two pairs of white-rimmed eyes staring at Neleta. They seemed to be floating in the dark like ghostly spectacles. After some palaver the trouble was explained. Would Mnombibi provide a charm to keep Anthony's soul in him while he slept?

He would—for a consideration—and on his own conditions. He must have something belonging to Anthony, a nail-paring or hair, for instance. Also he must be allowed to visit Gallegos surreptitiously and see for himself how the land lay there. Especially, he must see the artificial cave of the white wizard with the dead tree before it. He had heard much about it. He questioned Neleta closely about Brother François.

The half-breed girl felt herself between two fires here. As a nominal Christian she feared the priest; a savage at heart she feared Mnombibi more. Her answers conveyed nothing to the wizard but further aroused his jealous suspicions of the white man's magic. It was said that those in the white wizard's charge, the children, wore charms about their necks which prevailed over all native spells. They were freed, he had heard, from the spells of the forest and river. How was it done? Who was the white man's *Duppee?* Mnombibi would find out.

Late afternoon saw Neleta and Mnombibi gliding back to Gallegos in a swift canoe. In the bottom of the boat was the wizard's kit. It consisted of two small bags tied at the neck, an ebony box, and a shaggy cocoanut painted with a devil's face. This occasionally rocked itself from side to side as if alive, while from within came clicking noises from time to time. Neleta sat saying nothing, both pleased and terrified. Two scared, young fishermen shovelled the canoe along rapidly.

They arrived at Gallegos an hour before sunset and considerably ahead of Ferdinando, who had gone to visit Mongo Tom. Neleta sighed with relief. It was easy enough to smuggle Mnombibi into the big house. She left the gate open at the man's bidding. From one of the bags he took out a dried baby's head and placed it on the threshold with the wizened face looking inward. It was a charm which nothing African could pass.

Once in the house he tied on a hyena's tail behind and began running about on all fours, sniffing in every room and corner. He nearly scared the maids to death, including Cheecha. They cowered grey-faced against the wall. Over Cheecha he lingered for some time. Finally he thrust his hands into her breast and pulled out something on a chain. It was the chameleon Anthony had given her in Havana, now large and fat. He broke it from its link and went on. Cheecha collapsed.

Arrived in the room where Anthony and Neleta slept, Mnombibi was doubly particular. So far he had not been able to smell out anything or anybody himself. He intended to make doubly sure now. The chameleon he suspected, but he knew how to dispose of it. He now opened his second bag, and bidding Neleta stand on a stool, waited.

Presently the large, flat head of a blind snake rose from the sack. There was a white fungous growth over its eyes. It looked like Mnombibi. He addressed it as "my dear nose," and bade it smell well for him.

The snake began to glide about the room. With its black, forked tongue it seemed to taste its way through space. Finally, after about fifteen minutes of apparent searching, it calmly returned to its bag and subsided there in oily coils.

Mnombibi snorted.

It was as he thought. The evil influence was not in the house. He would have to look outside. As a precaution, however, he fed Cheecha's chameleon to the snake. For some minutes a double-headed animal seemed to be peering from the bag. The small arms and head of the chameleon with rapidly blinking golden eyes protruded from the snake's mouth. Neleta still stood on the stool fascinated.

Mnombibi now spoke to her while he secured the snake. She left the stool and going over to a chest took out Anthony's hair brushes. She plucked several brown strands from the bristles. These she delivered to Mnombibi. He now opened his ebony box and rapidly began to fashion from beeswax and ashes the rough semblance of a pronouncedly male figure. In the wax he carefully incorporated Anthony's hair.

He now demanded double his fee and received it. He was sophisticated enough to know the value of gold coins. Until they were paid into his right hand he continued to hold the wax image in his left. Neleta had no doubt whatever that it was her man which Mnombibi had in his clutches. She was therefore glad to ransom him at twice what she had at first promised.

Mnombibi next gave her some further directions, and the horn of a black goat to hang under her bed. He told her that if he could prevail over the white wizard she should have a child. Her husband's soul, he said, would stay even at night as long as she kept the figure safely. He asked some further questions about Brother François and warned her against going to him. Any mention of the afternoon's doings would break the spell, he said.

He finally left after removing the dried head from the threshold. It had worked. The maids, who had made a bolt for the gate as soon as his back had been turned, had been stopped by it in the courtyard. He rattled the shells on his feet at them and promised them baboons for husbands if they ever mentioned his visit. He showed them the painted cocoanut shell and they shrieked. The last they saw of him was his broad, evil grin disappearing through the gate under the glare of his white spectacle-like eyes.

Neleta locked the wax figure of Anthony in her chest of drawers. A small spider that seemed to be spying on her she killed with her slipper. She was pleased to find that from that day forward her slightest wish was law with the maids.

———•———

Ferdinando, who was returning from a day's visit with Mongo Tom, stopped to light his pipe on the way up the hill just where the path turned out to Brother François's little settlement. He stooped low behind a rock to keep the tinder in his box from blowing away, and got out his flint and steel. It was at that moment that Mnombibi coming downhill passed him like a shadow and disappeared in the thicket. Ferdinando paused with his steel in the air. Then he realized he had not been seen by the witch-doctor, whom he had recognized. Full of curiosity, he slipped his feet out of his pumps and followed noiselessly.

From time to time he caught sight of the black figure gliding through the plantation. Presently they both came to the edge of it near the little chapel. Mnombibi concealed himself in the long grass. Ferdinando crouched and watched Mnombibi. Some minutes passed. The chapel seemed to be empty and no one was about. A low hum of conversation could be heard coming from the huts, and the voice of the stream. Ferdinando at last became impatient. Why had the witch-doctor come here?— he wondered.

Just then Mnombibi wriggled out of the tall grass like a snake. He passed over the short space of lawn on his belly and made for the door of the chapel. He was careful to avoid the shadow of the cross that near sunset stretched long and black across the sward. At the door he paused for an instant, pressed close to the wall and peering in.

What Mnombibi saw was a perfectly smooth stone hut with one window, the cross bars of which threw the same kind of magic shadow on the floor that rested on the lawn. At the far end was a stone table with candlesticks on it. "Seven-headed snakes," thought Mnombibi. This was evidently the table upon which the Christians ate their god. He had heard of that. The place was quite patently an artificial cave in which the god was kept locked up. There was even one small light hanging from a chain so that the god could see. The lamp had a red eye. Mnombibi was afraid of it. It seemed to watch him. But he must have a look at the god, nevertheless. The place was half dark, too. What was that against the far wall over the table?

Braving the guardian eye, he wriggled in half-way to the stone table and looked up. On the wall was the god of the white magician stretched out and fastened by nails on a tree.

"So—that was the way they kept their god prisoner! Perhaps, if the white witch-doctor could be caught and nailed up that way . . . eh! Then one would have both the god and the man who kept him, too. Both safely nailed on a tree! That would be a fine end to the white man's rival magic. And all the powers of the god on the tree would be in the keeping of Mnombibi. An idea—an idea to be considered carefully!" As a first trial of strength the witch-doctor made a face at the crucifix. That was carrying matters a little too far, perhaps—considering that watchful eye. He thought he saw the figure squirm in the shadows. It might get loose! He turned and crawled for the door. Suddenly he heard men walking and talking just outside. He rose to make a bolt for it.

Just at the door he met Brother François and the old Susu hunter, who acted as a sort of sacristan and was coming to ring the evening bell. For an instant the three stood as if petrified.

The red-rimmed eyes of Mnombibi in their white circles glared devilishly at Brother François.

Ferdinando stood up in sheer excitement to see better. In his confused mind, where the stiff Latin ritual of the cathedral at Barcelona, seen in his boyhood, mixed with the earlier savage memories of his mother's hut at Bangalang, he instantly saw implicit in the group before him a trial of supernatural skill. It was the witch-doctor *versus* the priest.

Greatly startled by the sudden apparition at his chapel door the priest made the sign of the cross. Mnombibi instantly hurled the painted cocoanut at him, dived into the grass, and wriggled away like a snake, the grass rippling behind him. Brother François was so surprised at this curious procedure that he actually caught the strange missile that had been hurled at him and stood holding it, half-bewildered, turning it over in his hands. The bestial face painted on it glared up at him. An extraordinary series of events now took place.

The old Susu took one glance at the devil's head in Brother François's hands, and giving vent to an angry and frightened howl struck it from his grasp. He kept shouting something in his dialect, evidently a warning to the priest. The nut rolled some distance away. Meanwhile, the old warrior kept dashing about frantically looking for something. Finally he darted to the bank of the stream and returned with a heavy boulder. He poised this over the nut and brought it down with great force. The thing cracked open and a colossal tawny spider darted out. It crouched back in the grass fiddling with its mouth. It emitted an indescribable, locust-like sound. The blood of all those looking at it ran thick and cold. Suddenly the Susu attempted to spring on it and stamp it flat. It ran up his leg. The man flung himself into the air, twisting and spinning. A shrill, whistling scream tore from his lips. Brother François and Ferdinando saw the spider leap from his extended arm while he was still in the air. It made for the ledge of rocks.

"Kill it, father," shouted Ferdinando, now darting forward. "Kill it! Kill it!"

The priest was terribly startled. He had not known Ferdinando was there.

They seized sticks and made after the thing. But it was too late. Once they caught sight of it again, but it made off into a rift in the rock strata.

"It has stolen the man's soul," shouted Ferdinando who gave some signs of being hysterical and was twitching all over.

"Come, my son, you are too good a Christian to believe *that*. Mon Dieu!" said Brother François. He laid his hand reassuringly on the half-breed's shoulder. Ferdinando shook it off.

"You will see, father. Por Dios, you will see!" he snarled. "You cannot help him now."

They returned and found the old man lying on the grass face downward. He had blanched a slate-grey all over. When they turned him over there was foam on his lips.

"He will die," said Ferdinando, "in a few days. That devil has gone off with him. This is only a breathing corpse."

Brother François, who had been horribly shaken, could not find a mark on the man's body. From sheer nervousness and pity he began to shed a few tears. Ferdinando looked at him with contempt. They carried the old warrior to a hut together.

"You will not say anything about this, will you?" said the priest humbly. "The people here would not understand."

"They would understand well enough," said Ferdinando. He stood watching Brother François working over the man. "No use," he added. He stood a little longer. Finally he shrugged his shoulders.

"Good night, father." He said it contemptuously, and left.

On the way up the hill a spatter of rain hit him in the face. What a tale he would have to tell Neleta at supper tonight! There could be no doubt that Mnombibi had won. He felt a greater contempt than ever for Brother François. In this country a priest was no good. What was he doing at Gallegos anyway? He wished Anthony would come back. Caramba! he had better hurry himself! It was coming on to rain with a vengeance. He started to run.

Over the steaming forest and plantation the roar of the oncoming rains set in, modulated by growls of distant thunder. Ferdinando was soaked. He drenched himself inside with rum and hot water that night. Neleta had to help him to bed. She was greatly worried. Anthony should have returned before this. She took the little image out of the drawer to look at it. She had forgotten that her chest of drawers stood all afternoon in the sunlight. To her horror the figure had partly melted. She ran out on the porch in her night-gown. There was no sign of Anthony's canoe having returned.

Westward toward the Atlantic the lightning snaked through the clouds that now hung low over the coastal forests, vomiting rain. Neleta shivered and went in. The bed was cold.

44. THE HARD METAL RUNS

The rain that had soaked Ferdinando overtook Anthony on the river half-way to Gallegos. He had delayed at the barrier beaches far too long.

Nevertheless, the last morning there had dawned as clear and golden as any that had preceded it—and the rains usually announced themselves by several days of scud and showers driving before.

But not this time. The vast, low-hanging cloud of the main deluge had simply lifted itself over the horizon about noon and driven down on them with lightning zigzagging along its inky front. Thunder rumbled and stumbled along the coast for hundreds of miles. The low, continuous mutter of it had been their first warning. Then the cloud came with high, billowing thunderheads and cut off the amber light like a sliding shutter. Men wandered about under it as if in an eclipse. The world had instantly slumped from clear, cheerful sunlight into grey gloom. A steaming rain, which grew colder hour by hour, slid down upon them in slanting cascades that dashed off their shoulders faster and faster.

They had hastily packed their few belongings in the rowing canoe and fled up-river before the cloud. But not fast enough. The first full deluge and the violent squalls that always accompanied it caught them toward evening ten miles below Gallegos on the Rio Pongo.

It was dark as the inside of a tar barrel. The forest moaned, washed and crashed. The gusts seemed to be trying to lift their light boat out of the water and spattered the river around them with torn branches and leaves. They could steer only by flashes of lightning as night came on, and the tide failed them long before they could make Mongo Tom's. To force the boat upstream against both the ebb and the rapidly swelling current was soon impossible. There was nothing for it but to try to land and wait for the turn of the tide. To tie up, or to drift and bail, would be to court disaster from the loose débris of the forest that now began to hurtle at them suddenly out of the darkness.

Landing was not to be so easily accomplished as thought of, however.

The mild drainage ditch of the dry-season, Rio Pongo could now scarcely be recognized in the boiling, swirling current full of dead trees and forest garbage which flashes of lightning revealed streaming down upon them like a broad brown ribbon hurling itself out of the darkness. Already the river had overflowed its low banks. To be battered over the fallen trunks and root-knees in the shallows was sure destruction. They paddled anxiously along the edge of the rapidly submerging forest looking for some slight rise of ground but found none. It was scarcely possible to make headway now. Then an eddy sucked them upstream, and a jagged bolt, that seemed to strike the river itself just ahead, revealed a grotesquely shaped sandbar with a few trees on top still rising above the flood.

They paddled under the lee of it and flashed their one dim lantern along its pitted banks. A large hole under the great roots, and a sickening smell of carrion caused one of the Kru boys to call out a warning. He was too late. Anthony caught the gleam of the lantern on two yellow eyes under the roots, and then the beast was on them.

A crocodile disturbed guarding its festering nest acts impulsively. This one tried to climb into the boat. One of the Krus thrust his assegai into its mouth. It swerved. But the boat was half full of water and the lantern out. Then the tail of the monster came around and struck the craft a shattering blow.

"Pull," roared Anthony.

Luckily the Krus stuck to the paddles. Their last stroke shoved them into the bank. Everybody swarmed out and up over the roots and stood on something flat and solid in the downpour. Anthony began to shout their names. They were all near him—and all there—somewhere in the darkness.

A great scrambling and thrashing broke out on the bank below.

"Madre!" screamed Juan. "He's coming up after us!"

Another flash revealed the determined saurian coming across the low plateau of the sandbank straight for them. In the intense dazzling glare the fanged, lizard smile, the flaring curve of the upper lip and the swift preposterous waddle of the squat legs of the thing seemed to be rushing upon them for an eternity. Beyond was the brown, bubbling slide of the river, and against it the bare branches of dead trees thrashing despairing arms into the air.

Darkness swooped again.

Anthony found himself with that vision still seared on his eyeballs while he sat high up in the limbs of one of the trees. His action had been absolutely automatic. The tail of the beast went battering about down below. It jarred the thick tree perceptibly. He felt it through his tightly gripping hands. By God, that fellow meant business!

Anthony and Juan were sharing the same tree with a young Diana monkey. It whooped and swore at them till the steadily descending downpour, which varied from a drizzle to drowning cloudbursts that drummed on the river, silenced it. In lulls they heard its teeth chattering and their own were soon joining in chorus. In the infrequent lulls of wind and thunder the miserable men in the trees called to one another. The voices of the Kru boys already sounded weak and thin. The hopeless twittering of these drenched and shivering human birds first suggested to Anthony that they would probably perish here miserably. Hours passed while the mad rain beat upon them.

A boat came down-river beating a gong. They set up a noise like the wailing of souls in purgatory but a squall drowned them out. When it was over the boat had passed them and gone downstream. Those on board would be looking for a light.

Morning it seemed would never come. It was impossible, Anthony felt, that only a few hours ago he had been warm and dreamfully happy on the beaches shining with sunlight. This was a different world he was in now. Its signs were darkness, furious rain, cold, and the vision of the crocodile charging in the lightning glare. How could one night leave him so weak? He fastened himself to the limb with a belt.

The wind died toward morning and the rain let up. The light finally filtered through a dark, bulging canopy softly flowing over the tree-tops close above. A new misery now developed. In the calm unnumbered swarms of gnats and mosquitoes fell on them. A Hindu god with fifty hands could not have defended himself. They were bitten till they felt they were going mad. The mosquitoes lit in grey patches and drew blood.

It was possible to see where they were now. It was a flat sandbar about a hundred yards long and twenty wide. Its sharp nose pointed upstream and its top was only a few feet above the flood. It was the cherished abode of scorpions and a caravanserai for crocodiles. How they had ever landed safely in the dark and got as far as the trees was a mystery. As the water kept rising the number of saurians large and small that came out from under the roots where the sand was rapidly being washed away was astounding. Five or six of them started to roam around under the trees snapping at each other. All of the Krus had lost their spears. Their boat was no more. The monkey looked about him and moaned scratching his orange-coloured thighs. Juan looked up from a lower limb with a face so swollen and red that it looked like the ape's behind. But no one laughed.

"What next, master?" said Juan with swollen lips.

"Breakfast," said Anthony trying to grin.

"Sí, for the crocodile," said Juan. He leaned against the tree a symbol of swollen despair. The Krus dripped from their branches like so many black scarecrows on a grotesque gallows, silent.

Quite obviously there was nothing to do. They did so. They sat. Anthony felt on fire all over, dull and feverish. He moved into a more comfortable crotch and tried to think. He dozed instead. The wind had driven off the gnats. But he was thoroughly poisoned. His eyes were swelling shut. Suddenly everybody began to shout at once. A constant dismal screeching went up from the treetops punctuated by the howls of the monkey. Down-river they had heard a shot.

Suppose the boat should pass them again? It might. He could no longer see. Only a glimmer through his puffed cheeks. He pulled off his shirt and began to wave it and roar till he was hoarse.

The sound of the frantically beaten boat gong came to him as a reprieve. Then there were shouts and a great many guns went off. The crocodiles hated to leave home. It all seemed far away. He was too ill to care now. His arms and legs were too swollen to move. He was afire from head to foot. At last he felt himself being lowered dizzily out of the tree. Someone was pouring something heavenly cool and soothing over him. He choked on some good Holland spirits.

"A man could lie down and sleep now. No more lightning in the dark forest or mosquitoes. A man could lie down and sleep. A man could . . ."

Three hours later they were back at Bangalang and he was being carried up the hill. Neleta put him to bed weeping over him but he couldn't see her. It was she who had sent the boat. He didn't care.

"Let me sleep, I tell you, let me sleep." He dozed off in a kind of poisoned coma.

Two days later the swelling suddenly subsided and he was shortly able to get about a little. But he felt weak and had great white circles under his eyes in a face that was otherwise like a mask of bronze. The sun, indeed, had burnt him bronze all over but most of the good of the trip to the barriers had been undone by the night on the sandbar. And he would take no advice. Ferdinando kept on insisting that he take double potions of the cinchona drench to ward off the fever. But he was sick of the bitter stuff and began to smoke cigars constantly and take large quantities of rum, sugar, and hot water instead. He used up most of the Cape wine and was stupid after dinner. In that way he would get some sleep. Otherwise he would want to prowl at night with a cigar in his face.

Neleta was avid for him after his absence. She used him now. He tried to get some passive solace out of her desire. That only seemed to madden her the more. In the morning he would lie with marks of her teeth all over his breast, too indifferent to get up. Outside the rain streamed down for hours at a time. The forests steamed. Once in a while the sun would come out for a few minutes and turn the little courtyard and the room into a Turkish bath. There was blue mould in his shoes in the morning. His clothes were clammy.

A week of unexpected and exceptional clear weather brought him a little reaction of will power. He went down to the docks to watch the loading of the remainder of the slaves still in the pens onto *El Argonautico*, a ship direct from Havana. This cleaned the last of the people out of the barracoons. He felt relieved. There would not be any more for some months. Caravans did not come in what was usually the beginning of continuous rains. There was a heavy mail to go over, some of it from Livorno.

Mr. Bonnyfeather was dying—the letter was five months old. Probably the old man was gone by this time. He paused, surprised to find that the news caused him almost no emotion of any kind. He couldn't feel anything any more. He had some wine opened at the warehouse and drank in Ferdinando's office which he had never done before. Two bottles of Malaga brought a faint sensation of sorrow. Ferdinando kept worrying him about what to do in his books with the material furnished to Brother François. He cursed Brother François and Ferdinando and opened letters listlessly.

. . . Mr. Bonnyfeather has directed me to write Captain Bittern at Gibraltar to call at Gallegos for you and bring you back to Livorno. He is most desirous of seeing you before it is too late. The "Unicorn" is expected at Gibraltar almost any time now. Address Captain Bittern there, giving the latitude and longitude of the Rio Pongo. Be sure to communicate that data to him. He does not know the Grain Coast. The "Unicorn" has been making many prizes of late. The war with Spain is profitable to British privateers, etc. . . . How do you find life with the golden savages? McNab and our mutual Faith are both well. . . .

It was Toussaint writing. The rest of the letter was about European politics.

"How did he find life with the golden savages?" My God! He spat on the floor. He was too tired to write Captain Bittern. Let him find the Rio Pongo if he could. It was on the maps.

He turned over some letters from Havana. Cibo was sending the *Ariostatica* again in two months' time. "His Excellency is most desirous of slipping as many ships through the net of British harriers as possible."

Humph! Suppose the *Unicorn* should pick up a few of His Excellency's ships and sell them for prizes? He grinned at the thought. Would he go back with Captain Bittern if he appeared now? He didn't know. Probably not. He couldn't make decisions any more off-hand. He felt like—like a fish left on a hot beach.

He swept the mail into the drawer and went back up the hill. Perhaps it might help if he unburdened his soul to Brother

François. He turned in at the little gate and found the priest sitting disconsolate after having buried the old Susu some days before. Anthony had to listen to the whole story of the spider. It horrified him strangely.

Brother François had not been able to do anything for the man. After a while he had just stopped breathing. A terror rested over the little settlement since the event. The priest felt helpless in the face of superstition like this. He looked it. He kept on protesting. Anthony felt for the first time there was no help in him any more. He said nothing about his own troubles. His soul had been stolen too, he told himself half whimsically. He stumbled on up the hill.

In the sun the wine came on him strong. He felt dizzy and there were spots before his eyes. Brother François was no good any more, he told himself. He went in to his bed, fell asleep, and wakened with the shakes and fever. That night on the sandbar! Fever was in his bones, he felt his joints grind. The rains came on for good that night. Three days later he was nearly stricken to death again. The chills, the fever, and the rains went on. Malaria began to burn and freeze him.

—————◆—————

For the rest of his life that long rainy season at Gallegos remained in his mind as a vague but horrible nightmare. He got steadily worse. It was always dark outside. But within him it was darker still. In a few weeks the world appeared as if he were sitting far back in a cave. At a great distance, and in a curiously blurred way, things went on happening at the entrance to the cavern. He himself was chained in there. He began to wish he were dead.

Every three days something invisible crept upon him in the darkness and shook him like a rat. His teeth chattered and clicked. Then he burned and sweated. Liquor brought a temporary relief. He drank steadily, constantly, and increasingly. He drank a great deal at night. He was soon utterly confused. Neleta kept annoying him by trying to keep him in bed. He would fight with her, drive her off. Yet he knew he should not.

She meant well. He hated her now because she loved him. She would not go away. Ferdinando he would not have in the room for a moment.

The factor, however, took this philosophically enough. He was glad to find himself to all intents and purposes the master of Gallegos. Joseph soon introduced certain minor practices about the place which Pharaoh would never have countenanced.

Brother François for one fared ill. Neither Ferdinando nor Neleta welcomed him at dinner. Indeed, he would have ceased coming to the house on the hill altogether if it had not been that he longed to do all he could for Anthony. He was not able to break the clutch of the fever. As he sat by Anthony's bed he was always conscious of Neleta's eyes resting on him. They were baleful. She managed on one pretext or another to exclude him as much as she could. He had no knowledge of what Mnombibi had told her, of course. Nor did he know that Neleta threw all of his medicines away.

Anthony for most of the time appeared to be in a stupor. At any rate he would say very little to Brother François. He refused all offers of spiritual help and a suggestion that he should receive the wafer. In a dim but deep way Anthony was conscious of the struggle that was going on over him between Neleta and the priest. The atmosphere of the sick room when Brother François was present was very tense. Anthony begged to be let alone.

When he could think at all clearly he felt sure he was going to die. As he grew weaker and could no longer get drink for himself even at night the conviction grew upon him. Neleta, in fact, had gradually cut down altogether on the rum. Although she had undoubtedly saved him from killing himself more rapidly, and he looked better, his sensation of suffering was now more conscious and therefore more intense.

It was getting along toward the end of the rainy season. His chills and burning fever had continued for weeks on end. He was now frequently delirious. Of those days of burning and weakness in which external and internal events were hopelessly confused a few things afterward remained in his memory with the startling clarity of a prolonged, drugged dream. What was illusion and what was fact he could never entirely separate. Both the possible and the impossible seemed equally true. The real and the unreal presented themselves in a succession of ever-flowing images that merged one into the other. In them his moody thoughts were mirrored as if they were taking place in space subject to the dissolving effect of time. They became the equivalent of events for many weeks.

Space seemed to have prolonged itself. It was longer than it was wide, and the length of it frequently varied. Sometimes the ebony foot-posts of his bed were very close to his face. He could see the strange Ethiopian gargoyles carved upon them grimacing at him, now so close that the darting tongues of the grotesque beasts were about to lick his face, now a hundred feet distant with his bed stretching all the way between like a path to a gate.

Perhaps this triumph of length over breadth was aided by the fact that Neleta's looking glass stood on her chest of drawers exactly opposite him across the room. In it he could see himself and everything that went on in the room. Neleta had once covered it with a cloth, but the blankness before him he found intolerable and begged her to take it off. When she did so the world seemed to be re-created again. The concentration of light in the mirror seemed to reflect itself back into the gloomy cavern behind his eyes where he was now afraid to be left alone with himself in the darkness.

The glass was a large French mirror, the envy of all the maids. He had given it to Neleta when she had become mistress of the house. By stepping back a little she could see all of herself in it. The drawers on her chest were built to recede like steps and so she seemed to be standing before the glass at the foot of a low flight of stairs. Indeed, everything in the room led up to and found itself re-created in the glass in a kind of golden atmosphere which the glow coming through the lattice-blind from the courtyard accentuated, or the candles by night. All the life of the room went on in the glass in a sort of dreamful penumbra.

It was there that Anthony saw himself lying on the bed with the bronze colour gradually fading from his face as if the fever were melting it away while his features became thinner, his skin sallow, and his eyes large, staring, and haggard. Now, indeed, he could look into his own eyes for hours at a time, face to face with himself. In the mirror also sat Brother François who seemed to gather about him the light that filtered in from the screen. With this the ethereal kindliness and bright unfaltering affection of his smile blent as if of the same quality. Years afterwards it was the head of Brother François surrounded by light that came back to comfort memory as the enduring image of the man.

He must frequently have sat by the bed of the sick man for hours for with this memory alone was there afterward any voice. What it had said Anthony could not remember. But to it he had replied. They had talked together. Never a sentence of those surely ghostly conversations afterwards came back to recollection. But what was Anthony stripped of all habiliments, stripped, indeed, almost of the flesh itself, talked with Brother François. The import of it vanished but the comfort and refreshment remained. It was always Anthony's impression that it was this spiritual medicine which had permitted him to survive.

When Brother François had gone he would then see Neleta again moving panther-like about the room. He would see her bending over him, bringing him water, of which he now consumed enormous quantities, tidying up the chamber, putting flowers by his bed, smoothing his pillow and weeping sometimes when she turned away. Yet there was always a certain fierceness about her, an air of possession in her every movement. She would often lie stretched out on the bed beside him fanning him, dressed in a long spotted silk gown. She would raise the screen behind him whenever she could and he could see the waving green leaves of the plants reflected from the courtyard behind him. In the mirror it seemed as if there was a leopard lying in the forest by something stretched out helplessly. He would go to sleep with the cool breath of the fan and the warm breath of her mouth alternately felt upon his cheeks. He had come now to accept her utterly. Neleta was in the mirror, too.

There also came and went other things and people. The bearded face of a stranger who came to bleed him. He learned afterwards that this was the new mate of the *Ariostatica* who was by way being an amateur surgeon. At any rate the bearded man with the basin and lancet came several times. He felt quieter and weaker now. In fact after the third blood-letting he reached the nadir of existence. Luckily the *Ariostatica* and her "surgeon" sailed soon. But he knew nothing about that at the time.

It was while he lay in what was all but a fatal lethargy after the third bleeding that Brother François came for the last time. Just that day it was too much trouble to move his eyes to one side or the other. Besides, the world receded into a dizzy darkness everywhere except straight ahead of him. Brother François in the mirror was greatly excited, animated, protesting. He seemed to be trying to get the man on the bed to do something. Anthony saw it all as happening to somebody else in the mirror. Why did they trouble *him* this way? They might let *him* die in peace at least. He heard a sound of voices arguing.

"Oh, if he could only leave all this!"

Ferdinando and Neleta were in the picture now. Brother François was holding on to the bed in the mirror pleading. Suddenly he saw him rise and turn away. His face went out. It was quiet again. Blessedly quiet. Everything went out of the mirror shortly. It grew grey, the light faded. Darkness was filling his eyes. He lay very still, on the balance, just breathing. Something terrible had happened, something for which he could not be forgiven. Brother François had gone. Well, he would go, too. "I will leave them." He gave up. The world suddenly ceased.

———— ◆ ————

The poignant atmosphere of tragedy which had conveyed its emotional contagion to the sick man so near the brink as to be numb and insensate—lost, indeed, to all understanding of its cause and only dimly aware of its emotional effect—had been the doing of Ferdinando.

When the *Ariostatica* had arrived at Gallegos she found the slave pens empty, the last of those brought by Amah's caravan having been shipped on *El Argonautico* some months before. Sóller who was in charge of the schooner was impatient to return. It was the middle of the rainy season and no new supplies of captives could be expected for some time. Yet both Sóller and Ferdinando were peculiarly anxious to make an excellent showing on the books for Anthony when he should recover. No ship had ever been known to lie idle for long at Gallegos without receiving a cargo. Ferdinando was determined that the only case of one doing so should not occur while he was in charge. Sóller, who had been put in charge of the *Ariostatica* after the death of the captain some years before, still felt himself to be a doubtful case in the opinion of Anthony. He was now anxious to make good. He and Ferdinando now put their precious heads together.

Mongo Tom, it was found, had a number of young slaves in his pens. They were scarcely more than children, leftovers from the last shipment, and he was anxious to get rid of them. The youth of the batch put an idea in Ferdinando's head as he and Sóller looked them over. Why not seize the children under Brother François's charge and so make up a full cargo for the *Ariostatica?* It would also immediately provide a way to balance that irritating open account on Ferdinando's books and show a nice profit on the goods supplied to Brother François for some years past, goods the half-breed considered to have been wasted. Sóller was enthusiastic. He even saw an element of humour in carrying off the priest's flock. Healthy children brought from $25 to $50 apiece since the trade had been curtailed by the English war. Bueno!

The longer Ferdinando thought of the scheme the better he liked it. If Anthony recovered he felt his business acumen would be praised; if not—if Anthony died, he, Ferdinando, would be temporarily at least the Master of Gallegos. Well, he

432

would show his authority while he had it anyway. Brother François should be put in his place as an impractical beggar and hanger-on.

Whereupon the practical Ferdinando put the Gallegos blacksmith to work shrinking leg-irons to fit snugly about young shins. Taking a goodly supply of these in several buckets he and Sóller, accompanied by four or five Foulahs, sneaked down the path toward Brother François's little establishment on the evening before the *Ariostatica* was to sail.

The peaceful sound of the bell came to them through the trees as they neared the place and they found the entire population of the beehive village gathered before the small chapel engaged in the simple service which always marked the end of their day.

Even such entirely forthright and up-and-coming fellows as Sóller and Ferdinando were given pause by the sight of the priest at his own forest altar and engaged in prayer. They waited till he had finished and blessed his flock. Sóller, indeed, now began to hold back a little. He had once been a choir-boy in Spain. Ferdinando, however, with the triumph of Mnombibi thoroughly in mind, gave no signs of wilting. He called out to his men, who, without mincing matters, laid hold of those nearest and began fitting them with leg-irons. Startled by the appearance of so many strangers, some of the youngest gathered about Brother François and began whimpering. The rest stood in scared silence. Seeing the irons one of the women groaned.

"What are you about?" said Brother François coming forward swiftly, the colour mounting to his face.

Ferdinando drew back a little. The priest kicked the irons out of one of the Foulah's hands. The rest stopped work and looked up at Ferdinando who snarled at them to go ahead. The sound of chains and locking resumed. One of the youngsters screamed.

"Do not interfere, padre," sneered Ferdinando. "I am master here now."

"You?" said the priest.

"I!" said the half-breed. "*I* am master now."

"He is dead then!" said Brother François. "Why didn't you call me? You heathen!" His voice rose with a sudden scream.

Ferdinando shook his head. "Not dead!" he said, and looked defiantly at the priest.

"What does this mean, then?" said the priest.

"Cuba!" grinned Ferdinando.

"No! no! In the name of God—*no!*" shouted Brother François.

The next instant Ferdinando went down under the solid impact of a blow on the mouth that half stunned him. The priest had apparently gone mad. He was beating the half-breed over the head with a bucket. The little lawn before the chapel resounded with horrible cries and childish screams of terror. A worrying sound came from the throat of the priest who was shaking Ferdinando like a great dog dealing with a stoat. The children rushed into the chapel. Someone tangled with the bell rope and a brazen clamour as of fire bells broke out.

But the Foulahs, all lusty Mohammedans, now threw themselves on Brother François and pulled him off Ferdinando. The half-breed got up spitting curses and teeth. He ordered the priest bound. Sóller interfered.

"He is a white man, you know."

"Hold him, then," screamed Ferdinando stamping about crazy with rage and pain, and wiping the blood off his lips. "You might do something yourself to get these brats down to the ship," he gasped at Sóller.

"Never mind the irons, drive them down," cried the Spaniard. "Use canes!" He broke off a section of bamboo and began to round up the flock. Some of them broke away and ran to the priest. He cried out without words and struggled. Presently he grew calm and stood weeping. Ferdinando cursed him.

Unfortunately most of the children had taken refuge in the little chapel. These were now driven forth in charge of several big Arabs with long sticks. One or two others were rounded up after a chase and scramble. The entire flock was then herded pell-mell downhill. Only a few old women and one or two sick men remained.

"Let them alone," said Sóller. "They're no good."

"The curse of the Almighty God on you, Sóller," cried Brother François.

"What!" said Sóller swaggering up. "What's that!"

The two stood close together for a moment. Gripped in the arms of the two Foulahs, who were taking no chances, Brother François, who had been leaning forward as if he would throw himself at Sóller too, suddenly straightened up. He stood looking directly into the face of Sóller which was now poked close to his own, with a defiant expression on it.

"You do not know what you are doing, do you, Sóller?" he said almost gently. A puzzled, clownish look spread half belligerently over Sóller's coarse features.

"Well, I guess I know my business," he blurted out. "I guess I do."

"May Christ forgive you," said Brother François and let his clenched hands fall by his side.

"Now that's what I call being a Christian," laughed Sóller, and set off down the hill whistling. He was secretly relieved at having the curse removed. Feeling quite sure that he had frightened the priest into forgiving him, he swaggered somewhat in his walk. Ferdinando had rushed off to bathe his face.

The two Foulahs, lacking further orders, and somewhat abashed at holding a white man prisoner, now let go of Brother François and walked away. He sank down at the foot of his cross and lay there. Presently he was joined by the woman with her breasts cut off. She began to make soft, hopeless sounds in the growing darkness. In the cluster of beehive huts there were no lights any more. Only the little stream continued to rush on through the valley filling it with a sound of watery voices like those of children far-off and at play.

Towards midnight Brother François rose and went into his chapel to be alone. He lit the candles and celebrated mass.

It was the following morning that he had gone to make his final plea to Anthony. The *Ariostatica* had not sailed yet. She was still swinging at anchor waiting for the down-tide. Brother François had small hope of finding Anthony in a condition to interfere, or even understand, but he could not let even the slim last chance of retrieving his flock go by. It was then that Anthony had seen him in the mirror for the last time.

But Anthony had been too ill to respond. He had in fact lapsed into unconsciousness while the priest, almost beside himself, had pleaded with him to interfere. Neleta much frightened, convinced that Mnombibi was certainly correct and that Brother François was a hostile influence, had called Ferdinando. The two had literally carried him from the room and thrust him from the door. From the hill he could see the *Ariostatica* getting under way. He watched her till her masts were veiled by the long point as she drifted past Bangalang. It was a half hour of sheer despair.

He went downhill to his deserted little hamlet. He knelt for a while in the chapel and was finally able to say, "Thy will, not mine be done," with a sincere heart. Then he called to the two old men and the three women who still remained to him and told them to pack up hastily. Two small donkeys that grazed near by were caught and loaded with a few pots, kettles, nondescript bundles, and the meagre furniture of the little chapel. The bell he threw into the stream. The wooden cross from before the chapel door he strapped over the back of the largest ass. He would not leave that at Gallegos.

The small procession headed by Brother François, with the only musket of the party over his shoulder, started uphill through the trees and passed through the stockade gate. The large cross on the small donkey waggled with the beast's ears. The Foulahs on guard had often seen Brother François go and come. They made no effort to stop him. They watched the priest, the donkeys, the two crippled men armed with spears, and the three women with bundles on their heads cross the rough clearing on the other side of the stockade and descend toward the wall of the forest. Half-way down Brother François took off his sandals and shook the dust off them.

He put them on again, and disappeared into the jungle that stretched toward the rising sun and had no end.

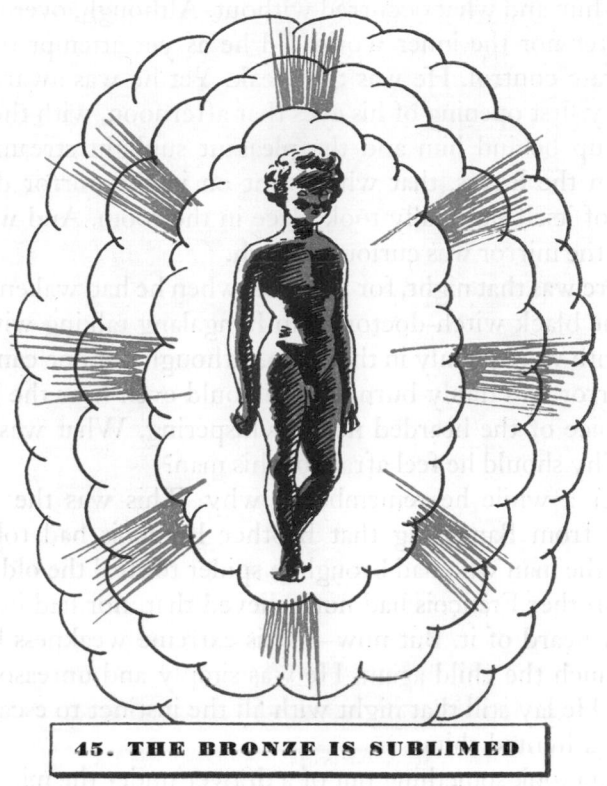

45. THE BRONZE IS SUBLIMED

THAT peculiar quality of sunlight, at once soothing and cheerful, which strikes through broad and lush green leaves, filled the eyes and the room of the sick man when at last he became aware of his surroundings again.

How long he had lain helpless he had no idea. So deep was the oblivion of weakness after the fever finally left him that he had lost all sense of time. Time did not seem to have been going on as he had always felt it to be going on during the night while he slept. This time existence had paused, and he had awakened after a distinct lapse.

But he was now fully conscious and rational again, he told himself, conscious of the difference between what went on within him and what occurred without. Although, over neither the outer nor the inner world did he as yet attempt to exert deliberate control. He was too weak. Yet he was aware from the very first opening of his eyes that afternoon, with the blind rolled up behind him and the pleasant sunlight streaming in through the leaves, that what went on in the mirror did not occur of itself but really took place in the room. And what he saw in the mirror was curious enough.

There was that night, for instance, when he had wakened and seen the black witch-doctor from Bangalang talking with Neleta. Both were plainly in the room, although but one candle by the mirror was dimly burning. He could even hear the husky, bass voice of the bearded negro whispering. What was going on? Why should he feel afraid of this man?

After a while he remembered why. This was the witch-doctor from Bangalang that Brother François had told him about, the man who had brought a spider to steal the old Susu's soul. Brother François had not believed that, nor had he when he first heard of it. But now—in his extreme weakness he was very much the child again. He was simply and unreasoningly afraid. He lay still that night with all the instinct to escape notice of a hunted thing.

Neleta took something out of a drawer under the mirror and showed it to the man with the white spectacles painted about his eyes. When you could not see him in the shadows you could still see his eyes floating in the glass. They came and went. You lay still. The man was much excited by what Neleta was showing him. When he moved about there was a sound as if a baby were playing with a rattle somewhere; *shuck-shucka-shuck, shuck-shucka-shuck.*

He was squatted in front of the mirror now doing some kind of monkey-business. He waved his arms about and burned feathers. There was a little fetish placed on Neleta's chest of drawers just before him. Mnombibi was making dantica to it.

How the burning feathers did smoke! It was an outrage—making a stench like that in a sick man's room. An outrage!

"Neleta!"

He began to make protesting noises in his throat and coughed. Then he saw Mnombibi on his hands and knees crawl past the bed and scuttle through the door. He saw that, and it was not in the mirror. And yet here was Neleta soothing him and assuring him it was nothing at all but a bad dream.

Well, well, perhaps? But what was the stench of burning feathers then? And that damned little manikin before the mirror, where did it come from?

It stayed there nearly all night. He saw it again and again. Yet next morning it was gone. It was all very confusing to a head still swimming dizzily.

And he had thought he was getting so much better!

He pondered all this till he grew tired and gave it up. Neleta still swore that he must have been dreaming. He lost confidence in himself. It gave him a decided set-back in recovery. Thinking the matter over, he decided he was not wholly rational yet after all.

He grew a little stronger day by day. Nevertheless, it was a long, tedious process. Trying to sit up, the whole room had reeled. He lay back and decided not to force matters. The man he saw looking back at him from the glass was more like the youth of four years ago than the bronzed Master of Gallegos who had greeted him there only a few months back. He was very thin again. The hard lines in his face had relaxed. It was not nearly so mask-like and determined. Yes, he was more like— "like Anthony,"—he thought. It reminded him of old times.

Neleta was silent. She acted at times as if she were frightened or holding something back. His mind dwelt meanwhile a good deal on the past, the Casa da Bonnyfeather, and even the convent came back vividly again.

In this moody vein it comforted his reminiscent fancy to insist on having his madonna brought out and set up before the glass on the chest of drawers. Something so familiar would give him a comforting sense of reality again. There could be no doubt what was before the mirror now. If any fetish was to appear there before his eyes, let it be one he knew—his own.

It was extraordinary how difficult it was to prevail on Neleta to get the shrine and to have her put it just where he could see it when he went to sleep as he had as a little boy. Surely he was entitled to so harmless a comfort, a souvenir of old times, he told himself. Yet he had to insist; to send for Ferdinando at last and bid him open the chest in the fireproofed shed; *to go and get it,* and no more nonsense about it.

It was Cheecha who finally took off the cover in which Faith had wrapped the shrine at Livorno. Neleta would have nothing to do with the madonna. She even appeared angry and worried. He had had to caution her that he valued it highly and would not have it touched.

So there she stood again. He had forgotten how beautiful she was. The blue of the heavenly little canopy, the gorgeous robe of the Virgin, and the mother-of-pearl at her feet glowed in the bare room. He almost felt like talking to her again as to an old friend; or that Father Xavier might come into the room at any moment. Would that he could, good man! But where—

"Where was Brother François?"

Suddenly it struck him that he had not seen Brother François lately. Why didn't *he* come to visit him? How strange!

He had gone on a journey, said Neleta. Doubtless he would be back shortly. She put Anthony off as best she could. Brother François, he remembered, had often been away for as much as a week or two at a time.

"Very well then, ask him to see me as soon as he returns."

Neleta promised. Both she and Ferdinando were now worried. What would Anthony do when he learned why Brother François had fled into the forest? Ferdinando said the returns from the sale for the *Ariostatica's* cargo would come back on *La Fortuna,* which was expected in soon. Then he would be able to make a fine showing with his books. That would be an acceptable excuse, he felt sure. At most there would be some grumbling, perhaps a perfunctory reprimand. He was complacently certain of it.

"You fool!" sneered Neleta.

Ferdinando felt uncomfortable again. Neleta knew Anthony

better than he did. He had learned that much. Perhaps he had better conceal the matter as long as he could.

Neleta was glad enough to have Brother François removed, even if it should cost Ferdinando his place when Anthony found what had happened. But she felt that it was Mnombibi who had been the real cause of Brother François's departure. For a while the conjuring and her plan had seemed to be working well. Not only had the Christian priest been driven out and his supposed influence over Anthony removed, but Mnombibi on his last visit to the house had reconstructed the melted manfetish. In this Neleta believed lay her influence over Anthony and her hope to have a child by him. It was the Christian priest, of course, who had caused the wax to melt. But that set-back had now been overcome. It *had* been rather awkward to have Anthony wake up that night and find Mnombibi in his room. But she had been able to reassure him about that, she thought. All was going smoothly when Anthony had insisted on having the madonna placed before her mirror. She feared it. In that virgin image she instinctively beheld a threat to all Mnombibi's conjuring of fecundity. She determined to get more advice at Bangalang.

As soon as she could she made another surreptitious visit to the Kru town. She and Aunt Ungah and Mnombibi had a long discussion upon the new turn of affairs. Neleta was for destroying the madonna, but Mnombibi laid his interdict on that.

The witch-doctor was really greatly puzzled and somewhat afraid of the white man's fetish that Neleta assured him was an important one in Spain. But although he saw in it the possibility of unknown trouble, he also thought it would provide him another opportunity to visit Gallegos with the usual reward in view. However, it seemed best to wait until he should hear what Brother François was doing. For the Christian witchdoctor was the power who might make the new fetish dangerous. Mnombibi had already set inquiries afoot about the whereabouts of Brother François, whom he considered to be his one dangerous rival and an interloper in the neighbourhood. Yes, on the whole it would be best to delay.

He retired to his hut and kept Neleta waiting in Ungah's until it was almost dawn. He thumped his drum and made dantica with his spirits.

Neleta was much bored. She sometimes suspected both priests and wizards. The smell of fish was very strong for one who had become used to a civilized house. And there was nothing but a hard wooden pillow to put her head on. When Mnombibi finally emerged he announced that if Neleta so much as touched the Virgin her own fetish would fail. She returned with a wry neck and gave Mnombibi nothing for his trouble, at which he took to his drum again.

Mnombibi's was not the only drum along the coast by any means. That spring there was a good deal of thumping and "wizard-talk" from village to village, especially on dark nights. Ferdinando noticed it, and so did Anthony as he lay awake through the long night hours. That drum at Bangalang was interminable!! To Mnombibi, however, came the news, tapped out and relayed over miles of jungles from inland villages, that the white witch-doctor had settled down in a new refuge established in the hills. Runaway slaves were welcomed and protected there. The dead, black tree was planted again before his door. That was what Mnombibi wanted to know. So the tree *was* the main fetish after all! The drums suddenly ceased. Mnombibi began to lay his plans.

At the house Neleta was mortally careful not to touch the madonna, which she now disliked the more for being afraid of it. The dry season had set in again. Anthony began to recover more rapidly. The caravan from Futa-Jaloon came down from the hills.

Anthony had forgotten his promise to Amah-de-bellah to visit Futa-Jaloon. But the escort to take him back to the Ali Mami's capital had been punctually provided. He was confidently expected to return with it. Both the messages and gifts which had been sent him were flattering. If he accepted the welcoming-gifts he could only do so as the approaching guest of the forest potentate. If he refused them it would be a deadly affront—and he was largely dependent on these hill-people for his trade. Indeed, Gallegos might not be tenable without their friendship. Certainly it would be uncomfortable and dangerous.

Despite that, Anthony hesitated. He was still weak and comparatively helpless. The journey up-country might finish him, he felt. Neleta was unalterably opposed to his going. She clung to him. It was old Mehemet Ali, the leader of the caravan, who finally persuaded him to leave.

He was a gay old fellow with a large paunch, a ribald sense of humor, and an ingratiating smile. A huge pair of horned spectacles under a snow-white turban lent him, when occasion required, an air of gravity and wisdom. The combination of these qualities was hard to resist.

He promised to provide a horse-litter for the trip up-country. He extolled the healthy air of the hills as the best way to recover from fever. He gave such an enticing account of the hospitality in store at Futa-Jaloon that the difficulties of the hundred-league trek thrugh the jungle and hill-country rapidly took on the aspect of a happy adventure. Finally, with tears in his eyes, the old rascal pleaded with Anthony not to be the death of him. If he returned without the expected guest, he said his head would no longer remain in that happy conjunction with the lower parts of his body which he claimed to have found highly satisfactory and hoped to continue to enjoy.

"Do not, my son," said he, "be the cause of such a sad parting —and remember, I cherish the only solace of twenty-one wives."

"My father, prepare the litter," said Anthony laughing, and despite Neleta's vehement protests he gave orders to pack.

He sent for Ferdinando and gave him off-hand but minute instructions as to the conduct of affairs at Gallegos during his absence. Ferdinando listened carefully, and decided to say nothing then about Brother François's leaving. He regarded Anthony's departure as a happy solution of that difficulty. Why bring it up now? He had already sent Juan on a trip up the river for ivory. He now cautioned Neleta to behave herself and keep her mouth shut.

It was the middle of June when Anthony finally set out, and the long hot days had already turned the lowlands about Gallegos into a vapour bath through which the stars glimmered only as blurred lights when evening came. It was high time to be breathing the free air of the hills again, he thought as they wound day after day along the narrow caravan trails through the steaming forests. He realized that in his debilitated condition he could never have survived another miasmic summer on the coast. An unconquerable weakness and lethargy seized upon him. He swung from side to side helplessly in the cradle-like litter that had been contrived for him. Most of the time, overcome by lassitude and the sleepy motion, he slept.

They moved perforce very slowly. Only after five days did they begin to ascend. On the sixth they camped at evening amid the hills.

Their camp fires twinkled along a dry, rocky height under clear, keen stars. Anthony had not seen the constellations wink and glitter that way for nearly four years. A heavy stone seemed to have been lifted off his chest. His lungs no longer laboured. They expanded eagerly and easily, drawing in the cool, dry air faintly perfumed with sunburnt grasses.

All the sensations of his body responded and became a joy to him again. He lay in his tent experiencing a sensation of lightness akin to intoxication. He was still giddy when he moved about. But it was heavenly to lie quiet, feeling as if gravity itself had relented. Only a little more and it would release him entirely. He remembered how a stranded boat seemed to become lighter as the tide rose, till it floated away.

"I have escaped all that fever in the furnace below," he thought,— "come up under the clean, clear stars again. Perhaps I was not melted and cast into hard bronze down there after all. Anyway, I shall live and go on now. I shall keep going on. My other, my real self is not going to die. Tonight I feel something alive and stirring within me as if it knew it will soon be set free to go on with the tide."

For the first time in months he was able to merge into sleep happily. Like a healing spring he felt the waters of rest begin to permeate him.

Presently he seemed to have made an unalterable decision— or it had been made for him. He could not state to himself exactly what it was. But he was utterly content with it. In the space between wakefulness and slumber he felt abundant joy flow through him, a feeling of having come to a conclusion eternally right. Energy flowed into him from beyond himself. It gradually flooded and refreshed his being with a great sense of peace and well-being. Why had he cut himself off from this refreshing river that flowed from the same eternal source and was the spiritual counterpart of light? How long he had been using only a stagnant little part of it! His own will had shut the valves of his soul against it! He was tired, worn-out holding them closed. Now he had given up and life-giving waters swept through him.

Now he could let his body stretch out at peace with the life within it; at one with its contained self. He knew he would awaken from sleep refreshed. He would not have been holding himself against the tide all night long, swept this way and that by evil dreams, almost torn apart. He would awaken one with himself. And through the day?—

No longer would he pass the daylight hours as at Gallegos— like an actor in an endless play with a futile meaning and a logical little plot; a play where every motion must be the result of consciously exerted will. Acting! How tired, how exhausted that had left him! What a vile stage was Gallegos, and how hollow was the animated metallic figure that had moved upon it, worn out, burned out by fever of mind and body, empty of itself. That figure had melted down at last and now lay almost sublimed. Was it about to float off leaving nothing but a few burnt-out ashes behind?

For he *had* succeeded in becoming that impervious, expressionless bronze boy that stood watching the river of existence flow through the fountain; not caring whence it came or where it went; interested only in the interplay of shadows and pictures on the little pool at his feet where for an instant the eternal water flashed into the light for him alone. And he had become tired of it at last, because finally he could see nothing but his own shadow falling there. That shadow had blotted out all else. Yes, he had succeeded in becoming the Bronze Boy who had lost his living twin; who stood looking at his own shadow on the water till his eyes had gone blind. He had succeeded in damning himself! Yet tonight?

Surely tonight some mercy had been vouchsafed him! He was being swept on with the waters again; being bathed in their strength. No longer would he stand and only look across their surface. They were running deep now, down, down . . .

Very deep in him, just at the verge of sleep, lay the images which expressed life to him. They were the primary semblances of things upon which his blank eyes had first feasted in infancy when he played about the fountain in the convent courtyard under the plane tree. There the dream within the dream had first begun.

For him those images were always there. In the daytime they might be sunk beyond sight and crowded down, but still there; the unseen ones who at the direction of the unknown master of the drama pulled the moving strings of his emotions behind the scenes. Yet they could always be seen again when the depths of his being were stirred. And then they moved in a drama of their own, his drama, having taken on the meanings of meaning for him through the accumulated experience of years.

These subliminal dreams of his soul in which he saw his own life mirrored and dramatized were not childish to him no matter what the nature and appearance of the dreamful actors might be; no matter how beautiful, grotesque, outrageous, or obscene the mimes became. This play moved beyond the petty censorship of common sense, wrapt forever from the carping of logic, under the rules of socialized morality, safe from the wakeful world which it triumphantly caricatured or glorified with the free imagery of a primal poetry that transcended reality. It was his glass of truth, like a mirror provided by God. The reflections upon this glass of sleep made him laugh, weep, love, hate, burn with lust till the seed spouted of itself from his loins. They comforted him with visions of the dead-alive again; they fascinated him with strangely glorious landscapes, and forgotten things; they sent him reeling through caverns pursued by dripping monsters of his own begetting, shrieking with fear. Any play is *the* thing, the presentation of life in the terms of life itself. But there is also the play within the play.

Anthony had always known this instinctively. It was his faith *in* himself. For the greater part of his existence he had lived by it. The last three years at Gallegos he had tried to deny it utterly.

Tonight in the little tent under the stars, where he breathed the light mountain air again after weeks of fever, the sudden release, the sudden relief of having been rescued had almost cut him loose from his physical moorings. He was, in fact, at the crisis of his inner and outer sickness, and what sustained him from within, that which he had so long denied as true now threatened to withdraw.

His first impression of returning strength and renewed determination as he went to sleep that night had been due to the sensation of comfort experienced from a complete relaxation upon being carried up into the cool hills. It was due to weakness as much as anything else, and that weakness now released him too far. What had for a few minutes been a feeling of delicious ease soon let him down into an utter lassitude, an increasing numbness that began to verge upon nothing at all. Almost asleep, as if something had whispered a warning to him he began to realize the necessity of a last desperate effort of the will to escape from approaching oblivion.

He was gliding down a steep slope in the dark with sickening speed. There was a tremendous cliff at the end. Somewhere in the billowing mists that filled the empty abyss at the end of the world was a far-off glow, a smudged, cloudy glory in which the madonna had wrapped herself.

If he could only speak to her she would save him. But he had refused to do so for so long that he was unable to cry out now. He filled his lungs to try. A hand came down out of the darkness and clamped itself over his mouth. He struggled. He was nearing the verge . . .

"Madre . . ." he choked.

Then he fell. He kept on falling—

Down . . .

Down . . .

Down . . . ice-cold waters closed over his head. He had finally become the bronze boy and he sank like heavy metal.

He touched bottom and lay there . . .

Air! He was drowning. Give him one more breath! One!

With a *tremendous* impulse he shot himself upward again through the dark, cold water.

He came out!

He seemed to burst through and fill his lungs again.

The heavy dew had by now stretched tight as a drum the fabric of the tent in which Anthony lay. A late, cloud-troubled moon had gradually climbed above the tops of the surrounding trees. In the shifting black-and-silver shadows in the tent, where the filtered moonlight seemed to concentrate and congeal like à semi-gaseous fluid, the man who had just hurled himself up from oblivion by a last desperate effort now opened his eyes still filled with the horror of his dream.

There had been an overpowering sensation of speed to his return. As he opened his eyes the impulse of it seemed to be carried forward into something else beyond him, and to leave him. Something rose up from his body and was carried by the momentum of his return into the misty light beyond as if he had projected it out of himself.

It stood naked in the shifting moonlight.

He had seen it before—when it was younger. It had had the face then of the child who had laughed back at him from the fountain before Father Xavier came and told him it was only a dream. It was "Anthony." It was the dear first playmate, the lovely child who had laughed down at him from the branches of the plane tree while the filtered sunlight danced over him . . . that face in the miniature . . .

But now it was older. It stood naked in the mist, now wrapping itself in shadow and now burning clearly in a figure of light again. The face of it, noble with a man's strength, was also sad with unfulfilled desires and hopes; with dreamful eyes like wide, undiscovered seas. Flowing out dimly and more dimly into the darkness, flickered its brush of burning hair. In that nest a phoenix might be reborn; might rise suddenly and soar away.

So for an instant it stood as if bewildered at having been cast forth into the cold outer moonlight. It shivered and turned to look sadly at him, its eyes wide with a strange wonder like those of a child looking upon a dead playmate; wild with a grief-stricken and lonely surmise. The lonely twin stood looking for a while at its birth-fellow. Then it turned to go . . .

He threw himself upon it.

He wrestled in the moonlight over the floor of the empty tent. It was more powerful than anything he had known. He was in love with what was choking him and struggling to be gone. The breath of his throat rattled as he struggled with it. He wound his arms around this strong impalpable thing more precious to him than a dying child. He clasped it close and felt it burning into him again. The chest of it seemed to collapse into his own and to fill his lungs with fire. Every breath was a fiery agony . . . His veins glowed . . .

He cried out with a terrible voice, "Water! Water!"

The hoarse, throaty cries from Anthony's tent filled all the sleeping camp with alarm. The sentries who had been on watch against a possible lion came running. They stood listening now to the silence. Old Mehemet Ali tore open the flap and found the guest of his master lying exhausted on the floor of his tent with the contents strewn about in intolerable disorder.

Finally they brought him a drink. He *could* breathe now. He was going to live!

Old Mehemet stood by uneasily peering through his foolish, wise-looking glasses. "Now, my son," said he, "you will get better. Those who come up into the mountain air to recover from swamp fever are sometimes given to fits. Your cries were terrible. I thought you were fighting with a lion."

449

"I was," said Anthony feebly.

"There, there," said the old man soothingly. "We shall not leave you alone again until you get much stronger."

It was near morning. The camp did not go to sleep again. The men built up the fires and waited for dawn, getting what comfort they could after such an eery alarm from the tones of their own voices in casual conversation. Here and there a few laughed at the white man's nightmare.

All the rest of the way into the foothills Anthony slept. Some days later they heard the distant thunder of the snake-drums at Futa-Jaloon throbbing their greeting. It would be a long visit for him, he knew. He must really get well this time. He steeled himself for the indescribable tumult of an African welcome to an Arab town. Already the war-horns, the neighing of horses, the drums and musketry sounded as if a battle were in progress.

———— ◆ ————

Six months of a barbaric but bountiful life in the hill-country about Futa Jaloon had more than put Anthony on his feet again. Indeed, it had put him on four feet, for he had been made free of the splendid Arab stud kept by the Ali Mami. For the first time he had tasted to the full the joys and benefits of noble horsemanship. Over the wide plateaus, the opulent valleys, and through the open forests of the foothills surrounding the town he and Amah had chased the deer, coursed antelope, and hunted leopards. They had camped under clear stars in thorn bomas about the leaping fires in lion country. They had returned to the little capital to experience a literally royal welcome. For while at Futa-Jaloon Anthony had seen a palace revolution take place. The old Ali Mami had died and Amah-de-bellah had succeeded him, not without a little street fighting marked by the timely demise of several nephews. Now Amah sat on the ivory stool tasselled with ostrich plumes, which passed for a throne.

But this unnoted ripple in an otherwise blank page of history had caused little change in Anthony's status as a guest. If anything, it was for the better. He and Amah-de-bellah had become, despite the barriers of blood and language, very genuine and fast friends. Language, indeed, had not stood between them long. During his convalescence Anthony had taken pains to master the bastard Arabic of the Foulah hill-country, if one can be said to "master" a dialect in which the vocabulary is strictly limited and most of the grammar forgot. As for blood—any strain that produced so splendid a figure of a man as Amah deserved admiration. In spite of the fact that he really was one, Amah-de-bellah looked and acted like a king. That is, he was a free man, sovereign enough to impose his will on his fellows and himself at the same time. His was a good will.

The bond between him and Anthony was one which, though nowadays rare, once developed in more heroic states of society perhaps the chief moral virtues in man. It was friendship based upon an essential compatibility in manful attitudes and pursuits; in war, hunting, barter, and the frank relaxations and conversations of the camp fire, the tent, and the town.

The Arab hill-town, to be sure, was neither heroic nor Utopian. Outwardly it was merely a collection of a thousand or more white, flat-roofed houses clustered about a large rambling building of sun-burnt bricks known as the "palace." Through the centre of the town ran a loud mountain stream, and there were pleasant enough open squares shaded by palms. The place was surrounded by a double stockade with a packed earth parapet. There were wooden watch-towers over the gates and several miles of date trees, palm-nut groves, and market gardens around about. These were by far the most pleasing feature of the Foulah capital.

Six or seven thousand Arabs of a very mixed strain, ruled over by a few families of purer blood, lived here and dominated a surprising extent of territory by continuous and ruthless raiding of their darker, heathen neighbours. Slaves for both domestic use and for barter were a drug on the market. They were, in fact, the debased, sweated currency of a constantly fluctuating realm.

From Futa-Jaloon to the coast stretched about three hundred miles of low, hot forest region largely unknown. This was a no-man's-land of obscure forest tribes who raided one another and in turn were raided by the Foulahs whenever their own territory to the east amid the high hills had been hunted out.

The climate of the place was salubrious; the soil ridiculously fertile with the mixed abundance of a temperate hill region near the equator, where crops succeed one another in an endless round. In addition there were flocks of black native sheep, herds of cattle, and immense droves of half-wild goats and swine. Game of all kinds abounded.

It was not altogether surprising, therefore, that Anthony had remained at Futa-Jaloon month after month.

His hitherto retarded convalescence had here been rapid. At the end of half a year he was stronger than he had ever been before. The six months at Futa-Jaloon marked a sort of mental pause in existence for him. The atmosphere of the place was timeless. He lived only for the day and had cast off for the first time in his life cogitations about the past; plans and worries about the future. After his nearly fatal collapse and the struggle that night in the tent on the way up from Gallegos he had realized that he must devote himself to regaining his strength and becoming thoroughly reintegrated, no matter what happened to his affairs. Existence, and not the ways and means of it, was now the end in view.

In this, Amah-de-bellah had proved himself an understanding and solicitous friend. There was no limit to the hospitality and courtesies of the princely Mohammedan. To the stranger who had come ostensibly for purposes of trade, the house of his host soon proved to be the most comfortable and hospitable roof under which he had ever been. Anthony was nursed back to health by Amah's mother and sisters, who, though they never dropped their veils, were none the less skilful and solicitous nurses. Nor was it the first case of complicated swamp fever they had dealt with. They purged him, fed him, and cheered him back to strength as if he had been one of their own blood. As he grew able and anxious to converse again Amah had come and talked with him for hours, squatting on a low clay bench covered with the skins of various beasts. Dressed in the long white robes of his tribe and rank, with the water-pipe bubbling musically at his feet and the sweet smoke curling from his fine clean-cut lips half-parted in a pleasant open smile, Amah emanated a high-bred courtesy and an engaging charm with every word and gesture. This was all the more striking due to the somewhat hawk-like cast of his features and his glittering black eyes that Anthony felt might just as easily and naturally take on the pitiless stare of the falcon who has been shown a swan.

Strong friendship begins with respect, traverses admiration, and ends in a trust and affection which continues to combine the first two. The process is greatly accentuated if the friends in the making are both willing to confer and receive favours without conceiving them as obligations or weights on the scales of influence which must ever be kept nicely readjusted and precisely balanced. A true friendship transcends this mere tit-for-tat game of influence played between urbane self-seeking acquaintances. It finds its equipoise in the discovery that both parties have a trust and belief in some eternal relationship beyond themselves. Then, no matter how differently they may approach that common centre, they understand their actions and attitudes to be upon a mutually permanent ground.

It was so with Anthony and Amah. They had begun by respecting, even by fearing each other a little. They had opened their minds to each other during the long hours of conversation and had each been agreeably surprised and moved to admiration by the qualities of the other. And they had, as their reserve vanished by mutual degrees, discovered that each had at some time in his life given himself up for lost and knew that he still continued to exist as if by an extended act of mercy and not by his own transcendent strength and cleverness. In this profound compromise of their egos, differences of race, creed, and custom seemed trivial.

As became a Mohammedan, Amah's outlook upon things was somewhat fatalistic. He might strive and will; Allah would decide. His mortal dangers had been met and had passed him by in foray and battle, for he had been a warrior since boyhood. Arrows and spears had been loosed at him and had been turned aside to quiver in the hearts of others stronger and wiser than he. Thus, said he, "God has tempered my pride."

Anthony had won the same sense of his place as a servant of a superior will by internal rather than external strife. It was the vision of light upon the barrier beaches which had finally brought him to a mental acknowledgment and conviction of himself as a living atom of the whole, but as an atom nevertheless possessed of an atomic will of its own. It was the struggle with himself in the tent that night on the way up from Gallegos that had shown him how to use that will. That it had also been a struggle with death he had no doubt.

But he had been permitted to return. He had been permitted more than that. He had been permitted to see and to understand what kind of being he was; to recapture and retain himself. That curious entity that lies in so many of us forever unknown, an entity that when outraged sometimes strikes back at us like a mysterious enemy, or becomes weary to be gone—had been revealed to him naked. It was the quality of his mind so to see things—to see them rather than to hear them and to make words about them. The emotional meaning of that vision of his outraged and departing self were plain. Plain also was the departing glow in the mist which he had called upon but which had answered him no more. The temptation to become a mere ruthless doer for the sake of doing had been passed. Gallegos had passed him by like one of the arrows of which Amah had spoken. True, it had also like them fleshed itself in the hearts of others and he was partly responsible for that. He had helped aim the arrow.

But the nearly vital wound which he had given himself was going to heal. Had, indeed, already closed. His triumph in that was so great as to preclude much thought of the wounds of others. How he could liquidate this experience, how close-out at Gallegos he did not yet know. The method, the impulse for that must be disclosed by events.

For a while he was too weak and exhausted by his long fever and the fever of the spirit that had accompanied it to make any practical decisions. Something must help him to that. He prayed while he still lay ill for something to strengthen his will to enable him to make the break. His will was weak and tired now after years of forcing himself against himself. In his heart he acknowledged this weakness. He was no longer the strong, self-sufficient Master of Gallegos. Knowing more now, seeing much more clearly—he felt he might still fail. But there seemed no immediate answer to this impasse. He left it, waiting. For the time being he wiped the slate of dreams and cogitations blank.

Thus it was that Futa-Jaloon became for him a kind of dateless experience. As he looked back at it afterwards, it remained forever like a halt in time. It had about it a bit of the calmness of eternity, a place where he had slipped out of the swift troubled rhythms of the West into the changelessness of the East. Futa-Jaloon, indeed, was a small outpost of the Orient. And it was all the more marked with that feeling because, for Anthony, it lay between two distinct epochs of his life.

Early impulsive manhood had gone. It had died, had been burnt out in the fever; passed with the era of the Bronze Boy in the fierce furnace of tropical heat and mad desire. Henceforth he knew himself not as merely becoming but as to a great extent become.

This inward conviction undoubtedly reacted upon him physically. He not only grew well again, but the process went further. Once having conquered a constant internal doubt and conflict, he now gave outward signs of inward rest, of greater strength and assurance. He became heavier and stronger, less brittle and metallic in his body. Yet more sinewy and tougher. He became less liable to be broken and shattered; more resilient and flexible. By day he was tireless, and at night he lay down and slept like a child.

He thanked God for this. He told himself that he had won through onto the untroubled table-land of mature middle life. It now seemed to stretch before him to an unbroken horizon. At least he could not see beyond that imaginary line. Meanwhile, he lingered on the plateaus about Futa-Jaloon and in the house of Amah-de-bellah, comforted at the world's end by unexpected and generous hospitality; by trust, and as time wore on, by affection. He seemed suddenly to have found not only himself but a brother and a family in that house. He even had a horse and a dog. He had never known the dependence and devotion of animals before; how deeply it tried and tested a man. And here too he had not been found wanting. All the gold of the Indies could bring him no more. All that was wanting was a wife and children. Amah on more than one occasion had said so laughingly. Soon he had grown more serious.

All this, however, was suddenly put an end to by the un-expected appearance of Juan with disconcerting news from Gallegos. Anthony had heard only twice from Gallegos since he had come up into the hills. All had been "as usual" and "going well," according to the quite literal Ferdinando. But now his writing was different.

La Fortuna was lying in the reach again waiting for cargo. Petty trouble had developed between Don Ruiz and the factor, which, to judge by both their letters, promised to become seri-ous. In the midst of this an English ship called the *Unicorn* had suddenly appeared in the Rio Pongo and now lay covering the channel below Gallegos with her guns. The English ship was commanded by a horrid, determined gentleman by the name of Bittern who claimed to have come to take Señor Adverse to Italy. And he would not depart, nor let anyone else depart, until he had seen the said Señor Adverse to whom he insisted the *Unicorn* belonged.

Here Ferdinando's letter broke into a wail. Was it possible that this was true? If so what was to become of them all at Gallegos, with England and Spain at war, and an English armed ship owned by their master in the river? Wasn't this rather hard to explain? Also what did Anthony think Neleta was doing all this time? etc., etc. The factor permitted himself a few per-plexed but rather tart liberties.

At all this Anthony felt somewhat inclined to laugh. Don Ruiz and Ferdinando faced by the implacable Captain Bittern was not without its humorous aspects. But his smile faded as he read on. Ferdinando had now seen fit, at a safe distance, to illu-minate his employer about the departure of Brother François.

Furthermore, the cargo of children had been sold at a considerable profit. This point the factor took some pains to drive home. Anthony was some two hundred pounds better off by the transaction, he discovered—when he was able to look at the paper and see the neat copper-plate writing of his clerk again.

And [said Ferdinando, evidently sure of himself] *it is on the whole, señor, much better that we are rid of that padre once and for all here at Gallegos. He has attempted to set up again at some place about the headwaters of the Rio Pongo, I hear. This has caused a great stir amongst the coast tribes whose slaves have been slipping off to his crazy settlement.*

So far has this matter gone since you left that our own trade is being interfered with, too. A great gathering of the coast tribes recently took place at Bangalang and after a deal of drumming and witch-finding set off yesterday inland. I think this bodes no good to the padre. We wish him no harm, of course, but I did not think it necessary to interfere. Mnombibi, of whom you have heard, is his enemy, and I did not desire to antagonize the natives so near at hand upon whom we must depend. What we now fear is that on the way back they will be crazed with the war-fever and attack the settlement from the land side. We shall then be between these devils and the deep sea, with the Englishman waiting down river. Come home, Señor Adverse. We are short handed . . .

The letter ended in a thoroughly scared whine, a half-breed left alone to his own resources!

Anthony flung the letter on the ground with a round curse and looked up to see Juan's eyes resting upon him.

"Juan," said he, "it is my fault. I have stayed away too long. I know . . ."

"Sí," answered Juan looking at him reproachfully. "I have come myself this time to be sure you hear the truth. It is much worse than you think. That man Ferdinando is a half-breed wolf. He would sell his own children. Everything! He and his sister—caramba! She is a bitch without brats. Someone should give her some. It is 'Cheecha, Cheecha,' all day long now—and the sound of the whip at the house on the hill. Ah, pardon, señor, but it is true. Sí! I have come to tell you, and to bring you the letters of Captain Matanza. Without Don Ruiz we would be in a bad way. I have been living on *La Fortuna* myself for a month past. Your factor when he is drunk is the kind of a man that makes the knife itch to go home, ugh! If you are a man, señor, you will come back now. Brother François gave me this on the way up. I found him! From his hands I received the holy food. He is well but . . ."

"You *saw* him!" cried Anthony. "Give it to me!"

He tore open the small scroll of native matting. Inside, written across the torn page of a missal in some dim vegetable fluid that had run he made out very faintly:

A moi, mon ami, for the love of Christ—and the peace of your own soul. I appeal to the last . . .

The rest was a hopeless blur. But the import of it was like an explosion in Anthony's brain. "Mnombibi—Brother François."

———◆———

Juan had reached him where he and Amah had come out to hunt some leopards that had been causing the villagers trouble in the level tract of country just below Futa-Jaloon. It was a wide, park-like plateau that stretched out from the foothills to plunge down suddenly into the coastal jungles some leagues to the westward. The hunt was to begin on the morrow. It was a full-moon night. Hyenas were laughing somewhere in the distance and the pack of eager hounds they had brought with them was baying with melancholy harmonies at the cloudless, copper disk just beginning to rise redly through the trees and the smoke of the evening fires.

Anthony tossed Ferdinando's letter into the flames.

"Can you still ride, Juan—after your long journey?"

"If it is with you—homeward."

Anthony nodded and led the way to Amah's fire. Something in his gait and demeanour made Amah look up and grow tense.

"What has happened?" he asked.

"My brother," said Anthony, "the hand of God has been laid upon me. I must go."

"Bismillah!" exclaimed Amah, "but you will not go alone!"

"No, lend me men and horses, my friend, I too will go hunting tomorrow, but in the forest below for those who trouble a holy man."

"Allah be with you then," said Amah, and gave a shrill whistle. In five minutes twenty men were armed, mounted, and waiting expectantly just below the chief's fire. They were used to forays by night. Anthony's horse was led up.

Amah rose suddenly and facing Anthony laid his hands on his shoulders.

"My brother," he said, "for seven moons now we have eaten salt together and we have deeply tasted the same savour. Is it not so?"

"Allah reward you for it, Amah my friend," said Anthony much moved. "The savour of your bread and salt has been sweet to the tongue."

"Ah! It comes upon me suddenly I shall not see you again," said Amah. "May the glory of the face of Allah light your path forever." He raised his hands high above his head in a mantic gesture seeming to release a sudden force as he opened his palms to speed his blessing upon them. The men waiting below shouted.

"Wait," said Amah, "there is something I would send with you." Then he hesitated as if he had changed his mind. "My friendship will follow you," he said.

"Farewell." They both said it together and laughed. Anthony mounted.

"Go!" cried Amah.

They swept out over the level grass land with the fresh night-wind in their faces, the little troop galloping hard, and close together.

Amah saw them pass over the grey face of the rolling grass country like a small, white cloud scudding under the moon.

"Kismet," he murmured.

Presently he made a sign to one of his men. "Loose Simba," he said.

At the first halt, as they drew up to breathe the horses, Anthony was overtaken by the powerful hound that he had been hunting with for some time past. It ran up and lay down at his feet. He knew it was a parting gift from Amah, who valued his brave dogs more than his gold. Amah's friendship would follow, as he had said.

They were in the saddle again in a few minutes, speeding over the gentle, mile-long waves of the hill pastures with only the next horizon and clumps of trees here and there, like ships anchored on a sea of moonlight, to guide them. Shadows of antelopes and jackals fled before them. They galloped long and hard, they rested—and galloped on again.

By morning they had come to the great escarpment where the plateau fell away sheerly and then tumbled down through several miles of eroded foothills to the low, coastal forest two thousand feet below. A grey cloud through which here and there, on a few isolated high places, the tops of tall palms wrapped in mist thrust themselves upward with a funereal effect, stretched as far as they could see. Three days westward through those orchid-hung, steaming depths lay Gallegos.

Juan pointed out a range of low hills toward the far horizon which was already beginning to shine in the dawn while all else still lay drab and level as far as the eye could reach in that direction. It was there he said Brother François had made his refuge. Those hills lay a good ten hours' journey along the caravan trail to Gallegos. Anthony's heart smote him to think that he must have passed them close-by on his journey up. "If he could only have known—have seen Brother François then! Now, perhaps, it was too late."

Reproachful voices seemed to rise up to him out of the forest below. He turned away sad and sick at heart; full of foreboding. Those hills seemed far-off, dark as Calvary. Yet he must not permit himself the disconcerting luxury of remorseful reverie. He must save himself to press on. If he could only arrive before Mnombibi and his tribesmen! *If* he could only do *that!*—all might still be well.

They settled themselves on the edge of the plateau for a brief halt. It was essential to let the horses rest and get their last belly-ful of the good grass before plunging into the leafy gulf below. Between them and the coast there was nothing but dark forest. It was the country where he had lost himself, Anthony thought. He longed for a glimpse of the sea beyond, for the free path across which, under the clear stars, ships came and went. In one of them he could sail away.

But would he?

Would he, when he got home with Brother François safe again, have the courage to make the final break from Gallegos? Neleta, the much cherished plantations, the whole order of the existence he had built up for four years would be there—reach-ing out for him. At the top of the cliff, before he plunged back into the forest again, he tossed in his blankets and wondered. What would mere dreams in the hills be when once more he lay in Neleta's arms in the castle he had built for himself? He was strong now, stronger than ever before, and the fire of life beat in his veins.

As the first heat of the morning poured over the pleateau and turned the forest below into a thousand smokes, they rose, saddled their beasts, and plunged downward through the bare, clay foothills. An hour later and the roof of the jungle had closed over them.

The narrow caravan trail, forever lost in glimmering half-lights, led hither and yon. It looped and twisted through swamps and made detours to strike the muddy fords of black, sleepy streams. Not a ripple of breeze stirred the palm-tops a hundred feet above them. Eternal silence, and the immemorial twilight of the primeval forest bathed in stupefying heat closed them in. Now and then they halted while vines that had grown across the trail were being cut through. It was evident that the trail followed the tops of slight ridges through trackless reaches of swamp. Bad as it was, it was one of the best roads in Africa from the hill-country to the coast. Horses could follow it if they could survive the flies and insects. They halted at noon in a forest clearing, an inane paradise of orchids and vines covering the fire-scarred sites of native huts. It was here they heard drums. They were very distant. It was a shaking of leaves rather than a sound. It shook Anthony like the leaves.

He now pressed his men and horses to the limit. They began to rise out of the swamp again. About three o'clock Juan pointed out a fork in the trail they might otherwise have passed. They took this and rose rapidly. Evidently they were now among the nest of low hills they had seen that morning. Presently they could trot again. They did so, stopping frequently to listen, and with scouts out ahead.

Suddenly they emerged into a series of open glades. Great springs broke out clearly from under masses of black, volcanic rock. Here was the source of one of the main forks of the Rio Pongo, the Foulahs said. They turned sharply to the right still following Juan's lead and entered an open, bowl-shaped valley. At the upper end the embers of what had been a cluster of huts only a few hours before still shimmered with heat and smoked hazily into the afternoon sunlight.

They were too late.

Anthony sat his horse drearily. He cursed himself and his luck darkly. Here and there in the grass he saw the glimmer of dark bodies. Several vultures flapped away. There was the busy noise of flies. Mnombibi's people must have raided the place some time that morning. It was the drums going down-river that they had heard—after the raid! Most of the people they would carry off.

"And that devil Mnombibi had been in his room that night with Neleta!" He ground his teeth.

But Brother François, Brother François, where was he?

Someone gave a dismal shout and pointed.

Against a black outcrop of cliff several hundred yards away Anthony saw a white body apparently suspended in the air. It did not move. His spine crept.

He slid down the neck of his horse, which was cropping the grass, and stumbled forward in a tumult of agonized horror. He looked for the rope. The arms were held out stiffly. At first he did not see the dark beams of the cross against the black rock in the cliff's shadow. Now they suddenly seared themselves on his mind forever—and the man hanging there.

The cross stood before a little cave which Brother François had evidently made his chapel. He ran and fell down by it. He cried out so that the hound which had followed him cowered and whimpered and was afraid to come near.

After a while the man on the ground grew silent and lay still . . .

"Why did this have to happen to him? It was more than he could bear. Now he was lost. He was in hell *now*. If time would only pass. Let it be a year from now, instantly!" He tried to pray.

"Father," he cried, and looked up.

There were none of the comforting conventions of the carved crucifix there. The naked body, welted from the shoulders down, was bound to the beams with thongs of rawhide. These had drawn tight in the morning sun, which had passed slowly, blistering the tonsured head. The dark, clotted locks hung down before the face like a scorched curtain. Through the hands and feet were thrust long mimosa thorns that dripped slowly into black clots on the stones below. But the shadow of the cliff had now advanced beyond the little cairn of rocks where the cross had been planted. Already it was enveloped in advancing shade. It grew cooler.

The man on the cross shivered and opened his eyes.

"I."

"Tonight thou shalt be with me in paradise. . . ."

"I?"

Not yet! This was the terrible earth yet. Hands, feet, fire!

"A moi," he cried raising his face. His head sunk again and he looked down through his hair, hanging.

He heard a voice below him. He saw dimly. After a while he remembered.

"Anthony," he whispered, "my son . . ."

The sound fell into the ears of the man below like dry burning leaves.

"Alive yet!" cried Anthony. He stood up. He could do something. He looked.

Not too late . . . ? Yes—yes, too late—and forever too late. . . . Oh!

"You are dying."

The leaves of sound began to fall again. The cross shook. The man on it was trying to speak to him. He looked up again at that agony. It was for him. *His.* The wind blew the hair back from the face. It was only the body fighting there he saw—fighting. Suddenly Brother François's face, the beloved face Anthony had known, peered through it. The lips moved not of themselves but to the music of the mind.

"It is you who are dying. Not I."

Anthony stood fixed, turned to stone. He saw that face lift to the sky.

"Remember me . . . Jesu . . . I still live . . ."

"I LIVE," he cried with a triumphant voice.

"Go!"

The body of him leaped upward against the thongs and thorns. The cross rocked against the sky. Then it was still.

Silence again.

A column of ants approached and began to ascend the cross.

The man below stood looking up but seeing nothing. After a while a cloud seemed to be passing across the top of his mind. He seemed to be looking up from the bottom of a well. Presently he knew it *was* the sky he was looking at. He fell backward out of eternity into time, and caught himself. He fled up the hill.

When he came to himself he was lying on the grass with a circle of dark faces peering down at him and the hound Simba licking his hands.

"Not worthy of that," he thought. He caught them away.

Then he threw his arms about the animal and burst into an agony of weeping.

It saved him from going mad.

They stayed in the valley all night and built great fires to keep the beasts off. It was necessary to appeal to the Foulahs for help. Luckily the only one of them who could read his Koran remembered that Mohammed had said Christ was one of his prophets who had come before him. It might therefore be permitted to help bury Christ's servants who had been slain by the heathen. After some urging, and the promise of gifts at Gallegos, they were persuaded to set about gathering large stones for a tomb. But they would not touch the body on the cross.

Anthony and Juan were left alone to that. In the flickering light of the leaping fires they unbound the now shrunken form from the tree where it had suffered. They wrapped it in a rich cloak Amah had given Anthony. They laid it on the rough stone altar at the end of the cave. It was a naturally cloistered cavern. They stood the long cross lengthwise against the low wall of the place. Juan left and returned with some white rock-flowers he found near by. He spread these about softly and wept. Anthony saw that he had left his shoes at the entrance.

"Look, señor," he whispered. "They have stolen the silver crucifix that the good padre kept over his altar. There must have been Christians among them."

Anthony shook his head. He could neither weep nor speak.

The torches began to go out. The night deepened. Anthony thought of Brother François's face under the light of the vine that day at Regla.

"The light has taken him back to itself. I saw him go," he thought. "It is well with him now. I cannot bear it here any more. I am only a man."

"He will pray for us," said Juan when they stood outside under the stars again. "Our sins will be forgiven." Anthony pressed the simple fellow's hand. He waited while Juan went for the Arabs. They blocked the narrow entrance of the little cave, piling one great rock on another. They brought the earth down over the front.

The sound of the stones falling one on another was the language that night of Anthony's thoughts as he sat alone with Simba by the fire. The others might sleep. Yesterday had altered him beyond the language of the tongues of men. In an indescribable way he felt himself to be a totally different man. Like the blade of a sword taken hot from the fire he had been suddenly plunged into cold eternity for a moment and permanently tempered. When he had reeled back from the foot of the cross he had stumbled into time again. But his metal had been changed.

How this new man would act, who he was in fact, he must now find out for himself. Nor did he feel that the tempering of himself had been the end intended for what had happened to Brother François. "No, no, a thousand times no!" He was beyond any egotistic superstitions about this martyrdom which to his own inner world had been like a cosmic catastrophe, a spiritual earthquake which for a few moments had left him standing alone like the only man left on earth, face to face with God. It could have been intended for him alone no more than an earthquake could have been aimed at him or a storm at sea.

Yet he had been involved in it. He had even been instrumental in both a wilful and involuntary way in bringing it about. Looking into the embers of the dying fire in that valley of the shadow that night, he faced all the implications. And his own part in this happening and the meaning of it to him, accidental as that might be,—or providential if accidents were part of providence,—was part of them. The meaning of it remained with him alone.

Alone among those present he had had eyes and ears to understand. The Foulahs could only gather stones to make a tomb. The others slept while he watched and in his own manner communed.

Even Juan slept. Poor fellow, the marks of tears were still there on his simple, peasant face. In his handkerchief, wrapped up in sweet-smelling leaves and hidden in his breast, were the three thorns that had pierced Brother François's hands and feet. He had asked for them. Anthony knew they would eventually go to the little chapel overlooking the sea in Juan's native village in Spain. There the pious tale of the returned sailor would go round. There would be pilgrimages from the local countryside, perhaps. It would be like the "miracle" at Regla. Surely, surely *that* could not be the end of Brother François—three thorns in a gold box on a country altar? No! no! Someway, somehow, he must yet learn how, he should carry that light farther. When the time came he would light it again. He would take up the torch he had left burning out in the cavern. Perhaps Juan would take up the one he had left there in his own way. Perhaps, the thorns on the altar and pilgrimage were one way of remembering, of keeping the torch lit. But he must find his own way of shedding that light. Now he knew what the madonna had been holding out to him. The child in her arms had leaped into the man on the cross.

He wrapped his cloak about him closer in the darkness and gazed into the dying embers, not asleep, but lost at last in a wordless reverie. The night passed. The titanic fingers of the sun thrust fanwise through the eastern clouds. The tropical dawn came with a single stride. Suddenly the intolerable sun smote him on the eyes.

"Let there be light!"

"Go!"

"Go. May the glory of the face of Allah light your way," Amah had said.

"Go!" It was the last utterance of Brother François, whether addressed to his own spirit or to Anthony's, Anthony did not know. It would have been like him to have thought of another even at the last. Now the entire universe seemed to be filled and to be thundering that word accompanied by speeding bolts of light that struck the hills themselves into day.

The beams sped on into the west where that word of action was the way to salvation or damnation. In Futa-Jaloon, in the east where the dawn came from, men might sit and let the fate of Allah overtake them. They might wait for it there. But he, Anthony, was going back home. He must go now. He must *go!*

He called to the sleepers and they rode out of the shadows of the valley as if they could leave them behind forever.

46. THE "UNICORN" CHARGES HOME

On the same morning that Anthony was slashing his way through the forests toward Gallegos, Captain Bittern of the good ship *Unicorn* was walking the quarter-deck with a faster tread and shorter turn than usual. He had been lying—and stewing—in the Rio Pongo for over six weeks, and he was thoroughly fed-up with the landscape just below Gallegos and immediately opposite Bangalang. With this view of things, a thoroughly monotonous one, the entire ship's company was for once in exact agreement with their captain.

Only once since they had arrived in the Rio Pongo to fetch home their new owner—about whom rumours were rife in the foc's'le—had the prospect from the deck been changed, and then only enough to shift the angles of things in the view very slightly. Yet this change, to the eyes of the captain at least, had been quite important.

He had warped his ship about a half mile across the bay from her first anchorage to take advantage of what is known to admirers of the art of artillery as "defilade space." In this case it simply meant that the guns from the hill-battery at Gallegos would be forced to over-shoot the *Unicorn* in her new berth, due to the prominence of a small rise of ground on the long point of land between them and the ship.

Captain Bittern had picked out the one safe spot in the broad reach between Gallegos and Mongo Tom's with the canny eye of a privateersman who had cut-out many a tall ship and felucca from under the noses of barking Spanish shore batteries. Although he had now come on a peaceful private mission to an out-of-the-way spot, he bore an English letter of marque, the Spanish flag waved at Gallegos—and he was taking no chances. He still regarded minute protuberances in the landscape, such as now shielded him, as small but important works of God in favour of British enterprise. In a world where the majority of mankind persisted in disagreeing with him and his countrymen about the superior nature of British institutions, he had trained himself to see eye-to-eye with the deity in regard to defilade space and other small matters—and, oh, the difference to Captain Bittern!

Hence, from the quarter-deck of the *Unicorn* the view was not quite so devoid of interest as it was from the fo'c'sle, where the beauties of defilade space were not fully understood. As the captain paced back and forth he noted with some satisfaction that the *Unicorn* was not only safe in the precise spot where he had moored her bow-and-stern with springs on her cables, but that a few turns on the capstan would bring her broadside to bear on the river channel just where ships rounded the long point coming down from Gallegos. For a full half-mile or more he could simply "lack them through and through" before he got a gun in reply. And the same would also be true for any hostile craft coming up the river to the south of him. Besides, both Mongo Tom's and Bangalang lay directly across the flats within easy range of his guns. Both places, therefore, continued to furnish him with fish, green provisions, fresh water, and other small comforts, with alacrity—but at prices which were only less ruinous to them than finding themselves all blown to hell, which was the alternative named.

Don Ruiz had taken all this in through a glass from the main top of *La Fortuna* where she lay by the new quay at Gallegos. If the Englishman intended to blockade Gallegos until Señor Adverse came back, he, Don Ruiz, could do nothing about it. He would simply wait until Señor Adverse returned to solve the difficulty. In the meantime, he would continue to take dinner every night at the big house with Ferdinando and Neleta. Perhaps, after all, it was Neleta who kept the blockade from being broken. *La Fortuna* was more heavily armed than the *Unicorn*, and Don Ruiz was a brave man.

But this particular morning Captain Bittern was by no means satisfied with the view. He kept man-o'-war discipline on the *Unicorn*, but the crew had just come aft in a body to inform him respectfully that tomorrow would be New Year's Day, 1801, and the articles under which they had shipped would "hexpire." The question was: should he try to wait any longer for the new owner of the *Unicorn*, who seemed to have disappeared into the interior and might be dead of fever, or should he up-anchor and make sail for London, where considerable sums in prize-money as well as pay and discharges awaited him and his crew?

"After all—what was he doing here? And why should Captain Bittern boil himself and his men any longer for what had been the whim of an old man—and a dead man at that? He had served John Bonnyfeather faithfully for thirty-seven years, but now that he was gone, and his affairs were being administered by *Baring Bros. & Co.*, why was he bound any longer to serve them or this young Mr. Adverse, who was only the heir by law and no relation to his old employer? No! Perhaps he had been a bit too grateful to the past in undertaking to bring the *Uni-*

corn to the Rio Pongo. And a devil of a time he had had finding that muddy ditch. The charts were crazy.

"What luck some people had! Mr. Adverse—who was *he?* A pleasant young dog who had been smart enough at learning his ship's accounting at Livorno, he remembered. But, good Lord, the old man must have left him a cool hundred thousand at least! And Mr. Adverse seemed to have been doing remarkably well here, too. Maybe there was more to it than appeared on the surface? McNab had hinted at something once over a demijohn or two. Sandy McNab, that grand old crab, and Toussaint— what would become of them all at Livorno now? Where would that woman Faith go? She could take care of herself, he'd warrant. A very smooth piece, she was! Perhaps he should have spoken to the old man about her being in the house—and all that. A woman that would kneel down over a chair and let a man . . . pshaw! Whose business was that? It had been a wonderful night in the cabin. And now they would be selling the ship at auction soon. The chair, that leather-padded monument of romance, would have to go. He might buy it in for about £2. For £2?

"*£2—£2—£2 . . . going. £2 and* 1. *Do I hear the seafaring gentleman with the rings in his ears say £2 and* 1? *Good! Ah, £2 and* 2 *now. Thanks, father in Israel. £2 and* 2, *£2 and* 2 *. . . going . . . going. Do I hear sixpence more? The captain with the rings in his ears again, do I hear* 2½? *Yes! Going, going, going, gaw—£2.3 . . . Gone!—sold to the father in Israel for two pounds and three shillings. Take it away!*

"Farewell chair, farewell.

"Captain Bittern has no more use for chairs—had only once, only once. He was raised up a pious man. He has had his own reward. Now he is going to live in a cottage in Chelsea with his niece and her two yellow-haired 'orphans.' *She* trusted in man. Served her right, served her right! But they are nice little girls, little girls. No more chairs for Captain Bittern. Of what use now are chairs except to sit upon?

"On Sundays—on some Sundays—he would take them all in a hack to the Muggletonian chapel at Spitalfields, where he had sat as a wide-eared, wooden-faced youth and listened to the Prophetess Johanna Heathecote expound the scriptures. How mouse-like his mother had been with a little brown tippet wrapped about her, sitting meekly on the cold chapel benches. A silk-weaver's daughter, she was. A mouse—he wondered now how his father had ever got her with him. It must have been a surprise to her, a distinct nervous shock. She wouldn't have believed there *could* be a woman like that Paleologus girl. She enjoyed it. It wasn't even sin with her. Maybe the prophetess would have understood. She had worn a deep, respectable bonnet too. Prim you might call her. But now, now that he came to think of it, she was a fire-ship, a fire-ship in disguise, by God, sir! She would have drifted down on you with the church pennant flying, and then—grappled with you—and spouted flames in the dark. *Ha, ha . . .*"

Mr. Spencer, the young gentleman purser, who had been taken aboard at the request of Sir Francis Baring to represent the executors, nearly stepped on his wrist as he heard the grim captain suddenly burst out into a loon-like laugh. He took the news forward. It might mean they were going home. He opined hopefully.

Jenkers, the sailmaker, shook his head.

"You don't know 'im like hi do," he said. " 'E's jes thort o' suthin' narsty. 'E's figurin'! An' if we gets hall our prize-money wen we gets t' Lunnon, we'll be bloody lucky, we will."

"I shall speak to the new owner about it when he comes aboard," said the purser loftily.

"Aye?" sniffed Jenkers, "*wen* 'e comes aboard. Wen will that be? That's wot we hall warnts ter know. You might himpart your hinformation to the marines. Tell 'em the ole man larfed."

"Now look here, Willum Jenkers . . ."

But it was just then that both Mr. Spencer and Jenkers heard the sound of drums and tom-toms. They were apparently away up-river yet—but coming down. They both leaned out of the port to listen.

"Belike it's them Bangalang 'eathens comin' 'ome again,"

said Jenkers. "You might tell that to the ole man. 'E's a bit deef, 'e is." Mr. Spencer returned aft.

Meanwhile Captain Bittern had come to a decision about going home. He would wait the last day of the old year out and sail on the morrow. He could legally hold his crew to the end of the voyage. But it would have to be a bona-fide voyage, under sail. He couldn't dawdle any longer in the Rio Pongo and pretend he was cruising. He might but he wouldn't. It was time to go. It would take him some time to square things with the Barings when he got to London, anyway. The *Unicorn* had been out since '96 off and on, and had made a lot of captures. And now he would get his own share and let the Barings settle with Mr. Adverse if they could find him. He couldn't—and he had done his best.

It was the Barings who had given him instructions when he had last put in to Gib to sail for the Rio Pongo to get Mr. Adverse. Sir Francis Baring himself had written. He was a schoolmate of John Bonnyfeather and very anxious to find Mr. Adverse to do the right thing by him, it appeared. Spencer had also let slip that the affairs of Mr. Adverse very much needed his return to Europe. It would pay him to give them personal attention, he said. There was Mr. Bonnyfeather's estate, there were the dozen or more prizes the *Unicorn* had taken, and there were large sums of money which Mr. Adverse had been smuggling through from Cuba by foreign bills of exchange.

Well, whatever came, he would see that his crew got their pay and their prize-money out of it. Even if Mr. Adverse never showed up it would be an admiralty and not a chancery case, thank God! Four years of privateering at the end of a long career, and the last of the Bonnyfeather fleet! He had kept the old house-flag flying to a profitable tune on the *Unicorn*, long after it had been hauled down at Livorno. Well, it was all over now for him. Mr. Adverse would have to look after his own, and if he was dead . . .

"*Well*, Mr. Spencer, what is it?"

"*Drud—druda*—drums, sir," shouted the purser. "Coming down-river fast, sir," he bellowed.

"Damn you, do you think I'm deaf?" said the captain.

He went to the taffrail to listen. The *Unicorn* was swinging free with her stern pointed up-river toward Gallegos. It was a clear, hot day and the long point stretched over the water a mile away upstream like a sharp pencil laid on glass.

Captain Bittern heard the drums.

———◆———

They were certainly loud and insistent enough. There was a certain triumphant slam in their rhythm that grumbled over the water insolently. A large fleet of war canoes was emerging from the forest just where the river first swung east into the jungle above Gallegos. More and more kept coming around the bend.

On account of the point Captain Bittern could not see them yet. From the docks and hill at Gallegos they were soon in full view. From the decks of *La Fortuna* Don Ruiz counted three score and four. It was the combined armada of the Kru coastal villages which Mnombibi had assembled for the crusade inland. A number of allies from Mandingo villages farther upstream could be picked out by their longer spears and leaf-shaped paddles. All were now returning to celebrate at Bangalang the success of the expedition.

A formidable gathering which it would be best not to meddle with, thought Ferdinando watching from the porch of the residence. In his time, even as a youngster at Bangalang, Ferdinando could not remember seeing so many war canoes. He was glad they were not coming home by the land side. He hoped devoutly they would pass and go down-river without making trouble or asking for rum. This fellow Mnombibi had raised himself into the position of a war prophet for the whole region. He might be hard to deal with in the future. Yes, he certainly hoped that this fleet of war-maddened, grotesquely-masked warriors, with blue light flashing from hundreds of spears, with the thump of tom-toms and the roar of drums and conch shells rolling over the water would go by.

Don Ruiz beat to quarters on *La Fortuna*—and Captain Bittern heard that.

The canoes passed Gallegos with obscene gestures shoreward and loud shouts of triumph. Something had broken their fear of the white man. His prestige about Gallegos had vanished. Ferdinando could guess why. On the bow of the long, black war canoe from Bangalang, which had not been taken from its shed for a generation, capered a man with a white-spectacled face, waving a silver crucifix in one hand derisively. The fleet bunched lower down where the current swept them together in a slowly swirling eddy just before it streamed around the point. Here they gathered about Mnombibi's canoe, with much *boo-booing* on conch shells and the roaring of bull-whistles, to hold a palaver.

The success of Mnombibi's raid on Brother François, although trivial from the standpoint of loot, had been immense in morale. Some lack of plunder had been made good at the expense of several unfortunate villages on the way back. The witch-doctor's influence was now paramount. Not only had he nailed the white man's wizard to his own tree, but he had carried off the white man's fetish and now held it in his hand. There it was, nailed down too. It could never get away. All its strength was his now. The secret power of the white god had passed to Mnombibi. It was Mnombibi and his followers who were henceforth in possession of the white man's magic superiority. It was they who were now invincible.

Mnombibi believed this thoroughly, although with him the raid had been a mere matter of professional etiquette and business. Brother François had set up a rival shop, and had paid the penalty. But some glimmerings of reasonable doubt had caused Mnombibi to pass by Gallegos and the big ship there which had so many guns. These qualms he knew had disappointed his enthusiastic followers. But he had other plans. There was the smaller ship in the reach below just off Bangalang. His suggestion that they should take the *Unicorn* to the beach, burn her, and share her copper rivets as the dividends of certain victory met with pandemoniac approval.

This decision, though popular at the time, must have been regarded later by the small minority who survived it as mysteriously unfortunate. On Mnombibi's part the error was a theological rather than a tactical one. His acquaintance with the complex nature of Christendom, with the doctrines of certain obscure Protestant sects in particular, was sadly limited. His plan was to drift down easily upon the *Unicorn* and engulf her. In much the same manner he had quietly walked in upon Brother François—and there had been no trouble at all.

But Captain Bittern was a Muggletonian. There were only two hundred and eighty-three of those Saints left alive in the entire world on December 31, 1800. Being in the minority, however, had never troubled them. Even in England not one of them had ever been known to resort to compromise. Nowhere in the inspired book of Lodowicke Muggleton, *The Divine Looking-Glass*, which the captain read every night, was the doctrine of non-resistance pressed upon the Saints; quite the contrary. It was not even mentioned. Captain Bittern would no more have thought of submitting to crucifixion, for instance, than it would have occurred to him to preach a sermon to seagulls.

Curious as it may be—all this, when taken in conjunction with the invention of the late Friar Bacon, held a bellyful of surprises for Mnombibi and his sixty-four canoes. As they rounded the point and began to drift down upon the *Unicorn*, a voice resembling an annoyed sea-lion's barked on her quarterdeck.

A sound like a large clock being wound up drifted across the still water as the ship walked around to her anchor and faced the flotilla. The twelve eyes in her side opened all at once with a small round pupil in each. Like a beast of the Apocalypse she gazed across the glassy sea at the approach of black Apollyon.

Mnombibi on the bow platform of the leading war canoe moved a little uneasily. But it was too late to turn back now. His prestige was hopelessly involved. He began to take a few chaste dance steps, mindful of his attendant spirits and the balance of the canoe; and to chant softly to his twenty-four rowers, "*Goling, golah, ssh* . . . *goling, golah, ssh* . . ." The sharp overhanging prow shoved across the flat water that whispered beneath his feet at every stroke. *"Goling, golah"*—five hundred yards . . .

A yellow cloud rolled out from the side of the *Unicorn*. It billowed higher and higher shot through with incandescent flashes of red lightning accompanied by terrestrial thunder. The intolerable tattoo was both regular and incessant. When the gun at the stern was through firing the bow gun was ready to resume, and the red flashes passed through the sulphur cloud exactly five times.

Don Ruiz, who with the rest of his crew had scrambled into *La Fortuna's* rigging, wild with excitement, now sat there green with envy at the Englishman's gunnery. Under the concentrated hail of grapeshot that beat the river into foam and bloody spray the black flotilla dissolved. Only five or six canoes could now be seen landing frantically at Bangalang.

In an interval of eery silence the smoke curtain slowly rose from the *Unicorn* upon what proved to be the next act.

Her capstan began to clank again as she brought her unused broadside to bear on the town. Her twelve starboard guns let loose as one. The volley of chain-shot cut through the piles of the huts at Bangalang as if a man had taken one long swing at that village with a giant scythe.

Aunt Ungah-gola's shebang slipped slowly sidewise into the river and then hung precariously on only one stake. It was too well-built to collapse. So, she still sat in the high corner where she had been cleaning fish just a moment before. One of them flopped gasping down the tilted floor and swam away. The frame of the house shook again. This time Aunt Ungah screamed. Through the hole in the floor the genial, young crocodile which had flourished for some years past upon her superior garbage was now coming home with a fixed smile.

In the morning calm the smoke drifted slowly away from the now silent *Unicorn* across the bay toward Mongo Tom's. There was not enough wind to scatter it. The Mongo sat with a jug on the veranda somewhat dazed by the rapidity of events taking place before his rheumy eyes. He scarcely knew what to make of them. Trade would certainly be ruined! From time to time he scratched selected islands on his head. Suddenly out of the sulphur murk to windward three canoes came tearing for his beach. He called his overseer and gave orders to lead the survivors to the nearest barracoon. "It's an ill wind—" said the Mongo, "even on a calm day."

As Captain Bittern sat in his cabin that evening over a mess of salt pork and palm cabbage, he quietly remarked to Mr. Spencer that fresh fish from the river could not be considered a delicacy any longer. "Otherwise," said the captain, "they would go well with these greens."

"Yes, sir," replied Mr. Spencer, turning a little green himself.

"Most of the mess that still floated went down with the tide, but you never can tell."

"No, sir, you certainly can't," agreed the purser.

"Not that it will make much difference," mused the captain, "now that we're leaving. It's too bad we can't wait any longer for Mr. Adverse. But at least our visit here will be remembered. I think—"

He bolted the centre of the cabbage.

"Quite!" exclaimed the clerk.

"Tell Mr. Sharp when he calls the larboard watch to ask Mr. Aiken to step down to see me."

"Yes, sir."

"Good night to you," grunted the captain abruptly.

Mr. Spencer lingered a while over his errand. He was much bored at going to bed every night at eight o'clock. He would rather have messed in the steerage. But as a gentleman representing the great house of *Baring Bros. & Co.*, Captain Bittern had done him the honour of the cabin table and he could not help himself. He knew only too well that whatever the captain said was fate. Mr. Spencer after speaking to Mr. Sharp went to bed.

The captain snuffed the wicks on a pair of fat ship's candles and sat down to read as usual. He opened *The Divine Looking-Glass* at the last page and took out a fringed canvas book mark. On it his mother had embroidered when he first went to sea:

A 1757 *D*   *Thou art responsible to God alone*

The book had been printed in 1656, and the captain had divided the unbroken, solidly-printed, square pages into 365 paragraphs by ruling them across with red ink. He read one paragraph every night of the year, and either the first or the last paragraphs, which were identical, he skipped on leap years. Thus his spiritual as well as his earthly navigation proceeded by regular observations, and his exact position in both spheres could be precisely entered in his brass-bound diary. That book reposed, together with a King James version of the Bible, in a rack with a strap across it. Beside the Bible and the diary, there was room in the rack for *The Divine Looking-Glass*, a table of logarithms, and a treatise on the use of "Napier's Bones."

On this particular night the captain carefully printed, in a minute script on the back of the canvas marker, *"Finished reading for the 43rd time, 31st Dec. 1800"*—and this time read the last paragraph of the book of Lodowicke Muggleton, which now lay open before him:

And lo, and behold, the spirit within me was quickened and spake, saying, "Thou art immortal from both before and after, and the Kingdom of God on this earth is within. Arise, recollect it, and make thy share in it plain, lest thou be like unto a beast of the field that remembereth not; neither is he remembered. Behold the grass springeth and the mark of the beast is washed away. Enter thou into the kingdom as becomes a man and remember what man is like." And I cried out, saying, "Lo I remember." And the spirit said unto me, "Take thy pen then and write." And I saw two small angels of God like unto manikins that did ride upon little saddles upon my pen. And one was a dark angel, an evil servant of the Lord, and the other did glister like the bright waters of the rivers of Heaven. And the angels talked one with the other. And what they said I wrote, understanding not all of it but setting it down, for those that sat upon the saddle rode hard, and faster than I could follow. And they did open up the heavens and the earth unto me like unto a

479

box of mirrors wherein the reflection of one thing is cast upon the glass of another so that the origin of the image is reflected back upon itself. And therein I saw not my own face but all things else. And there was nothing about which the angels spake together and pointed out to me that I could not remember as though it were yesterday becoming his own tomorrow. And this is the memory of the sons of God, and of men, and of the heavens, and the earth and the oceans and the beasts thereof that I have set down and sealed with my name that bare witness to it in the divine looking-glass.

Not understanding these things, but being much moved thereby, Captain Bittern, after a short entry in his diary covering an eventful day, prepared to turn in. He heard the watch called as he did so. The first mate stepped in.

"You have orders, sir?"

"High tide's about dawn tomorrow, Mr. Aiken. Stand by to take the ship down with the ebb. Have your people get the stern anchor up now. You might outen the candles there. Good night."

Mr. Aiken seemed to hesitate.

"Well?" said the captain looking through his night-shirt with which he was having a terrible time.

"The new owner has just come aboard, sir."

"The devil you say!" snapped the captain. "He must have been damned quiet about it then."

"Yes, sir. He and one man came up by the stern in a small boat. And you're to send your gig up to Gallegos tomorrow to fetch a dog aboard," said the mate with a ghost of a chuckle.

The beak of the captain suddenly rose triumphantly out of the night-shirt.

"Did you leave him rotting on deck like an old sail?" he roared.

"Yes, sir," gulped the mate.

"Be damned to you, Aiken, *that's* no way to treat your owner. Pshaw! Mr. Adverse, Mr. Adverse, where are you?" the captain shouted going on deck in his night-gown.

"Standing on my own deck at last. And thank God I am," said Anthony. "Is that your ghost, Captain Bittern? You look like the captain of the *Flying Dutchman*."

◆

Anthony had heard the rumble of cannon early that morning while he and his troop of Foulahs were slashing their way as best they could through the jungle toward Gallegos. He listened, filled with misgivings at the distant mutter of what to him was a mysterious fusillade. He wondered if Mnombibi's people were attacking the establishment, or whether the *Unicorn* and *La Fortuna* had at last fallen foul of each other. He pressed on now even more rapidly than before. But the path which he had ordered Ferdinando to keep clear for some miles inland was half overgrown through neglect, a mass of vines and creepers piled with ants' nests. The bridge at the five-mile creek had been riddled by termites and they had to make an exasperating detour through a swamp where the leeches clung to the horses' legs. Hurry as fast as they could, it was several hours after dark when the well-known stockade finally loomed dimly across the clearing and they rode through the open gate without being challenged. All this did not speak well for Ferdinando's care and discipline. Anthony's wrists beat anxiously at first at the silence. Then he saw all was well. But it was plain from a hundred signs of neglect that the Master of Gallegos had indeed been away.

Yet how familiar it all was. One glance from the hillcrest, and he could tell even by the few lights burning here and there through the trees and over the harbour that the place only awaited his return, and in peace. The moon began to rise. Beyond the long point he saw the *Unicorn* riding at anchor and his heart leaped. They were taking in her stern anchor. He was just in time then. In time to go? How beautifully the moonlight lay through the black stems of his palm groves; how mellow were the golden squares of *La Fortuna*'s ports glowing by the quay. The night breeze brought him the heavenly perfume of orange trees in blossom.

Under the moon Gallegos lay like some Arabian Avalon

asleep in its palm groves, redolent of spices, twinkling with the green lanterns of a million incredible fireflies carrying the intermittent lamps of their dim loves through the silver blur of the nocturnal atmosphere. And all this enchanted garden he had made; planted the trees, nursed the blossoms—and stolen the men. How many bits of paradise amid the forests had perished that his might be patched-out here? In the dark house there Neleta would be asleep now. And in the bay below lay the *Unicorn*. And he was going to go? He was going to leave—Circe! Yes, he had found the holy sprig of moly hanging on the tree. He would go now. But, oh, he had forgotten how lovely was the song of the Sirens in the moonlight. And he had not bound himself to the mast yet. Quickly! Let him do so, or even now, even now it might be too late.

He told Juan to lead the Foulahs quietly to the little valley that would be deserted now, and to see that they were well looked after there. The huts would be empty—very empty now! He warned him not to rouse Ferdinando nor to let it become known that he had come back. The tired men led their horses to the brook eagerly while he turned in at the path to the house.

He had considerable trouble in getting any one to unbar the courtyard gate. It was Cheecha who finally came. She would have cried out if he had not stopped her. He told her to stay at the gate and to waken no one. He left her there weeping large Ethiopian tears of joy at his return. For the first time it came upon him fully how faithful Cheecha had been. Poor Cheecha, poor soul!

And Neleta?

He turned down the hall quietly and entered the room.

Instantly the sheer familiarity of the place defied his resolution to leave it. Everything was exactly as it always had been. The same bars of moonlight fell across the same woman on the bed, asleep, waiting. Surely nothing could have happened to him since he had seen her last. No, he was only coming home at the end of the day to go to bed as he had the night before—and the night before that. Tomorrow they would get up and have breakfast and he would go on as usual. Why, what had he been thinking about? All that had happened for months past, the entire experience in the hills, seemed to have been suddenly cancelled. He would simply go to bed with her and take her in his arms.

How silent it was. Only the forests far-off, roaring and grunting to the moon. They would go on forever. Here in the room—

Her regular breathing coming and going deeply through the darkness was the unbroken connecting thread of life and passion upon which all these familiar things, and all the emotions and meanings that surrounded them from one end of Gallegos to the other, were hung. Neleta was the life and centre of Gallegos. He felt suddenly that she was the mysterious cause of it. Without her it would never have been. He could not have made it. It was Neleta who had made him master of Gallegos, and Neleta was mistress of it all.

So he stood there haunted by her. It was not desire alone. The magnet that drew him to her was more immense than that. She was simply the pole of it, of all the life of the Grain Coast. In her the lines of all its attractions met and centred. And he felt them now like palpable things pulling him toward her where she lay asleep on the bed. How could he be the negative to that? He just managed to look away—whether to begin from old habit throwing his clothes across the well-known chair there or not, he never knew. He sat down and began to take off his shoes—and he happened to look up.

On Neleta's dresser across the room the moonlight gathered in the mirror with a concentrated silver glow. And in this dim effulgence, dripping with a white, watery light, stood the madonna just where he had left her months before.

She too was familiar.

But with the familiarity of other things, of past days and places, that rushed into his mind now so that the room and all within it, except the little statue with the dim glow about it, was driven outside and lay plainly and objectively beyond him again. He was no longer merely a part of it. He slipped his feet back into his shoes and went over to the chest-of-drawers where the figure stood.

He remembered now. He was going to take her away with him—along with a hundred other little, personal things he could no longer bear to be without—comforts, and remembrances which a man cannot replace, things he had missed sorely time and again lately. That comfortable set of razors Cibo had given him. Lord, how he had missed *that!* Certain favourite clothes— and the cuff links Dolores had sent him. Dolores!—where was she tonight?

Lost! He had lost all of them. Angela his lover, and sweet cool Florence Udney—the feeling of northern spring and violets, the cool strong burgeoning of innocence and youth. What fire had melted all those snows away that should have melted kindly to the moon? It was the hot tropical sun—and Neleta.

Why, he had staggered into her by chance like a drunken bee that falls suddenly into a flesh-coloured orchid hanging on a hot wall! And the flower-trap had closed over him; the little hairs of it covered with honey dew and the great smooth inflamed petals with tawny speckles on them. God! How he had lain there dying of ecstasy with his wings folded and gummed. Caught! With the light far-away, and the green forest beyond. It was still roaring tonight. It would roar like that forever. It was imitating the sea . . .

"But the sea is my home," he said. "And I will go."

He took a grip on himself and began looking for the tinder-box. It was not in the usual place. He stumbled over Neleta's shoes. Damn! Cheecha had always put things away. It was Cheecha who had really run the house and made life physically tolerable. Not Neleta. Neleta was legs in the spasm, eyes rolled back, confusion, things in heaps, perfume—and a sudden witch-radiance at dinner when the orchid hung over the wall. My God! where *had* she put the tinder-box now? On her best shawl, of course,—and a great hole burned in it—he lit the candles—the shawl from China. Don Ruiz had given her that. Let him. Anthony would make use of it now.

He spread the madly figured shawl on the floor and began

to throw things into it helter-skelter. After it was "packed" he would waken Neleta and tell her . . . would he? Yes. But defer it now. Pack. Wait and see. He began to ransack his chests like a burglar working speedily—but not quietly. The things were his—weren't they? The bundle grew. So did the racket. A lid fell with a vicious smack. He laughed.

Neleta opened her eyes. She understood instantly what was happening and without saying a word got up and threw herself on him.

"No! You are not going. No! No!"

Her passionate negative was as resolute as his positive intention of leaving—more vehement. It was much harder to go than he had supposed. It rapidly began to become doubtful as she clung to him, pleading, commanding, suggesting, enticing with a thousand variations and tones of "no." This was not an argument. It was Neleta. How to resist her in the flesh? No, it was impossible that he should do this thing.

At any rate he found himself dragged onto his knees and kneeling by the bed; leaning over her with her arms around his neck. She begged now, whispering to him. Pity for her began to overwhelm him. He put his head on her breast. She began to smooth his hair and draw him closer. He felt tears on her cheeks. Some of them were his own. His arms stole about her. His hands went under the pillow to bring her head closer to put his lips on hers again.

Then his fingers clutched something hidden under the pillow.

It seemed to be shaped like a forked radish, smooth, softer as he held it—wax! Suddenly he remembered Mnombibi rocking himself before the mirror that night. Could it be . . . he would see.

He rose with it in his hand, powerfully, tearing himself loose from her. Her coiled hair whipped smoothly across his neck as he drew back. He took the thing over to the candles where the madonna stood. Yes! It was the witch-doctor's horrible little manikin, a fetish with an enormous thing cocked up at him, a blind, silly face. He saw his own hairs running through the half-transparent wax.

So it had been no dream that night. Neleta *had* brought that devil Mnombibi into his room. She had procured this. Somehow, somehow Neleta had been the cause of horrible things. Brother François! And Anthony had been sold to the devil, too—for what? As he looked at the grinning fetish he turned sick. A noise behind him caused him to whirl about.

She was crawling over toward him through the moonlight. She had left the bed stealthily. Some of the covers dragged behind her. They came off. She was naked, crouched, ready to spring. It was the fetish she wanted! "To hell with it!" He smashed it on the floor and trod on it. The next instant he was trying desperately to prevent her doing the same to the madonna.

She carried him back for a minute. She swarmed up him biting like a great cat. She wrapped her arms and legs about him. She gave the hated virgin figure on the bureau a kick. It rolled over and smashed. She screamed with delight. He held her off, wrestling with her as he had wrestled that night in the tent. A complete horror and hate of her, a burst of fury gave him full strength.

What had he been born a man for?

He bore her back to the bed and bound her there hard and fast with a twisted sheet. It was degrading, even funny for an instant—and painful. Then it was fearful and horrible beyond usual experience. The abysmal face of the dark woman looked up at him, thrown back, the long white teeth longing for his throat. Her eyes smouldered with yellow and green glints. The incomplete, man-eating soul of her lay revealed twisting on the bed like an unformed thing half torn out of its cocoon. But dangerous, strong, hungry, furious. Like Faith—witchcraft!

This was what he had been trying to mate with—a body alive. Madre! He might have had children by it.

She had forgotten her Spanish now and raved at him in some mad gibberish. His spine crept. One of the candles burnt out. God! He would be left alone with her in the dark again.

He swept the madonna, and everything else on the floor and the dresser, into the shawl. The big mirror fell with a hard smash on the remaining candle. Pieces of it rained about his head as if someone were hurling them at him. He dashed out of the dark room dragging the bundle after him like a thief. Her voice followed him down the hall.

Cheecha stopped him at the gate. He stood there half-mad with rage and the pain of his bitten arms. He felt like wrecking the house. For some time he did not know that Cheecha was clasping him about the knees. Then he shook her off. He was looking for something to kick . . . he stepped over her.

"Master, take me with you," she cried after him. "Master . . ."

He turned around, touched by something desperate in the tones of the woman's voice. She had sunk back on her haunches in despair.

"Neleta will kill me now," she said looking up at him in a last appeal. "Tomorrow . . ." horror convulsed her features. "She will think you care."

Poor Cheecha, poor soul!—he knew it was true.

"Go down to the docks, I will look after you. Go now." She fled before him into the darkness.

A few minutes later he found her waiting dumbly. He whistled for Juan who came out of the shadows. The three of them got into a small boat and rowed out to *La Fortuna* while Cheecha held the bundle, wrapped up in Neleta's shawl, like a child in her lap. It was all that Anthony was taking from Gallegos. He made her leave it in the boat, and whispering something to Juan, sent them forward.

Don Ruiz was engaged in a game of solitaire. For the sixth time he had had an extraordinary run of luck with himself that night. He was amazed but genuinely glad and relieved to see Anthony.

"What had the cannonading that morning been about?"

"Oh, you should have been here, señor." He explained at great length and graphically while Anthony sat looking grim enough. So Captain Bittern had swallowed Mnombibi and his people at one gulp—just as he remembered he used to drink soup. That plate was clean.

Don Ruiz went on to say that things had been going from bad to worse at Gallegos since Anthony had left.

While Anthony was putting himself into decent shape again after Neleta's mauling, by the help of the captain's wardrobe, Don Ruiz kept pouring complaints into his ears about Ferdinando. Cibo, it appeared, had been greatly put out over various transactions in which the factor had overreached himself. "Make a dog a king, señor, and the whole court will soon be snarling." Anthony gathered that Don Ruiz and Cibo had become bosom friends in Havana. He was glad of it. It suited his plans. He led up to the point he had in mind by relating some recent events.

Don Ruiz, Anthony was glad to see, could still be shocked. He was all for hanging Ferdinando for murdering a saint. Anthony shook his head.

"I have thought of that," he said. "But there must be no further vengeance. Brother François would not have it so. The slaughter this morning must have been horrible. Under the circumstances I cannot blame Captain Bittern—but no more. Besides, such men as Ferdinando are really savages. I know that now. According to his light he tried at first to serve me. The rest was my fault. I was deceived as to the man's real nature by his delicate manners. But he is a half-breed, you know, captain. His mother came from a hut in Bangalang. As for his sister—"

Anthony paused. Whether this was news to the captain he could not tell. Don Ruiz's expression did not change. Anthony hurried on while hastily donning a new shirt, his own having been ripped to tatters.

"It is my intention, captain, to leave Gallegos tonight, to go aboard the *Unicorn* and never to come ashore here again. For many reasons I am finished with Africa forever. When I am gone there will be nothing to prevent your taking over the establishment. Ferdinando's blunders, as far as the ledgers go, are small ones. In the main you will find a going concern in excellent shape. You and Carlo Cibo will have to handle the Havana end of the game between you. I shall write Carlo, of course, the first opportunity. I shall from now on devote myself to my own affairs in Europe. You can count me out here as having left six months ago. That is fair enough. Now what do you think?"

"One minute, señor. Let me consider." Don Ruiz who had been walking up and down rapidly sat down and played out his uncompleted game of solitaire. Anthony went on dressing.

"That is extraordinary," said Don Ruiz after a little, "for the seventh time tonight I have played out on the same card." He held up the queen of spades. Then he reshuffled the cards slowly, laid one out on the table and laughed.

"Yes," he said. "I will do it. Have you no stipulations, señor?"

"One or two personal ones," began Anthony, pausing now and then while he carefully tied back his hair in European style again. "The woman Cheecha who is now aboard, is to be taken to Havana on this ship and turned over to Carlo Cibo to be given her freedom. I shall see that she is taken care of through him. Also see that the Foulahs who came down with me are properly entertained and sent back with gifts to their hearts' content. Later, from Europe, I shall send you certain cases which I wish you to forward faithfully by the first caravan to Futa-Jaloon. They are for Amah-de-bellah. By the way, cultivate his good will."

"And the señorita?" said the captain drumming a little on the table.

"Let her stay in the big house as long as she wants to. I expect to arrange for certain sums to be paid her quarterly through Spanish bankers. She can claim them at Havana if she has a mind to. They will come to her regularly, but it will take me some months to arrange for them. In the meantime—"

"Perhaps, she had best remain at Gallegos till *La Fortuna* sails —after this next trip," suggested Don Ruiz. Anthony agreed.

"That is all," he said.

They shook hands on it.

The captain's eyes took on a far-away look.

"It is not true, then, señor, that you married the lady just before the padre left—when you were so ill? Ferdinando gave me to suppose . . . ah, pardon me. I understand now. Pardon."

"So that was the reason Ferdinando had been so anxious to get rid of Brother François! If I had died Neleta would still have been mistress here. No one could have contradicted them. Ferdinando again! What shall I do with him?" he thought.

Nothing! He would do nothing. He would let that remain like his own account, to be settled with Providence. He was guilty himself. He would not judge and punish Ferdinando. No, he was done with Gallegos and all its affairs. He put on his coat and sent for Juan.

"Don Ruiz," he said as they walked together to the ship's side, "I am leaving you at the edge of the world here. You can easily fall off. There is no law here except what men can find in themselves. I tried to make my own and could not live by it—others died. But you are in charge now. You can settle certain matters to suit yourself. I go for my reasons; you stay for yours—the cards, for instance—but I warn you." He paused by the binnacle and bared an arm bitten from wrist to shoulder. "And that is only one thing. There are other marks, deeper. These that you see are only on my arm."

The captain of *La Fortuna* bowed and smiled. "You are fair enough, señor. I thank you for the warning. But I am not afraid. In my country there is a proverb, 'When you go among the women take your whip along.' But," he added hastily, "I am a man of honour, a caballero."

"So I have been told," said Anthony a little bitterly.

Don Ruiz replied vehemently. "Believe, believe me, I also have learned by sorrowful experiences. I know, for instance, that it is not just the woman who is driving you away. No, you go on account of many things; because of yourself, to be a free man. Is it not so?—And you do not wholly credit me with knowing that. I am a man of feeling, too. And there are many ways to feel. My way may be right for me."

"That is true," said Anthony. "I beg your pardon."

They shook hands again. "Good luck—good luck."

"Farewell, amigo," cried Don Ruiz looking over the side now. "I shall do the best I can. It is my fortune here. Yours there. But we shall not forget the good man we saw in the little valley that day. Never. You know. Adiós, adiós, but I won't say good-bye forever. Ah—quién sabe?"

They shoved off.

In the small boat with the bundle sitting alone in the middle of it Anthony and Juan slid rapidly downstream and rounded the point. A few minutes later Anthony was standing on the well-remembered deck of the *Unicorn* shaking hands with Captain Bittern.

There was only one thing he had forgotten. It was the hound Simba. He sent a boat back to Gallegos for him a little after dawn. Don Ruiz returned him a note.

I have everything in hand this morning and am holding hard. Fire a gun when you leave and you shall have from La Fortuna *an honourable farewell in reply. Here is your Havana mail, which I forgot last night. Adiós.*

But they weighed anchor quietly and slipped down with the gathering ebb while the river was still misty. Juan piloted them out. The *Unicorn* seemed to greet the open sea with delight.

"Look, señor," cried Juan, pointing happily to the long barriers where they had spent the days of light together, "that was the best of Gallegos. Let us remember that—and the padre." He crossed himself. "Now we are out in the open sea again, I turn the ship over to you. Ah! We shall see Europe again, Spain! You will let me go home for a while, won't you?"

"If you will promise to come back to me," smiled Anthony.

"Sí, wherever you are I will come to you."

A few minutes later Anthony heard Juan's guitar on the deck below. Beginning mournfully, it continued some time in a melancholy strain. Then suddenly the strings released themselves into a mad tumble of lyric joy. The voice of the hound Simba joined in, whining with excitement. Anthony held on at the wheel himself. He did not look back. By noon the low coast lay behind the eastern horizon. He heard the ship's bell again marking the relentless march of time—and went below for the midday meal with Captain Bittern in the cabin.

Other things besides the dinging into his ears of time and tide reminded him he was back in the midst of his own world again. One was the way Captain Bittern drank his soup. He raised it on an even keel to his exactly horizontal mouth; he looked across the level surface of it as if he were taking an observation and saw ice on the horizon. The slit in his face opened. The plate tilted and the soup vanished. It was gone! Eating to Captain Bittern was part of the grim business of life. If he ever tasted anything, no one, probably not even Captain Bittern, knew it. There was no time for it. Anthony was swept back again to the remarkable gastronomic legerdemain of the captain at Mr. Bonnyfeather's table. The Casa da Bonnyfeather rose up before him and all those who had sat about the board there. And the great pile of correspondence that awaited his attention completed the sensation of having come back to the world with a vengeance.

Baring Bros. & Co., Mr. Bonnyfeather's executors, were clamorous in ink to have him come home. Their agent awaited him at Livorno. It was now essential to close-out the affairs of the House of Bonnyfeather in Italy and on the spot. Anthony grinned at their assurances as to the trustworthiness of their agent at Leghorn.

. . . Herr Vincent Nolte, a young man with a rising reputation for able banking in difficult times, the heir of an ancient concern with which we have long dealt. You may have every confidence in him, and he is authorized to advance you . . .

A long accounting followed.

He looked at the totals in amazement. It was thrust upon him now and at last with a full and keen realization that he was rather, yes, decidedly, a rich young man. He could go where he liked. He could do what he wanted to. So the "lonely twin" was going to be free. Why had this favour been shown him? he wondered. Through what inexplicable channels the waters of events took their way. Where would they next break into the light again and spread out before him? Oh, let them run deep and quietly for a while underground. It had been a terrible pool into which that other Bronze Boy had been plunged. He at least was gone forever—only the lonely twin remained. He, by the grace of God, had somehow been set free.

He leaned forward putting his head down on his arms amid the clutter of his papers on Captain Bittern's table. He shoved aside *The Divine Looking-Glass* which the captain in his hurry had left lying open the night before. The canvas book mark with its broad, black letters fell out under his eyes. He read what was written there with profound astonishment and considerable awe.

After all—what was an accident?

At any rate, he would not forget this one—either. He felt the ship quietly sweeping on. Into another world again! The bell on deck began to strike musically. . . .